CITIZENS CREEK

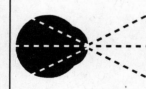

This Large Print Book carries the
Seal of Approval of N.A.V.H.

CITIZENS CREEK

LALITA TADEMY

WHEELER PUBLISHING
A part of Gale, Cengage Learning

GALE
CENGAGE Learning·

Farmington Hills, Mich • San Francisco • New York • Waterville, Maine
Meriden, Conn • Mason, Ohio • Chicago

GALE
CENGAGE Learning®

Wheeler Publishing Large Print Hardcover.
The text of this Large Print edition is unabridged.
Other aspects of the book may vary from the original edition.
Set in 16 pt. Plantin.

LIBRARY OF CONGRESS CATALOGING-IN-PUBLICATION DATA

Tademy, Lalita.
  Citizens creek / Lalita Tademy.
    pages ; cm — (Wheeler publishing large print hardcover)
    ISBN 978-1-4104-7393-6 (hardcover) — ISBN 1-4104-7393-7 (hardcover)
    1. Slaves—Fiction. 2. African American men—Fiction. 3. Creek Indians—Fiction. 4. Alabama—History—19th century—Fiction. I. Title.
PS3570.A248C58 2014b
813'.54—dc23   2014035782

Published in 2014 by arrangement with Atria books, a division of Simon & Schuster, Inc.

Printed in the United States of America
1 2 3 4 5 6 7 18 17 16 15 14

To my husband, Barry Lawson Williams

Other things may change us,
but we start and end with family.
— ANTHONY BRANDT

■ ■ ■ ■ ■

PART I
TOM

ALABAMA, 1822

■ ■ ■ ■ ■

CHAPTER 1

His master's voice, testy, from the direction of the main house. He had to obey, eventually, but pretended not to hear, giving himself time, sliding his hand along the stomach line from dewlap to udder, feeling for an unfamiliar bulge or irritated patch. Good. Nothing for worry. He was sure what awaited him was another meaningless chore, or errand easily assigned to one of the others. A task not worthy of a *hilis haya*. A healer. He was just turned twelve, mostly a man.

"Tom!"

Hadjo chewed a lazy cud, her eyes calm, but he knew better than to believe she couldn't just as well deliver a fast kick, whether hurt or merely displeased, and kept his body from her firing line. She still showed no sign of shakes, thank the Great Spirit. She was full of personality among her dimmer colleagues, a bit of a show-off.

11

He'd named her himself, Hadjo, the Creek word for jokester. No one else would understand his choice of favorite. They'd choose the cow that calved often and gave the most milk, or one with big haunches for a tasty stew, or the strongest, or they'd refuse to pick at all, unable to see differences, as if one cow substituted for another. She might not fetch highest price if put to sale, but Tom preferred clever.

A week ago, when Hadjo refused her suckling, and turned from the grass at feed time, he worried she'd caught milk sickness. But now he thought it nothing more than a passing malady, without potential to hurt the tribe. He personally hand-fed Hadjo grain mixed with oil from the dried, ripe seeds of the flax plant, in the way of Old Turtle, and already saw improvement in both appetite and movement. Once sure she posed no danger, he would return her to graze with the others as she passed her time on this earth until her end, providing her milk for the tribe and her meat for the tribe, or until she was sold for currency held by Chief Yargee for the benefit of all. Once Tom ran her, he'd know whether Hadjo was infected with the slows. If her legs didn't buckle, he would declare her well. If she weakened and fell to the ground, he would separate her from the others until she succumbed, and bury the remains deep so none could feast on her poison. He owed that much to the People. If beef of milk-sick cows was eaten, or milk drunk, the system of the People would be contaminated. He'd seen it before, in the time of his old master, before Chief Yargee. First came the person's loss of energy for days or weeks, followed by the terrible shaking, followed by the final gasp of breath. And the cow long dead. Old Turtle taught him the connection.

"Tom!"

He patted Hadjo on the rump, not daring to ignore the call again.

"Back directly," he promised in Mvskoke, and then again in English. He practiced every chance, the words in both languages true on his tongue.

Hadjo continued about her business, unconcerned.

Tom sped cross-pasture and nudged Old Turtle where he nodded under a moss-draped live oak close to the sluggish stream.

"Chief Yargee calls," Tom said. "I'm gone from the herd."

"Humph." Old Turtle tightened his lips and squinted hard at Tom. The intense sun and passing years had turned his skin leathery, burnished to the color of dried figs, his expression unyielding. "Don't show too smart, boy. Mind your tongue around master."

"He calls for his *hilis haya*," bragged Tom. "Second healer," he immediately corrected, not wanting to offend. "Next to you, best in the tribe."

The advance of blindness and age slowed his mentor, but rheumy-eyed Old Turtle was still better in the healing of cattle than the most able-bodied man in Alabama, black or Indian. And Tom was the young *hilis haya* of the five hundred cattle in the herd, having watched Old Turtle minister to livestock on first Master McIntosh's plantation, and now, among the Upper Creeks on Chief Yargee's plantation.

"You and me, we're as much slave on this place as the last, though the master be more tolerable here," said Old Turtle.

"But we're Creek too," insisted Tom. He touched the red strings in his turban for luck.

"We are what we are. Owned by tribe's not the same as tribe," said Old Turtle. "Straight off now and see to what the chief wants. And don't overstep."

Tom followed the banks of the Alabama River, tromping through the tall grass in the direction of the chief's house. He rounded

14

the corner of the side yard's vegetable garden.

Two unfamiliar horses lazed in front of his master's logged cabin, a three-hand roan with a fancy horned leather saddle and a smaller paint with broad pinto spotting, draped with a coarse wool riding blanket. He knew now why he'd been called. Visitors.

Four figures stood in an awkward knot outside the house, waiting, a different flavor of annoyance written across each distinctive face, Indian, black, and white. He caught the eye of the other Tom on the plantation, a tall pecan-colored slave two years his senior, already sprouting the beginnings of a mustache on his upper lip, caught up in the net of the same name. The other Tom answered the call more quickly, most probably from the stable, where he shod the tribe's ponies. They'd found themselves in this situation before, the two Toms, and after the briefest flicker of recognition, Tom concentrated on his master, figuring how much trouble he might be in for taking too long.

Chief Yargee threw up his hands when he saw Tom. He seemed more nettled that he had to deal with a white man than that he'd had to wait. His master didn't take to strangers, especially English-speaking strangers. Yargee was full-blood, devoted more to old ways than new, and if the chief could have lived his life through without ever seeing a white face or being vulnerable to the confusing ways of the Wachenas, he would have died a man content.

"What took so long?" asked Yargee in Mvskoke.

"Cattle trouble," said Tom. He thought of Old Turtle's warning and said nothing more, holding his breath as he waited for Chief Yargee's reaction.

Distracted, Chief Yargee skimmed past Tom's delay and waved away the other Tom with an impatient gesture. "They talk crazy," he said.

The two strangers looked uncomfortable. The short white man was smaller than the chief, dressed in a mishmash of clothing, some Indian, some store-bought cloth and American fashion, like Tom had seen before on the old plantation. The dark-skinned man wore a feathered turban, a blanket wrapped around his body Indian-style, and breeches with fur around the bottom.

"I am *yatika.*" The black stranger spoke in thick-tongued Mvskoke, so heavily accented he was difficult to understand.

"What's he say, Tom?" Yargee asked.

The situation came clear. Chief Yargee had little tolerance for unfamiliarity with his language. Tom had thrown himself into mastering Mvskoke as well as Creek customs and dress when Yargee bought him into the nation as his property. This white man had the foresight to bring his own interpreter, but Yargee didn't approve of the abuse of the language in the black man's mouth.

"I am *yatika* for Chief Yargee," Tom said in English.

He ignored the black man's look of surprise and the mirrored expression of the little white man. Tom was used to doubt, to challenge, to underestimation, because he was twelve and looked younger still.

"Chief Yargee asks the reason for your visit."

This time the white man spoke, in English. He too had an accent, but Tom made internal adjustments for his odd lilt and speech, and found him understandable.

"I'm passing through, writing about Indians in Alabama. For my own amusement. Yes?"

Tom wasn't sure how much Mvskoke the black man really understood, so he mostly performed a straight translation of the white man's words for Yargee without commentary or shading, but he left out the part about amusement. Chief Yargee wouldn't respond well, and he wanted to keep the exchange going, fascinated that a white man brought his slave dressed Cherokee-style with him as he traveled through Alabama.

"We feed them," Yargee said in Mvskoke to Tom, "then they go."

"The chief invites you to sup," Tom translated, "before going on your way." The white man seemed grateful at the offer, so Tom added, "You and your *estelvste.*"

The black man straightened up at this last, his face suddenly flinty.

"I am not his," he said in English, pulling his blanket tighter around his shoulders. "I am a free man, belonging only to myself. I have papers for proof. I travel without permission."

This man was as dark as Tom, maybe even a shade darker, his hair kinky beneath his turban, his face broad without the slightest hint of Indian blood. Every black man, woman, boy, or girl Tom had ever known was owned by white or Indian. Masters differed in temperament and treatment, in wealth and in influence, but so far as he knew, any with one drop of Negro blood were slaves. He'd seen official papers before, sheaves of parchment his former master

18

kept in a locked rolltop desk no one was allowed to touch, except to keep dusted. Master McIntosh used to pull these papers out each month and worry over them, scratching black ink across the pages with a goose-quill feather pen. He'd add new sheets to the stack whenever he made a sale or a purchase on the plantation. Tom wondered if the black man's proof papers looked like those.

Tom wasn't supposed to know how to read or write, but Master McIntosh sent his son to the white man's school, and in the beginning, the boy showed Tom the individual squiggles of letters he said were the mortar and pestle of the white men's books in his father's library. Tom practiced them when alone. That was before the son outgrew their small-boy friendship and went on to embrace the life his father laid out for him, where Tom's function was to serve, not accompany. But Tom could write his own name and pick out some words. Once he came to Yargee, the chief didn't care one way or the other if Tom could read, so long as he performed his chores. Yargee had no knowledge of the written word, and cared about only the valuable cattle-tending skills gained for the tribe when he bought in Old Turtle and young Tom together.

Tom looked to Yargee, but his master had scant interest in an exchange in a language he didn't understand and which promised to impact him little. Still, Tom translated the black man's words, the freedom declaration.

Yargee didn't comment, but didn't laugh either, or protest the absurdity of the claim. A free black man. Sometimes you had to see a thing to know the possibility of it. He'd ask Old Turtle later.

"Mightn't I ask Chief Yargee about his life as Upper Creek in Alabama?" asked the white man.

Tom translated.

The chief grabbed up his bois d'arc bow and a full quiver of arrows. "Have cook lay supper and food for them to carry away," he said in Mvskoke.

"Chief Yargee meets with Council now, but asks me to see you eat and drink to your fill."

He'd get these men to himself before sending them off. If only he could learn how one came by freedom, with papers as proof. Or glimpse a world beyond an Alabama plantation.

The white man seemed particularly disappointed, but that didn't burden Chief Yargee. He pulled Tom to the side.

"From now, won't be two Toms," Yargee whispered in Mvskoke. "Your name is Cow Tom, and his is Horse Tom, and you come soon as I call."

"Yes, Chief Yargee."

Yargee headed toward the woods without a backward glance, leaving Cow Tom to handle the visitors.

Later, alone, with the two men fed and on their way, Tom found the twinkle of the star that never moved in the northern sky to accept his nightly prayer. He conjured up his most precious memory. His mother, her callused hands so warm at the nape of his neck, humming some nameless, soothing tune as she tilted his head and spooned her concocted herbal brew between his lips as he lay sick of a childhood disease on a straw pallet. A pause to her crooning, and something cool on his forehead, and the timbre of her voice, rich enough to tame pain or hurt that he still played back the melody of it whenever he fell into sadness. "Come, boy," she said then. "My Tom. Be well. You're meant for special things. Be well now."

He missed her.

His star called to him. First, he wished his mother safe. He wished she would come back. He wished for guidance on how to be

21

special. And now he had something new to add to his list. He wished he was paper-free.

CHAPTER 2

Cow Tom stared at the sway of Amy's hips as she walked toward him. She carried a slab of warm Indian bread on a wooden paddle, and extended the flat loaf to her brother, who tore off a sizable chunk and squatted in the dirt to eat. Only after did she come to him, her eyes not bold but without surrender. Eyes dark and deep, sable brown, like he remembered his mother's.

"Water," said her brother, barely looking up. She produced a cowhide container, which he tipped to his lips and almost emptied. Tending the herd was hot, thirsty work, but for one so young, Cow Tom thought, the boy had promise. He displayed a real feel for cattle and showed almost as much potential as he himself had once demonstrated at Old Turtle's side. But as a man of twenty-three, Cow Tom had other things on his mind than cattle.

She brought the container to Cow Tom.

Her walk was solid, as if she were a part of the earth. He had water left in the flask at his hip, but accepted her offering, if only to be closer to the warmth and scent of her, and took his time in the drinking. He'd watched her ripen, just a few years behind his own maturation, from the time of girls' stickball in the compound to her joining the circle of women at their baskets. He had known for some time she would be his, long before she put up her braids and assumed her duties. She was the girl closest to his age in the slave population on Chief Yargee's ranch, but his attraction was deeper than that. His approval as she developed mastery at bread making and tending the vegetable gardens and the time-consuming task of dressing deer hides had lately developed into an accompanying ache each time he saw her, a fever to explore the planes of her face and the curves of her ample body. Sometimes the effect she had on him overwhelmed, and he had to guard against falling too deeply under her spell.

Months before, when Cow Tom asked Old Turtle what he thought of Amy, he poked out his lips and made his pronouncement.

"She'll do," his mentor had said. Old Turtle's specialty may have been the peculiarities and diseases of cattle, but he had a firm opinion about every other topic under the sky.

But Amy would more than just do, an easy pairing. If Cow Tom was *hilis haya* for the herd, Amy had the makings of *hilis haya* for the People. She was young yet, but learned the art of healing with herbs from her time with the Seminoles, before Yargee. Already some members of the tribe sought her out for the strength of her potions. And she'd taught him all the Hitchiti phrases she knew, the words fresh and crucial to Cow Tom's ear.

In the last years, Old Turtle's health, already poor, had failed further, and Cow Tom took the lead in managing the herd. He thought of his mentor each time he saw Hadjo out to pasture, old, slow, and spent, as Old Turtle was now. He pushed away the thought of either selling or slaughter as he would any other milk cow past her prime. She'd served the tribe well, and he'd protect her now in her last days. Times were, for the most part, good at the plantation in Alabama, with sufficient food for anyone willing to hunt or forage or plant. If the tribe ever had true need of Hadjo's meat, Cow Tom would deliver her up without complaint.

Amy stood in the dust of the oak tree,

slowly spinning the beaded bangle on her arm, neither settled into staying nor attempting to leave. Cow Tom pointed to a far-off spot in the south field and ordered the girl's brother to look after a calf too close to the woods. The boy bounded off at a fast clip. The calf was in no danger, but Cow Tom wanted to show Amy that he was in charge of the herd. That he was in charge of her brother.

"I have to go back," said Amy, but she made no move to return to the square.

"Meet me in the woods tonight after supper," Cow Tom said.

She surprised him by saying nothing. She was usually as eager as he to find a place where the two of them could be alone, and they had a well-used meeting spot by the split oak where they could be together beyond the curious eyes of the tribe or the Negroes in the Commons. Her two-room Commons cabin housed three, including her brother and Sarah, the woman who did the cooking for Chief Yargee, and the log cabin where Cow Tom lived was little more than a pass-through point for single males on the way to manhood or beyond coupling, including Horse Tom and Poke-Eye. Amy's brother would soon be too old to stay with the women and needed to take his place in one of the men's cabins. Many nights Cow Tom slept under the expanse of the moon and sky, sending prayers upward to the stars, more content outdoors among the cattle than imprisoned in a dank room with snoring young males and liquor-soaked old men.

"What say you?" he asked.

She drew her mouth tight. "Spotted Deer is younger and already jumped the broom with Ezekiel."

She bent to retrieve the flask from Cow Tom's feet. He caught her hand in his, and moved his thumb upward slowly, past the bangles at the wrist, stroking her bare arm until he felt the resistance melt.

"Someday," he said, barely giving thought to her complaint. A stronger notion had begun to crowd his mind of late. His life was bound too tight, and he dreamed more and more of some world where he could roam wherever the winds blew, exploring new territory, meeting new challenges. It confused and frustrated him, this cruel aspiration, impossible as the slave of another man.

"There's a baby," she said, pulling away from him, but she didn't break her gaze, searching his face.

Just at the copse line of trees at Amy's

back, an emboldened hawk dipped and sliced the air close to the ground before it continued its rapid upward flight and disappeared from view. Cow Tom brought his attention back to Amy.

He felt the long, flat line of his life crowd in, settling heavy around his shoulders. Cows. Wife. Children. Crops. Cows. Something deep inside him chafed.

"One day soon they'll move the Creeks from this place," Cow Tom said. "The government wants the land."

"Did you not hear? There's to be a child."

"I saw the assigned territory as scout with Chief Yargee a few years back," Cow Tom said. "North and west beside a river, not so rich as this. Some Lower Creeks are already gone there."

"What of their slaves?" Amy asked. She placed one hand on her stomach and held it protectively, but there was nothing Cow Tom could see that was any different from yesterday. Not a bulge, not a bump, not the familiar waddle of women he'd seen all his life, black or Indian or white.

"Some taken along, some sold and left behind."

"Chief Yargee's never sold any of us," Amy said.

"But if he does, we'd be white owned.

Scattered."

Amy stripped a low-hanging willow's branch of some of its leaves, balled them together, spit on them, and threw them over her shoulder.

He'd become used to her not-quite ways — not quite black, not quite Creek, not quite Seminole, not quite white. Sometimes Cow Tom recognized a starting point, could trace from which of her ownership lives a warding-off superstition stemmed, but other times he suspected she made it up as she went along.

"There's nothing we can do about it," she said.

"There's always something to do," snapped Cow Tom. Amy winced, but he didn't try to smooth it over, fighting to hang on to his belief that his words were true. Her humbugs sometimes made him uneasy.

Cow Tom could still recall the fierceness of the free black man who visited years before, carrying freedom papers with him like a shield. From that day, Cow Tom had scrounged and saved, but he didn't have enough yet to buy himself, let alone a wife and baby. For every quarter or dollar Cow Tom earned on the side, Chief Yargee deducted his share and held the rest against Cow Tom's future purchase. Cow Tom sold over fifteen scrub cattle he'd raised as a small herd on his own, for three to four dollars apiece. He knew given more time, he would negotiate a far better price for the two fine calves recently presented to him by Chief McIntosh as a reward for saving the lives of the mother cows last year. Chief Yargee held over one hundred dollars to put toward freedom papers. A start, but not enough. His price was $400.

"What of us, today?" Amy asked.

"I'm going to be free," said Cow Tom.

"Maybe," said Amy. "But your son comes on his own time, no matter."

Amy was so sure of her place with him, he was tempted to believe he could be content. Cow Tom wavered. Attachment was risky. People always left in the end, whether their fault or no. But a son, a physical mingling of himself and Amy, a well-built boy he could teach to hunt and track. Another sudden image replaced the last, and rolled through him, hot and sharp. A port-wine-stained woman, spirited away as Cow Tom watched.

Torment still came upon him often, regardless of years passed, and if not careful, pitched him into foul darkness for days, strong flashes of memory he couldn't purge. Himself as a young boy, staring across a field of cotton, full bucket of water in his hands. Two men, two horses at a gallop away from the back of the main plantation house, his mother thrown across the saddleless blanket in front of the larger man and held down tight. Tom didn't move right away, frozen, registering a random smattering of detail. The men didn't seem Creek, neither one, but wore cloth turbans, and one sported a silver gorget across his chest. His terrified mother, screaming, the birthmark stain at her temple red and flaring, a short, dark woman in worn homespun and a head scarf, with rope at her wrists and the paper-thin cracked leather of one shoe exposed beneath her skirt. The other foot bare and kicking until the man shouted something in a language Cow Tom didn't know, and silenced her somehow. Finally, Tom's legs propelled him across the wide expanse in their direction, and he took up the screams his mother no longer uttered, but the gap between them steadily widened until the two men rounded a bend in the road and disappeared from view. By the time Tom found the Graysons, his mother was long gone, and his master's pursuit of the abductors only resulted in failure.

Later, Old Turtle brought him supper, but he couldn't eat. Unable to hold back choking sobs, he described the Indians he'd seen. The old man speculated from clothes and speech that Seminoles stole Cow Tom's mother, and most likely took her somewhere in the wilds of Florida to hide among themselves. One day Cow Tom had a mother, and the next he had none.

Tom battled the image gone, and blinked away the searing residue, bringing himself back to Yargee's plantation.

"There's got to be more than cows," Cow Tom said to Amy.

"Family," she said. "Now we make a family."

"I want . . ." He stumbled to find the words. "I want to be part of the world, not just here."

Amy was unfazed. She looked so young, her hair wrapped tight in a cotton scarf, a sureness in her dark eyes that seemed to catch sight of parts of him he didn't recognize himself. The tiny mole on the right side of her face pulled him toward her lips as if he had no say.

"I know who you are," said Amy.

But did she really? Did she understand how much he wanted something he couldn't name or describe, something more than passing an empty life doing someone else's bidding, tending a herd not his own, trapped on a patch of land, no matter how large, the landscape too soon familiar and the circumstance too hedged? How he yearned to make good on his mother's prophecy before she was ripped from him, that he become, somehow, a man special enough for her pride? Did Amy understand how the soles of his feet itched and his heart ached when outside visitors came to talk to Chief Yargee for one reason or another, and he couldn't mount a pony and follow when the time came for them to leave, off to someplace fresh, and unknown, somewhere with new things to learn?

"I won't always be slave," he said.

Amy nodded. "We fit, you and me."

It was true. After his mother was taken, he had never been drawn to another person, or opened himself to any other, except Old Turtle.

"Family," he repeated.

"And soon our son joins us."

Cow Tom was struck by the beginnings of a longing that muted the image of the port-stained woman. A boy. His boy. He wanted a son. He wanted to be part of his growing up, to protect him. And Amy was right. The two of them fit well. His unease shifted. He met Amy's gaze.

"The time is come for us to marry," he

said. The words tumbled out, and he wasn't sorry. She bewitched him.

Amy smiled, not wide, but definitely a smile, and Cow Tom found his voice again. "You've no parents for permission, and your brother is too young to seek agreement there, and my people are gone. We'll get Chief Yargee's consent to jump the broom."

"But not before the full moon," said Amy.

Cow Tom was used to her injunctions. She'd been right when the *stikini* screeched all night in the tree close to Lucinda's cabin, and Amy predicted death close by. Sure enough, they'd found Lucinda's baby stopped of breathing in the morning.

"Bad luck for us to marry before passing of the first moon," she said. "After, my brother takes your bed in the men's cabin, and you move into ours with me."

He didn't mind that she'd already worked this through. He was content she was so capable. Although marriage came sooner than expected, the transition didn't have to be difficult. Amy would make a fine wife.

Marriage. A son. Freedom. He wanted all of it.

CHAPTER 3

On a bright summer Tuesday, Cow Tom found them together on the banks of the river, Old Turtle seated, shoulders hunched, his back against the cypress tree and stout stick on the ground next to his feet, and Amy holding a gourd to his lips, the fullness of her jutting belly straining at the fabric of her tunic. Three women, two Negroes and one Creek, washed clothes farther downstream, their voices rising occasionally above the slapping of wet cloth on the rocks.

Exhausted from a long day in the pasture tending a sickened heifer, Cow Tom wanted nothing more than to collect Old Turtle and lead the blind man back to his cabin for the night before taking supper. But the sight of Amy and Old Turtle, the two people he most prized, caused him to pause, and he hesitated, considering them both. Amy had become even more grounded in the carrying of the child, more attuned, as if she heard a song in her mind to which only she knew the notes. She talked so softly to Old Turtle that Cow Tom couldn't make out her words. Usually Old Turtle rambled on, and Amy patiently listened, but today Old Turtle was calm and compliant, without his usual grousing, allowing her to guide the gourd without struggle. But he only sipped, laboring under each swallow.

Every morning, Cow Tom led Old Turtle out of his cabin, and settled him in the out-of-doors with his corncob pipe and guiding stick. He propped him up at the stout base of the same cypress tree by the river, in the shade, spreading a blanket over his legs, and left Old Turtle to fend for himself while he worked, leaving a supply of river water and a bean pie or slab of cold *sofki*. Toward evening, Cow Tom returned him to his shack. Either he or Amy looked in on Old Turtle as best they could throughout the day.

Amy looked up first, and Cow Tom quickened his step to join them.

"Ready?" he asked Old Turtle.

Completely blind, his hands in constant tremble, Old Turtle turned toward Cow Tom. "Time for me and you to talk," he said.

Amy stood. "I'd best be getting to fixing

supper," she said, and she slipped away, leaving him alone with Old Turtle. Cow Tom squatted in the dirt and waited.

"She gone?" Old Turtle asked.

"Yes."

"She's the right one for you. Amy."

"So she swayed you to her side," said Cow Tom.

"You jumped the broom, married now, a man full-grown. And soon enough, a father."

Cow Tom nodded, though Old Turtle couldn't see it, sure there was death talk to follow. Old Turtle lived less and less in this world, and more within his preparations to depart.

"My time is coming. Everybody needs somebody on this earth, 'specially you. Choose wise, but careful to give back in kind. You're not the motherless child no more."

Cow Tom held himself tight. After his mother was snatched from the Old Place, Old Turtle never talked about her, or said her name, or referred to her even in passing, and Cow Tom didn't push, as if by asking, his mother might slip from his grasp entirely.

"You're the closest I got to family, and now you've age enough to bind my claim of fours," Old Turtle said. "I been watching, all these years, from the Old Place to this. You got your ways to make things come out one way over another. When my time comes, you the one to do the digging. Don't let them leave me alone until I go in the ground, four days later. The night before, hold service and talk good about me. Bury my walking stick and my drinking gourd and a cup of coffee and an apple with me, and you and Amy give me the farewell handshake. Make sure the grave is covered complete, and keep the rain from over my head till I'm gone west. Build a house over the grave so when my spirit wanders for a bit and makes the last visits, it knows where to come back to. And gunshots, four, one in each direction."

"I can do most," said Cow Tom, "but Chief Yargee won't shoot guns for us."

Old Turtle lit his pipe, a slow process. He had to feel for the dent of the bowl, tap in the pinch of tobacco. He didn't want Cow Tom's help, except to marry the flame.

"We might get Saturdays and Mondays for ourself, and could do worse owned by other than Upper Creek and Massa Yargee, but slave is still slave. Don't forget it." A bit of tobacco spilled from the bowl of the pipe and fell down the front of his shirt. "That said, you got powers to do what I ask," Old

Turtle insisted. "Those shots give my spirit time to go the way of the sun, to join family and friends gone before."

"Why would Chief Yargee listen to me?"

"Don't talk foolish. I don't have time enough," said Old Turtle. "You know you got something big in you, boy."

"What I know of cattle I learned from you," Cow Tom admitted.

"I showed you this and that, and you took to it, but it's not cattle I'm talking about," Old Turtle said. "Maybe that's most what Massa Yargee notices right now, but it's matching up words to people and meanings and happenings that serves you best."

Old Turtle felt around, his trembly hand patting at the blanket. Cow Tom thought he'd lost his pipe in the folds until he realized the blind man was searching for him, for the touch of him. Cow Tom leaned close, and awkwardly put his hand on the quilt covering the old man's knees.

"Your mama, she was smart that way too," Old Turtle said.

Cow Tom quickly drew his hand back. He covered his confusion by hoisting Old Turtle and helping him to his feet.

"Time to get you inside," Cow Tom said. He led Old Turtle to his cabin, matching his gait to the old man's, and got him settled.

"Remember what I ask," said Old Turtle as he left.

Next morning, Cow Tom came to collect Old Turtle for the day. The small cabin, always dim, seemed a different shade of black inside, cold and foreboding. A dim glow of embers remained in the fireplace, mostly ash now, but there was a stillness hung over the room. Cow Tom stepped slowly into the darkness, and knew before he came to the narrow cot that the figure under the threadbare cover had crossed to the other side. He didn't have the right to touch or handle the dead, not until he drank the red root and purged, but he sat on the old three-legged stool next to the cot for a moment to collect his heart, permitting himself to stare once more at the old man's face. He couldn't stay, a day of chores and the herd needing his attention, but he couldn't leave just yet. He waited until the last ember in the fireplace turned black, and the fire ceased to be.

Old Turtle was dead. His mentor had left him.

And Cow Tom's last link to his mother was gone.

CHAPTER 4

Cow Tom thrashed about the better part of the night trying to figure how to persuade Chief Yargee to fire guns at a slave's funeral.

"You'll find a way," Amy said into the darkness beside him, but his mind still churned after she fell into a soft snore.

The next day in the pasture, he practiced first one speech and then another on his cows, the knot of his stomach pulling ever tighter than a fist, but no argument seemed quite right, quite convincing enough, and time ran short.

He came straight from his work in the pasture to Yargee's log house, and presented himself at the back door. Sarah, the cook, let him in, a skinny Negro woman twice Cow Tom's age who ate better than anyone black or Indian, but never put on the weight of someone whose stock and trade is food. He stood in the kitchen for quite some time until Yargee was through with his evening meal, reminded the while by the rumbling of his stomach that he should have stopped for his own supper first.

Finally, Yargee met him on the back porch. The chief towered over Cow Tom, unusually tall for a Creek. He seemed in a foul mood, annoyed at being called out, and Cow Tom considered coming back in the morning, when he might be more receptive. The chief was changeable, ill-tempered and rigid one day, and full of humor the next. But Cow Tom plunged ahead.

"Old Turtle's dead," Cow Tom said.

Chief Yargee softened a bit. "I am sorry to hear," he said. "We'll put him to ground tomorrow, before sundown."

"He asked after the Creek way. Buried in four days."

Chief Yargee considered. "That'll be all right."

"I'll dig the hole," said Cow Tom. "People be coming by the cabin to see him the night before. He'll be ready."

"All right." Yargee turned to go, their business finished.

Cow Tom thought of Old Turtle, how sure he'd been his charge could represent him.

"He wanted shots fired," Cow Tom said, before he lost Yargee back into the house. A throbbing started up at his temple, gaining speed. He wondered if Chief Yargee could see it. He had to fight to keep his voice even. "A service with shots fired. I thought to clear that by you."

Yargee squinted at Cow Tom, his face clouded. "Shots are for warriors. Upper Creek warriors."

Cow Tom tasted a sickening sourness at the base of his tongue. "Old Turtle served the tribe," he said. "Served the tribe better than most." The words pushed out hard and fast, far louder than he expected.

The tightness in Chief Yargee's face deepened, and he folded his arms across his chest.

Cow Tom knew then that he was done, that he'd been denied, but he couldn't seem to stop. "Old Turtle saved the whole herd from milk sickness after we first came here. He thought himself Creek. Like the rest of us."

Yargee's voice turned cold. "He'll have a fitting service. Go along now."

The throbbing turned to a hammer and pounded out everything else. "We *are* Creek. We *are.* Old Turtle earned those burying shots."

"You forget yourself, boy. Back down or pay the price."

Cow Tom looked down at his hands,

balled into tight fists. What Chief Yargee meant was that Old Turtle would have a fitting service for a slave, despite his high-handed talk about how they were members of the tribe too. Yargee loved a good celebration, whether for life or death or any reason in between, and Cow Tom should have appealed to that instinct in seeking permission for gunshots. Instead, he'd squandered his one opportunity without figuring out how to read the man properly. It was a mistake. His mistake. A coward's mistake. Slowly, he unclenched his fists and contorted his face to a docile mask. He backed out of the house and made his way back to the Quarter.

Coward, he told himself. He was a coward. He couldn't show anger. He was slave. But still. He didn't have it in him to be special.

Cow Tom failed. He'd failed Old Turtle.

After the burial, they gathered outside Old Turtle's cabin, all the slaves, but Cow Tom's mood turned dark. Once Amy performed the purification, he went back to his cabin and fell onto the thin mattress as if drunk, although he hadn't a drop to drink. Something had been severed, a ragged incision that left him without defense. He was alone, pinned in place on the sweated cot. Old

Turtle was gone, his faith in his young charge misplaced. The bitter sickness eating at Cow Tom's insides reminded him of those days just after his mother was taken, and the world around him turned more and more gray, until little had meaning. He finally fell asleep, or something close to it, but jerked awake in terror, searching out something familiar. The night was pitch-black, no light coming through the small window, and Amy sat beside the bed. She had put a poultice on his forehead, and he grabbed at the wrapping cloth and flung it across the room. She was talking to him, but he didn't hear what she said, he didn't care what she said. He turned his back to her and curled up into himself, his hands over his ears until the talking stopped.

"Tom."

Amy again. Must be morning this time. No difference, so long as he didn't slip back into sleep, and his mother's port-stained face, mouth open in scream, awaiting him in every dream. His limbs seemed too leaden to lift, his eyes hurt too much to open, and his ears were too tired to listen.

"You have to get up. I told him I'm treating you for the fever, but Chief Yargee can't be put off much longer. You have to go back

45

to work."

Dark. It was all too dark for Cow Tom to see.

"Tom."

Her voice was far away.

"If not for you, or for me, for your son," Amy said.

His wife's voice was measured, impossible for him to block.

"Get up for your son, so he knows from the start how a man does."

If she had shown panic, or desperation, or anger, if she had pleaded, Cow Tom wasn't sure she could have broken through his fog. But as she repeated herself, over and over, he considered the curious possibility of following the clear, bright line of her voice from the depths of the hole in which he found himself, just for awhile, just to see where it led, and then he opened his eyes, bringing her into focus. She was calm, in a chair by the bedside, sweating lightly, one hand on the high bump of her overripe belly, a strange intensity in those sable-brown eyes that held him steady.

With the connection made, she spoke new words.

"I will give you sons," Amy said in Mvskoke.

"We are your family," she said in Hitchiti.

46

"I will give you sons. We are your family," she repeated in English. "Go on. Get up now."

Cow Tom struggled to his feet, fighting the pull to crawl back under the covers. The sun had barely broken the seal of the night. He was still in his grieving clothes, shirt and leggings, his moccasins on the floor, close to the bed. Amy must have removed them. Cow Tom put them on slowly, and set off to the pasture to relieve his wife's brother in the tending of the herd. He was bone tired, and he was hungry, but comforted that Amy would bring his breakfast out to the field to him soon enough, surely before the sun rose too far in the sky.

Within one week of Old Turtle's passing, Cow Tom became a father. The tiny, dark baby emerged with a full head of hair, wailing. A girl.

They named her Malinda.

CHAPTER 5

The ground was still sodden from the sudden afternoon squall, but the sun was doing its best to dry the pasture, the fields, and the gardens. It was a less busy time of year, neither breeding nor calving season, and after leaving Amy's brother and another hand to tend the herd, Cow Tom came from the meadow a little early, splashing through puddles. He had business with Chief Yargee in the main house, but delayed in order to pass through the Quarter on his way. The jagged crisscross of paths between the small logged cabins was second nature, and he practiced his arguments in his head to present to the chief before he came to his own house.

His daughters played together on the damp ground, Malinda and Maggie, the older three and her sister one. Maggie mimicked Malinda's every move, patting gooey mud into a flat shape, as if making bread for supper. Sons would have pleased him more, but he was well satisfied with his daughters, and there was time enough for the boys who would surely come. Not far away, Amy toiled in the garden, hoe in hand. Cow Tom congratulated himself. He was aware of his good fortune, a wife who still excited him each time he caught sight of her. His detour to the Quarter, he knew, stemmed from the knot of guilt tugging at him, though he intended to hold steady to his course. Cow Tom was a man at war with himself, fighting the need to do right by his family and the deep hunger to be free, to explore.

She looked up, her face betraying both the carryover of their unfinished business from last night as well as concern.

"You're early. So you'll talk to him today then?" she said.

"It is Chief Yargee's choice," Cow Tom said, as if no time at all had passed since this line of reasoning failed in their argument of the night before.

Amy stared at him, her eyes tunneling into his until he was forced to turn his head, fixing his gaze on a neat row of green-topped onions in their patch of garden.

"I do what's best for us," he said. "All of us."

"You want to go," she accused. "You steered Chief Yargee into sending you."

He started to protest, but stopped himself. He couldn't deny the merit in her words. She knew him too well.

"Three hundred and fifty dollars, Amy," he said instead. "Freedom comes much faster this way."

"And if they Remove us while you're gone? What then? What of us, me and the girls? If you don't come back, what then?"

"The military man said the war nears its end. Just a few months to round up the last of the Seminoles in Florida. All Creek warriors and translators will be back to Alabama long before our Removal, February at the latest, in time to make the trip with you to Indian Territory, in time for first planting there with Chief Yargee."

"How can you know how long war lasts? Seminoles are stubborn. And cagey. We would do well to keep out of all their doings, Seminoles, government, and Creek."

"We *are* Creek," Cow Tom insisted, and though she held her tongue, he could see that Amy's lack of argument did not imply an equal conviction on her part. "Our good is bound up with theirs."

Amy set her jaw. "You'll do what you want," she said.

"There's no changing course now. The bargain with the army is struck. I leave with the others next week."

She picked up her hoe and began to stab at the clusters of weeds sprouting near the squash.

He almost told her then, and shared his desperate plan, but feared jinxing if he said the words aloud. He'd have to smooth things over later with Amy. For now, he needed Chief Yargee.

He found the chief near the crook of the stream, his favorite place. He sat on a large, smooth rock on the bank, staring out into the water, his unlit pipe in hand.

"Chief Yargee," Cow Tom said.

His chief looked as if he had aged ten years in the last twelve months, and he turned to Cow Tom only briefly before resuming his calm stare. Cow Tom wasn't sure what Yargee saw when he gazed at the blue of the water.

"I am loath to leave," said Yargee, in Mvskoke.

"It's been a good place," Cow Tom answered simply.

"My father, Big Warrior, was principal chief of Upper Creeks here after the Creek War. My brother was killed by whites here.

I brought down my first deer in those woods, and married both my wives here. And now they force us to go, like the land belongs to them alone."

"You'll take everyone with you? Negro and Indian?" Cow Tom tried not to sound too anxious. "We can all help rebuild in Indian Territory."

Chief Yargee seemed surprised by the question. "Yes. All will travel together, Creeks, Negroes, and as much stock as they allow. Removal won't be easy."

"But the land has been set aside?"

"Yes. Some of us are already moved. Lower Creeks mostly. I intend to wait until my warriors return from Florida to start the journey."

Before Removal from Alabama, the United States military demanded Alabama Creeks send seven hundred warriors to Florida, and the tribes didn't dare refuse. Chief Yargee had already picked six of his warriors, and two translators, including Cow Tom.

Cow Tom judged the time right. "The military man promises $350 for each translator." The possibility of that much money backed by the United States government for a few months of work almost made him lightheaded.

"Yes," said Yargee.

"Some of that rental money goes to the tribe, like always." Cow Tom rubbed his hands on his pants. "More than fair," he added quickly. "Amy and the girls stay behind to help the tribe while I do the job in Florida, like I've done for you so many years, translating English and Mvskoke to and fro. And some Hitchiti. I'll scout and track and round up Seminoles to Remove to Indian Territory like they say. The military will be satisfied." His palms were still damp, but he let his hands dangle loose at his sides. "I'll be back in time to help us Remove. And I'm hoping you'll put my bit of the rental money toward my freedom papers."

Yargee lit his pipe, and Cow Tom waited while the chief assured himself the tobacco was caught and he drew in the smoke.

"I will put it with the rest," he finally said. "For your return to the tribe."

"Half?" Cow Tom said.

Chief Yargee nodded.

Cow Tom made his face a mask to hide the sudden rush of exhilaration. Soon he'd leave Alabama for the first time in his life, and earn enough in just a few months to bring him closer to freedom. And now he would make good on his lifelong hope. Even if akin to tracking a single grain of sand, he renewed his pledge to find his long-gone mother in Florida.

All that was left was to make it up with Amy before leaving.

■ ■ ■ ■

FLORIDA

–1837–

■ ■ ■ ■

CHAPTER 6

Cow Tom ignored the steady trickle of sweat sliding down his cheeks, his nose, his chin, before dropping to the ground, just more wetness mixing into the Florida swampland. He stood a few feet from the general, eyes slightly downcast, careful not to feed into the man's agitation. Even when the second mosquito slipped down his shirt collar to feed, Cow Tom didn't swat the blamed pest or move a muscle, letting the general vent his gall undistracted. They were separated from the other military men in the scouting unit, and Cow Tom waited patiently to find out why the general had called him to his side.

Cow Tom was the general's favorite interpreter, cut by saw grass, made raw by insect bites, enduring drenching rain, noxious vapors, and scorching sun. He'd waded rivers, marched burning sands, crossed impassable swamps, been subjected to malaria, dysentery, alligators, and venomous snakes. He'd served as interpreter and government mouthpiece for countless treaties, even though he knew them full of half-truths and outright lies on both sides.

"Damned Seminoles!" the general exclaimed. "Millions of our money lost here, and for what? To gain this barren, sandy, swampy, and good-for-nothing peninsula? Sometimes I think it better to leave the Indians here in Florida, where God placed them."

The white man looked more haggard with every passed day, and as his forced accomplice, Tom could predict the man's frame of mind before the general himself knew he'd brewed up a temper. This latest had gone on for days, more than the usual swings of mood or fatigue from spilled blood or breathing fetid air while traipsing through the muck of Florida swamps. Hunting down Seminoles in their camps, carrying out orders from a headquarters so removed they didn't understand the realities of the field, and striking Capitulation treaties with rebellious and uncooperative Seminole chiefs took their toll.

Cow Tom said nothing. After ten months of service, he knew it was better to wait the general out when he got like this. He took his mind instead to the rolling hills of Alabama, absent here in Florida, and tried to fix an image of Amy tending the home fire, and Malinda and Maggie, fed and thriving. He wondered who looked after the herd in his absence, if there was still a herd to tend. They'd thought the war and his stint of service would be over months ago, a short-term rental before relocation to Indian Territory with his family by February, in time to resettle and plant for the new season. And here it was June, yet dragging on. Where were they now, Chief Yargee and Amy? Creek families were held as hostages for the good behavior of Creek warriors sent to Florida, but where? In a holding camp? At a military fort? Now all he wanted was to get back to Amy and his girls before the general got him killed.

"I tell you this," the general said. "By my hand, by the hand of the United States government, they *will* Remove. Every last Seminole in Florida." He thrust a stiff finger in the air to punctuate his point. "I'm tired of Seminole resistance, tired of stubborn chiefs and conniving counselors and blood-thirsty warriors and tricky black translators and antagonistic slaves, ready to die before honoring Capitulation."

Cow Tom could have pointed out that

Seminoles were only defending their family land, but the general was too wrapped up in his righteousness. The United States government was determined to move the Seminoles west, and the Seminoles were equally resolved to hold to the Florida ground of their ancestors.

"I want you to go to Fort Brooke," the general said. He relit the stump of his cigar and drew in a long breath before exhaling. The smoke coiled in lazy loops around his dark curls, and the sharp tobacco smell made Cow Tom long for a smoke of his own. "And report back any unusual activity."

Last year, when Chief Yargee rented Cow Tom out for his translator skills, sending him east alongside seven hundred conscripted Creek warriors to fight for the Federals, Cow Tom was assigned to the general. He'd arrived at Fort King green, a novice, amazed by every sight and sound and smell. The fort housed military and military hangers-on, men of both horse and foot. He saw men of prayer side by side with the profane, scholars and dolts, swaggering men of rank, youngsters new to gun and blade, fat men and lean, temperate and drunk, the bootless and idle watching the busy. Cow Tom followed behind the general from one such fort to another, and came to understand what a determined military man he was, ruthless, competent, and capable of deceit.

And now Cow Tom was the interpreter General Jesup trusted most, right hand to the man in charge of the entire Florida campaign of the Second Seminole War. The general turned to Cow Tom for not only words but ideas as well. Few white men could handle Hitchiti, Mvskoke, and Miccosukee, and few Indians English. The U.S. government needed the Seminoles to abandon their native soil, because they wanted Florida lands for themselves. That much was obvious to any thinking man. But some white men of great influence wanted more. They schemed to send the Seminoles west, with their slaves left behind as easy fodder to collect and feed to Southern plantations. But the last years of do-or-die fighting proved the Seminoles wouldn't easily comply.

"Yes, sir," Cow Tom said.

Fort Brooke. Cow Tom hated the idea of the sprawling camp, like many he'd come to know, holding pens for the dispossessed, way stations for people stripped of every familiarity and shuttled from one hard life to the next, hundreds or thousands of miles away, ripe to death, disease, starvation, separation, and melancholy. Yet this assignment was a perfect opportunity.

"Two is better than one," Cow Tom said. "Harry Island is a top linguister. Almost good as me."

The general waved his hand in easy dismissal. "Yes. Yes. Fine," he said. "Just report back to me immediately if there's trouble. The situation isn't . . ." He trailed off.

"Stable?" Cow Tom offered.

He'd handed the general an easy out. What he wanted to say to the general was that the situation was foul. He bore no great love for the Seminoles, two had carried off his mother after all, but this business of repeatedly moving them and all other tribes off ancestral land and taking away their way of life was worse than wrong. As bad as Indians had it, the slaves of Indians were in for even worse if stripped of their current masters and forced to the Deep South to cotton fields or plantations there. But he held his tongue, as he'd learned to do well.

"Yes," the general said. "Not stable." He looked as pleased with the word as Cow Tom knew he would. The general used it often to convey broke-spirit compliance with the government's will, and Cow Tom recognized the value of feeding the word back to him now. Translation wasn't the only tool of a good interpreter. "The Seminoles have known they are to Remove for three years, and still they threaten hostility."

Cow Tom considered keeping quiet, but what purpose to have maneuvered into his position if he didn't risk to protect those who couldn't protect themselves?

"They didn't expect slave catchers let loose in the camp," he said. "They believed the treaty."

The general flared, and turned to face Cow Tom head-on. "The job is to Remove all Seminoles from Florida. Suddenly your sympathies are with the Seminoles?"

"Peaceable removal of the Seminoles has to include their Negroes," Cow Tom said simply, keeping the edge from his tongue. "Otherwise they'll keep resisting, and fighting never stops."

For generations, the Seminoles had held their in-name-only slaves, intermixing, intermarrying, fighting off the government, or hiding side by side deep in the swamps of Florida. Leaving their slaves behind would mean, too often, leaving family behind. Outnumbered and outgunned, the Seminoles surrendered to army-run emigration camps only after the general's personal assurance they could take their slaves with them when they left.

The general squinted his eyes as if he had a headache, his high forehead prominent. He ran his hand through his thick mane of hair. "The government decreed them Removed, and they will Remove, whether I bring them in one at a time or burn their camps down where they sleep. Your soft heart is of no consequence. Creeks set no store by the Seminole, nor Seminole to Creek."

"My wife was owned by Seminole before Creek," said Cow Tom. "That's how I come by the language."

The general stared at him, taken aback, whether from the fact that he had a woman in Alabama, or that Amy had been slave of Seminole before Creek, or that Cow Tom had never offered personal information before, he wasn't sure. The general didn't ask anything else, letting the matter drop, and Cow Tom made no further offering either, as the general took the disclosure and quickly threw it aside, disinterested.

"As soon as a few more bring their horses and cattle for the quartermaster to purchase, we sail," said the general. "Seminoles who come in peaceably to the camps will Remove first. With slaves." He stared baldly at Cow Tom, daring his response, authority

64

plainly painted on his face.

He was lying about something. Cow Tom was sure of it. He'd made a study of matching men's gestures with their words, practicing for years on Chief Yargee before this bigger test of Florida. The general's breathing slowed and he gave the appearance of calm whenever he lied in negotiations, and his demeanor mirrored that now. There were already reports that some Seminole slaves expecting to emigrate west at Fort Brooke were first segregated in separate areas, and then "reclaimed" by anonymous white men allowed into camp. Several disappeared, either escaped or spirited away to the South. The general surely understood this was a direct violation of his personal promise. He might be a rigid man, but for all his faults, he wasn't merciless. He didn't enjoy the spectacle of suffering, even as he caused it to occur. Cow Tom calculated this wasn't the time to try to push the general further into a corner he had to defend.

"The sooner the ships come to take the Seminoles and their Negroes together, the better," Cow Tom offered. He waited for the general to share a timetable with him, to let slip some information that would give him hope for the future of the detainees.

"All I need from you is to go to the camp

and tell me if there's trouble," the general said. "Let me know if Chief Micanopy means to keep his word to Remove."

The general turned his back to Cow Tom and rejoined the other military men, and Cow Tom took his chance for a quick smoke.

He was trapped in Florida, that was given. But so long as he was here, until he could get back to Amy and his daughters, he would continue his own mission, one not swaddled in stalking and bloodshed and double-crossing. He had free rein to search this detention camp, as he had so many others, and seek his mother.

CHAPTER 7

For the better part of a day and night Cow Tom, Harry Island, and one of the general's dragoons navigated the military road from Fort King into the detention camp at Fort Brooke by Tampa Bay. They arrived without incident, midmorning on ration day, the damp heat oppressive, riding in for the last few miles in the wake of a convoy of forty supply wagons and fifty pack mules. The racket overwhelmed, and they paced the horses slow, afraid the marshy ground would trip their steeds. The moment their three-man party rode through the gate, a soldier called them.

"You there," he said. "We need attending."

Cow Tom, Harry, and the dragoon dismounted and helped unload supplies, while convoy soldiers began to break barrels and sacks down into quantities for individual distribution. Others jockeyed their animals into position to water and feed.

"Put muscle behind it!" the soldier shouted to the sweating men. "We got a turnabout to make."

Too hot to move this fast, Cow Tom thought. The supply wagons had only just arrived, yet they intended to drop the load and clear out again. A long line snaked around one of the outbuildings, Seminole women waiting in the scorching sun, more than one wrapped in the cotton feed bags used to hold corn for the army's horses. Cow Tom studied them all: long, straight black hair, complexions fawn and russet and olive and mushroom and copper, but even the darkest among them weren't the deep coffee color of his mother. He refused to let his disappointment get the better of him. There was more of the camp to search.

"Leastways they boast rations," he said.

Two young Seminole braves began to pass out the weekly corn and flour to the line, under the watchful eye of a dragoon, along with mismatched lengths of coarse cotton cloth.

"Where are the guards?" Cow Tom asked. At the turret, there was only one dispirited soldier with a musket.

"Measles outbreak," Harry said. He had to almost yell to be heard. "Soldiers here sick or dead. First they thought smallpox, but the doctor declares measles. The convoy's dumping supplies and hightailing. They won't stay overnight."

Cow Tom was never exactly sure where Harry secured his information, but had come to both trust and depend on it. He enjoyed the company of another African Creek forced to serve as guide and translator. Harry Island's owner lived not too far north of Chief Yargee in Alabama, but Cow Tom hadn't known Harry before they met in Florida one sticky afternoon, each at the heels and ears of their assigned military men.

"Sickly season in Florida is a crazy time to wage war," Cow Tom said in Mvskoke to Harry, so the dragoon couldn't understand the criticism. "For both sides."

Once finished with unloading, the three led their horses to the stables. A young soldier, alone, groomed one of the horses, without enthusiasm, a healthy brown roan with a darkish mane. The soldier's uniform seemed several sizes too big, and the tuft of sandy brown hair under his cap was dry and brittle. From farther away, the soldier had a farm-boy look, fresh faced, but when they came closer, they saw the ravages of dried pustules and spots not yet faded dotting both cheeks. The dragoon was first to say what Cow Tom was thinking.

"You got the pox?" he asked, taking a step back.

"Not the pox," the young soldier said. "Doctor when he come said measles. I spent my time in the sickbed, and measles come and gone." He fingered his face, touching the still-swollen skin as if exploring a foreign territory. "More than three-quarters of the soldiers here in the infirmary, burning up with fever. I'm better off than the others."

"They let you out?"

"Once you can walk out, that's what you do," the boy said. "If fever breaks, you're through with it. Doctor says you're done carrying."

"They let you handle the horses?"

"Nobody else here to do it," he said. "But don't matter to me whether you leave your horses or not."

After a bit of negotiation and pulling of rank by mentioning the general's name, they left the tired animals with the young soldier to dress and put up.

"Best stay away from the infirmary," the soldier warned as they left the stables.

The dragoon disappeared by himself into the bowels of the fort, off, Cow Tom assumed, to find drink and English-speaking companions more to his liking. Cow Tom and Harry kept together and explored by foot. Deportee camp or no, there were bad feelings between the Creeks and Seminoles, and hostilities didn't evaporate overnight because of a shift in the balance of power. Conditions were as they had come to expect, the women in the most desperate state, clothes scant and tattered, mood subdued and depressed. Groups of Seminole men were scattered around the grounds, adjacent to the dots of makeshift housing on the sandy soil.

"Must be seven or eight hundred Seminoles here," Harry guessed, in Mvskoke.

"But for rations, the chiefs would never come in willingly," Cow Tom said.

"Especially with Osceola at their heels," said Harry. "He can't be happy they've given up the fight."

Cow Tom switched to English, though none seemed particularly interested in two black men talking. "Murderers, the lot of them. Micanopy and Jumper killed almost as many whites as Osceola. I never believed to see all turn themselves in at once."

They wound their way around the encampment, mingling with the Seminoles, pausing to listen wherever men clustered, straining for news, but for the most part, they met stony silence or outright suspicion. Cow Tom compared Fort King to this encampment in Tampa Bay. Setting aside the likeness of steamy heat and sand and vicious fleas, the difference came down to people. Only the occasional woman appeared at the margins of Fort King, usually of the roughest, military-follower sort, but here at Fort Brooke, large numbers of women settled into domestic life alongside their men, their children playing games among themselves as children did anywhere.

A sallow-skinned brave lay prone on a coarse horse blanket, alone under a sycamore tree, chewing slowly on a tobacco leaf. He coughed several times, hoarse and unsettling.

"You all right?" asked Cow Tom.

"The white man brings us to this place to give us smallpox," the brave said.

"No," Harry said in Miccosukee, "measles. The white man brings measles."

The brave glared, unimpressed with the distinction. They left him and walked the camp, and came upon a small group of women pounding coontie root with a flat rock. The women never slowed their rhythm. They hadn't touched their ration of corn or flour, set off to the side under an oak tree, wrapped in gunny. Instead, for bread making, they used the plentiful root found everywhere in this part of Florida, foraged outside the encampment.

"You see what I see? Or more like it, don't see?" said Harry. "Not a single Negro, free nor slave."

"Balls!" Cow Tom swore. The government already separated the Negroes from the Seminoles. His mother wasn't at this camp. Understanding the general's strategy didn't calm his anger. A free black man or woman facing re-enslavement was the most potent ally the Seminoles could have in their bloody fight to keep their Florida home.

"So much for easy information," said Harry.

"We best find Micanopy," Cow Tom said.

Cow Tom and Harry widened their loop around the camp once more. At the periphery, under the shade of an old oak, a cluster of men sat in a circle, passing a smoking pipe. Cow Tom recognized almost all of them, the same group he and the general met for the Capitulation six months prior. They looked the worse for wear, thinner, scruffier, defeat written in the language of their bodies. Micanopy sat at the head, flanked by his henchman Jumper. The old chief held himself slightly apart, sitting cross-legged on the ground. Micanopy gave instruction to a young brave in the circle, who leaped up, coming back moments later with a piece of bread still warm from the women's fire. Micanopy was twice Cow Tom's age, maybe more, and in contrast to the others, so overweight he barely moved at all, except to give a slight turn of head to see who approached, but he didn't acknowledge their presence. Micanopy accepted the bread without thanks, devouring half of the large piece of flat dough with the first bite, crumbs a-tumble down his massive front. The brave silently resumed his seat.

Cow Tom and Harry drew nearer, too close to ignore, directly in the chief's line of sight.

"Governor," Cow Tom said.

Micanopy fixed him in a steely stare. But then his expression changed, as if suddenly aware of something to be lost or gained.

"Jesup's man," Micanopy acknowledged.

"Yes. Cow Tom. Come at General Jesup's request."

"Report back," said Micanopy in Miccosukee, his voice a mix of fatigue, pride, and loss, "I brought my people in." Cow Tom easily adjusted to the Seminole dialect of Hitchiti. "My advisers worry Washington won't do right by us, but I have the promise of the big white chief." He looked to Jumper and the other lesser chiefs. "They follow my word."

Cow Tom knew differently. Micanopy was, indeed, Pond Governor of the Seminole Nation in Florida, head chief, but by heredity, and his opinions and advice often went unheeded in Council. Cow Tom observed the dynamics firsthand when he met with the general and Micanopy at Capitulation, hammering out the terms under which his people would be willing to emigrate. Micanopy leaned heavily on everyone else — his counselors, his lawyer and sense bearer, his Negro translator Abraham — always choosing the path of least resistance. Although surrounded by younger and more reckless Seminoles still possessing the passions of youth, Micanopy's eagerness for conflict of any kind played out long ago. He preferred talk of peace or whatever the white man wanted to hear so long as he didn't actually have to do or risk anything.

"No trouble here at camp?" Cow Tom asked.

"Trouble? No. But now is a bad time for us to Remove," said Micanopy. "Better in the fall. Tell General Jesup."

The same suggestion he always expressed. No matter when they talked, Micanopy said the right time to leave would be next month, or next year, or five years hence. But somehow Micanopy managed to get young braves eager for revenge to lay down their weapons and surrender. Or more likely, one of his counselors had.

"Where is Abraham?" Cow Tom asked. "Where are the Negroes?"

"Taken. To Fort Volusia, down the river," Micanopy said. "To ship on separate boats."

Impossible, this chase. What if his mother wasn't in Florida after all? Twenty years gone since he'd seen her. Yet already Cow Tom's mind spun to figure how to get sent to Fort Volusia, to look for her there.

"Are your people ready to Remove?" Cow Tom asked Micanopy.

Micanopy concentrated on his bread, stuffing the last piece in his mouth, as if he hadn't heard Cow Tom speak. He'd lost interest in the exchange.

His lawyer answered instead. "We need more corn," Jumper said. He was perhaps forty, small and scrappy compared to Micanopy's girth. In negotiations, a whisper by Jumper in Micanopy's ear at the right moment often caused the chief to change course. "We left crops in the field to come here. And weapons. We need weapons to hunt."

"Terms of Capitulation are for the government to provide all food until Removal," Cow Tom said. "And one year beyond."

"Terms of Capitulation also say our bona fide property, our Negroes, emigrate with us," said Jumper. He spoke in English, emphasizing the word *property*, as used in the treaty, his distaste and defiance both clear. "And where are they now?"

Cow Tom took his time. He considered telling Jumper they would reunite in Indian Territory, but he himself wasn't convinced, not since the general failed to inform him the Negroes were already sent away from Fort Brooke. Empty words would do nothing to reassure Jumper. He abandoned the official platitudes so often repeated in translations at the general's request.

"The Seminoles are friends to the black man," he said. "I admire Abraham and his place in the nation. It is best for all if Seminole and Negro stay together."

Jumper considered this, without comment.

"What about Osceola?" Harry asked. "Will he Remove now you've turned yourselves in?"

Micanopy cocked his head, suddenly uncomfortable, and Jumper and one of the other petty chiefs exchanged a quick look.

"Osceola is his own man," Jumper said.

"Bound by none but himself."

"Will he revenge against those who surrender?" Cow Tom didn't expect honesty, but sought a statement from which he might try to wring truth, something to report back to the general.

"Osceola is fearless, with many followers in the Seminole Nation," Jumper said.

The men in the circle turned inward then and passed the pipe in silence, without offer to Cow Tom or Harry, and the translators took the gesture as dismissal.

Once out of earshot of Micanopy and his advisers, they speculated as to what the exchange meant.

"I don't know," said Harry, "but just the mention of Osceola set them squirming. I wager you this. Some sort of shecoonery is afoot."

CHAPTER 8

Cow Tom and Harry kept themselves apart from the others, Seminole and military both, and set up bunk outside near the storehouse, sharing the jug of moonshine Harry liberated. The fiery liquid burned, but they drank to the bottom of the jug, and the menace of the fort seemed more distant. They wanted no part of the free-floating hostility permeating the camp, and less of measles. The evening proved thick and warm, but they slept in their clothes, scant protection against the biting sand fleas.

Cow Tom woke to war whoops. The moon was at its height, full and bright. Harry bolted upright, alert, and Cow Tom held his arm to prevent him from making a sound. They unsheathed their knives, and crept slowly in the direction of the outer wall of the fort, toward the front gate. The lone sentry slumped seated, his back propped against the upright like one of Malinda's rag dolls, blood at a line on his throat, dead.

Seminole braves appeared from every direction, some barefaced, some with faces striped with mud, half-black, half-red, fanning throughout the grounds and weaving in and out of the buildings, pulling the few soldiers they found from their beds. Cow Tom and Harry scattered, but not before Cow Tom saw one young brave goad forward the dragoon they rode in with from Fort King by repeated jabs with a beech club to the small of his back.

Cow Tom managed to slip behind an upright beam, neither hidden nor exposed. He'd lost sight of Harry and stayed frozen, trying to think his way out of this mess. But the warriors were everywhere, hundreds, and finally he began to run. He tried to circle around to the stables, but two braves were on him before he'd barely built up momentum and they pinned his arms, pulling him backward toward the open area where rations were distributed. Harry was already there, along with the dragoon and several others. The supply convoy from earlier in the day and all the accompanying soldiers had left the fort before nightfall, and what remained were only the few soldiers permanently stationed at Fort

Brooke. The measles outbreak had reduced the number of healthy soldiers significantly, that number less than ten. The diseased were relegated to the infirmary. The camp was more Seminole than military, more sick than fit.

Detainee Seminoles poured in from the surrounding areas of the fort, great masses of them, abandoning tent and sand and makeshift blanket. Women in flour-sack dresses stood alongside Seminole warriors dressed for battle, corn husks in their hair, faces streaked with red ocher. Cow Tom guessed at least two hundred warriors had descended on the fort, as from nowhere, more surging through the front gate even now as though they owned the entire garrison. Cow Tom waited with the rest of the captives, and the detainee Seminoles whispered among themselves in a loudening buzz. He heard the name from several directions at once.

"Osceola."

His bladder went weak. Until now, his jobs had mostly been physical labor, or thickets of words to translate, or swamps to scout, or foxing the general, or spinning bold strategies to impress. This was life-and-death. He hoped he wasn't a coward. There were more stories of Osceola than all other chiefs put together, the symbol of the resistance to remove all Seminoles from Florida. One quick glance at Harry confirmed. Harry was as panicked as he.

The night was bright, and Osceola stepped into the middle of the detention camp gathering, not far from the clutch of prisoners. He was nothing like Micanopy, in temperament or carriage: commanding, even magnetic, average height, and older than Cow Tom, somewhere between thirty and thirty-five. His face, neck, throat, and the back of his hands were streaked with red ocher, and he pulled his scalping knife from his war belt.

Osceola held up the knife, and the crowd quieted.

"I am Osceola," he announced. A guttural cheer went up.

Cow Tom singled out faces in the crowd. One of the women who pounded coontie root. The brave who refused to talk to Cow Tom and Harry. The brave who fetched a piece of warm bread for the ranking chief. Micanopy and Jumper stood close by.

Osceola pointed to the prisoners. Cow Tom tried to swallow, but found he could not. Even if they had weapons, they were less than a dozen against a field of two hundred warriors and seven hundred detained Seminoles who greeted Osceola as inspiration.

"They cannot hold you here. They have no power over you. They confine you and spread their sickness among you. You are free to return to Seminole lands in Florida instead of making the trip to the holding pens in the west."

The crowd cheered again.

"I will make the white man red with blood; and then blacken him in the sun and rain, where the wolf shall smell of his bones, and the buzzard live upon his flesh."

Osceola pointed his finger at Micanopy's chest.

"You led your people here, but they know moving from the ancestral land is not the way. You are principle chief of the Seminole, and must be respected, but a true chief will lead his people away from this place. A true chief will continue to fight. A true chief will not Remove."

Micanopy stood rooted, flanked by Jumper. For all his girth and title, he looked small and vulnerable alongside Osceola's slimness and surety of purpose.

"The military have guns, and food, and might," Micanopy said. His voice sounded whiny in the night air. "The search teams track us like deer and drive us deeper into the Everglades to starve. What chance have we in Florida now? At least in Indian Territory we will not be hunted."

Osceola played to the crowd. "Any who surrender are our enemy. We brought wagons and horses, and we will be on our way to Palaklikhaha before the break of day."

Old man Micanopy seemed at a loss. Jumper inched closer to his chief, but before he could whisper into his ear, Osceola lowered his voice to speak directly to Micanopy.

"Micanopy, if you don't lead your people out, I will, and I will leave you here for the enemy in your own blood."

Micanopy assessed the sea of Seminole faces surrounding him. For this, he needed no adviser. He held up his hand.

"The Seminoles are a great people," he announced in a thunderous voice to Osceola and the crowd, "and we will take up arms and fight the white man until our last breath."

Once again there arose a group cry of support, and Cow Tom understood their time was short. All that remained was to loot the fort and flee into the Everglades. No need leaving prisoners alive to pursue them, or to alert the U.S. Army. Cow Tom wondered how Osceola would kill them, whether fast or slow, personally or through agents. His guess was fast, since they had to move so many in one night. He wondered whether it would be him or Harry who'd watch the other die first.

As if Cow Tom summoned attention with his thoughts, Osceola looked in the direction of the prisoners, assessing his options. They stood in wait, ringed by war-painted warriors.

Osceola motioned toward Cow Tom and Harry.

"Blacks," he said.

Four braves grabbed Cow Tom and Harry by the arms. Cow Tom's knees had gone feeble, and he thought they might have to help him move, but he refused to be dragged like a cow to slaughter. He straightened his legs and walked, until they were so close to Osceola he could see for the first time the burls of pitted scars down both cheeks. The braves closed behind them like a curtain, separating them from the others. They prodded Cow Tom forward. There was no point resisting. Whatever was going to happen was already on its way into being.

"Who do you belong to?" Osceola asked.

Cow Tom found voice first, although he couldn't quite marshal his thoughts, and answered the first thing that came into his head. "General Jesup sent us yesterday to the fort to report on conditions, but we came to seek out Abraham. My mother is with the Seminoles, and I'm trying to find her."

Osceola considered this, deliberating. Cow Tom's thoughts scattered, random images flitting through his head, of Amy's strong hands flattening Indian bread for the fire, of his daughter's waddling walk alongside the creek bed. But then he imagined the first lance of the knife's sharp blade, the picking of vultures through his bones after his broken body was left to dry in the sun. He could only hope the end came swiftly.

Osceola was quick with his knife. As if in one motion, he pulled at the tip of Cow Tom's ear and sliced clean through from top to bottom, and held up the bloody flap. Red spurted, and dripped down to Cow Tom's collar, and he cried out, as much in surprise as over the stinging burn where his right earlobe used to be. It came so fast Cow Tom barely associated the bloodied mass as his until the pound and throb brought him to focus, and he clutched at the right side of his head. Osceola watched him through narrowed eyes, and Cow Tom sensed an unexpected hesitancy. He forced himself to straighten up, as if momentarily caught off guard by nothing more than a wasp's prick, of little consequence. He stifled both the scream of pain and the scream of terror competing to surface.

Jumper stepped forward. The counselor made no pretense of going through Micanopy, and the fat chief didn't protest. He seemed as irrelevant as Cow Tom in the exchange.

"He did ask after Abraham this morning," Jumper confirmed.

Cow Tom's head wasn't clear, some angle to figure he couldn't quite grasp. If Jumper involved himself, there was indeed an angle. It took Cow Tom's full concentration to remain upright.

"Where is Abraham?" Osceola asked Jumper.

"They took him to Fort Volusia with the rest of the Negroes," Jumper said.

"We need our black warriors to fight by our side." He turned again to Cow Tom. Osceola's stare was fierce, but Cow Tom saw how deeply fatigue played at the corners of his mouth and his eyes, how hunger and want weighed down his features. "Are you government?"

Cow Tom allowed himself a faint flicker of hope. Sound came to him as if confused by its own echo, both muffled and clear simultaneously, but he willed himself to focus. "We go where our masters say we must, work for who we must. The general pays our masters, and we translate. That is the way of it. We are not government."

Osceola thought about this. "Tell Abraham we wait for him to lead his people out to join us."

Cow Tom nodded, mutely. He didn't volunteer that he didn't really know Abraham, and had no authority to go to Fort Volusia. He didn't ask Osceola how unarmed blacks were supposed to break free from a fort surrounded by white men willing to siphon off any slave who couldn't prove ownership by a Seminole. Osceola had already shifted his attention elsewhere, finished with the burdensome talk of blacks and Indians.

The braves who held them released their hold, and Cow Tom and Harry stood where they were. Harry touched Cow Tom, lightly, on the arm, and made the first slow move away from the congested center of the swarm of Seminole detainees organizing themselves to flee. Cow Tom followed, the flow of blood slowing, but still dripping down the side of his face and soaking his shirt, and they eased their way toward the stables.

Their horses were still there, put up for the night, and they claimed them, saddling quickly and walking them out toward the front gate of the fort, where they mounted and waited.

"Our chances are better in plain sight than trying to hide until Osceola clears out," Harry said to Cow Tom.

The night wind played havoc with Cow Tom's ear, a strange humming set to tune.

"If they leave us our horses, we might beat this yet," Cow Tom said.

CHAPTER 9

Cow Tom mouthed a silent prayer, his pony solid beneath him as they waited by the fort's gate. He wasn't sure how long they'd been there, he and Harry, but surely two hours at least. The pain on the right side of his head had settled to a constant thrumming, as if his heart sought escape through the absent ear. But they were still alive.

"We aren't clear yet," said Harry.

Harry stated the obvious, and Cow Tom found amusement in the man's seriousness. Something wasn't working quite right with Cow Tom's mood, as if he'd stumbled into some territory beyond fear whose mother tongues were acceptance and fate. Prudence seemed to have fled in the memory of Osceola waving his bloody ear flap before the crowd.

"If spared, I pledge the rest of my life to the Negro cause," Cow Tom said. "Freedom and justice for every black man in the tribe.

Bar none."

A grand gesture. He imagined himself reflected in Harry's gaze, his head leaking blood, grossly outnumbered, but offering up negotiation points. A true bargainer. A true linguister. He was almost dizzy with his boldness.

"I join you in that pledge," said Harry. "A pact."

"A pact."

Cow Tom and Harry kept themselves unthreatening but visible, watching passively as the detainees emptied the storehouse, took military rifles, gathered their few belongings and meager, hoarded supplies, and prepared for escape into the Everglades.

By the hundreds, the Seminoles spilled out of the camp and into the nearby woods, where horses and wagons waited, Cow Tom and Harry atop their ponies at the fort's gate as they streamed past. Osceola gave an order and two of his braves slit the throats of the captured soldiers, including the Fort King dragoon. They didn't take time to scalp, but left them for dead, unceremoniously sprawled on the ground where they fell. Osceola seemed surprised to see Cow Tom and Harry as he passed through the Fort Brooke entrance, but finally nodded, as if remembering his earlier act of leniency.

They remained motionless until they were sure Osceola was gone. Only then did they dismount, and Harry doubled over, retching, and stayed down for some time. Cow Tom fought hard not to follow suit, waiting for Harry to right himself. He touched his ear, the blood no longer aflow, but soft-crusting, the steady throb familiar to him now.

They checked for survivors among the prisoners, but the soldiers were dead, and Harry and Cow Tom left them where they fell. They searched the rest of the camp, leading their horses. Among the detritus left behind, they came across a young Seminole woman who had stayed, ragged and frightened, hiding on the far side of an overturned wagon, holding a small, naked baby.

"Why didn't you leave with Osceola?" Harry asked in Miccosukee.

She wouldn't meet his eyes, continuing to look down. Harry asked again, less gently.

"Tired," the woman finally said, and clutched her listless baby tighter to her bony chest. She refused to say more, rocking her baby, rocking herself, claiming her patch of littered, sandy ground.

They moved on, and secured the horses to a hitching post.

"We have to check inside," said Cow Tom.

In the first of the fort's outer buildings, they discovered several small bands of Seminole women in hiding who hadn't fled. They eyed Cow Tom and Harry with caution, and the translators left them undisturbed, and entered the main building. They found a lantern with a small reservoir of kerosene in a side office, and struck a match to light their way. Osceola's people had stripped the storage room of its contents. Spilled flour and stray husks of corn were scattered about. The lantern threw ghostly shadows against the walls, and they proceeded slowly, delaying the moment. Cow Tom went first, and then Harry, and they entered the outbuilding at the rear, set aside for the sick.

They heard groans as they entered the hallway, and braced themselves for the worst. The odor of sulfur and putrefying flesh hung heavy in the air. One swing of the lantern revealed at least two dozen single cots pushed close together, some elevated, some on the damp floor, some with more than one man inhabiting the space. By beard and look, Cow Tom assumed them all soldiers, although none were in military dress, stripped down to their dirty, sweat-stained civvies. The room was packed with the sick — moaning, feverish, calling out for water, trapped in troubled sleep, but alive, throats uncut, scalps attached.

Neither Cow Tom nor Harry wanted to enter. The room itself was dark, and as they approached, a man on the cot closest to the door threw up his hand to shield his face, closing his rheumy eyes tight against the lantern's light. His face was a swollen swirl of lesions, red and angry, and followed a line of advance down his body, speckling his arms and legs.

"Water," he rasped, voice barely audible, the words almost lost in a round of brassy coughing.

Something fell and clattered on the floor, and Cow Tom swung the arc of lantern light toward an interior door.

"Come out," Cow Tom warned. He felt for his knife but it had been taken by one of Osceola's braves. The door slowly swung toward them, revealing the young soldier who had handled their horses in the stable yesterday. He couldn't be more than eighteen, still in uniform, a pistol in his unsteady hand.

"What are you about there?" Cow Tom asked.

"They let them go then?" the young soldier asked.

"No," said Cow Tom. "The soldiers are dead."

A twitch played havoc about his mouth. "The Indians?"

"Most followed Osceola to the swamps. All Seminoles with fight are gone." Cow Tom spoke slowly, his eye on both the gun and the boy's face.

The soldier lowered his pistol. "Seemed best to hide," he said. "Better measles than a lost scalp. They took one look and left this room be." The soldier raised his pistol again and pointed. "Why didn't Osceola kill you?"

"Didn't consider us soldiers, I guess," Harry said.

"What name you go by?" asked Cow Tom.

"Billy."

Cow Tom took a step backward, farther out of the darkened room.

"Well, Billy, I've no interest in measles," Cow Tom said.

The boy considered. What little resolve he possessed evaporated, and he lowered the gun a second time. He kept to the outskirts of the room, walking toward them, and sat down on the floor near the open door. "I couldn't truck being left like this, no food, no water," he said. "A week ago, was me on that cot."

"Harry and I can fetch water, and you give

it to the men. Osceola's people pretty much bankrupted the storeroom, but we'll bring round what's left, and scout for more."

The boy agreed and Harry and Cow Tom left him there, relieved to be outside, away from the stink of disease and misery. Outside was death's leavings, inside was toxic affliction. They preferred outside.

Harry and Cow Tom salvaged what they could find scattered around the deserted camps. They weren't the only ones foraging. Some of the Seminoles who stayed behind had already lit fires, and huddled wordlessly in small groups. They didn't talk to Cow Tom or Harry, and the translators didn't talk to them. Each went about their business, waiting for daylight. Cow Tom and Harry found containers, drew buckets of fresh water from the tower, and dragged them to the door of the infirmary. Each time they returned, they saw Billy holding to his part of the bargain, distributing water to those crying out for it, although the boy had no real talent at the sickbed, and stopped often to rest. He left food by the cots, but most of the sick's appetites had fled, and the corn bits and hardtack were as likely to be consumed by rats as by the fevered men.

After a last delivery, Cow Tom and Harry returned outdoors. They skirted the slaughter ground, avoiding the soldiers' corpses, resigned to leave them where they lay until morning, and found a remote spot, not too far from the protective walls of the fort but not too close to the infirmary, and spread their blankets for a second time that night. One kept watch while the other slept. Although the straggler Seminoles left behind seemed passive in their decision to Remove peaceably, neither Cow Tom nor Harry had desire to be caught by surprise a second time.

Come morning, they tackled the gruesome task of burial. There were eleven in all to be put to ground, including the dragoon the general sent with them from Fort King, and an unlucky soldier from the infirmary who spat up blood before his choked breath stopped in the middle of the night. Billy helped them dig, and Harry said some impressive words over the bodies, but Cow Tom was so tired he could barely remember from one moment to the next. Without the dragoon as escort, they knew they had to return directly to Fort King, along the military trail. They couldn't risk being caught alone, two slaves with neither Indian nor white to claim them, vulnerable to slave catchers, vulnerable to hostiles, vulnerable to road thieves.

And how could Cow Tom maneuver a trip to Fort Volusia now, to search for his mother? He feared that opportunity as vanished as Osceola.

CHAPTER 10

Cow Tom and Harry kept mostly to the main military road, ducking into the woods if they heard a traveler. Often, on the trail, Cow Tom touched the makeshift bandage on his missing ear to reassure himself he was still alive. They arrived back at Fort Brooke in less than a day.

Cow Tom barely took the time to knock the dust of the trail from his moccasins before rushing to the general's office. The general was a volatile man, lately more paranoid than ever, and Cow Tom didn't want any parts of their story to drift back to the commander without explanation. When he entered the room Jesup used for business, the general sat behind his desk, cleaning the blade of his small boot knife. Though all the windows were open, the room carried a musty smell, and Cow Tom took a deep breath before announcing himself.

"Are the chiefs still ready to Remove?"

the general asked, his tone mild. He didn't bother to look up from his papers.

"No, sir," said Cow Tom.

The general gave full attention then, and when he noticed the crude bandage where Cow Tom's ear used to be, his manner changed. "Egads, man, what happened to you?"

"Osceola," Cow Tom said. He hurried to share the worst news. "The Seminoles escaped. Almost all. And ten soldiers killed."

The general pounded his desk, his eyes gone flinty. "How?"

Cow Tom launched into an accounting of the twenty-four hours spent at Fort Brooke, the lack of sentries, the measles outbreak, the hoarded rations, the midnight raid by Osceola and his braves, Micanopy's change of heart, the slashing of his ear, the looting of the fort, the killing of the soldiers, the few straggler Seminoles, the confounding pardon of himself and Harry Island at Osceola's hands, the infirmary, even young Billy. He waited for the general's reaction.

"You and Harry Island were the only healthy men to escape — not by hiding or throwing in your lot with the soldiers, but by . . . ?" He stopped to light his cigar, and let his thought trail off. The general's icy calm was not a good sign.

"It was whim," Cow Tom said. "We've no notion why he spared us."

"Remove the bandage."

"Sir?"

"The bandage." The general moved fast for a big man, around the desk and at Cow Tom's side in a flash. He ripped the bandage from his head and examined the wound, poking at the exposed flesh. "So," he said, "it's real."

Cow Tom knew better than to complain, though the general's touch set off a deepening round of the stinging pain, and bleeding started afresh. He reattached the bandage as best he could.

"Osceola —" Cow Tom began, but the general interrupted.

"A year ago, I started out with over seven hundred Creek warriors to help round the Seminoles up for Removal."

Cow Tom had no idea where the general might be going with this line of thought. When the general ranted, it was always best to stay silent until he calmed. But when the general went cold, it sometimes served better to introduce some new consideration before too late. He decided to respond. "Yes, sir, I rode east alongside them."

"We thought to use the natural bad blood between the tribes, and match fierceness of

Seminoles with fierceness of Creeks. But that is not the way it turned out."

Cow Tom projected his listening face, assumed his attentive, ready-to-be-taught demeanor.

"I find the Creek warrior doesn't have much stomach for the job we have here. Even toward a natural enemy. So the Creek warriors are suddenly tired. The Creek warriors are suddenly sick. The Creek warriors can't find the Seminole camps or their trails. The Creek warriors drink so much they prove useless in the field. The numbers dwindle until there are only a hundred, not seven hundred. Like a fever, this attitude spreads. Like a contagion. And before you know it, everybody catches the fever. Instead of the discipline of a soldier, this weakness, this fever. From soldier on the horse to tracker and translator in the field. More and more, I'm forced to use non-Indians to round up Seminoles. Why is that?"

Cow Tom wanted a drink, something to steady himself. He pushed away the thought of the families of conscripted Creek warriors held hostage in camps somewhere as guarantee of their good behavior. He sent out another silent prayer about Amy and brought himself back to face the general.

Jesup jabbed a finger in Cow Tom's chest,

his face just inches from Cow Tom's nose. "Are you in cahoots with Osceola?"

"No, sir."

"I ask again. Did you help the Seminoles escape?"

"No, sir. We didn't expect Osceola, but there he was. We counted on the Seminoles to Remove peaceably. You saw them sign the agreement at Capitulation. They swore to Remove when they turned themselves in."

"I send three to Fort Brooke and only two return. Both Creeks. Black Creeks. At final count we had the main chiefs, the war near over."

"Osceola took my ear," said Cow Tom. He fought the assault of the general's withering gaze. "Sir. I'm serving the right side. I serve you."

The general calmed a bit and paced the room. Cow Tom didn't think the matter finished, but Jesup appeared to have moved on.

"We had them. We had most all in one place waiting for the damned boats!"

"Osceola brought hundreds of braves."

The general fixed Cow Tom with a stony stare. "So he forced them. Osceola forced the Seminoles to break pledge?"

"Micanopy maybe would stand Removal, but found his advisers primed to join Osceola. So all followed, except a handful." Cow Tom judged the moment right. Now or never. "They were angry their Negroes were separated from them at Fort Volusia, and the agreement broken. It might be helpful to send me to Fort Volusia to sense the mood there."

The general didn't respond. "And my soldiers at Fort Brooke?" he asked.

"We buried eleven before we left," said Cow Tom. "One from measles, the rest at Osceola's hands."

The general continued his pacing of the width of the small room.

Cow Tom made one last attempt. "Some of the Negroes at Fort Volusia lived alongside Osceola and Micanopy for years. They'd know hideouts, habits. I could learn much."

The general didn't bother to disguise his distaste, suspicion written plainly on his face. "I'll never trust the word of an Indian again," the general said.

Cow Tom could have pointed out that both the general and the Seminoles had broken trust in equal measure, but the general was in no mood to listen. Did he include Creeks as well as Seminoles in his new resolve against all things Indian? And what about Cow Tom himself? Did the general consider him Creek or Negro, or did his classification vary depending on circumstance?

"The sooner we get every Seminole loaded on boats west," the general said, "the better." His voice turned cold. "With or without the Negroes. That's my job. Measles or no, we tighten security on all forts. We will find Osceola and Micanopy and the rest, and when we do, we'll burn their camps to the ground until they have nowhere else to turn. Most sold their horses and cattle to us before they played their little trick, so their livelihood is gone. Mayhaps this time they drew some months' rations, stole government supplies, and left me an empty fort, but I promise, that will not repeat."

There was nothing more to say. Of one thing Cow Tom was sure. The general had been humiliated, and someone would have to pay.

CHAPTER 11

Less than six weeks after the Osceola affair, in a routine roundup of a dozen starving Seminoles in the woods, mostly women and children, one of the smaller captured boys threatened that warriors "from the big village by the lake" would rescue them. Cow Tom's further interrogation was fruitful.

"I might have found Micanopy's camp," Cow Tom reported to the general. "Inland. West of Fort Brook, deep in the heart of the Everglades."

"Did the boy call him Micanopy by name?" the general asked.

"No, but he called him the fat chief. My bet is Micanopy."

The general played with the idea in silence. Cow Tom's ear, or what remained of it, was on the mend, at least enough that he wasn't scratching or rubbing or thinking about the itchy nub every minute, but it bothered him now. Still, he waited patiently.

A capture this large would surely win back the general's trust, and he could search for his mother in the camp.

"Worth the gamble," said the general. "We take a contingent and ride out in the morning." He didn't hide his scrutiny of Cow Tom. "Can you scout us there solo?"

Harry was already assigned as translator elsewhere, upstate. Cow Tom would have welcomed his friend's company and counsel, but in truth, a part of him was greatly relieved Harry wouldn't witness his bald attempts to please the general.

"No issue," said Cow Tom.

They traveled for days, soldiers and horses and scouts, to get to the area the boy described, through scattered pinewoods and intermittent swampy ground. On the night of the third day, the rain came in force, and they camped out under dripping palmettos, only to rise early the next morning for a predawn start. The sky was clear, and a cutting wind from the northeast brought cold and foreboding. They tromped through shallow puddles from yesterday's downpours, and miles of fresh, gummy mud sucked at their boots, slowing their forward progress to almost a crawl in the worst of the swampy stretches. After three miles of marching, they approached a wide stretch of boggy marsh, and just beyond, elevated, a dense cypress hammock. They led their horses in.

The mud and water were knee deep, with sharp, rank saw grass growing five or six feet high. Unless they found a different way, less marshy, the horses were a liability in this terrain, bogged to their bellies after a few steps and useless. They needed to leave their horses and supplies behind, all save guns and knives. There was no way to get the horses through the swamps, and the general ordered them pulled back to firmer ground. The soldiers dismounted, awaiting orders.

The general chose two raw volunteers for horse detail, along with Cow Tom. "Stay back with the horses," he ordered. He prepared to slog ahead on foot with the rest of the military men.

"I can survey," Cow Tom quickly offered. Cow Tom wanted the credit for finding the Seminole village, and an acknowledgment of his loyalty from the general, and how could he get that guarding horses and baggage? But the general seemed unmoved. "The boy put the village in the middle of the hammock," Cow Tom added. "But could be a trick. No need to risk all without a further look."

The general nodded, but assigned two kersey-wool-outfitted dragoons to shadow Cow Tom, an advance party of three. All these months of faithful service, Cow Tom thought, and still the general doubted him.

Cow Tom was first to plunge into the knee-high sludgy waters, and quickly, the mud shifted under his feet until he was almost up to his waist. He held his muzzle-loading flintlock musket and powder container aloft over his head, so heavy that a sharp burst of pain shot through his arms and shoulders, but he pushed forward with as much speed as he could marshal. He was well aware that his musket was only good for close-in combat, less accurate than what most armed Seminole braves carried, their smaller-bored rifles better for marksmanship at long distance. Unlike the Seminole braves, only one in twenty of the soldiers had rifles — men of rank like the general — but there would still be hell to pay for giving even a musket up to carelessness. Cow Tom slogged his way slowly through the slimy black ooze and muck of the swamp, at one point able to gain purchase only by putting one foot precariously upon a clump of saw grass roots and feeling ahead for another such clump. The going was slow and exhausting, but the three men made their way up the slanted slope to the hammock.

Once on the surer footing of the raised ground, Cow Tom took the lead, with the two dragoons on his heels. He was a decent tracker, not the best, not the worst, but as they drew farther into the cypress hammock toward higher ground, the Indian signs would have been unmistakable even to a novice. Grass and mud pounded by moccasins, hides and bones of slaughtered cattle, footprints going hither and thither. The hammock was only three or four hundred yards long, and opened to a prairie, fairly dry, with both cattle and Indian ponies grazing. In the distance was the smoke of multiple campfires. For so many cattle and ponies to graze, there had to be another entranceway to the village.

Cow Tom stuck to the dense trees, a dark line of shadowy cypresses, where gently swaying Spanish moss was the only moving thing. The settlement seemed large, several hundred at least, and bringing so many in for Removal would be a challenge for the relatively small number of military, but Cow Tom was satisfied he'd found the community. He swung wide of the village, and within the hour, found another swamp on the far end, but not so deep, passable for horses and men in either direction. They'd entered on the back side of the village, and the advance party set out to return to the general with the news, following the higher ground out and across the prairie, circling around until they rejoined the military party from behind.

"I found the village, sir," Cow Tom reported back to the general, "and there's a better way in, over drier ground."

The general looked to the dragoons for corroboration.

"We saw it too, sir," said one of the soldiers.

The general regarded Cow Tom, his eyebrows knit in assessment, although the hardness of his features remained intact. "Well done," he said. He turned to the rest of the men. "Mount up," he ordered. "Follow Cow Tom. We take the village."

Cow Tom made his face a mask as he rode to the front of the phalanx of soldiers, processing the while his surprise. He'd received a rare compliment from the general, in front of the other men. Maybe his favored status could be restored.

On horseback, Cow Tom led the men away from the deepest swamp and through the woods abutting the prairie. They made good time, both cavalry and army together, picking their way through the wooded terrain, until they were at the lip of the tree line, still providing cover, but within sight of the village.

"Torches," called the general.

A dragoon quickly produced five torches, branches wrapped in cloth and soaked in kerosene, and awaited his orders. This was the part that disturbed Cow Tom most, watching helpless as the general's men burned down Seminole villages. He usually hung about on the fringes, back turned, waiting for the deed to be finished. His usefulness came afterward, in translation duties with the victims, newly homeless, stunned, and defeated. He explained the terms and mechanics of Removal to them in Miccosukee as they stood or squatted in the midst of scorched, choking air, their homes now nothing but smoldering ash. After, he rounded up confiscated cattle and ponies to drive back to the fort.

Cow Tom backed away, separating himself, closer to the tree line, and waited.

"Formation," ordered the general, and the men lined up, ready for the charge to storm the village. They needed little instruction, having played out the scenario many times in the last few weeks.

The general called out the two dragoons who'd accompanied Cow Tom in the advance party, and two others selected at random, and he scanned the other men around him. His eyes, bright and filled with purpose, settled on Cow Tom.

"You found them," the general said. "You burn it down."

This wasn't part of the bargain. Cow Tom wanted recognition for finding the settlement, not responsibility for destroying it. His own mother might be in there. But the general's unyielding gaze was upon him.

He accepted one of the torches from the dragoon, and several sulfur friction matches, but didn't let go of his musket, a clumsy undertaking. Cow Tom had seen this process enough times to know the sequence, but he'd never before set flame. They made a quick plan, who would take which part of the village, and mounted, the five of them, and set the torches alight. Cow Tom dug his heels into his horse's sides and they were in motion. He rode at something less than a gallop with his blazing torch, and peeled away from the others toward his assignment, the southwest corner, all the while plotting a way out, how not to be a part of burning the village down. Out of the general's sight, he would go through the motions, he promised himself, nothing more. He dallied as much as he dared.

The settlement was larger than he initially thought. In scouting, they'd skirted around only half of the periphery, but there were hundreds living here, a hut city of open-sided housing on stilts, with raised platforms and roofs thatched with palmetto leaves, supported by poles. On horseback, Cow Tom watched two plumes of dense, dark smoke, one crosswise to his position and another off to his right. The other dragoons had done their work, flames beginning to rise above the palmetto roofs. It sickened him, the transformation, the village alive with upheaval, like a disturbed anthill. Panic let loose, Seminole women in tunics running, confused children wailing, already alert to the destruction even before the general's scream of "Charge" and the sharp bugle blasts behind him.

He pulled up on his horse to watch the crackling blazes stretch skyward in height and intensity, and scanned the village for dark faces. Of a sudden, a black Seminole brave stood on the ground on his other side, an egret feather in his cap, bare-chested, dressed only in breechclout and leggings, a long rifle pointing at Cow Tom's chest. Behind the man were two boys, eyes wide in terror, the same age as Malinda and Maggie were when he left them back in Alabama.

The black man's lean, dark face was accusation laid bare. He was not that much younger than Cow Tom, no more than twenty-five, with a deep mahogany sheen to his skin. A long, silent moment passed between them.

Cow Tom didn't know what to make of the wordless exchange, but registered both anger and disgust from the man. He wished he could stop and explain to this black Seminole how he came to be holding that fiery torch, burning the village, threatening his sons, following orders he knew were wrong, when all he wanted was to get back to Amy, and his girls, and his tribe. The seconds stretched long, until Cow Tom had the presence of mind to throw the torch toward the man's feet, scramble off his horse, and roll to the ground. He sprang back up in a defensive posture. Only Cow Tom's quickness prevented the bullet from finding a home in his chest instead of ripping through his breeches and merely nicking his thigh. There was a sting, but barely any blood, and Cow Tom still had his senses.

The brave set about shoving in another load, methodically, expertly, but the tight rifling of his superior gun meant a slower reload, and in the chaos and noise all around him, Cow Tom grabbed his own musket from the horse's saddle, loaded and already primed, and pointed it toward the man. But the brave never let up his reloading rhythm, except to bark an order in Miccosukee.

"Find Mother!" he said, and pushed the boys away from his body, out of this particular harm's way, and they were off in a flash, bare feet slapping the mudded hammock, running toward the center of the burning village, away from him.

"Don't," said Cow Tom to the brave, in Miccosukee.

The brave's hands started to shake, whether from fear or nerves or frustration, Cow Tom didn't know.

"We don't have to do this," Cow Tom shouted. "Give up. Remove."

The black brave paused this time, the muscles in his face rigid but the deep brown of his eyes bottomless and fierce, and what Cow Tom saw was a free man, on his own land, with no intention to Remove. Not for Cow Tom, not for the general, not for the government, not even for his sons.

Buzzards circled overhead, and in the distance, a single flat pop of an American musket was answered with a sharp ring of an Indian rifle. The acrid smoke of burning gunpowder and the dense black smoke of palmetto aflame married and made it hard to breath. A turkey-bone whistle shrilled, drums beat, and human voices, both high-pitched and guttural, reached the two men at a standoff. A solitary keening chant that seemed of no beginning also had no end. The bugler began his play again.

It was as if only the two of them inhabited the hammock, young black fathers caught up in the making of life in a hostile world. They could be brothers, one free, one slave. Suddenly the Seminole fumbled, his grip loosed, and his rifle slipped from his grasp onto the ground. He looked from Cow Tom to his rifle and back again to Cow Tom, but he didn't stoop to pick up his weapon.

Cow Tom wanted an end to all this. He brought his musket to his shoulder and fired, point-blank. The force of the blast sent the brave backward, and he went down, sitting in the mud, a stuttered pattern of expanding red exploded across his chest and belly. Even as his life drained, he didn't look surprised, only resolute until the last, when he crumpled to one side, dead.

Cow Tom squatted in the mud next to the body, for how long he wasn't sure, but all shooting had stopped, and the hiss and crackle of the fires seemed louder than all other sounds. Finally, he rose, straightened the brave and arranged him on his back. He left him there, and led his horse to the roundup.

The smoke made it difficult to see and to breathe now, from thick, choking fires and gunpowder residue both, but most of the villagers huddled together waiting, corralled and defeated, watching the flames take the last of their homes, as always happened at the end of these raids. There were some injured, but only one dead, the black Seminole, lying where he'd fallen.

Cow Tom scanned the listless crowd of captured Seminoles, guarded by several dragoons. Most of the military attention went to Micanopy, the fat chief, recaptured at last. But of the thirty or so Negroes gathered, none was his mother. He recognized the two small boys from earlier. They stood with a rail-thin black woman, on either side, with her hands on their backs pulling them near, claiming them. The boys stared at Cow Tom, and then whispered something to the woman, and she pressed them closer to her body as she squinted against the sun and the smoke as if to memorize his features. They each looked to him then, mother and sons, as if he was the devil incarnate, and Cow Tom couldn't deny their judgment.

"Linguister!" called the general.

Cow Tom, mind a-churn, responded, his debrief chores at their beginning.

He had done this. His own mother could have been in the captured camp. He had taken pride in delivering up an entire village of people to turn them off their land. He was the only one in the raid to steal a man's life, another black man, and rob these boys of a father. Rob the mother of her husband.

No one must ever know the part he played today, he thought. Not Harry, more clever, who would have figured some way to avoid this outcome. Not Chief Yargee. Not his children. But especially not Amy, should they reunite, who would surely see him as less of a man.

No one must ever know.

CHAPTER 12

A part of Cow Tom never rose from the mud of that Seminole village, side by side with the dead brave. He couldn't shake the last look of contempt from the mother and her two fatherless boys. But he continued his work. What choice was there? He tracked the treacherous Florida Everglades, led the general and his soldiers through muck and mire and ambush, and concocted Miccosukee arguments for defeated chiefs to persuade them to abandon their native land. In vivid dreams, he strangled the general and left his body for the swamp's disposal, but in light of day, he knew that wouldn't stop the assault of innocents, or deliver him home to Amy. And so he rode alongside the general on more early morning raids, and watched the wrenching scatter of helpless Seminoles as their homes burned to the ground around them. He performed whatever was asked of him, torching and shooting with others. He always searched for his mother among the surrendered, but he expected little. Better to concentrate on the real, the possible, getting home.

"You are needed no longer," the general said in September.

Cow Tom wanted nothing more than to get shed of this Seminole War, but the sting of the loss of his position surprised him.

"Am I to reassign or detach?"

"The remaining Creek warriors will muster out, and you as well."

No more early morning raids on Seminole camps, the smell of scorched earth after torch set camp to blaze. No longer defined or defiled by the general's foul moods and suspicions.

"Am I dismissed to Alabama next week with the Creek warriors?"

"A ship of Seminole slaves leaves for Indian Territory this week."

"But my wife and daughters will be with my chief, wherever they hold the warriors' families." Hostage, he wanted to add. Wherever they'd been holding the warriors' families hostage. He'd hoped as long as Amy stayed close to Chief Yargee, his family would stay whole. Yargee could prove ownership, so they wouldn't be subject to slavers. "Might'n I sail with the Creeks next week?"

"In the end, they Remove to the Creek partition in Indian Territory. You meet them there," said the general coolly.

The set-aside partitions were divided between different tribes, so Cherokee didn't have to live among Choctaw, or Comanche with Creek, and each received their own swaths of land. If Creek and Seminole were forced to mix, there would be trouble every day, with memories of the Florida wars too fresh to forgive.

Cow Tom's mood plunged. The general's heart, such as it was, remained closed against him. But this was the last he would ever see the general, and he wanted to be heard a final time.

"The linguisters served you as well as we were able," Cow Tom said.

The general looked to him with renewed interest, as if he were a tiresome pet that had suddenly risen from four legs to stand on two and spoken aloud.

"When do I leave?" Cow Tom asked simply.

The general cleared his throat, twice, in the throes of decision, staring at Cow Tom the while.

"The other boat docks in a week. You and

the other linguisters ship out with the last of the Creek warriors on the *Paragon*," the general answered. "We're almost done with Florida."

"Yes, sir." Cow Tom turned to leave the smoky room, eager to share the news with Harry and compare notes over a flask.

"Say," the general called to him. Cow Tom faced him square on.

"Times of war call for extraordinary sacrifice. We can't always follow rules."

Cow Tom waited for something more. Did the general apologize for blaming Cow Tom and Harry for Osceola's raid at Fort Brooke? Was he defending his orders to burn Seminole camps from one end of Florida to another? Expressing regret at faulting the conscripted Creek warriors for their lack of enthusiasm in chasing down Seminoles? Cow Tom waited, but the general went back to his cigar, his lips firmly clenched around the soggy base.

"Yes, sir."

Cow Tom left as quickly as he dared. He was going home. Home to earn money enough to buy himself freedom or die trying. Home to purchase his family one by one, however long that might take. He was no longer a green recruit familiar only with tending cows, but a proven man who had survived a war, escaped a scalping, and for a time, influenced a general of the United States government. But he was also the man who looked into a black Seminole's eyes and killed him nonetheless, and broke his family. Who burned entire villages to the ground day in and day out. He'd have to carry that secret shame home with him.

This phase of his life was almost over, but the question still remained.

Where and what might that home be?

CHAPTER 13

Below *Paragon*'s deck, Cow Tom and Harry Island passed the flask between them, on the quiet. For Cow Tom, the relief of whiskey was a newly acquired habit since leaving Alabama, but neither could swill enough of the contraband to get mercifully drunk. Their stomachs churned off tempo with the boat's heave as they inched along the Florida coast. In the next few days, they were scheduled to stop at their first inlet destination at Tampa Bay, and the old, small 135-ton steamer had plenty of excess room for this beginning leg of the long trip home.

The *Paragon* carried a mishmash of evacuees — one of the last detachments of Creek warriors mustered out of the general's service and away from Florida, black translators being returned to their rightful owners, military men dispatched to maintain order and deliver the Creeks on board out of the United States and deep into Indian

Territory, a pair of Seminole braves in dotage — as well as a few heavy-bearded civilians hitching a cheap ride westward, the ship's captain and assorted deck and engine room crew, and a lone doctor, white, middle-aged, disheveled, and only minimally sober from the time the ship left port.

Cow Tom and Harry kept to themselves. None of the handful of returning black translators sprinkled among the fifty or so returning Creek warriors was bound or restrained in any way, not yet anyway, and the two thought to spend most of the boat trip in an alcove behind the boiler room, apart from the others. They'd made themselves as comfortable as possible among the choke of steamed heat and the stacked cords of split sycamore logs still lousy with Florida's spiders and other pests, storing their few belongings in the room's far corner.

They went mostly unseen at their post near the boilers, and could sip unchallenged the whiskey Harry had bought from the vendor selling cheap spirits before they boarded. No doubt Harry lied to the shore vendor, a rotten-toothed and bearded man, and said he purchased alcohol at the behest of one of the Creeks, or one of the military men, but in truth, the vendor was unlikely

126

to care one way or the other. As long as the coins proved good and came into his pocket, it wouldn't matter to him how Harry came by them.

The disadvantage of their location was the constant heat, noise, and damp from the boiler room itself, as the crew shoved pine knots and wood splits into the roaring fire, and sprinkled rosin over the coal to raise more steam. Despite the chill in the air elsewhere, the two firemen stayed stripped down to shirtsleeves, both arms and cloth streaked dark and muddy with a disagreeable mix of sweat and coal dust as they tended the boilers. The firemen possessed an entire barrel of whiskey for themselves, from which they drank often and freely, and they quickly proved to be a quarrelsome pair, full of loud and meaningless argument to pass the time.

"Could be worse," said Harry.

"Always could be worse," said Cow Tom. "How so?"

"Leastways no shackles."

"Guess they figure if we had a mind to run, we'd have tried already in Florida. Besides, they got our families somewhere."

"No putting us on half rations. Sick on all sides, but we both come out healthy." Because of Cow Tom's and Harry's proximity to the general, even as slave, even when out of favor, their grim duty year had left them lean but fit.

"You. Linguister."

A military man with bushy, dark whiskers covering half his face and an oiled, fancy mustache stood at the doorway. Cow Tom didn't recognize him, but Harry did.

"Yes, sir," Harry said.

"The doctor needs talking to a sick Indian. Follow me."

The military man led Harry away. Cow Tom retreated to his corner and his dark thoughts, closing his eyes against the thought of those two black Seminole boys growing up fatherless. Drinking seemed the best idea, and he took another pull. He grew more morose than before, restless. He couldn't affect the speed of the steamer, or the number of stops along the coast to pick up more people to transport or the capricious weather, and his translation duties, for the moment, were at an end. He was relieved to put Florida behind him, but had to admit that there had been excitement, an unexpected thrill in worming his way into the general's confidence for a time. But he couldn't wait to reunite with Amy and his daughters.

Cow Tom went topside, up the narrow

stairs, gripping with both hands the cold metal rails, careful to coordinate his movement with the rolling of the ship. Two Creek warriors hugged the side of the long topside balustrade that wrapped around the length and breadth of the ship, their heads hung over the side, retching to the point of exhaustion. Drunk or sick, Cow Tom couldn't tell. On sad display on deck were the last of the conscripted Creek warriors sent back from Florida, none sure where their people might be. All they knew for certain was that their tribes and their families were no longer where they left them.

Cow Tom quickly returned belowdecks and tried to sleep, but sleep wouldn't come. After a time, Harry also found his way back to the nook and sat cross-legged on the floor adjacent.

"Bloody flux," Harry said. "We got bloody flux on the boat." He held out his hand and Cow Tom passed over the flask. Harry shook the container, holding it gently by the throat, noting the deficiency, but he said nothing, just tipped it back and drained the rest.

They passed time in silence, but after almost an hour of calm seas, the boat began again to buck and pitch, as earlier that morning. Cow Tom made his way again to the deck on unsteady legs, pushing past small, listless groups of Creeks. He stood on the lee side for a few moments, patient, and finally emptied the contents of his stomach over the rail, holding on tight and leaning his body out as far as he dared. The wind behind him served to clear his head a bit, and restore his spirit, but also brought back the cruelty of his situation. He left the railing, and when he got back to Harry, his friend produced a full flask. Harry drank deeply, and offered the container to him.

"Where's it from?" Cow Tom asked.

Harry inclined his head in the direction of the firemen's barrel. Both of the crewmembers dozed, backs to the wall and chin to chest, and Cow Tom didn't push further as to whether they had given or Harry had taken.

The brown liquid burned going down, and Cow Tom relished the punishing jolt when it reached his stomach. Thank goodness for Harry.

"What do we drink to?" he asked.

"Getting out alive," said Harry.

"Alive," said Cow Tom. "And no more Florida."

"To no more alligators."

"No more sand fleas."

"No more treaties."

"There will always be more treaties," said Cow Tom.

They passed the flask between them for another round at the truth of it.

"To going home," said Harry.

Cow Tom grunted, the sadness returning and claiming its rightful place. "We don't have a home," he said.

They both let the thought linger. He'd had no definite word of Amy and the girls, whether they were still with Chief Yargee. Or if Yargee himself was alive or dead. He could only hope the rumors were true, that they waited for him in one of the holding camps. Or were already in Indian Territory, waiting there. Harry took another long pull on the flask and handed it over. One of the firemen stirred and shoved more logs into the fire before falling off to sleep again. The clanging from the boiler room made it harder to think a thought all the way to the end, and so Cow Tom gave up and drank instead. The boat chugged forward at a steady pace.

"To whatever waits," said Harry.

At least they knew their intended route, shared by the general's aide-de-camp before embarking. Pick up another load of Seminoles awaiting Removal from the camp at

Tampa Bay and on to Mobile, along the coast to Pass Christian, Mississippi, then to New Orleans, Louisiana. There, they'd change boats for the final leg of the trip, up the Mississippi River, then the Arkansas River, and then overland to Fort Gibson and resettlement to a new home in Indian Territory.

Cow Tom lay on the wooden floor and propped himself up onto one elbow. His queasy stomach taunted him but the thoughts aswirl in his head gave him even greater unease. "How about a tune?" he asked.

Harry's fiddle, never far away, was in his knapsack, but he didn't make a move toward it. He slipped into slurred Hitchiti. "I'm in no mood," he said.

"They'll be there, waiting for us," Cow Tom said. He tried to sound convincing, but the sentiment was more wish and hope than fact. He couldn't stop thinking of Amy and his girls either. Harry's concern was the white-haired woman on the plantation he came from who acted as mother for most of his years. He'd described her so often Cow Tom felt he knew her. Auntie Mim. She'd already fallen into old age and bad health a year ago before they left, and from their far perch of Florida, there had been no way to determine whether she survived the deprivations in Alabama, and if she had, whether she could endure the Removal from Alabama westward.

Harry didn't answer. He rearranged the splits of wood, tucked the flask into the waist of his trousers, and curled himself on the floor. Within minutes, he fell into a deep sleep. For a while, Cow Tom lay, eyes open. The boiler clanged at his back, insistent, and Harry's nasal snoring grew louder, as if in competition. Cow Tom stretched out full length and lay on the floor by the wall, closing his eyes against the day.

The sea pitched, but finally, he too slept.

CHAPTER 14

Except for a few forays to use their translation skills at one of the military men's request, Cow Tom and Harry Island kept to their alcove with only brief visits to the more populated deck. They fit into whichever attitude their situation demanded, alternating between making themselves useful and making themselves invisible, as most slaves could. Above board, they watched the Florida coastland glide past until they got their fill. The open space helped reacclimate their bodies to the roll of the sea, and they passed two days and nights in this way, down below and up above, until the steady progress of the ship down and around the horn of Florida broke pattern and they prepared to dock in Tampa Bay.

Sailors uncoiled ropes, calmed the fires, shouted instructions, followed the buoys set apace adjacent to the shoreline, and jockeyed the boat in. By then, everyone was on the deck, including Cow Tom and Harry, amazed by the great mounds of additional supplies delivered to the dock and lying in careless stacks of various heights and shapes, guarded by two military men in blue uniform and cap, rifles slung over shoulder. The terrain was marshy by the dock, with a white sand beach common to coastland Florida, but quickly gave way not far inland to a green, dense forest, with limited visibility. If there was an encampment of refugees here, it lay beyond the trees.

They tied into port. Sailors on board the *Paragon* were first to disembark, and after catching a quick smoke or emptying bladders, they began to load the supplies onto the ship while Creeks watched from the deck. One of the sailors motioned to Cow Tom and Harry, and singled out, they helped carry great quantities of corn and bacon, cloth and blankets, and a replacement supply of coal and corded wood onto the boat.

Two military men strode off by foot and disappeared inland through the thicket. While Cow Tom and Harry made trips back and forth between dock and ship, half the Creek warriors walked ashore, stretching their legs and savoring the stability of firm ground under their feet.

"Boiler room's empty," Cow Tom whispered to Harry after their third back-and-forth carrying loads of wood and coal for the next leg of the steamer's journey.

The firemen were ashore, and while Harry stood guard, Cow Tom refilled their empty flask from the open barrel of whiskey, after a long drink directly from the barrel.

It took a good hour of heavy lifting to transport all the wood onto the ship, but as they finished carrying the last, they made certain to leave space for themselves in the corner. They'd gotten used to their spot now, and considered it their own, and hoped their claim stood when others came aboard. But, the supplies transferred, they were happy to rest their muscles for a time and joined those ashore mingling aimlessly at the dock. Cow Tom still had a bit of tobacco, and as they waited, he and Harry smoked a cob pipe at the bay front awhile.

In the distance, a ragtag group on foot, flanked on either side by military men on horseback, approached the boat. There were more people than Cow Tom expected, men, women, and children, maybe a hundred, maybe more, advancing in a tired shuffle, kicking up dust as they trod. The Negroes of defeated Seminoles would easily outnumber the Creeks by at least two to one. The

Creek warriors onshore didn't seem pleased at the sight, muttering among themselves in complaint, but the group steadily trudged closer.

"No chains," said Cow Tom.

The planned route called for them crossing into southern territory before reaching their final destination in Indian country, a circumstance usually calling for restraints of one kind or another. For all his shuttling to and fro between owners as a young boy and a young man, sold or rented out, his movements between plantations, his travel between different states of the Union, Cow Tom had never been put into irons, leg or arm or neck, not once, and just the thought of them brought a rush of bile to his stomach. He'd seen them, of course. Shackles. He'd seen the dull glow of them wrapped around the wrists of a coffle of slaves passing through at Master McIntosh's, but Chief Yargee didn't employ their use, ever.

"Best get back aboard and protect our spot," Harry said to Cow Tom.

Cow Tom boarded the *Paragon,* following at Harry's back.

They secured their belongings below-decks, and came back above board as military men steered the new group up the gangplank onto the steamboat. Most of the

Negroes stood about in uncertainty, shoulders slumped, eyes yellowed, cheeks sunk, arms bony, clothing ragged at the hem. One unusually tall woman elbowed several others out of the way and made a quick scramble to stake out a corner near the wheelhouse. She set her face to stone and fanned her three children, all under the age of five, behind her like a deck of cards, daring anyone to intrude. Her marked territory appeared to hold. No one questioned her.

From their elevated post at the rail, Cow Tom and Harry watched waves of unresisting men, women, and children herded on board the *Paragon,* as military men steered them up and onto the boat. At first, Cow Tom peered into every face, but saw only averted eyes, resignation, and weariness. The new crop of Negroes varied widely in appearance, from those who could have just stepped off the boat from Africa to those who could easily pass as Seminole fullbloods. They didn't move singly, but clumped together in groups, babes in arms, children clinging to a mother's tunic, boys and girls of the same age holding hands as they headed up the plank. Cow Tom turned away to collect himself, but in the end, couldn't resist, and stared again at the oncoming wave of humanity. They all looked exhausted, and hungry, and several sickly, helping one another forward.

Three-quarters of the refugees were already boarded, the others waiting on the sandy swath of land beyond the gangplank for their turn. A white man appeared at a distance from inland, running his two-horse wagon team hard. He angled his winded horses directly alongside the ship, set the brake, and jumped down from the riding platform. He was civilian, plump and scruffy. An enormous, unkempt brown curly beard came all the way down to the middle of his chest, hiding much of the crumpled jacket beneath. Long loops of heavy chain and manacles lay in his wagon bed. The man made for the gangplank and tried to board the *Paragon,* but one of the military men blocked him. The man waved a paper, increasingly agitated.

"Take me to the man in charge," he bellowed.

The soldier talked to him quietly, but the man was having none of it, and he made such a ruckus that the soldier finally sent for the captain, who met him at the foot of the gangplank.

"Some of these are my Negroes," the man said, again offering up the papers. "They can't be allowed to leave Florida."

The captain barely glanced at the pages. Cow Tom saw easy dismissal of documentation enough times in his work as translator to posit that the captain of the *Paragon* most likely couldn't read.

"We have a transport contract with the military," said the captain to the white man. "This is no concern of mine."

"I'm here to take my property with me. I demand to board and claim my property."

"If there were claims," the captain said, "they should be handled before now. My agreement holds with the government, and the cargo is arrived. Payment is based on the number of heads I deliver. The only amendments I recognize, sir, are with the government."

"There!" the white man said. He aimed a long, crooked finger at a dark face on the boat. Cow Tom caught only a quick glimpse of gunnysack and a printed head scarf, swirled, before the accused melted back into the others and disappeared from view. He was fairly certain she was a woman, short and dark-skinned. "See her? That one is mine."

From the shore, the man continued to scan the clutch of bodies. "And that one!" he declared, pointing at a stocky man just to the other side of Harry.

Almost as one, the Negroes shrank back from the railings, cloaking their bodies as best they could, lowering their gaze and hiding their faces, easing their backs to the man on the shore, as if they too might soon be singled out.

"I demand their return. And there must be more. I demand to search the boat."

He advanced toward the gangplank, but the captain put himself directly in his path.

"This is my vessel. This is my cargo." He whispered to one of his sailors, who began to move the last few Negroes up and onto the boat. "There's to be no open poaching on my ship today."

The white man reddened. "You dare stand in the way of regaining rightful property?"

"Take it up with the government," said the captain. "We depart within the half hour."

The man turned to the military men still on land. "Let me on this boat."

"We have our orders," one said. The other shrugged a sheepish agreement.

"You haven't seen the last of me," he said to the military men and the captain. He directed himself to the occupants of the steamboat. "Don't think you've seen the last of me," he shouted.

He jammed his hat back tight on his head

and stormed to his wagon. He jerked the reins, and drove the horses as hard as he dared on the shifting sand, back the way he'd come.

A cautious, almost indistinguishable murmur started on the boat, and grew until heard over the commotion of the sailors making ready to set sail. A child began to cry, a little boy, far too young to understand exactly what had just happened, but old enough to feel the upset around him. And then another let loose, until muffled sobs were all round the ship.

"We best clear out of the way," said Cow Tom to Harry.

Just minutes before, he'd pitied the Seminole Negroes, as if their plight were poles apart from his own, but with a sudden chill, he was reminded of his mistake. With the new Negroes on board, he and Harry were suddenly indistinguishable from the others, no matter the facts that the two of them were fresh from working directly for the general, that they had fought side by side in the Everglades with the warriors from the Creek tribes, that they had each earned significant money for themselves and even a measure of respect for their service.

In the eyes of the government, one Negro was the same as the next.

CHAPTER 15

The Indian agent, physician, and four additional military men boarding the *Paragon* at Tampa Bay didn't separate the Negroes from the rest of the Creeks, or restrict their movements, and all were open to roam the crowded decks at their will. The military had rifles, but they produced no chains. No whips. But with few exceptions, blacks drew together from all corners of the ship, whether having lived among Creeks or among Seminoles, like the irresistible pull of magnets toward one another. They needed no order to keep separate. They did so of their own collective mind, gathering in pockets, but especially near the boiler room.

Cow Tom went among them, walking freely, talking to them in their own tongue and giving what reassurances he could, which weren't many.

"You will be fine," he repeated, in English, in Hitchiti, in Miccosukee, in Mvskoke.

Their need was great and immediate. The newly boarded from Tampa Bay were close to starving. After existing in holding camps for months, with food scarce and hunting scarcer, they'd brought their hunger and camp diseases with them. Most just wanted their ordeal over, to reconnect with the people they'd lived among for years, sometimes as landlord, sometimes as husband or father or warrior. This was a different breed of Negroes to be sure. Poor, yes, defeated, yes, adrift, yes, and visibly afraid of the future, but with a history and mind-set of independence unlike the Negroes Cow Tom had run across in Alabama.

On deck, two old men fought over a ragged blanket, more pushing and shoving than bare-knuckled or weaponed skirmish. Cow Tom didn't get between them, but instead decided to find the Indian agent on board and make an appeal. He started his search at the wheelhouse, and before showing himself, heard several voices from inside.

"We should lock them belowdecks," said one. "Creeks are restless with so many aboard. As am I."

"I'll not run a slaver," the captain said.

"No one wants that. But that man won't be last to make claim."

"Cheeky bugger. Not all bad, though. This

way, they know better the possibilities. My ship is the safest place to be for now."

"They could mutiny."

The captain gave a snort of incredulity. "And go where?"

Cow Tom made himself visible. The room itself was small, dominated by the navigation wheel and a windowed view off into the distance on three sides. In addition to a mute helmsman were four men in the small space, including the captain of the *Paragon,* the Indian agent, one of the military men who had embarked at Fort Brooke, and another who had just come aboard at Tampa Bay. They were so engrossed in their conversation they didn't see him. He cleared his throat and gave a small cough and one of the military men finally turned. He stared at Cow Tom, and after a bit, his face betrayed a moment of recognition.

"You were General Jesup's man at Fort Brooke, yes?" he asked.

"Yes, the general's man," Cow Tom repeated in English. "Linguister."

"You and the fiddler fellow."

"Harry Island. Yes."

"The fiddler was useful with that Seminole," the military man said. "Poor bastard."

Cow Tom wasn't sure what he meant.

"What happened?" the new soldier asked.

"Gripping guts. Didn't last the day. Nothing for it but to put him over the side."

Neither he nor Harry followed up on the sick Seminole from the first leg of the trip, but he wasn't surprised. He'd seen enough cases of bloody flux to fear the consequences, both for the sick and those around them. A sudden turn of dice could determine one man's swift decline and watery grave, and another's good fortune to view the rising of tomorrow's sun. If Amy were here, she surely would have drawn a circle around both their heads to ward off such tragedy.

"Come in," the captain said.

Cow Tom advanced into the small room. The setting sun sparkled off the blue water, and the whitecaps broke before the bow's steady progress. From this vantage point, with the captain next to the big wooden wheel and armed white men in uniforms flanking him, it seemed as though these men had control of the sea and, by extension, the land. He could understand why such men felt powerful, with tools such as these at their command.

"State your business," said the Indian agent. He was a tall white man gone part native, with a coonskin cap and worn moccasins.

"Blankets and corn," Cow Tom said. "Negroes will settle if we give supplies straightaway."

He was no more sure this was true than his reassurances to the Seminole Negroes that they would be fine on board this vessel. He purposefully said "we" instead of "you" to hold himself apart, to be an element of solution instead of lumped in as problem.

The Indian agent studied Cow Tom, assessing his worth, his age, probably calculating the risks of listening to his theories. Cow Tom must have passed the test, because the agent didn't order him gone. "Supplies are scarce and must last. We have more stops."

Cow Tom had advantage in knowing how much was on the ship, and where stored. His muscles still ached with the transport of them. He thought of these men in the same way he did in dealings with the general, or Chief Yargee, the need to plant a seed now in the hopes that if it didn't catch immediately, it might still bear fruit later. "Even a few blankets now, a show of good faith. And the promise of a quick meal. Corn, a little bacon for flavor. Maybe some of the women assigned to prepare."

He stayed quiet while they took his suggestion under advisement. The newly boarded military man, so fresh-faced he

147

brought to mind a schoolboy, spoke up for immediate distribution. But the Indian agent worried about Creek hostility, some already arguing to withhold rations from the slaves of their enemies. At the end, the men in the wheelhouse decided on half measure. Cow Tom promised to round up four women to prepare the first onboard meal, and he followed the military man to a padlocked storage area. Pulling a key from his jacket pocket, the soldier opened the room.

The storage area was packed from ceiling to floor, with foodstuffs and blankets, wooden crates and burlap sacks, and loose medical supplies in baskets — adhesives, sponges, Epsom salts, castor oil, a cork-screw, a spatula, a dental tooth key, even a pair of forceps. While the military man located a stack of wool blankets against the far wall, Cow Tom fixed on the contents of a poorly constructed crate on the floor, the top pried off and askew, as if someone had recently taken inventory of what was inside. Manacles. Chains. A metal nightmare of iron cuffs and shackles. He hadn't carried this crate on board, Cow Tom knew that for certain; he would have buckled under the weight, heard the rattle. He stared at the crate, unable to avert his gaze, as the military man returned with the blankets.

They locked eyes for only an instant, and then both looked away. Cow Tom made a show of fixing now on the blankets, the bins of corn, the bags of flour, anything but the crate. The military man said nothing. Cow Tom expected no different. Cow Tom was, after all, one of over a hundred Negroes here, and he had heard before of ships headed west where they chained not only the slaves but the Indians as well. He thanked the military man, and, a little awkward under the bulk and weight of blankets now his to distribute, set out to put distance between himself and the storage area, before any change of mind.

He tried to shake off the image of the chains, instead putting his mind to work calculating how most fairly to hand out blankets. They were small, but adequate, of a fairly coarse wool, a bit moth-eaten, but decent quality. Good enough to wrap the upper body against the wind and cold, good enough to use as a pad beneath a sleeping head, good enough to warm cold legs and feet, but not all of those at once. Cow Tom had only additional blankets for one of every ten of the Negroes aboard the *Paragon*. Some, such as himself and Harry, already had sufficient covers, and some from the wooded camp brought along both adequate and inadequate blankets in various stages of disrepair. All would want additional warmth if they could get it, especially as winter inched closer. Cow Tom was king of the blankets, an awkward position, as he hadn't met many of the new people. He had neither an understanding of their individual circumstance nor knowledge of who might be a leader among them capable of making decisions of this kind.

But he did know where he wanted the first blanket to go. He sought out the young mother he'd seen earlier when she first set foot on the boat, the tall woman with three small children and only one threadbare blanket between them. He warmed to her at once, envious of the tightness of their family. She reminded him of Amy, not in physical presence, but in her determination. He remembered how she made a place for herself without wavering, a place to keep vigilant watch over her children. She had a sharp, pinched face and bony frame, and she was filthy from head to foot, but she gave off an air of toughness, a strength born of protectiveness. She was barefoot, as were the children.

"A blanket for you," said Cow Tom in Miccosukee. "And the little ones."

She didn't hesitate, snatching the blanket from his arms. After a small nod in his direction to acknowledge her good fortune, she rearranged herself and her brood to accommodate the unexpected gift. Her oldest, a boy about five, lightly touched Cow Tom's jacket. The boy's longing look made him uncomfortable, as if the child carried around some hollowness he expected Cow Tom to fill. The way Cow Tom supposed he had looked toward Old Turtle when he himself was small. The way the two small boys had looked to their black Seminole father before Cow Tom shot him.

"Thank you, mister," the boy said in English.

Cow Tom caught the gaze of the mother again. Her face softened.

"I'm Ilza," she said.

"Cow Tom."

"Like my oldest," the woman said. "His name is Tom too."

The boy followed his every move, eyes wide.

"Tom Too," said Cow Tom, and the boy beamed, as if given a present.

"We all thank you," Ilza said.

He saw resolve on her dirty face. He'd seen deference to this woman by the others, and befriending her could prove prudent.

"Cooks are needed," he said. "A woman at the galley pot is sure to be in a better position to get a fair share for herself and her children."

He watched her internal struggle, weighing the benefits of a guaranteed meal against the requirement to leave her children behind, alone. In the end, food proved the greater inducement.

"I can cook," she said.

Cow Tom nodded. "Go down belowdecks to the galley. Tell them Cow Tom sent you."

Ilza delivered quick directives to the oldest boy, wrapped her children against the cold settling in as the sun disappeared, and left them.

Cow Tom continued on, but already the word had spread that he controlled additional blankets. As he passed among the Seminole Negroes, he found three other women to report to the cooking area. At every step, reaching hands pulled at him, voices pressed, and soon he lost his ability to distinguish between them. He gave out the next few blankets to those with the loudest claim, or most pitiable plea, until he had only one left, and went back to the military man to ask for more.

And then he saw her again. The woman with the printed scarf. Although he hadn't seen her face, he remembered the scarf's distinctive swirl pattern and was sure she was the one who disappeared into the crowd the day before when the slave hunter came to the boat. She sat alone amid the press of people on the open deck, her back to him, a thin swatch of cloth that looked like the tattered remnants of a flour sack pulled around her small frame, oblivious to the wind that drove gusts down the ship's broad deck. She seemed delicate, but not altogether defenseless, and Cow Tom was drawn to whatever her story might turn out to be. There were so many tales that could be hers, so many variations — flight and escape from a cruel master into the swamps of Florida and adoption into the Seminole tribe as a young woman, or born among the Seminoles, second- or even third-generation free, with no memory of any other way than living off the land, or marriage to a Seminole warrior and half-blood babies. But here she was now, alone.

Cow Tom clutched tighter to the blanket, for a moment unwilling to speak or draw attention to himself in the uncertain silence. But she seemed to sense him standing there, and when she turned to face him, her profile, dark and sculpted, was as familiar to him as the missing piece of rawhide braid on his knife handle, as the veins crisscrossing the backs of his own hands, as the small mole on the right side of his wife's face. The woman had a splash of color along her temple, a dullish port-wine stain from hairline to cheek, and it took every fiber of his being not to reach out to rub the pebbly texture of it.

She didn't betray any knowledge of him, but she didn't draw back from his frank stare either, meeting his gaze with an equal mix of vague curiosity and wariness.

Cow Tom swallowed hard.

"Do you not know me?" he said.

She focused on his face, as if in trance, but there was no recognition there. Her eyes were moist and sable brown, but with a flat blankness, and for a moment, Cow Tom questioned what he thought he knew. How could it be?

"I'm Tom. They call me Cow Tom now."

She barely blinked, casually searching the planes of his face. She seemed a cipher, a ghost, levitating on a pocket of air, almost oblivious to her surroundings. A change came to her eyes then, small but distinct, both a softening and a new focus, as if she were returning to a long-abandoned homestead after an exhausting journey, only to find a stone-cold fireplace and tangles of dandelion weeds in the neglected yard. She seemed almost shy.

"Tom?" she repeated. "Where's your ear gone, Tom?"

He sat down directly in front of her so they would be on the same level. "Gone," he said. He reached out for her hand. She drew back from his touch, settling her hands in her lap in a tight, interlaced grip.

"Ma'dear?" Cow Tom said.

She stiffened her back, turned her face away, and stared out at something in the distance. A bird flying overhead? A monotonous strip of white-sand beach at the shore? The rare sparkle of November sunlight on the water's churning surface? Her features set themselves back into vagueness, a disengagement. She'd left him behind. Again.

He tried another approach. "Are the slave catchers after you?" he asked. He kept his voice smooth and unchallenging.

She gave a small shudder, and turned back to face Cow Tom. "Yes," she said. "And he won't give up. He won't ever give up."

"Mayhaps I could help you," said Cow Tom. Much as he wanted, he was careful not to lean too close, or to try again to touch her.

"Slave to slave. There's nothing we can do against them," she said, her defeat apparent. "They'll have their way in the end." She paused, as if piecing together a difficult puzzle. "Why would you risk on a stranger?"

His thoughts broke in every direction, but he held himself firm. "I want to help you if I can," Cow Tom repeated.

She stared at him, without commitment one way or the other, waiting passively for his next move.

"This blanket is for you," he said.

He handed her the last of the blankets, and she draped it around her shoulders, clearly pleased with her new acquisition.

For two decades, of the countless times in his life since the age of seven he'd spent conjuring up possible images of this day, the thought never once crossed Cow Tom's mind that if he could ever find his way back to his mother again, their first meeting would be like this.

CHAPTER 16

Cow Tom guided her down to the shelter near the boiler room. She didn't resist.

"This is Harry Island," he said.

Harry shot Cow Tom a look of puzzlement. Cow Tom conveyed a silent plea in return. They had negotiated together long enough to pick up each other's signals, and Harry played along. He talked to the woman about unimportant and nonthreatening topics, about whether she was hungry, and the chill in the fall air, and although she wasn't chatty, she warmed to Harry, a little, more quickly than she had to Cow Tom.

"What name you go by?" asked Harry.

"Bella," she said.

"Pretty, pretty, pretty," said Harry.

He rummaged around in his belongings, pulled out his fiddle, and brought it to his chin. He drew back his bow, and made up a fast and catchy tune of trills and riffs, and in a deep voice sang a refrain for a chorus whose single word was Bella, liberally repeated.

Harry's music attracted a small crowd on the ship, drawn to the tight space to listen, even one military man. They formed a jagged circle around his notes and his voice, and he entertained Creek and Negroes at large, but he kept his focus primarily on Bella. Cow Tom kept a close eye on his mother, who at first sat on the cold floor, both transfixed and timid. But after a time she clapped with the others, and let the music take her. She seemed stronger, almost as if without worry, and Cow Tom seized the moment to lean closer.

"Reminds me of a fiddler used to play in Alabama when I was a boy," he said. He didn't call Old Turtle by name, trying to go slow, but they had listened together to those plaintive notes strung on the narcissus-scented night air, mother and son, on many a Saturday evening on the plantation after the day work was done.

She showed signs of agitation, tugging at her swirl-scarf, threatening to go inward, and Cow Tom backed away from his attempt to draw her out. He contented himself to sit alongside without further engagement, stealing a glance at her whenever he got the chance. Harry by then was in full swing, improvising from one tune to another without pause, encouraged to continue by the crowd's enthusiasm. By the time Harry put down his fiddle and joined them, and the others drifted elsewhere on the ship, she relaxed a bit.

"Where they taking us?" she asked Harry.

"Most likely Alabama first," said Harry. "Then New Orleans. But at the end, all go to Indian Territory."

Bella grew quiet. She turned from them.

Cow Tom couldn't decide what was best. Try to reassure her? Leave her to her own devices? Continue to let Harry take the lead?

"He'll come for me there," she said. "Alabama."

"Who?" Cow Tom asked.

She shook her head, a quick, evasive gesture.

"You have people?" Harry finally asked, and Cow Tom tensed.

"My people are gone," she said. "All long gone."

Pain blossomed along Cow Tom's right side, as if a wild animal used teeth and claws to get out. The pain always passed, eventually. He drew a deep breath, unable to look at his mother.

"My man got the fever, and died. So many

of us starving, we came in by our own," she went on. "For food. To stop them hunting us anymore."

Before now, he had only considered his side of loss. His boyhood abandonment. His hurt. His confusion. For years, he'd quietly nursed what sometimes came as crippling anger, with no place to go, only exercised in private, if at all. In the far past, he sometimes focused the anger toward the big house on the Alabama plantation, breaking some petty rule now and again if he thought he couldn't be caught. On occasion, a dark wave washed over him after remembering the horse's gallop as it rounded the bend of the long road with his mother thrown across the front like a sack of grain before disappearing from view. The aftermath was always the worst, hours of brooding before he could right himself.

But his anger spilled to his mother as well. She hadn't come back for him or sent word of her whereabouts, nothing to muffle the deafening speculation looping round and round in his head for days after, and weeks, and months, and then years. He'd wondered whether she was truly taken to Florida, wondered what Florida was compared to Alabama, if all slave life carried the same constancy, if being owned by a Seminole

160

was different from being owned by white or Creek, whether she'd had another little boy to take his place after leaving him behind. He'd spent so much time on his own wounds he hadn't given thought to what their separation had done to her. And now he knew. This wasn't the woman he remembered, the stern but sometimes playful woman he'd preserved as young and vibrant in his mind.

Cow Tom's stomach burned. Harry stepped into the silence.

"I only have my nana from the old place," said Harry. "She's old, and no good for travel. I hope she's in a pick-up camp on the way."

Bella absorbed this. "And you?" she asked Cow Tom. She didn't call him by name. "Your people?"

Cow Tom forced his words beyond the bitterness threatening to block his tongue. "I have a wife, and two little girls," he said, "supposed to be in a camp for families of Creeks sent to Florida. If they haven't already moved west." He felt he should add something more. "I fix to buy myself, and after, buy them too."

She seemed interested then, leaning forward toward him, sharing a secret. "Seminoles act different than Creeks. In the

Everglades, we lived free," she said. "Worked hard, but not to serve." She lost her moment of animation and leaned back in resignation. "But that's gone."

"Who's to claim you once off the boat?" Harry asked. "The man from Tampa Bay?"

"He's only an agent, holding the paper, sent to bring me back," said Bella. "He works for a man in Alabama." She leaned her back against the wall. "Better dead than back there," she said, her voice small.

Once again, they settled into uncomfortable silence. Once again, Cow Tom tasted the cruel sting of helplessness. He left them both and went above deck, to see if there was any good he could do there.

The boat made steady progress on the open sea, but never ventured far from land. Cow Tom threw himself into action, walking the length of the ship, checking the status of the newly arrived. Anything to blunt the dread and confusion he couldn't control. In his mind, there was only uncertainty on all sides, about Amy, about his daughters, about his mother, about a new home. He cleared his mind as best as he was able, and went to free more blankets. But this time, he identified four families, all women with small children, and only then, without promises, did he go back to petition the military man he started to think of as Schoolboy, Lieutenant Sloan, a formal-lessoned man from the North.

They made another trip together to the padlocked room, where Schoolboy allocated not only four additional blankets but also small runs of cloth, several metal needles, and a spool of coarse thread. By the time Cow Tom took the goods to the families, the first wave of boiled hominy was out from the galley belowdecks. The crew ate first, and then Creeks, by order of the Indian agent, and then Negroes last. Some possessed wooden bowls and took their meal in that, but most shaped the corn mixture into their open palms and ate where they stood, or carried portions to others. Before nightfall, everyone was fed, with hominy left for morning. Cow Tom's biggest fear of hunger-fueled unrest didn't come to pass. No outcome would be worse than to unleash a lockdown mentality among the military men.

Bone weary and ready to let go of the day, Cow Tom returned belowdecks. His mother lay asleep, curled into herself in a semiprivate corner fashioned from a slight rearrangement of firewood cords. The new army-issue blanket was pulled to her chin despite the damp heat, and her inky black hair splayed around her head like a buffalo's mane. Harry was still awake, on the other side of the wood line that now separated their sleeping area from Bella's. He'd liberated more whiskey from the boiler room, and gotten a head start, brightening when he saw Cow Tom and motioning him over.

"Who is she?" Harry whispered.

Cow Tom shrugged, loath to loosen the tangle of his secret hurt and hope. "She matters to me."

Harry didn't press further, pulling a long draft from the flask before dropping immediately to sleep. Even the bickering firemen were quiet in the boiler room. Cow Tom was the last awake, sure his mind would get the best of him. He hadn't time in the packed day to figure out much of anything, including how to handle Bella. But next he knew, the firemen were yelling, blaming each other for letting the fires burn too low, rushing in and then out again to carry more wood to the boiler room.

Morning.

The night wasn't long enough. Cow Tom dreamed of Amy, a too-familiar and unsettling recurrence, the dream in which he returned home to find his wife disappeared, without a trace, leaving him in an empty cabin surrounded by a pack of wolves. It always took him a moment to shake off the aftereffects of that dream, and the impossibility of Amy gone. He squeezed his eyes tight, reorienting himself to the realities of the world and not the trickster images echoing in his head.

"Morning."

Bella was at the ready, up for some time by the looks of it. Her flour-sack dress hung overlarge on her small frame, but she secured her swirl-scarf around her head in a tight back knot that made her look more in charge of herself than yesterday. She'd found a straw broom somewhere, and held it suspended in front of her with both hands, as if a dance partner.

Harry snored softly.

"Morning, Bella," he said. "Passable sleep?"

He would have liked to hear his own name come from her mouth, to measure the sound and tone today against what he remembered. When he was Tom. When she was Ma'dear. But she hadn't once called him in his name since she'd come on the boat.

She came closer, her voice barely a whisper, whether out of deference for the sleeping Harry or a natural reticence, he couldn't tell. "I brought back *sofki,*" she said.

He was wide-awake now. She was trying to look after him, gone early to the galley. He hadn't bothered to take off anything but his cotton jacket last night, balled under his head as a pillow while he slept, and he stood, clothed, and stretched his cramped muscles, at her level now.

"Three portions," she said, the pride obvious.

Cow Tom fought the suddenness of his disappointment. She was looking after Harry too, not just him.

"Thank you, Bella," he said. She had taken the bark from one of the smallest and flattest logs in their alcove and used it as a tray to bring back three large mounds. Cow Tom helped himself to one, stuffing the food in with his fingers until gone. "No one gave you trouble?"

She laughed, a bit smug. "In the galley this morning, in the waiting line, I said I was with you and Harry Island," she said. "There was no trouble." She paused. "The woman serving, Ilza, she sends her regards."

CHAPTER 17

Bella worried over their small corner of the boat, caretaker to the two young men who came to an older woman's rescue. She tidied up their quarters with a presumption that surprised Cow Tom, shaking out and airing blankets and oft-worn bits of their clothing in sore need of washing, humming the while.

As if come to unspoken agreement, Cow Tom knew he daren't broach the endearment of Ma'dear with Bella again. He only left the overheated alcove when he had to. Between himself and Harry, one or the other of them was in constant demand, whether as liaison with the Negroes or between the Creeks and the military. He'd been called to service half a dozen times before midday.

In the afternoon, Schoolboy poked his head into the anteroom, and with a measure of visible distaste, came into the alcove of stacked wood.

"I was told where to find you," he said. His face quickly went from pale to a rosy pink, and he pulled off his jacket. "Hot in here." He looked around at the disarray, despite Bella's best attempts at cleaning. "Not pleasant. Not pleasant at all. Most dangerous part of a ship, you know."

The man interested Cow Tom, his unconventional turn of mind, his unexpected craftiness not grounded in either domination or weakness. In less than a full day, Cow Tom had formed a better connection with Schoolboy than any other authority on the ship.

"We get by, Lieutenant Sloan," said Cow Tom.

Schoolboy eyed Bella, standing frozen in a corner, refusing eye contact, but didn't remark one way or the other on her presence. Harry was absent, having been fetched not long before by one of the crew to help move some Creeks farther away from the wheelhouse.

"Let's us step outside for fresh air," Schoolboy said.

Cow Tom grabbed his jacket and followed him up the stairs, wondering about the purpose of this visit. The bracing wind felt good after the stuffiness of the alcove, but a sudden gust whipped through his jacket as if he stood bare-chested. He drew his jacket tighter.

"So you served General Jesup," Schoolboy said to Cow Tom.

Cow Tom nodded.

"I admit to fascination with you African Creek and African Seminole linguisters, in the middle of action, not fish nor fowl. You've more influence than people grant. Those I've met are mostly clever fellows."

Cow Tom nodded again, not sure where Schoolboy tried to lead him, prepared to wait him out.

"What were your impressions of our great General Jesup?" Schoolboy asked.

"The general seemed made for war," he said carefully.

"Surprising, really. I knew Thomas before he became quartermaster general. Before he was a military officer. Before his assignments clearing Creeks from Alabama or Seminoles from Florida. Those days, he contented himself moving supplies from one place to another, not fighting Indians. Was a time he found sussing out food and water and horses and shelter for an army man the highest calling. He turned out quite the ruthless man in war. No telling yet whether he'll be a humane man in peace."

Cow Tom hadn't heard anyone call the general by his first name, ever, let alone speculate about his beginnings. He'd been around military men enough to know that a lieutenant speaking thus of a general might well lead to future problems.

"You worked with the general too?" asked Cow Tom.

"Worked for," said Schoolboy. "Years past. But I'd still rather find a blanket for some poor, starving woman on a cold night than hunt her down in the swamps."

Cow Tom wasn't sure if Schoolboy admired the general or was disappointed in him, but the conversation had taken an odd turn. There was no way he could allow himself to be dragged into talking badly about one white man to another. No good could come of that.

"Those blankets all went for good," Cow Tom said, switching tracks. "Nights at sea come fast and cold." Schoolboy seemed relaxed, in a sharing mood, so he pressed further. "How many days more before port?"

"Captain lost a little time along the Florida coast, but should dock at Mobile Point in two days. Monday latest."

The lieutenant pulled from his jacket a pipe and tobacco pouch, and stuffed the bowl. It took a few tries to get the tobacco lit, but he finally managed to draw smoke down the stem, inhaling deep and long before exhaling. The sweet aroma drifted on the air, and Cow Tom closed his eyes, imagining the taste.

"You smoke?" asked Schoolboy.

"When I can," said Cow Tom. Schoolboy wouldn't offer his pipe to another man, most especially not a slave, but the peculiarity of the exchange made Cow Tom more bold than normal. "Always carry my pipe, just in case."

Schoolboy retrieved his pouch again, and Cow Tom produced his poorer version of the lieutenant's pipe, fashioned from a corncob. Schoolboy tapped a smaller amount into the bowl, and Cow Tom drew strong, savoring the flavor deep in his chest. They stood smoking their pipes for a while in silence, Cow Tom waiting for Schoolboy to declare his intent. He didn't.

"I'm hoping to find my people," Cow Tom said.

"Who do you belong to?"

Cow Tom let the reference slide without challenge. "My people" meant Amy and his daughters.

"Chief Yargee holds my papers. Upper Creek, in Alabama, along the Alabama

River. He sent me to Florida as linguister along with six of his Creek warriors. I've not been back in over a year, or heard word of my woman or children."

"There's a holding camp at Mobile Point. Thousands of Creeks waiting, gathered since spring. Chances are, your chief is among them."

Cow Tom had seen enough holding camps in Florida to fear the worst. If Amy and the girls were there, they'd been since spring, and it was already October. "What of the Negroes?" he asked. "Did they separate us or keep with the tribes?"

"Together, most likely, but certain things happen in the field to cause a modification in procedure." He looked pointedly to Cow Tom to see if his words were understood.

Cow Tom hadn't spent the last year in the general's employ to be cowed by fancy English words, particularly the same phrase he'd heard the general use many a time. "Modification in procedure" mostly meant locals or military gone rogue. "My prayer is for my woman's well-being," he said.

Schoolboy nodded. He looked directly at Cow Tom, didn't hide his favorable assessment, as if the interpreter had passed a test. "A military man in charge can make a difference."

He said this last as if it should have special meaning. That meaning was still vague, but whatever Schoolboy wanted would clarify soon enough. It always did with the white man, usually sooner rather than later.

"You've seen this camp in Mobile?" Cow Tom asked.

"No, my dealings have been in Florida, but I'm briefed."

"And the conditions?"

Schoolboy hesitated. " 'Twas necessary to move the tribes quick from Alabama, get them under Federal protection. Alabama got to be a place not safe for either Creek or black. The locals didn't make it easy for Creeks to linger, once they knew the treaty was signed and land soon up for grabs. There were incidents. We knew of the need for camps, but the requirement came much sooner than expected."

"Is there food? Medicine?"

"I'm told provisions cost dear anywhere near the camp. Bacon twelve to fifteen cents a pound. Corn a dollar a bushel. Fresh beef not had in any quantity."

"Creeks will hunt, if there's game."

"Yes, but they alarmed the citizens, and aren't permitted to roam the countryside without escort. They're confined to the camps. That causes a bit of a difficult situa-

173

tion, I understand."

"So food is scarce," said Cow Tom.

"Food is a problem, but it is reports of sickness that distress," said Schoolboy. "Smallpox, influenza, cholera. Others."

"Can't they carry them elsewhere?"

"Not yet. The final destination is up the Mississippi to Fort Gibson, in Cherokee territory," Schoolboy said. "Once there, every major tribe gets their own partition of land. Cherokee, Creek, Osage, Choctaw, Chickasaw, Seminole."

"Yes, I've been there," said Cow Tom. "I've seen the settlement area for Creeks in Indian Territory." He made great effort, with success, to keep the sharpness from his voice. He could not afford to alienate Schoolboy.

"How is that possible?" asked Schoolboy.

"Ten years ago. Chief Yargee needed an English speaker, and took me as part of a scouting party of Upper and Lower Creeks sent to accept land and sign a treaty to Remove. Soil not so rich as Alabama, but good enough, and reasonable for grazing. Only then did they agree to relocate."

"We must Remove those at Mobile Point, soon. We can't assure safety much longer, and conditions worsen by the day. Mobile is the largest camp, but there are others."

"Why tell me all this?" Cow Tom asked.

"You could be of use to me for the rest of the trip. And I reward those who are helpful."

"Helpful?"

"Keep peace among the blacks on board. A hungry, desperate man is more dangerous than a hopeful one."

"Why me? Why not Harry Island or one of the others?" Cow Tom asked.

"I've watched you, how they react to you. You've been to the storage room. You understand there's other ways another officer might go about this. I'd rather not put anybody in chains. But if there's threat we won't dock in Mobile Point with all heads accounted for, chains it will be."

Schoolboy stared off into the distance, letting his words sink in.

"I'll do what I can," Cow Tom said. He thought of Bella, of the man pursuing her, and wondered if he would follow the ship to Mobile, as Bella hinted. "What of slavers making claims at the other end?"

"If an Alabama slave belongs to them, and there's proof on Alabama soil, we must turn them over. There's no other way. If the man at the dock in Tampa Bay presented himself before slaves were on the boat, by all rights we should have examined his papers and decided then and there, but the ship's captain overstepped, and the military men were lower level, inexperienced."

The *Paragon* hit a rough patch of water, and they both grabbed hold of the rail to steady themselves. Schoolboy's pipe almost went over the side; his knuckles turned white as he gripped, hard, but he kept his face calm and easy, as if without care. The military man neither revealed much nor did he miss much.

"Your call would differ?" Cow Tom asked.

"Mayhaps I would have sent the catcher packing, and declared the black off-limits, owned by a Creek tribe member, and Removed."

Cow Tom nodded, weighing Schoolboy's words. The military man had seen his attachment to Bella. Was he talking about her? Hinting at a way around her predicament? What did he know?

"Removed where?" Cow Tom asked. "Who to?"

"To where the claim might be made among the Creeks. Surely a potential owner might step forward."

"With papers?"

"Not all papers are proper, and once in Indian Territory, not all can be tracked. My mission is to deliver Creeks, Seminoles, and blacks to Indian Territory. My orders are clear, and I intend success in performance of my duty. With good fortune, most will survive the journey and start over on new land. But much can happen in the next few weeks. It will take luck and careful thinking to accomplish the goal, and with that aim, I enlist whatever help I can secure, from whatever source. And I am a man who doesn't forget."

The day wasn't as cold as previous ones, and the sun, however feeble, felt good on Cow Tom's face. It was true, he thought, what Schoolboy said. Cow Tom was the case that proved the point that a hopeful man truly was less dangerous than a desperate one.

"I am here to serve," said Cow Tom.

CHAPTER 18

On the second evening after Bella came aboard, the hour drew late, and Harry didn't make it above deck to empty his stomach. After Bella scrubbed up the sick, she pulled at Harry's jacket.

"Too much shine," she said, and retreated to her corner, turning her back to them. Even Harry in his sad state was taken aback.

They both drank less in front of her after that, although Cow Tom or Harry still ensured a full flask whenever the firemen turned their backs. But for long hours at a stretch, night as well as day, the men were employed elsewhere on the ship, and Bella spent much of her time alone.

On the third day out of Tampa Bay the temperature dropped, a hazard of October's changeling weather, and the ship below-decks swelled with both Creeks and Negroes seeking shelter as rain swept through. There was little to do but endure, try to keep dry and warm, and fight for a fair share of the scant rations handed out each day. Some slept, some talked, some played cards or dice, some couples managed to find not-so-hidden corners for a quick tryst. Those who had tobacco smoked, those who had liquor drank. Another Creek warrior died, with a quick-rising fever and bloody flux that carried him off in record time, and then two more blacks. One woman, limp and malnourished from the time she came aboard, was stricken in the early morning hours and struggled throughout the long day and night, too ill to care for her child, a small boy, barely crawling. Ilza stepped forward to see after the soon-to-be-orphaned child, and late that evening, once the mother's body went over the rail, took the boy up and added him to her own. An old, toothless man Cow Tom remembered from shipboard rounds succumbed in an expulsion of blood.

Before the sun rose on the fourth day, Cow Tom felt a nudging at his shoulder, rousing him from a deep, dreamless sleep.

"Mr. Cow Tom." A small boy shook him. "Please wake up."

Ilza's son.

"Tom Too," Cow Tom said, fully alert now, fearing the worst. "What?"

"Lieutenant Sloan sends for you. Says come to the wheelhouse. You and Mr. Island both."

"Get him up then," said Cow Tom, pointing to Harry, on the floor, snoring off either the exhausting night or the flask. Maybe both.

To the boy's credit, he didn't shrink from the task, but shook Harry until he awoke.

"What do you think you're doing . . ." began Harry, but he saw Cow Tom, shoes on and ready, and began his own quick preparations.

"The lieutenant wants us," Cow Tom said, and Harry righted his cap and followed.

Cow Tom and Harry navigated the ship in the darkness, shadowed by Tom Too. There was busyness everywhere around them, the crew out in force. When they came to the wheelhouse, Schoolboy was deep in conversation with the captain.

"Ah, there you are," said Schoolboy. "We dock shortly after dawn. Reassure the Creek warriors their families likely await. They should ready themselves to leave the ship in less than one hour. Once we match up families in Mobile Point, we ship out again westward."

"And the Negroes?" Cow Tom asked. "What of our families?"

"If reports are correct, they should be settled in the camps by town alongside their holders. But the Seminoles' blacks won't be matched until New Orleans. Maybe not until Fort Gibson."

Cow Tom couldn't calm his belly's jitters. He might be only an hour away from Amy and his daughters. One final hour. But he also flashed on Bella, whether someone would claim her in Mobile and pack her off to some remote locale, whether her fate was to disappear into the bowels of Alabama, or into the Seminole-designated part of Indian Territory, or some other place he couldn't guess.

He made the rounds, spreading the word, but those on board already sensed the change in the wind, and didn't need telling they would soon dock. Everyone crowded the deck.

Cow Tom went back to the alcove, where Bella sat cross-legged on the floor. He'd given her one of the metal needles, and she mended a hole in his sock, drawing together coarse material, dipping the needle in and out until the gaps disappeared. She began to hum, soothing and sweet. As he lingered, she began an old lullaby, a song he remembered, the voice resonating deep in his marrow, and it poured into him like tonic. He

181

needed no proof she was who he knew she was, that he hadn't made her up out of some need to satisfy a boyhood invention, that her voice was indeed beautiful and the memory not false, and yet this song confirmed again everything for him.

She looked up. Her face brightened when she saw him, although her cheeks sank inward within her gaunt face, a markedly unhealthy effect. She'd taken off her scarf, and her coarse hair lay sweat-flattened against her head. Yet she looked at peace, the beginnings of a smile playing at her lips.

"You've let your things go to ruin," she said.

"But now you're here," Cow Tom replied.

He watched Bella's face close to him, her small smile evaporating. She dropped her head and slipped her full concentration into the loop of her stitches.

"We must prepare to go ashore soon," Cow Tom said. "We're almost at Mobile Point."

With a resigned shrug, Bella put aside her mending and gathered her few things, including the blanket he'd given her, and followed him to the deck.

The inlet was wide, but a large ship headed out of the bay, and the *Paragon* gave it berth, maneuvering around, finally pulling alongside the dock where two stern military men kept vigil. As they drew closer to shore, neat stacks laid out on the flat of the wharf came into view. Cow Tom assumed them supplies, until he made out details.

They were bodies, dozens of them, placed with care in rows, head to toe, as if a checkerboard for a colossus.

They made no move to disembark. Only Schoolboy left the boat, and they all watched his lone figure descend down the gangplank. He talked to the military men for barely a few minutes, and returned directly back aboard. The *Paragon* lingered in Mobile Point for less than an hour, and only that to allow two men to go ashore to procure wood for the boilers, before the steamboat set out again for open sea.

CHAPTER 19

Nervous speculation fast became all-out panic, from crew to military to Creek to black. Tangles of voices in a myriad of languages carried hysteria but little information, and by the time Cow Tom elbowed his way to the wheelhouse, Schoolboy was under siege, his face tight and closed to the assault of questioning. He spotted Cow Tom and waved him to his side.

"Calm them," he demanded. "Dysentery and fever. Tell them the living are carried to Mississippi, where we go straightaway."

Cow Tom obeyed, repeating the message time and again around the ship, as then did all the linguisters to their own constituents, but his thoughts were of Amy, whether she had transported to Mississippi or lay on the Mobile Point wharf. He tried to reassure, but his voice had gone shrill, and he couldn't find the correct words in any language.

He left the rest to others, and set off to confront Bella. By all that was holy he would tell her about Amy, and his daughters, of his life with Chief Yargee, of his distress. Whether she responded or no, he meant to make her listen, to see him for who he was, to force the connection. He found her humming as she performed her fruitless sweep of the filthy floor. She cut him off before he could begin.

"Harry told me," she said, and smiled, as if all was right with the world. "No Alabama."

Harry's name came easy to her, but not once since meeting had she uttered his.

His resolve vanished. Cow Tom turned on his heel and rushed out of the alcove, almost tripped by a split of firewood on the floor. He kicked at the log, unmindful of the alarm on Bella's face. At the base of the narrow stairway leading to the deck, a hollow-cheeked young man bullied an older woman for her blanket, trying to pry it from her hands.

"Leave her be," Cow Tom said.

"Who you think you are?" the man challenged.

Without a word, Cow Tom punched him square in the face, not once but several times, until the blood ran. He only came to himself when he felt the pain in his hand. The stunned man loosed his hold and backed away. The woman gave him a strange look, equal parts bafflement and gratitude, and settled her blanket more snugly around her. Cow Tom left them both and climbed topside. He claimed a place near the wheelhouse, where he spent the night in the cold and in his own silence, refusing anyone else's problems.

Toward morning, a land-based lighthouse appeared in the distance, marking the point where the channel to Pass Christian began. The tapered brick structure rose out of the surf like a watchful parent. Buoys marked the outer turns in the muddy water, and the captain and crew went hard at it, guiding the *Paragon* in toward the Mississippi mainland.

His mind more stable, Cow Tom roused Harry and Bella, but didn't encourage talk. Once again, they gathered their small bundles, as they had at Mobile Point, and flanked Bella at the railing, prepared to dock at Pass Christian. They waited, and this time, once ropes were secured and the plank attached to the wharf, they, along with the others, disembarked and followed the military men who met the boat.

As relieved as Cow Tom was to leave the

Paragon and walk firm ground, his patience was scraped bare. The soldiers told them their families were at a place called Henderson Point, and they trekked inland, coming at last to an enormous clearing, with tents and bark huts in every direction. There were thousands of Indians in a series of squalid, abutting villages. Cow Tom scanned for any familiar face in the vast landscape but saw none. Returned Creek warriors, informed to meet again tomorrow for the formalities of mustering out, began to canvas the encampment, looking for their own. The military corralled the Seminole slaves together, more careful now they were off the boat.

There were several white men milling about, watching the new arrivals. Cow Tom wasn't sure if they were slavers or no, but he didn't like the hungry way they eyed the gathering Negroes, as if waiting. One of them approached Schoolboy, gesturing with his hands in explanation of something, waving a paper as the slaver had in Tampa Bay.

Now or never.

Cow Tom broke off from the pack as the Creeks had, gently leading Bella by the arm, wading through the nearest thicket of tents, and Harry stayed close behind. Cow Tom caught Schoolboy's eye, just a glance, but the soldier made no motion toward Bella, or acknowledgment at all, and kept talking to the white man, changing the position of his body a step to the left, enough so that when the man moved in response, he now had his back to Cow Tom and Bella. Cow Tom tucked his head and struck out.

They wound their way past filthy, dazed children and dispirited adults, most idle, all thin, lying on blankets by smoky campfires. Except for women cooking, there was little industry; no guns to hunt, no corn to plant, no livestock to tend. Henderson Point was a random re-sorting of Alabama Creek towns, squashed together, reconstituted on lesser land and devoid of supplies. He needed to find Upper Creek. He needed to find Chief Yargee.

They asked at tent after tent, following lackluster but conflicting directions of where the Upper Creek families from the Alabama River might be housed, without success. This search was no good, there was no method to it, and now they were under no one's gaze who might protect him, not Schoolboy, not Chief Yargee. And should Cow Tom fail, Bella had no chance.

When they came to a muddy crossing, more trickle than stream, Harry Island recognized an old man from his town,

Negro, sitting in front of a crude shelter of blankets.

"Pompey?" asked Harry.

The man nodded. "Harry?" Pompey's eyes were watery, as if burned by the sunlight. "Another brave just come through. All the Florida men back?"

"Brought us by steamboat," said Harry.

"River's high enough, then," Pompey said. "Mayhaps they let us off here now."

"You know Chief Yargee?" Cow Tom asked him. "Upper Creek? Alabama?"

The old man shook his head. "But bunches of Negroes back that way."

He pointed off between a copse of trees, as good a place to look as any, and confident Harry had found his place, Cow Tom prepared to say his good-byes and continue his own search. As reluctant as he was to leave Harry behind, time was critical. There was no telling when or where slavers might appear.

"Good luck," Harry said. He headed toward his master's tepee, and Bella followed close behind him.

Cow Tom caught her by the arm to pull her away.

She balked. "No."

He came closer and whispered in her ear. "If you don't want to set loose slave catchers, you must stay quiet with me."

Seminole and black alike from before the age of speech knew the importance of silence for survival. After years of pursuit in Florida, Bella was no exception. She went immediately docile, and Cow Tom led her away without further trouble.

They walked from camp to camp, but none of them was Yargee's. Cow Tom wondered how long he could keep his own fear at bay, and Bella from spooking. Already he had soaked through his shirt, despite the cold.

That's when he saw her, from the rear, the round of her back so familiar, squatting at the cooking fire, her hair done up in cloth, two small children playing in the dirt nearby.

Amy.

CHAPTER 20

Amy wore a dirty, rough-weave cotton garment, hardly fit to call a dress, grayed to almost black, though it may once have been some other color. She turned in profile, and her cheeks were drawn and hollow, her feet bare, with winter already upon them.

"Amy?"

She found the focus of his face slowly, taking a while to register, as if it might be a trick. Her face showed a total tracking, first possibility, then fear of misidentification, then recognition and wonder. She seemed almost to levitate from her position by the fire, on her feet now.

The woman he left more than a year before hobbled toward him. She had a strip of bloody cloth wrapped around one foot, and winced each time she put weight on it, and he hurried to meet her, so intent was she on coming to him.

"Is it you, then?" she asked. "Is it you?"

When he got to her side, she leaned heavily on him. "We waited on you," she said, and the trust in her voice pierced him.

Cow Tom was loath to take in the horror of this place, and willed it to background. Notwithstanding the fetid air that clung to the camp like fleas to a mangy dog, he took his first deep breath in over a year, something wrong righted. He'd seen all this before, the cramped camps, the filth, the idleness, the hunger, the sickness, and yet Amy in the midst worsened the impact tenfold. Cow Tom pressed a piece of jerky he'd liberated from the ship into Amy's hand, another excuse to touch her.

"We saw bodies at Mobile Point," said Cow Tom. "I thought you . . ." He couldn't make himself finish.

"We are well enough," said Amy. "Compared to others. Though death and misery follow close wherever we go."

She took his hat from his head, to get a better look, following the curve of his face with her fingers as if there were only the two of them on this earth. She flinched.

"What's happened to your ear?" she asked, alarmed, touching the nubbed rim for the first time of many.

"Osceola," he said, but the name meant nothing to her.

Amy called to the two small girls, ragged and dirty. They came immediately to her side, the older holding the hand of the younger. Each clutched a different part of Amy's dress, hiding behind the skirt, peeking out. His daughters were bigger than he remembered, raw-boned and caked in mud. Malinda. Maggie. His heart broke and mended itself, seeing them thus. Alive.

"Girls, your father's come."

They seemed almost afraid, but Amy pushed them forward, and he touched each on the head, amazed by the wiry force of each. With one hand, Amy waved a circle in the air, encompassing all of them, and spit on the ground.

Cow Tom eased Amy to sitting, as the girls behind stared. Only after did Amy notice the frail woman standing at Cow Tom's elbow.

"This is Bella," Cow Tom said. "She came on the *Paragon* too." Cow Tom dug out another plug of jerky. "Bella, take this over yonder and split it with my girls."

Bella brightened, and took them off a small distance, within sight, but not hearing. Bella's manner with the girls pleased him, and Cow Tom squatted next to Amy.

"Who she belong to? This Bella?" Amy asked.

Bella squatted in the dirt with the girls, eyes on him the while.

"The story is long, for later. Maybe she belongs to us."

Amy didn't push.

"You look fed," she said to Cow Tom. "And mostly whole."

"Florida was a trial but I am returned," he said. "How came you to be here?"

"Whites came sniffing round not long after Chief Yargee sent you away. We tried to wait for the warriors to come home from Florida, to Remove together, but settler gangs weren't agreeable. They raided us, drove us off the land, and the army walked us to the hellhole at Mobile Point. And nowhere near Indian Territory yet. Between runaways and sickness on the march, for each five we lost one."

"Who is lost?" asked Cow Tom.

"Chief Yargee kept us together, but Sarah the cook is gone, exhaustion, and Peter's gone, fever." Peter was Yargee's youngest son by his youngest wife, a frail boy since birth, but the chief's favorite. "Couldn't do nothing for neither, slipped past my herbs' power to remedy or ease. We buried them both by the trail, barely time to add stones to the graves to feed the spirits of the dead."

Cow Tom revived, latching on to a grim

194

possibility in this sad piece of news. He wondered if Yargee losing a member of his family would make his case easier or harder to argue.

"Mobile Point was sickness and death from the start, even before the yellow fever," continued Amy. "We struggled for months, scratching to stay alive. When the military finally let us break camp, we were ready, anything better than staying put and waiting to die. They told us we'd go by boat, to be on the wharf ready to leave the same night, so we brought the sick on litters. But for two days, a storm blew and the boats couldn't lay alongside the wharf. The military ordered us to return to the old camps, but we said no. We wouldn't go back, none of us. Malinda was too sick to move. Everyone with a taste of dysentery or fever. Creeks. Military. Officers. Agents. Negro. Once the boats could land, we set sail."

"And then here?"

Amy nodded. "Pass Christian, Mississippi. Better than Mobile Point. The whites don't raid, yellow fever mostly passed, and rations flow, but we can't stay on here. We been waiting for the Arkansas River to get high enough for a steamboat."

"Did Yargee save anything? Cattle? Seed?"

"Alabama's gone, but they say Chief

Yargee hangs yet to a bag of the tribe's money from selling the cattle to the government," said Amy.

She set her jaw in the manner he knew well, but something was different. She'd lost a tooth.

"Part of that is my freedom money," Cow Tom said. There was little time to waste. "Is Chief Yargee here?"

"Yonder." She pointed. "He wouldn't Remove until his braves came back."

"Your foot?"

"Too much walking, carrying the girls. It'll heal, given time."

"I got business can't wait," said Cow Tom.

He left her with Bella and his daughters, she favoring one foot over the other, and Bella buzzing about them all, making them comfortable, as if she'd found a role she could understand. Without turning round, he was aware of Amy looking after him as he disappeared into the darkness, but there was nothing for it but to try to spin his plan.

Chief Yargee wasn't hard to find, now they were in the right section. The chief sat with one of his wives inside a cowhide tepee. Cow Tom stood before him, waiting to speak.

"War went on so long, thought none of you might come back," said the chief.

Only a year gone, but Chief Yargee looked much older than when Cow Tom had seen him last, his braid dull and sloppy, his shoulders stooped.

"My service with General Jesup is finished," Cow Tom announced. "They take us all to Fort Gibson now."

Chief Yargee nodded.

"Not all returned." Another of Yargee's linguisters perished in Florida, and Cow Tom detailed the movements of those he knew about, braves and Negroes, a bearer of new information.

"Months they kept us waiting here," said Chief Yargee.

"Today's tide is high, and soon as everybody's mustered out, they plan to set to sea again before the week's change."

"So we move on," said Yargee.

"There's opportunity here," said Cow Tom. "A special case."

Chief Yargee's wife brought him a pat of tobacco and his pipe. He looked weary, not eager but not indifferent either. Cow Tom talked on.

"As your linguister, I bear the brunt of dealings with Wachenas," he said. "My loyalty is always to the tribe."

Chief Yargee nodded, patient.

"I know a woman who can become part

of the tribe."

Chief Yargee sat upright on his worn deer-hide floor pelt, listening and smoking. He was interested.

"The Wachenas may try to claim her, but she will be loyal to you." Cow Tom went off script. "She is my mother, and must be claimed. None need know that connection. The great Chief Yargee must begin again, on new land. She'd be of use, can take Sarah's place, skilled in cooking and sewing. Or work harvest."

"I've no appetite to get in the middle of ownership for someone belonging to another," said Yargee in Mvskoke.

Cow Tom could still read the man. Chief Yargee was cautious but not immovable.

"I do all talking with officials," said Cow Tom, "in translation."

Yargee grunted, considering, the pot not yet sufficiently sweet.

"If money held for my own freedom is safe," Cow Tom added, "it goes toward my mother."

Chief Yargee pondered, now fully engaged. He wasn't a greedy man, but perhaps considered the tribe's needs for replacement cattle, for seed, for tools, for Cow Tom's sweat in working the new place. Maybe he was just tired of so many months surrounded by Wachenas without Cow Tom as buffer. "Some cattle were stole, but gold and paper are with me still," he said.

Cow Tom had nothing left to bargain. Chief Yargee held the future now. He remained silent, letting the chief come to his own mind.

"I'll not turn her in, but won't argue claim should another submit a case."

"Good enough," said Cow Tom.

CHAPTER 21

By the first sundown at Pass Christian, Bella warmed to her role as the girls' companion, and sat in the dirt with Maggie and Malinda playing a child's game. The girls developed an instant fondness for her, trailing after wherever she went, and Bella, among the filth and squalor, blossomed with the attention.

In private, Cow Tom took Amy aside and described who Bella was, and his mother's strange blankness. He left nothing out. In all their years, he'd told Amy the barest minimum of his beginnings, but if there was risk to take, he thought it fair she know now. He laid out his plan, dreading Amy's reaction to his proposed gamble, her worry for the rest of them should Bella be caught out in the masquerade.

"Whether she knows or not, she's family," Amy said. "We must try."

Cow Tom let out a long breath he scarcely

knew he'd been holding. "I guess some families are trickier to be part of than others," he said.

Amy didn't try to hide her surprise at his rare attempt at light-heartedness. And when she chuckled softly, he believed they had a chance at carrying out the scheme.

"We got to make Bella and the girls ready," Amy said.

They found the threesome behind the jury-rigged blankets. The dim gloom of encroaching night had closed in, the wind a-howl, and Cow Tom drew close to make out Bella's features. She sobered at his proximity.

"We're taking you to Indian Territory," he said. Bella's eyes went wide. "You mustn't speak except by demand, and from now, Sarah is your name. Only answer to Sarah, no matter who or what. Chief Yargee is your master."

Bella dropped her head. She wouldn't look at him.

"Understand?"

She nodded.

"Any strangers come round," Amy told the girls, "keep behind the blankets with Aunt Sarah."

Cow Tom tucked his mother away with the others in the cramped space, out of sight behind the rude tangle of branches and wood-bark roofing and strings of blankets and mud. He slept the night in the frigid cold, despite the brutal bouts of rain, all of them now a part of Chief Yargee's entourage.

By the following day, he'd fallen into the rhythm of the camp at Pass Christian, organized around ration retrieval, idleness, eating, sleeping, and dying. He waffled between thankfulness and gripping fear. Thankfulness for reunion with Amy and his girls and Chief Yargee, thankfulness for future transport by boat, allowing more time for Amy's foot to heal before the marching sure to come, thankfulness for Schoolboy having turned a blind eye as Cow Tom separated Bella from the Seminole Negroes. But more often, Cow Tom obsessed on the slavers prowling the camp.

There were only a handful of them as near as he could tell, rough, low-class white men armed with pistols, and they lounged near the food- and supply-distribution points, or by the dock. Cow Tom made several trips round the encampment, assessing the situation, once catching sight of Schoolboy across the distance and tipping his hat, once seeking out Harry Island for a brief visit, but he was afraid to be gone for too long, and hurried back.

On the second day, the tide was high enough to allow the release of some of the Alabama Creeks from Pass Christian, Mississippi. Cow Tom followed along behind the commotion, as two hundred from the holding camp were selected, rounded up, and led to the dock. They'd chosen the *Paragon* for the initial departure, and Cow Tom's heart flagged when he realized that Schoolboy would sail without him on the first ship as it chugged its way up the mouth of the Mississippi. Yargee's party would be left behind to wait their turn on the flotilla of ferries on the next leg of the journey toward Indian Territory. He had counted on Schoolboy's sympathetic presence should things go wrong.

Worse, he watched the slavers spring to action once the *Paragon* began to load the Indians and their property — their Negroes and other assorted goods. No more lounging. The slavers insinuated themselves near the gangplank, checking each dark face as they trudged onto the boat. There was a fair amount of natural jostling in boarding, even pushing and shoving, and from his vantage point Cow Tom realized how difficult it would be to slip Bella undetected through that gauntlet when their time came. Difficult, but not impossible. They'd need luck.

That's when he saw the curly-bearded man from Tampa Bay who'd tried to board the *Paragon.* The man Bella feared. How he'd made it to Pass Christian so quickly, Cow Tom didn't know, but here he was, asserting his claims again. Cow Tom watched in horror as the white man plucked a small, dark woman from the mass of people before she could set foot on the gangplank, and separated her from the others, roughly yanking her by her arm, off to the side. No one stopped him this time.

Cow Tom ran all the way back to Yargee's camp, relieved to find Bella and the girls out of sight behind the blankets, at play. He was unsure whether to tell Bella about the slaver or no. She was skittish enough already, and he decided not to spook her further. When he described what he saw at the dock to Amy, she agreed. They needed a better plan.

Each passed day was a torment. Cow Tom made sure Bella stayed hidden, and spent hours on end with Amy. He pressed her for more detail of their ordeals in his yearlong absence, not only to understand what they'd been through, but also to hear the steady stream of her voice. He thought to find Harry again, but refused to leave their little encampment unprotected.

On the sixth day, toward dusk, Yargee's party was finally assigned to leave. They marched to the dock in a stormy squall, carrying their belongings. Amy leaned on Bella and Cow Tom, Bella's printed head scarf wrapped around her foot as binding rag. Cow Tom was bareheaded, the driving rain and wind pelting him as they pushed forward. It was Amy's idea, once Cow Tom told her the story of the *Paragon,* for Bella to hide any special marker a slave catcher might recognize. Bella pulled Cow Tom's hat down low on her face to cover the port stain, and wore a dead boy's leggings and tunic.

Cow Tom couldn't believe the number of Creeks at the dock when they arrived, and still they came, hundreds upon hundreds. A fleet of ferries waited, small sailing vessels that hardly looked equal to the windblown sea between Pass Christian and New Orleans, their next stop, where they would board larger steamships contracted by the U.S. Army. If they could get past the slave catchers here, Cow Tom thought, then he would worry about New Orleans.

Yargee's party huddled at the dock — three of his wives and their children, six returning Creek braves and their families,

Cow Tom, Amy and the girls, Bella-turned-Sarah, and the family of the other black interpreter killed in Florida. Several slavers buzzed about, but he hadn't yet caught sight of Curly-beard. Cow Tom tried to appear calm. Bella was close to breaking apart, and truth be told, he wasn't that far behind. They stayed close to Chief Yargee, both because he was their owner and because Cow Tom was carrying Yargee's sack of gold, their restart stake in Indian Territory. It seemed crazy to set sail in this weather, but the sooner they boarded, the better.

Several Creeks around Cow Tom began to complain, afraid, unwilling to start the journey in the dark. Even Chief Yargee grumbled, in Mvskoke, and one official offered up several bottles of whiskey for the passing. The official had partaken himself already, but the bottles weren't for Negroes. Cow Tom wouldn't have minded something to take the edge from this night, but he needed his wits about him. Some Creeks on the dock accepted the liquor, some did not. Chief Yargee declined, but dissatisfaction grew louder, until the announcement came.

"We sail tonight."

There began a process, with military men dividing Indians into groups for the available boats, pointing and shoving. Cow Tom still didn't see Curly-beard, but there were far more people at the dock than when the *Paragon* sailed, and he hoped they could get aboard without confrontation. He made sure all of his were accounted for, Amy and his girls and Bella, wanting to be near the front to board the boat as soon as they could, just before Yargee.

A military man finally made the assignment, and Yargee's group was given the *Borgne.* They joined hands or grabbed hold of tunics so as not to be separated, and Cow Tom pushed them all toward the gangplank. The night had grown darker, the moon encased in clouds, and the constant drizzle of the day turned to rain so heavy, dangerous waves smacked the sides of the *Borgne* like thunderclaps.

There he stood, a lone figure at the base of the gangplank of the *Borgne,* as if indifferent to the gale, a flash of lightning revealing the path of the rainwater through the curl of his brown beard. The slaver examined each dark face as best he could, but the night was dark and foul, and the crowd impatient to get out of the storm. Cow Tom saw his opening. He put himself on the side closest to the slaver, with Bella farthest away, and began a surge forward, pushing until all around him pushed too. The crowd turned unruly, stumbling, some even falling, following suit, all of a body at the gangplank at a pace too chaotic for the slaver to manage. Cow Tom lagged behind then, against the people tide, in the slaver's way for precious seconds, hoisting the heavy sack close to his face to block Curly-beard's view until he saw Amy had hold of both girls and Bella, and they had passed up the gangplank.

" 'Scuse me, sir," Cow Tom said. If he'd had his hat, he would have doffed it.

He headed up the plank, where they waited on him. His legs shook so badly, and his heart pounded so violently, he had to stop and rest for a moment before he could make himself go on.

Cow Tom led them all to a lower deck, where they could huddle dry and out of sight. As relieved as he was that they'd made it this far, he feared their luck might not hold for the next transfer in New Orleans. He barely slept, trying for some better plan to protect his mother, and in the morning, when they climbed toward the fresh air of the main deck, he saw New Orleans spread out before him, and heard the grumbles from the military handlers about the yellow fever epidemic raging there.

The ferries emptied, their tired human

cargo rushed by the military handlers across the portage from Lake Pontchartrain to the Mississippi River, where three large steamboats waited — the *John Newton,* the *Yazoo,* and the *Monmouth.* There was no need for hiding or deception this time. No slave catchers prowled, scared away by the epidemic. Yargee's party was assigned the *Monmouth,* a decrepit boat with sagged boards and rotted wood, and just before nightfall, they boarded in another frenzy of storm, unimpeded.

Cow Tom had learned much on the inbound trip, and remembering Schoolboy's distaste for their quarters near the boiler room, this time he staked out a prime place for Yargee and his people near the wheelhouse, the group much larger than he'd looked after on the *Paragon.* They were safe, all of them. And Bella was aboard, no questions asked.

When Cow Tom thought no more could possibly fit above deck or below, still they herded groups aboard, drenched and frightened, and again voices pleaded to wait for morning to sail. Seven hundred packed on the *Monmouth* before they called a halt to boarding, where there had been two hundred on the *Paragon.* At one point, Cow Tom saw Harry Island above deck, rejoined now with his master, as was Cow Tom, and an acknowledging gesture had to suffice, the boat too crowded to do otherwise, the relative freedom of Florida something distant. He lost Harry in the crowd, and attended to his own. His heart still raced, and although he was afraid of setting sail in such a storm, he wanted nothing more than to leave the dock.

Finally, the whistle blew, and they pulled away from New Orleans in the black, driving rain, up the Lower Mississippi en route to the Red River and beyond to Indian Territory.

CHAPTER 22

Crew and officers returned often to the great stacks of boxes containing whiskey bottles, in relief from the raging storm or to gain courage to push on, Cow Tom didn't know, and the overloaded boat chugged its way north.

Cow Tom peered out on a river so wide as to appear to be open sea. In the distance all was inky black, the curtains of water assaulting the ship and obscuring even the lantern in the wheelhouse, the only light aboard, throwing out scant illumination beyond a few feet. He feared another ship from the other direction, neither seeing the other in the night. After the voyage from Florida to Pass Christian, and across Lake Pontchartrain to New Orleans, he was used to the feel of the sea, the swells of water and unpredictable currents turning his stomach inside out. But this was different, as if the ship ran in loopy circles.

Cow Tom wasn't the only one to notice, drawn into the fray as linguister when a Creek brave, Timbochee, conversant with protocols at sea, begged the officers to stop until morning. Timbochee stated outright his belief the men charged with steering could not control the ship and keep on course, zigging and zagging. They didn't listen, more intent on their card game and bottles. There was no one of Schoolboy's caliber in authority for appeal.

They passed onshore lights, and someone called out the name Baton Rouge, but they quickly put the town behind them, thrust again into darkness. They were to approach Prophet Island Bend within the half hour.

Several on the *Monmouth* saw the ship coming at them, including Cow Tom. Not one but two shapes, maybe the latter in tow, the first vessel draped in a hazy luminescence of muted light, but not the second. Boats going upriver were to stay in the quiet waters close to the banks and, at the bends, cross to the far banks where the water moved slowest. Downriver boats were expected to follow the river channel out toward the middle, where the current moved fastest.

Suddenly, as if from one throat, cries went up.

"Stay to one side! Stay to one side!" Timbochee yelled. "Let the night ship pass!"

A shrill sound pierced the darkness from the wheelhouse.

"Don't you see it?" the pilot shouted.

The first thundering crash was followed by a sickening series of grinding scrapes and shaking apart as the unlit boat struck the *Monmouth.*

At the rail, Cow Tom saw bodies by the dozens from the lower deck spill into the dark river, swept out and away, while the upper deck of the *Monmouth* listed and dipped closer to the water. The other steamboats reversed to stop against the current. Amid the terror of screams and shouts, he fought his way back to Yargee's party. Amy clutched Maggie, the small girl's arms around her neck, and Bella held Malinda, and the rest of Chief Yargee's retinue clustered round him. Cow Tom closed the last few yards, pushing against the tide of Creeks trying to come up from below by the stairway connecting upper deck to lower, while quick and confusing shouts were drowned out by the constancy of the distress whistle, projecting its ear-piercing call into the dark night.

"Wait for the boats!"

"It's split in two!"

"We're sunk!"

"Swim to shore!"

"All drowned!"

Amy saw him, and reached her hand. Fortunately, they clung to one another, his family, holding firm, and Cow Tom propelled them all as one toward the rail. They stayed on the listing deck as long as they could. Those belowdecks, at least those not already pitched into the water, fought for higher footing, but the *Monmouth* was fast sinking, the deck already wet with Mississippi waters at their feet. Better to take their chance with a pick-up boat. In the water, those Indians not immediately swept away struggled desperately for something solid to grasp on to. The other army steamers from New Orleans circled around and men picked up what survivors they could.

They were almost level with the water now, and Cow Tom prepared to hand his girls to rescuers in a waiting boat. They were terrified, but Amy whispered something to them both and his daughters gave themselves over to him. He had Malinda by the waist, in midair, when he heard another creaking groan. The cabin of the *Monmouth* broke off, and thrust them all downstream alongside crew and hundreds of other Indians.

Cow Tom pulled Malinda back in close to his body, but they moved in a different direction now. He wiped spindrift from his eyes. The rescue boat had disappeared. He watched the new swirls of water, the fresh crop of bodies washed far from shore, but he was still elevated above the surface, still connected to a major piece of the boat beneath his feet, his family still around him. Amy brought Malinda back to her arms, holding both girls now, and Cow Tom tried to get a fix on where they were. They floated some distance, adjusting to this new reality, as if suspended in time. But then the cabin broke in two parts, as had the boat, and spilled them all into the river with the speed and force of a racing stallion.

The water was frigid, and in the suddenness of the upheaval, he got separated from the others. Shouts punctuated the night air, both screams of fear and calls for help, and Cow Tom heard yells in the darkness from several directions promising rescue.

"We're coming," a few strange voices called out, and a frantic chorus responded from different points all around him. "Here." "Over here." He recognized one of the voices as Amy's.

Cow Tom saw his wife, always a strong swimmer, drag Maggie toward a jagged piece of broken-off debris in the river and get her bearings, and was relieved to see a small rescue boat with a single lantern rowing in their direction. Close by was Malinda, but she was too far for Amy to reach without letting go of Maggie. Bella was nowhere in sight.

Cow Tom swam hard in the direction of his daughter, arm over arm, fighting the pull of the river. He came up to get his bearings, and struggling to see through the frigid spray and the driving rain and wind, watched as Malinda, panicked, began to thrash wildly. Bella's head appeared from beneath the water mere inches from his daughter, and within seconds, his mother had the girl propped up and her arms pinned back so she couldn't take them both down. Cow Tom took another deep breath for one last effort to reach them, and when he surfaced again, Bella had already pulled the girl close to the rescue boat, Malinda still fighting the while. Cow Tom could see Bella's fatigue, but they were at the boat, and he and Bella pushed Malinda up and over the lip of the side, and hands from inside reached out and pulled her in to safety.

"We got her. We got her." Amy's voice.

Exhausted, every muscle in his body aching and the frigid cold beginning to numb his mind, Cow Tom took a moment to orient himself in the water as he clung to the side of the boat, half in, half out of the torrent. Amy and Maggie were safe. Malinda was safe, and Bella had saved her. But where was Bella? The pelting rain made visibility almost impossible, but Bella had been right beside him just seconds before.

He dove under, but the water was so dark and there was so much debris, he made out only outlines and shifting shapes. But then he bumped Bella, her body a limp curl, spiraling downward in a loose fall. She had released herself to the water, tiny bubbles floating upward as she drifted down. He made his way to her and snatched at her shirt, making good contact on the second try, and pulled her up to the surface as quickly as he could, getting her head above the flow before he drew in air for himself. She was still, heavy and lifeless, but then her body bucked, and she began to gasp for air, sputtering and coughing, greedy for breath.

Cow Tom called out until he grew hoarse, as so many others were calling.

"Over here!"

Not one but two rescue boats raced toward them, at cross purpose to one another, and for the second time that night, Cow Tom experienced a moment of inescapable clarity as the inevitable collision came directly at them.

He hadn't come this far to see his mother hurt again, and he shifted position, spinning Bella out with one arm as if a dance partner, hopefully removed from harm's way, and jammed his hand in between the two boats, absorbing the brunt of the impact. The pain wasn't as much as he expected. He had the clearness of mind to puzzle out that the icy water lessened what would surely bring greater pain later, but even so, he felt the pincerlike pressure on his left hand and up his arm, and was certain of broken bones and escaping blood. He refused to go into the rescue boat until Bella was safely aboard, and once he saw her pulled up, he allowed them to bring him in too.

"Where is she?" he demanded, over and over, until they cleared a path in the small boat so his mother was in his line of sight.

Bella was slumped over, wrapped tight in a blanket, shivering, a little stunned, but seemed free of injury. She stared at him, her breath coming in short bursts. Cow Tom could no longer hold on to himself, and the next he knew, someone carried him to land.

Hundreds of Creeks lined the shore, both dead and alive. Bella refused to leave his side. He balked at staying put, and struggled to his feet to find Amy, despite the blood and his mangled hand, but Bella pushed him back down and wiped at his gory fingers with a strip of her tunic. When done, she helped him stand and took the lead, pushing him forward in the search, acting as his eyes and ears. Amid the dark and confusion, they came across Amy ministering to the deep leg gashes of a young Creek boy who had lost both parents to the water. The girls were at her heels. Amy didn't bother to blink back the tears when she saw Cow Tom, and threw her arms around him. She discovered the mess of his left hand.

"So much death," she said.

"You all right?" he asked his wife. Not back a full week, and she'd almost slipped from him again. Her arms were heavily bruised, whether from boat or water, there was no telling.

"We survived," Amy said.

She inspected his hand and unwound Bella's rag to use as a bandage.

"No way to save the fingers," she said.

Cow Tom heard her through a fog, his head once again betraying him. He had to sit. "How many?" he asked.

"You still got seven," she said. She re-wrapped his hand, and as horns and whistles and bells pierced the night, he couldn't prevent himself from falling into a deep sleep.

He woke several times throughout the long night, sometimes to Amy and Bella, and sometimes to only Bella, who refused to leave him when Amy left to minister to the sick who might still be saved. They filled him in on reports of the collision, as much as they knew.

Each time he woke briefly in the night, he felt a little stronger, more himself, and each time, Bella's port-stained face filled him until he drifted back to sleep. Toward morning, he opened his eyes, searching for fragments of the nightmare he'd carried so long, the little-boy terror of the galloping horse widening the distance between him and his mother, and him left behind.

"Bella?"

She sat next to him on the ground, cradling his head in her lap. Her eyes were clear and fully present, and she smiled at him in relief.

"Tom," Bella said. "My Tom."

He didn't stop himself this time. He reached up and touched the pebbly texture of the birthmark on Bella's face, and she let him.

He winced at the pain of his bandaged hand, but the penalty was small.

He may have lost three of his fingers, but he regained his mother.

CHAPTER 23

They spent the night at Prophet Island
Bend, the other two steamers from New
Orleans hulks against the dock, unwilling
now to set off again in the dark. A mist hung
low, soaking everyone to the skin. There was
no good solution; to overload and put
survivors on another steamboat invited a
repeat of disaster, but hundreds of wet and
shivering Creeks were without shelter. The
military loaded some Indians on the *Yazoo,*
but others balked, including Chief Yargee,
who decreed his people stay ashore, despite
the sleet and cold. At Henderson Point,
they'd had their bark huts, but at least the
military came in force now to pass out supplies and food and medicine. The Creeks
were much reduced, at least by half, and
pieces of the broke-apart steamer and
bloated bodies washed downstream
throughout the long night.

The next morning, not too long from

light's break, Cow Tom volunteered for death detail. Some selfish part of him wanted to stay asleep, his head in his mother's lap, but he couldn't lie still while others were far worse off. He thought of Harry, possibly a body unclaimed among the wreckage.

Alongside others working the riverbanks, he pulled bodies from the water, and positioned them inland for identification, ignoring the pain of his left hand, wrapping the bandage tighter, and favoring his right. Almost all the bodies were Creek, and Cow Tom hardened himself, as if pulling logs from the unforgiving river and not corpses. There were Negroes among them, and he studied the features of each, heartsick, but also relieved as each proved not to be Harry. He dragged ashore one of the bodies of the two non-Indians, immediately identified by a military man as the *Monmouth*'s fireman, and once more, Cow Tom thanked the Great Spirit they'd been up on the deck when the catastrophe happened, and nowhere near the boiler room.

He fetched another body from the water, turning the young Creek woman faceup for easier identification, and arranged her garments for modesty as best he could. The shore was alive with activity now, rescuers, rescued, those dealing with the dead. Family members formed grim patrols to find their missing amid the bodies strewn about, now a wretched detail, with no new survivors. Even in Florida, he'd never seen this many lifeless bodies at once. Midmorning he fell into despair, almost dropping in the mud from cold and fatigue. He was not yet thirty, his life an endless trail of death patrols. He tried to shake himself from his misery.

He sat on the river's edge, next to this latest body, just for a minute, he told himself, and closed his eyes to the ugliness surrounding him. There was no danger of sleep, but he found it increasingly difficult to think about opening his eyes or resuming his chore. He wasn't sure how long he sat, but felt a rough hand on his shoulder, shaking hard.

Harry Island stood before him. He'd lost his hat, and squinted against the sun, panic on his face, but other than that, appeared fine. Cow Tom revived, suddenly almost light-headed.

"You gave me a start," Harry said, "pretending ill." But then he noticed the bandaged hand. "You *are* hurt."

"Fingers lost to a good cause. Bella is still with us."

To his surprise, Cow Tom found himself pouring out the whole story. He'd meant to share only the change of name from Bella to Sarah, and the trick of getting her aboard the *Monmouth,* and her near death in the wreck, but he couldn't stop talking. He told Harry of his mother's abduction, his child's longing, and Harry didn't interrupt, nodding but silent. For an instant, Cow Tom even considered telling Harry about killing the black Seminole brave, but that was a story of a different sort, a tale of personal shame and dishonor, to be hidden at all cost.

"I came out looking for you this morning," Harry said when he'd finished. "Much better to find you mangled than dead. Soon you won't have body parts left to give up."

"I looked for you in the water too," Cow Tom admitted.

"We lost two in the crash," Harry said. "Those cussed fools in charge, packing us on that no-count boat. Most belowdecks gone. Three hundred dead. Maybe more."

"Not one of ours taken," Cow Tom said. A hard lump lodged in his throat, and he coughed it away. In the midst of so much death, he latched onto a moment of wonder. He still stood, with a family intact. And a tribe. And now a friend.

"Enough of the sea. I'm moving to shovels," said Harry, and Cow Tom agreed, falling in step behind.

They left the muddy bank and joined others digging burial holes in the interior for those already identified. They dug for hours, the work harsh and dispiriting, but Cow Tom felt steadier than he had for months.

"Rumor is, military opens claims this afternoon for property gone and dead Negroes," Harry told Cow Tom.

"Chief Yargee lost his money bag in the storm. My get-free money was in that sack. Scant chance they'll find it."

"Or return it if they do," said Harry.

"You don't try," said Cow Tom, "you don't get."

His fate was tied to Chief Yargee, his and his family's. He wasn't anxious to bring attention to their party, especially until Bella was safely out of the South and in Indian Territory, but he knew Chief Yargee's gold was important for the tribe, and would buy them all a faster start in the new land, for food and seed, for building supplies and cattle. No matter what happened, freedom would have to wait.

As Harry predicted, the military set up an area near the dock in the late afternoon.

Cow Tom persuaded Chief Yargee to be among the first to file his claim, and accompanied him to the makeshift area.

Cow Tom recognized one of the military men from the *Monmouth* under the shelter of a tree, and not far from where he sat, other officials combed through flotsam and jetsam washed up on shore, separating items still usable — clothes, shoes, cookery, planks, spectacles, instruments, weapons, blankets, baskets, watertight barrels — from the clearly useless or destroyed. There were any number of mounds of uneven heights, and a stream of men carrying additional recovered items inland added to them, dumping their loads before going out for more.

"Chief Yargee brought a bag of money from Alabama," Cow Tom translated. "Gold coin and paper. The sack was near the cabin when the *Monmouth* went down. He can single out the markings, a white-faced owl carved into a red deerskin rucksack."

The military man took down the chief's name, making scratches in his book, and when they gave a detailed description of the bag, he made notes about that too.

"Tell the chief we'll notify him should we come across such a bag," the military man said.

Cow Tom held little hope. Either the money was at the bottom of the river, or would soon be lining some official's pocket.

"What's he say?" Yargee asked.

"Chief Yargee asks if he can search now," Cow Tom said to the military man. "Search through the grounds."

At first, the military man wasn't inclined, but Cow Tom pressed the point for Yargee. The night and day had been long and wearing for the military too, and finally, in exhaustion more than anything else, he agreed with a shrug.

"Nothing gets carried away. Just look for your sack."

He and Yargee spent the next two hours sifting through sogged messes piled along the shore, culling through rubble. They split the piles between them, Cow Tom to the right and Yargee to the left, moving large items to uncover what lay underneath, searching for the tanned reddish color that held their future. Twice, Cow Tom jammed his bad hand in the stubborn debris and had to wait for the pain to subside before renewing the search. He and Yargee met again in defeat near the center of the piles, but before they could commiserate over their failure, they both saw the flash of the familiar color in an unexamined stack just unloaded downriver.

Chief Yargee was first to the heavy sack, and Cow Tom helped him drag it to the side, away from the other wreckage. The chief opened the large pouch, and discovered both the gold and paper money intact. The currency was water-soaked and stuck together, but all there.

The military man, when they told him, seemed surprised by their find, and when they led him down the bank and showed him the white-faced owl carved into the sack as they'd described earlier, he was quick to offer to dry out the paper money for them and return the sack later.

Cow Tom translated, and Chief Yargee told Cow Tom he was willing to come back that afternoon, but Cow Tom did a quick negotiation of his own.

"We could take the gold now, and come back for the paper," he reasoned with Yargee. The chief agreed, and Cow Tom presented the chief's wishes.

The military man didn't seem particularly pleased with this suggestion, but he released the gold to them, which Cow Tom carried back to the encampment.

They never saw the paper money again.

Two days later, they were assigned another

steamer, and proceeded up the Mississippi to Fort Gibson in Indian Territory. Compared to its beginnings, the remainder of the trip was uneventful, and when the time came to march, Amy's foot was much improved, almost healed, and both Cow Tom and Bella helped carry Malinda and Maggie. They were all received, processed, and recorded at the fort, and only awaited release.

Bella played her part, as did Chief Yargee, and Bella became Sarah, the cook. After a week's stay, the entire party struck out from Fort Gibson to begin again, staked with the meat from half a cow, a wagonload of corn, a flint and steel to start a fire, a big-eyed hoe, and an ax, all from the government in recognition of their Removal. And they had Chief Yargee's bag of gold coins from the sale of their Alabama cattle, in hopes of putting together a new home along the Canadian River.

INDIAN TERRITORY

–1842–

CHAPTER 24

Just past daybreak, Cow Tom picked his way through the mudded trails of Tuckabatchee village, outside North Fork, two days from Yargee's homestead. Although still within the relative safety of Upper Creek lands in Indian Territory, he'd trekked enough without a master to know that what defined rules of slavery in one jurisdiction wasn't necessarily protected in another.

He found the cabin along the road leading into the village proper. A man in his middle thirties sat on the porch in front of the small log house, and coolly assessed Cow Tom as he drew near. On his turban, three wild turkey feathers rose from the back of his head like a peacock's plume, and he dressed in age-dark deerskin leggings under his tunic and a loosely wrapped blanket about his upper body. An old fiddle of polished wood rested at his feet.

"Say, brother," the man called in

Mvskoke, "do you fear God?"

Cow Tom drew closer. "That I do," he answered.

"Do you drink?"

"I've passed the jug."

"Do you idle?"

"Too much needs doing to sanction a life slid past."

"Have you come to seek women?"

Tuckabatchee's two main businesses were whiskey stores and brothels. "I got all the woman I need," said Cow Tom.

"Have you come to listen to my sermon this fine day?"

"I'm fresh from the sale of a brood cow in North Fork," said Cow Tom. "But I'm come to visit my old friend Harry Island."

"Then welcome, brother."

"Too long past, Harry."

Harry jumped off the porch, his belt buckle clanking against the bone necklaces down his chest, and with great gusto, clapped Cow Tom on the back. Neither of the men could be considered tall, but Cow Tom had at least a couple of inches on Harry Island, and Harry circled him slowly several times, studying him head to toe.

"You've filled out since Florida," he said. "Not easy where good land is scarce and food scarcer."

"Not so many meals missed on your side either," said Cow Tom to Harry.

"Five years," said Harry. "Come to check our pledge?"

Cow Tom still remembered the damp of the evening at the gate of Fort Brooke, the uncertainty of whether he and Harry would end the night minus their scalps or as future agents of justice. Without thinking, he touched the nub of his right ear.

"Chief Yargee settled along the Canadian River, but I been too hard-pressed living to show much pledge progress," said Cow Tom. "You?"

"Doing my best," said Harry. He accepted Cow Tom's whiskey jug offering and set it next to his fiddle. "Away from home, wandering alone. You free?"

"Not yet. Chief Yargee lets me go off for business, but on a short leash. But this sale puts me almost to $400 in the clear for my papers; a few months, then I come to be my own." He'd already have the cash if not for Yargee deducting Bella's price coming into Indian Territory. And if one of his blasted cows hadn't wandered off before he sold her while he slept off a drunk. Amy deviled him about the loss, as if his fault. They'd argued.

"You always were a man to make good on

intention."

"After me is to buy Amy, before more children come. There's four already, all girls. Better born free than bought free."

"And Bella?" Harry seemed tentative, as if afraid to poke a wound.

"One of us now. She goes by Sarah, and cooks for Chief Yargee."

"Glad to hear," Harry said, grinning big. "How did you find me?"

"Harry Island is a name of great reputation," said Cow Tom. "Old Gouge is unhappy with you. He went to Council, red turban shaking, asking why the praying people abandon old Indian ways."

"I have a different path to follow."

"He wants Christian worshippers striped, and called you by name as the preacher from Tuckabatchee."

"We been beat, yes, but no striping yet," said Harry. "And still we preach. And still the faithful come. Today is special. Will you attend?"

Cow Tom studied his friend. The same feverish cast to his eyes as when they warriored together in Florida, the same sly defiance pushing at the bounds of abandon, but somehow always tamed to grit and calculated gamble.

"And the danger?"

"Waking to morning is danger," Harry said.

"You believe you do good for Negroes?"

Harry considered this. "It isn't only us attending my sermons," he said. "If past is judge, there'll be Creeks, half-breeds, and Negroes, both slave and free. See for yourself."

"You can't be persuaded otherwise?"

"We made us a pledge. And now I been saved, and am the better man. You can be saved too. I hold service this morning."

There wasn't a flicker of doubt on Harry's face. The wild man Harry was when they first met had developed into something different, a more focused instrument.

"Yes," Cow Tom said. "I'll come."

Harry offered *puska* and jerky, and they ate together. When Cow Tom pointed to the jug, Harry passed it to him.

"To getting out alive," said Cow Tom, and took a long swig. Before the alcohol itself had a chance to do its work, he untensed at the promise of it.

Harry didn't take the jug when offered, but toasted anyway. "To no more Florida," he said.

"To no more alligators."

"No more sand fleas."

"No more treaties."

237

"There will always be more treaties."

They lapsed into silence. It bothered Cow Tom that Harry wasn't drinking, but he hoisted the jug with his two-fingered hand and let the liquid wash through him.

"You miss it?" asked Harry. "Florida?"

Cow Tom thought about the life he lived on Tiger Mountain, domesticated, confined. The land along the banks of the Canadian River was fertile but uncultivated when they Removed five years prior, and conditions were harsher than Alabama. Homes washed away during violent storms, and warm, sunny days suddenly turned to freezing-cold nights. He'd devoted backbreaking years helping Chief Yargee develop the new plantation in Indian Territory, already almost the rival of the spread in Alabama, and built up a new herd. Chief Yargee allowed him freedoms, but Cow Tom was restless. He had much, but something was lacking.

"Some parts," Cow Tom replied. "The spark of living in the heart of a thing. You?"

"It was a letdown, coming back," Harry said. "I lost my way for a while, but found a new calling."

They sat on the porch for the next hour. Cow Tom described his life on Tiger Mountain, and Harry his in Tuckabatchee village.

"Couldn't do without Amy and the girls,"

said Cow Tom. "And Sarah fit right in."

"Ah, our Bella."

"She and Amy thick as thieves. Only now they both on me any time I slack off for a minute to unknot and spend a little time with the jug, talking about how I should be doing extra work toward freedom money instead."

"I had to let drink go," said Harry.

"Makes the day and night tolerable, but sometimes morning comes faster and harder than I thought," Cow Tom admitted. He took another swig from the jug. "I think Amy's trying to hex me from liquor when I sleep. Even Chief Yargee's started giving me the stink eye."

"You ever think serious on letting go of drink?" asked Harry.

"I'd no more give up drink than you'd give up the fiddle," said Cow Tom. He'd heard Harry was village fiddler of Tuckabatchee. "Say, what of a tune? For old times."

Cow Tom had trouble reading Harry. There was seriousness, a hardness just beneath the surface, but Harry finally smiled a sheepish smile, and picked up his fiddle and bow.

"For old times," he said.

Harry veered from one maniacal tune to

the next without pause, as if chased by the devil himself, in the same frenzy Cow Tom remembered from Florida. When he finally put down his fiddle, he seemed a man transformed, calmer, settled.

"It's time," Harry said. "They'll be gathered."

He grabbed his fiddle and the jug of liquor. The south wind was high, but the sun dominated, and they set out in only their tunics, no need for blankets, traveling by foot, not far, to a bigger homestead farther outside the center of the village. A Creek rancher, a sympathizer, had given over his house to the service, and fourteen Creeks, half-breeds, and Negroes waited inside.

Harry set his jug and his fiddle in the corner, and took to the center of the room. When he sang a hymn in Creek to Creek music, his congregation joined in. More plaintive than solemn, Cow Tom felt himself pulled into the curious rhythm, reassured by its familiarity. Harry's voice was strong and infectious, if not always tuneful, and he led a series of Baptist hymns in English, the words simple and shaped to fit the tune. Cow Tom assumed the songs made up, as Harry repeated "Farewell Father," with a chorus, followed by "Farewell Mother," and on and on until he exhausted sister, brother, and preacher. It was easy to participate, which Cow Tom did, including the final tune, whose only words were "I'm bound to go on," in English.

Harry held up his hand at the last note, calling for silence. He started his sermon, slowly, but built the tone and speed as he spoke of a wrathful God, a God who tolerated neither sin nor disobedience. He asked those in the room to show their commitment. A young Negro named Silas came forward.

"I want to be saved," Silas said.

"Do you fear God?" Harry asked, the same words he'd asked Cow Tom that morning.

"I fear God," Silas said.

"Will you give up ardent spirits for God?"

Silas shuffled his feet, his eyes downward toward the floor. "I am weak," he said.

"If you do not, you cannot enter the house of the Lord."

Silas hesitated.

Harry went to the corner, snatching up both the jug and his fiddle. "I am a sinner," he said, holding the jug in one hand and the fiddle in the other. "I am weak, but He is strong. I have drunk to excess. I have idled away my time for my own amusement.

But no more."

"Come out to the sunshine," he called, and marched outdoors. "Follow me."

Silas was first to go after him, out into the waiting wind, and they all followed, one after the other, as did Cow Tom. Harry staked his ground fifty yards from the house, the small crowd gathered round him.

"The Lord condemns whiskey," he said. He poured the contents of the jug on the ground, until the brownish liquid weakened to a dribble. The act shocked Cow Tom. The Harry he knew would never waste a jug of liquor. Harry's eyes were fire bright, as if in fever. "And so I will drink no longer. Spirits poison our minds and weaken our body. We forget our better selves. We forget our pledges."

He looked to Cow Tom, as if no one else was there. Cow Tom looked away.

But the quiet deepened, as Harry willed Cow Tom's eyes back to him. Cow Tom couldn't refuse.

Harry raised his fiddle and held it over his head, the same fiddle he'd carried into war, the same fiddle he'd played to cheer the warriors and console himself as their tour of duty in the swamps stretched beyond what any of them imagined. In Florida, Harry had slept under the stars with this fiddle cradled by his side, as careful with it as a newborn. He'd saved the fiddle when the *Monmouth* sank.

"One brother helps another be strong," Harry said.

For a moment, Cow Tom thought he meant to play, in the sunshine, as he had this morning on the porch, but Harry brought the fiddle against the tree with such force that leaves from high branches rained down as wood splintered into pieces. The catgut strings stayed oddly intact. Once more, Harry smashed the face of the fiddle against the stout base of the tree, and then again, until hardly anything recognizable was left to destroy.

"I am saved," he said into the silence. "And so can you be saved. Who will follow?"

A tension ran through the small crowd, a hush, an almost imperceptible shuffling of feet. Silas stepped forward, holding his arms out toward Harry. "I am a drinking man, but after today, I'll drink no more," he said. He dropped his arms to his sides, his eyes red and moist, and although Cow Tom wasn't convinced the man would keep to his promise, he was convinced Silas believed it himself at that moment.

"Welcome, brother," Harry said. He

looked around at the rest. "Who else will bear witness today? Who else will slough their corrupt ways?" He stared at Cow Tom and kept him in his gaze, waiting.

Cow Tom had attended more than one service put on by white missionaries passing through Yargee's lands, but they had been dry affairs, droning and high-handed, nothing like this. He looked at the splintered pieces of Harry's fiddle on the ground, the sure calm of his friend's face. Here, today, he found himself flooded with a sense of possibility. With release. He felt a catch in his throat and the spread of an inner light that warmed him, as if a soothing hand held his heart. He was moved beyond measure. Surely he was the only one who could know what that fiddle meant to Harry.

Harry chose a different path and seemed more content. Why couldn't he?

"I do," said Cow Tom, although his voice almost failed him. He'd seen the waste of too many, caught in the clutches of alcohol. He'd felt the slip of Amy's favor when she'd found him passed out in the corncrib, and he'd almost missed morning's call to work. He'd seen the question on Yargee's face where there had never been doubt of him before. If Harry could give up his fiddle, Cow Tom could give up the jug. Give up the shake of hand and the sour belly.

"I mean to leave off drink," Cow Tom said.

Harry nodded, as if he'd known all the while it would come to this.

"Welcome, brother," he said. "Anyone else?"

The rest of the congregation remained silent, and Harry launched into another hymn, this one in Mvskoke.

Cow Tom joined in, the reality of his pledge sinking in, already unsure if he could stay the course, thinking about the long trip home, back to Yargee's plantation, back to Amy and their daughters and his mother and his cattle. Back to Tiger Mountain. He was determined to try to atone for his past failings, to be a better man, a sober man, to take up Harry's good example.

He wasn't yet free, but now, at least, he was saved.

CHAPTER 25

Cow Tom rapped at the back door of Chief
Yargee's log house. He straightened his
jacket and brushed dirt from his leggings,
took off his turban and gripped it in trembling hands, but thought better and placed
it back on his head. Already he'd searched
for Chief Yargee in his usual places, under
the gnarled old oak by the river where the
chief liked to enjoy a quiet smoke away from
the domestic home front overfull with
women and children, down at the gulch
where braves gathered to swap stories, at
the sweat lodge. The day was too blustery
and the smokehouse too full for the chief to
be on a hunt.

Facing the closed door, with the distant
screech of a *stikini* and the whistling wind at
his back, his nerves, already stretched to
snapping, began to get the best of him.
Times like this made him sorry he'd given
up drink. He considered going round to the

front, but a short black woman in a home-spun dress swung the door wide.

"Morning, Sarah." Cow Tom touched his turban in two-fingered salute with his good hand, as he'd seen the white man do. Though he called his mother by her second name, he thought of her still as Bella, and was pleased anew at the place she'd made for herself in Yargee's house.

"Morning, Mr. Tom," she said. She looked him directly in the eye, studying him, and although she threatened a broad wink, she kept her face solemn. "Come in," she said, clearing a path for him. "Chief Yargee stayed close to home today."

Cow Tom followed her into the darkness of the kitchen. He'd spent a fair amount of time here, waiting to confer with Chief Yargee on one issue or another, and he mumbled his greetings to the other women working, tending the skillets and kettles, chopping vegetables, washing cups.

"Cold today," Sarah said. "Winter's early." She looked fit to bust. "A good day for special matters. For a special man."

Cow Tom nodded, mute, and followed his mother down the narrow passageway toward the front of the house. She deposited him there and, with an encouraging nod, retreated from the room. He felt like a little

247

boy, brought up before the tribal elders for an offense. Chief Yargee sat on a straight-back chair in the center of the room, flanked by two of his wives. One wove strips of flat reed into a basket, and the other pushed cut pieces of deerskin into what looked like leggings. Both of the sisters peered openly at Cow Tom, and Chief Yargee waved him in. A black-and-white patchwork mutt with begging eyes and a long jaw lay at the chief's feet, and neither growled nor barked. Cow Tom's presence in the house was not new.

"Any trouble with the sale?" the chief asked in Mvskoke.

"No, sir," said Cow Tom. "They hit the right cattle price. I have the gold here."

He pulled out the small sack from his jacket.

"Bring it to me," the chief said.

Cow Tom paid watchful attention to the dog, careful not to threaten territory too quickly, and placed the sack into Yargee's hands. The chief put it carelessly on the table by his pipe. "Good," he said.

Cow Tom cleared his throat, suddenly very thirsty. "My part for sale and translation comes to seventeen dollars."

Yargee grunted. "I'll put it aside," he said. "Like always." He tapped his pipe on the table to settle the tobacco, and lit the contents, drawing in great drafts of air.

"That makes $396," said Cow Tom.

"Yes. I believe it does."

"And I sold my scrub steer to them for another four dollars." He dug into a different pocket of his jacket and offered several coins. Chief Yargee placed them alongside the sack.

Cow Tom waited for further acknowledgment, but Yargee turned his attention to the dog. Cow Tom knew the story, as did everyone else in the tribe. Yargee had found him when he was a motherless pup, a scrappy survivor. He'd nursed him back to health and kept him close ever since. Yargee scratched the animal behind first one ear and then the other.

"That comes to $400," Cow Tom pressed.

Yargee grunted again.

"The time has come," Cow Tom said. He searched for how to proceed and came up empty. After a lifetime of waiting, he had lost the words he'd intended.

"What time?" asked Yargee. He barely made eye contact with Cow Tom as he talked, his stocky body loose and entitled, his attention more pulled toward the dog than either Cow Tom or the money. His movements were slow and sure, only enough to draw the short, smoking pipe to his lips and let out several curling puffs before returning the pipe to the table. The youngest wife let a tiny giggle escape before she composed herself, under the stern gaze of her older sister and fellow wife, her small mouth hidden behind her chapped, blunt-fingered hand. Yargee motioned the older wife, and she put down her basket weaving, picked up the sack and loose bills, and disappeared into a back room. Yargee tapped the bowl of the pipe against the table and waited.

Chief Yargee was playing with him. The old chief was a gregarious man, as fond of pranks as he was of stretching out a tall tale to make it last for hours, but Cow Tom didn't have his usual patience today. Today wasn't for tomfoolery. Today was only for seriousness.

"Time for free papers," Cow Tom said.

"Whose free papers?" asked Yargee.

"I come to buy myself," said Cow Tom, remembering his words at last. "I come to carry my own papers from now forward."

"I see," said Yargee. He exchanged a look with the young wife, and she dropped her gaze, concentrating on punching another small threading hole in the deerskin. "And the money?"

Cow Tom and Yargee had talked this

through already, before they came to Indian Territory from Alabama, before he married Amy and had children, before he spent the hellish year in Florida. Yargee's stated price for a black man's freedom was $400, cash, and to the chief's credit, he hadn't once wavered on the agreed amount despite the passage of time.

"There is enough, with money kept back," said Cow Tom. "With what you hold, and the sale last week of the sick steer I nursed through, and today's add. There is enough."

"Enough?" asked Yargee. "Did we say $450?"

"No, sir," said Cow Tom. "Four hundred dollars. You hold $400, all together." Cow Tom felt the sweat running down the sides of his face. Even his hands were damp and clammy, despite the chill.

Chief Yargee looked thoughtful, as if trying to decide between *sofki* with venison or ghost bread, each choice appealing and with merit, either decision possible and dictated entirely by his mood.

Cow Tom prided himself on reading people, one of the greatest survival skills a black man could possess. The chief could be playful, even at the expense of others, but as masters went, Chief Yargee was a reasonable man, not cruel, not intent on demeaning those belonging to him, nor overly harsh, even with warranted punishment. His attraction to money applied only to those things he could buy with it, like grain or seed or ponies or tools or cows. Chief Yargee was content to sit by the fire smoking his pipe all day while the tribe's lands were worked by his Negroes, retelling stories to younger braves, or attending day-long Council meetings and settling petty squabbles as final decision maker. He basked within the attentions of his three wives, watched his grandchildren play *ane-jodi* stickball or *chunkey* in the distance, their voices floating over the prairie as they slapped at the deer-hide ball with their hickory sticks and took aim at the wooden fish atop the twenty-five-foot pole. But Cow Tom also knew Yargee considered himself better than all his slaves, without exception, superior by birth, as Indian, as Creek, as full-blood, as member of the Muskogee Nation, as chief, as elder, as husband in possession of three wives and a dozen Negroes to work the land.

"Yes. Now I remember. Four hundred," Chief Yargee repeated, clearly sorry the game was over. "You will stay with the tribe?"

"Yes," said Cow Tom. "The tribe has been

good to me."

The chief's question was hollow. Yargee still owned Cow Tom's wife and children and mother. Of course he would stay with him. The freedom calculation was exact, the order of purchase mattered. If Cow Tom could, he would have bought his entire family at the same time and been truly free, but of course, that was impossible. If anything happened to him, the rest of his family were lost in the thicket of servitude, but once he purchased his own freedom, his wages would be his own, and he would work, no matter how long it took, until he shook every member of his family loose from Yargee's rolls. First himself, then Amy, so no future child of theirs would be born into bondage, and then their children before they came of age to have children of their own.

"You are free," said Yargee.

How many dark times had Cow Tom doubted he would ever hear those words? A wash of emotions fought his resolve — triumph, gratitude, resentment, exhaustion, disbelief. He wanted to go immediately to Amy, tell her he'd done this thing they'd dreamed for so many years, that her time was coming too. But he refused sloppiness, refused to let emotion overcome practicality.

"White men come through next week," said Cow Tom. "We can draw up new papers then."

"No need for the white man's paper," said Yargee. "We agree."

"The government is strong. Without the paper, they can make many claims," Cow Tom said. "Papers must be signed as proof you agree. For me to carry outside our village."

Cow Tom knew how much Chief Yargee despised dealings with the white men, the scent of them, the ugliness of their language, the capriciousness of their character, and the foulness of their ideas, the fact that they didn't properly respect the Upper Creek way.

"I will sign," Yargee said, "but then I want them gone."

Yargee turned his attention back to his dog, the mutt's tail slapping the floor.

Something drained from Cow Tom, and he was outside his own body, watching the release of a wild animal caught in a trap. He didn't move, unsure. He saw Sarah down the long hallway to the kitchen. She grinned openly.

Cow Tom turned back to Yargee.

"Thank you," he said.

He had walked into his master's house a

slave, but he was going back to his patch of land, to his wife and to his children, a free man.

He left by way of the front door.

■ ■ ■ ■

TEN YEARS LATER

–1852–

■ ■ ■ ■

CHAPTER 26

Amy joined Cow Tom by the river at his favorite spot, under an old scrub oak amid a cluster of cedars, where he most enjoyed a quiet smoke. The location always put him in mind of Old Turtle, and he cherished his stolen moments here, but his heart leaped at the sight of his wife.

"Is it time?" Cow Tom asked.

Amy laughed. "Soon enough," she said, her mood as high as his. "Edmound makes us wait."

Edmound. His daughter insisted on this. He hadn't known where Malinda came by such a lofty-sounding name, but she seemed sure as she carried the child in the swell of her belly, wide and low, that this time it would be a boy, and that the boy child would become Edmound. And Cow Tom had approved the Wachena name, without basis for real objection, eager as both he and Amy were for this male extension of the bloodline, after five girls of their own already born. Girls ran in this family, but now a grandson, at long last. Someone to carry on.

Amy sat next to him, and for a long time, they said nothing, the noise of the cicadas controlling the river.

"What I could not give, our daughter will," Amy finally said.

"Amy," Cow Tom said in warning, but he couldn't stop her.

"I promised you sons."

"I am content."

"You are a man born for sons, and for bigness. I know who you are."

Amy was attuned to the better man he'd worked so hard to become, but she could never comprehend who he'd been with the general, and for this, Cow Tom was thankful. Although all five of his daughters were precious to him, he'd had to resign himself to his inability to produce sons as his special punishment, retribution for that moment on the hammock in Florida when he robbed those two black Seminole boys of their father, and all the raids after. He could only hope the reckoning didn't spill over to his daughters too.

"I am content," he repeated.

"Malinda and Faithful will change the

course," Amy reassured him.

A part of Cow Tom wanted better for his eldest girl, a man more worthy than Faithful to father his grandchildren, a man of more fire, more ambition than sliding from day to day under the heavy haze of alcohol. But if Faithful could bring a boy child into their family, that would be enough.

"A child is a child," Cow Tom said.

He was afraid for Amy should Malinda deliver a girl. Amy had invested too heavily in the idea of a boy child and, after so many disappointments, was no longer reasonable about the subject. Yes, he was eager for a grandson, but Amy made the idea of a boy baby too large for easy retreat.

"He comes any time now," Amy said.

He hadn't seen her this excited since he'd bought the last of their children from Chief Yargee. She ran her finger down the ridged nub of his bad ear, a sign of her playful state of mind. He swatted her hand away, but she came back at him again, laughing, and he laughed too, happy at the sound.

The birth was difficult, off in a separate tepee removed some distance from the house, updates coming every few hours or so, from one woman or another or a messengering child sent by Amy, who midwifed.

261

By the second day, the tone became increasingly worrisome. Malinda was losing vigor, and the child wouldn't present.

Unable to sleep, Cow Tom walked the dark path and waited alone at the riverbank, where Maggie sought him out.

"There's two," she announced, "a boy and a girl." But a steady twitching in her face and the hesitation in her tone let Cow Tom know it was too soon to let go his caution.

"The boy was first, but small. He wasn't given enough breath," she told him. "And then the girl, smaller still, she fought her way out."

Cow Tom absorbed the news. He wanted to talk to Amy, for her to tell him all would be well, but he'd have to wait. Men were not allowed in the women's space, and Amy was still needed there. He concentrated on the positive. The long-sought boy had come, and with a sister. Edmound had come.

"The girl's name?" Cow Tom asked.

"No name yet," Maggie said.

He stayed out by the river, his need to be in the open overwhelming, and Maggie came once more to him there the next morning.

"The girl grows stronger," she told him. "She finds the breast."

His daughter gave more detail than he wanted.

"And the boy?" Cow Tom asked.

"He's gone," said Maggie. Her voice was flat. "He couldn't hold to life."

The idea had barely taken hold that there were two babies, before there was only one. Cow Tom closed his eyes, his dreams evaporating and carried off by the wind. Still, they'd look to him to set the mood.

"We bury him on Thursday," he said. "Four days hence."

He took up the ax and headed to the forest, where he cut firewood until his arms and back ached and he could no longer swing the weight of the ax above his shoulders. Death was a part of life, a transition, but if a departed spirit needed four days to visit old, familiar places and people before moving on, what would a baby do with all that time?

Cow Tom didn't move back to the house. He stayed by the river alone, two days, and then three, and Maggie brought him food and daily reports. Faithful was missing, not the first time, last seen senseless drunk in the north pasture trying to mend a fence. Amy stayed in the woman's space tending Malinda and the baby girl.

On the fourth day when Maggie visited,

263

one glance at her face and he knew something had gone wrong.

Maggie paused, some consequential words unspoken, words he would need to coax from her. Edmound gone filled his mind to capacity, and Cow Tom considered not pushing further, not giving chase to further news to disappoint.

"What more?" he finally asked.

His daughter stared out over the churning waters of the Canadian, gathering her thoughts, and Cow Tom regretted the ask. What could be worse than his grandson gone before he ever had the chance to take him buffalo hunting on the plain? To teach him to tell healthy cow from sick, or to lasso a steer?

"Is it the girl?" he asked.

She shook her head.

"Faithful?"

"We found him this morning, passed out in the corncrib," said Maggie, so matter-of-fact Cow Tom knew this had nothing to do with whatever Maggie came to say.

"Better just to tell it," Cow Tom said.

"Something's not right with Ma," she said.

This last took him unawares, and for a moment, he couldn't reassemble his thoughts.

"Has she fallen sick?" Cow Tom reached

out and took his daughter's arm, squeezing too hard, he knew, but bringing her to focus. "Speak quick, girl!"

Maggie blinked rapidly, though the morning had only begun and the day wasn't bright. "Not sick," she said. Her voice quavered, and Cow Tom saw her distress broaden to include him. "But she isn't Ma."

Cow Tom left his daughter where she stood, by the riverbank, first in a determined walk, and then almost at a run, turning in the direction of the women's tepee. The theft of Edmound was a cruel sting, hope thwarted, an affront that such injustice be allowed. But the concept that something had gone wrong with Amy went beyond, unthinkable. The world was a harsh place, guaranteed of quicksilver change and backhand slaps. But the constant throughout was Amy, calm and unflappable. Amy, the mainstay for them all regarding household or family concerns. He couldn't consider a circumstance without her. He was Cow Tom because she was Amy, like the flow of the river or the set of the sun, so ever present sometimes he forgot she was there.

"You can't go in the women's . . ." Maggie called after him, but her voice trailed, and he paid her no mind, hurrying toward the tepee with no real plan as to what he might do once there.

CHAPTER 27

The tepee came into view, set off to the side from the rest of the compound, the cowhide flap open. Cow Tom slowed as he got closer, the import of his intrusion into the woman's space breaking through at last, but he forced himself forward. He didn't announce himself, but stood in the opening and peered into the darkened space. There were two of them there in a frozen tableau. Amy stood with a wrapped bundle in her arms, and his daughter Malinda lay asleep and unmoving, only her head visible, a sheen of damp on her dark face and hair loosed from her kerchief in wild and tangled clumps, her form obscured beneath a sweat-soaked blanket. The smell from the tepee was heavy, earthy, of damp and doom.

"Maggie says the boy is gone," he said, from outside. His voice seemed to echo in the small, stuffy space, too loud.

Amy stared back at him, unresponsive,

and Cow Tom welcomed both the dimness and distance between them, giving him time to adjust to Amy's flatness.

There was movement from the bundle Amy held. Clearly the girl, swaddled and live, but the baby didn't cry or offer sound. Amy broke her gaze and looked down, made some adjustment to the piece of blanket, as if lost to him.

"She all right?"

Amy nodded, finally. The gloom over the space unnerved him. Cow Tom wanted to be finished with this.

"Where is he?"

At first, Amy didn't answer. "We're cursed," she said at last.

"Where is the boy?"

Still no answer. Amy sat down on the ground cross-legged beside the figure of Malinda, the recovering mother's breathing soft and barely audible, and she placed the baby in the hollow by Malinda's side on the pallet. Cow Tom suddenly feared their daughter was also at risk.

"Malinda all right?" he called into the tepee.

"She'll be fine," said Amy. "She'll rest awhile, to live another day."

"Amy, where's the boy?"

Amy fussed with the girl baby, picked her

268

up and stood again, this time moving her from one side of Malinda to the other, so the child could feel the warmth of the mother, even in sleep. Again she sat, as if Cow Tom hadn't spoken.

"Amy."

She looked up. The flat black of her eyes revealed an Amy gone to a deep, dark place he dare not follow, even had he wanted. Though he understood how much she looked forward to this grandchild as boy, Cow Tom couldn't imagine her dismay taking her to such a dangerous mood, but Amy had always been inextricably tied to her omens and superstitions in ways unknowable.

The space inside the tepee was not large, and Cow Tom was loath to enter. Still outside, he sought a sighting of the boy, and sensed the stillness in the corner of the tepee. Another bit of blanket, a rounded form, but no movement beneath. From behind, his other daughter had come up from the river and now stood almost alongside with uncertainty, only a footfall away, unsure how to handle the unprecedented male presence contaminating their sacred ground. For one moment, it seemed she intended to pass him at the threshold and enter the tepee, but she stepped back again, her internal battle betrayed by the indecision on her face, a tug-of-war between bonds of womanhood and duty of filial piety.

"We bury him before midday," Cow Tom said. "He must go to ground."

Cow Tom thought then that Amy would rouse herself to prepare the boy, but instead, his wife pressed at Malinda's forehead with a dampened rag. She cleaned and bundled the girl baby, but did not touch or acknowledge the body of the lifeless boy, nor did she speak.

"I'll see to him," Maggie said. She took a few tentative steps toward the entrance, but Cow Tom didn't give quarter, blocking her way. He shook his head, stopping her.

"It is Amy must do it," he said, making his tone hard, "not you." He put his body in between his wife and daughter. "I'll be back within the hour for the boy. Gather family. We meet at the clearing by the twisted elm in the east pasture. Tell Faithful to bring a gun."

He lingered just long enough to assure that Maggie left them to attend her task.

"Amy," he commanded into the semidarkness, his voice barely above a whisper. He hoped he did the right thing, nudging her back to her responsibility. "Have the boy ready by my return."

Cow Tom lit out for a part of the pasture prone to wildflowers, an area Malinda fancied as a girl before her hours filled with being a woman. He stopped at the lean-to supply shed along the way to collect a shovel. It didn't take long to dig the hole, so small as to be hardly more trouble than turning over the soil for a garden's planting, and when satisfied with the location and the depth, he threw down the tool, wiped his hands on his tunic, and returned to the tepee. As he got closer, he listened for Amy's voice, anything that could give him a clue as to what he would find. He made noise so they knew him coming and might prepare themselves, stopped once more at the threshold of the tepee, and peered in, feeling the fool all the while.

Amy still sat on the ground, just as he'd left her, listless. But now Malinda was awake, albeit droop-lidded and somber, propped up on the pallet with the girl baby at her breast. She started when she caught sight of him there at the threshold of the tepee, and did not try to hide her distress. Cow Tom didn't know the right thing to say.

"Malinda." He forced his voice to cheer. "The girl presents healthy."

271

Malinda looked down at the baby's suckling, and covered herself as best she could.

"Take the girl," said Malinda. Her tone, flat with fatigue, was edged with sorrow, and it wasn't clear who she talked to, whether herself or Amy or Cow Tom or God. "Take the girl away. I release my claim on her, only bring back my son in her place."

Cow Tom expected some rebuke of their daughter from Amy at this crazy talk, that she would take charge as she always did to coax reason from calamity, but Amy said nothing. His wife had yet to take her eyes from the mother and baby, or to acknowledge his presence at the threshold. Cow Tom had to believe that Malinda spoke from her exhaustion, and with time would weather Edmound's death, but if Amy set adrift, they were all lost.

"Did you prepare the boy?" he asked his wife.

His daughter's mouth clenched when he referenced Edmound, a slight shake to her shoulders as if chilled. Cow Tom became suddenly aware of three generations of women unfolding before him here, each under his protection, and his worry shifted from one to the next. His lot was to see after all three. Malinda was a strong girl, practical-minded and dutiful. She'd get beyond this. She'd lost the boy, but would come to accept the girl. The baby girl had already shown to be more warrior than her twin, and she would survive or not, as destined. Amy rubbed his heart most, her behavior puzzled him most.

Again Amy avoided his request, and Cow Tom forced his gaze to the back corner of the tepee. His grandson's body remained untouched, exactly as when Cow Tom left to dig the grave.

The thought was slow to come to Cow Tom's mind, but once it did so, there seemed no other way. Malinda was still too weak for practical matters, he had banished Maggie from the tepee in hopes Amy would come to herself, and now Amy was of no use. Unthinkable, and yet. Edmound hadn't managed to draw breath for more than the time it took the sun to rise and set, and now he must be set to ground. Custom be damned. What should fall to one of the women still needed doing.

Cow Tom entered the tepee, ignoring the looks of shock and disapproval from both daughter and wife. He lifted the corpse-child from the blanket where he rested, holding him close to his chest. The hole waited. He made one more appeal to Amy, but she folded her arms in defiant helplessness. He seized her arm to pull her to standing, made awkward by the child, and led her out of the tepee. She didn't fight him; she didn't help him.

"There is no curse," he said, although he wasn't convinced. "The girl still fights, and Malinda is young yet. No one knows what is to come."

They met Maggie on the foot-worn path outside.

"The family waits by the elm," she said.

"Go to Malinda and the baby girl," Cow Tom instructed. "See no harm comes to the girl."

He stopped at the supply shed once more, this time for a precious length of white cotton muslin he knew Amy saved for a special purpose. He grabbed up the material and headed for the river, pulling Amy along as best he could with his free hand, and when he was sure she would follow on her own, he went ahead with the boy in his arms, trusting her to come behind.

Once at the riverbank, he expected Amy to take over the duty from him, but she did not, watching him carefully, his every move recorded. She neither stepped up to clean nor to touch the small bundle, standing along the riverbank as spectator.

Cow Tom ripped the cloth into strips and

cleaned the child, wiping those smallest of toes and smoothing down the fuzz at his head, and he wrapped the stilled body in the white muslin until the exact form could no longer be determined.

CHAPTER 28

Cow Tom carried the white muslin bundle through the muddied pasture to a pinch of land he reckoned forevermore would be the family graveyard. Amy followed at his heel. He was oblivious to the ribbed globes turned deep orange on the ground, pumpkin time, his thoughts pulled too tight around loss. Unlike so many others in the tribe, black or red, Cow Tom had yet to bury one of his own here on this stretch of soil along the Canadian River, and that it should be thus, not of starvation or epidemic or someone's natural time, but before life even had a chance to blossom, weighted him like an anvil. The tiny body in his arms was light, shockingly light, a still, transient thing, and he tried not to imagine what could have been. Edmound.

Amy's step was close behind his own. She slid in the mud once, a slippery footfall, but righted herself without going down, and carried forward without comment. His arms were full. He couldn't help her.

"The girl still lives," Cow Tom reminded. Amy didn't answer, yet trudged along after. "And Malinda will come round," he added.

The family waited on them at the clearing, standing in a circle round the hole Cow Tom dug earlier that morning. Edmound's father, Faithful, wore his cloth meeting jacket, but atop his head, slightly askew, was the ceremonial red turban, the soft cotton soiled and fraying along the edges, but majestic nonetheless, and draped around his neck on a leather strip, his shell gorget necklace. Faithful did his best to rise to the formality of the occasion, but even standing still, he swayed in place, his head seemingly too heavy for his body, his red eyes blinking against the light, the reek of alcohol escaping from his pores. He carried his old hunting rifle resting stock down, barrel up at his shoulder, as a military man would on parade. Next to him stood Sarah, filled out and more matronly than those days so long ago on the *Monmouth.* Concern deep-etched her face like the carvings on Faithful's gorget shell, and she rushed over to throw her arms around Amy's shoulders and lead her into the bosom of their circle. Amy seemed to take comfort. Sarah didn't let go her grasp, and Amy didn't drop Sarah's hand as she took her place by the graveside.

Cow Tom knew how Amy would want the ceremony to transpire, full of her own distinct mix of ritual, Creek and African. He could give her this.

He took the lead, placing the form in the hole, laying strips of elm bark over the small body until the white of the cotton muslin was almost lost from view, stealing looks at Amy the while. Still, she seemed not ready, her face rock hard, which he expected, but her spirit too far from his reach, which he did not.

After, he motioned to Amy and Faithful, and they each threw in their handful of dirt, the farewell handshake. The rest of the family members followed, from youngest, barely able to form a credible fistful of dirt, to oldest, Bella/Sarah, who wept silently, even after her return to Amy's side. When they'd all had their turn, he finished the task, shoveling heaps of earth as cover and packing the soil down with his hands, careful not to stomp on any of the new dirt around the gravesite. Amy would accuse him of bringing sickness back to their own house if he had not done such.

He'd found three smooth stones, each the size of a winter squash, and placed the markers carefully at the top of the bulging mound, glancing over to Amy's bowed head the while for a sign.

Cow Tom had his musket, loaded and ready to fire, and Faithful his rifle. The boy would go with the proper send-off. He fired the first shot in the air to the north, and Faithful, though shaky, fired the second, west. Cow Tom rammed the next load in and shot south. Faithful shot east.

"Old Turtle watches after the boy now," Cow Tom said.

He sought to give Amy a vision, his vision, to make the letting go easier. They'd made their start under Old Turtle's eye. Cow Tom looked again to Amy, hopeful.

Amy met his gaze, the struggle plain. He could do no more.

She brought her hands together slowly, palm to palm. At first, Cow Tom feared she sought to rid them of the red, clinging soil. But she repeated the motion, again, and then again, until, with great relief, he knew it to be clapping. Solemn, she picked up the pace, and changed the tempo, lifting her head. With considerable effort, she smiled. A bit of a disquieting smile to be sure, laced with stiff and grimace, but born of her clear attempt to appear gay, to conform to her abiding belief in the public banishment of

sadness. She stared him down as she continued her constant beat until he too clapped
along with her, until he too forced a smile
where nothing but hollow lived beneath.

When at last she stopped the strange
percussion, he knew it time to build the
shelter. With stout branches for poles and a
canopy of elm bark, he built a little cover
over the mound to keep the rain from soaking down in the new dirt, protection until
the soul had time to depart.

They went back to the tepee then, and
Amy scattered some of her medicine
around, both inside and out, in the far
corners, along the seams of the cowhide,
low-talking under her breath. She killed the
old fire, still usable, scattering log and ash
in every direction before building another,
all new, and only then did she concentrate
on Malinda and the baby.

"No," Malinda said, pushing the baby
away.

"She seeks you," Amy said, and placed the
girl baby once more in her mother's arms.

"No. The boy."

The girl baby whimpered, searching,
prelude to a cry. Amy secured the child and
positioned her at Malinda's nipple.

"The girl is here, not the boy. No use
disrespecting fact," said Amy. Her voice had

grown stern, the voice of Cow Tom's memory after Old Turtle's funeral, when he took to his bed and Amy coaxed him from his dark place. "You will mother her."

Now the mother was weary and unconnected to the girl at her breast, and Amy, who worked with them both, encouraging the baby to suckle and the mother to nourish.

Cow Tom, already intruded in this women's business more than natural, made his decision. He never should have allowed the foolishness of the boy's name. They'd gone too far afield of themselves in Edmound. The girl would have a simpler name, a grounded moniker, neither too Indian nor too white. The boy had let go his grasp of the world, but the girl still battled for her place. Cow Tom appreciated such a spirit. A flower came to his mind, a special flower, able to defend itself. A flower thorned.

"Rose," he proclaimed to the startled household.

"Her name is Rose."

■ ■ ■ ■

PART II
ROSE

−1863−

■ ■ ■ ■

CHAPTER 29

The air gusted bitter cold, and Rose envisaged the sky pitting the Oklahoma mud with icy pellets and setting the Canadian a-sleet. Spring was reluctant this year, late in coming, but from her eleven years watching seasons come and go, Rose knew warmer weather could descend any day. The chill attacked every section of the ranch, from cow pasture to horse corral, from red barn to open fields. Even the crowded kitchen in the log cabin, Rose's normal place alongside her mother, Malinda, and grandmother Amy and great-grandmother Sarah, was nippy enough for a wrap over her long checkered dress and apron as she tended cooking pots and fires in the never-ending preparation of meals for twelve, including family and ranch hand.

"Baby's sick. I need life everlasting and slippery elm," said Gramma Amy to the kitchen at large. "Rose goes."

Ma'am looked for a moment as if she would challenge, but Gramma Amy cut short the possibility. "Malinda, the child has the connection. Twin will keep her safe. She can sweep the gravestones on the way. Off you go, Little Warrior."

Gramma Amy's word was law in the kitchen, grandmother trumping mother. Ma'am, rendered mute, forced the dough for Indian fry bread with the heel of her hand, underscoring her displeasure. Ma'am always was tetchy about Twin, prone to upset if Rose didn't keep the grave clean, but equally unhappy if Rose spent too much time there.

Rose grabbed up her moccasins from the puncheon floor, laced the buckskin tight around her ankles and calf, and chose one of the empty woven baskets by the door.

"Don't go too far," Gramma Amy called after her. "Pay attention."

Most neighbors fled long before, and yet, her family remained almost untouched on the ranch, tucked away from war. But just last month, chasing a quail, she almost stumbled over two white soldiers in the woods beyond the pasture. Lucky for her, they were Union, but they could just as well have been wild Indian or wild white or wild black, soldier or civilian, from one side of the war or the other. Men from both sides could be dangerous, but Lower Creek Confederates most threatening of all.

Rose ran all the way to the copse of trees along the south pasture, with the wind in her face and frozen sun at her back, the mud spongy and giving beneath her feet, the moist stalks of prairie grass so tall they whipped against her cheeks. She ran because the day was cold and running helped keep her warm. She ran because there was nothing but grass and sky to contain her. She ran because she knew Gramma Amy was impatient for her return to the kitchen and worried if she took too long. She was free of pots and pans and baby Elizabeth and Cousin Emmaline and Cousin Lulu and her scowling mother.

But still, the world was open to her, and she was ready to receive. Already she was considered an excellent cook, and Gramma Amy pushed her to master all of ranch life. She had assisted once at the birth of a baby, could grind seed to powder for medicines, shoot both bow and gun, lasso a small calf, ride a pony. Rose ran because she would be twelve years old tomorrow, and because she didn't like to keep still, and because the sky was big. But once Rose came to the lip of the woods, and the family graveyard, she slowed and entered the sacred place.

She cleared dead leaves and loose dirt with her hands from the three smooth river stones at the head of the sunken patch of rectangular earth, and brushed after with the stiff needles from a pine branch until the area looked groomed.

Twin. Her shadow, but male. Gramma Amy said Rose carried Twin's spirit in her, and she could see the glow with her special eye. Grampa Cow Tom said a little piece of Rose was rooted in the ground alongside Twin, allowing her a deeper understanding of the land. Ma'am said Rose snatched Twin's spirit from him so she could live in his place. But the others didn't understand Twin at all, not like she did, even Gramma Amy. Only Rose knew how wicked Twin could be, how reckless and disobedient.

When Rose sat on the bank of the river with her fishing line in the water, and she'd already caught enough fish for supper, and the sun felt warm on her back, Twin counseled her to pretend she didn't hear them calling her to come back to the house for her other chores. When her squirmy, bawling baby sister was born, and Ma'am and her new husband made such a fuss over what a pretty child Elizabeth was, Twin dared her to find the tender spot of new flesh on her little sister's bottom and pinch hard until Elizabeth shrieked. Twin put thoughts in her head. But he listened to her too, none of her complaints too small or petty. He was her best friend.

Rose sat cross-legged at the edge of the grave.

"Ma'am told Gramma Amy this morning I'd never find a husband," she said aloud to Twin. "War or no war."

If Twin had a physical self, he might have shed sympathy tears, or pulled the legs from a centipede one at a time. But Twin occupied a middle space, and could express himself only through her. Ma'am's words cut, but Twin did what he always did, and removed the sting. Rose relaxed into the pale blue light of Twin.

"If Papa hadn't died, Ma'am wouldn't be so mean," Rose declared. She didn't remember her father, not really, his face all but faded in her memory, but sometimes she could still summon the dense crimp of his kinky black hair, or the tart dampness of his smell. No one talked of him, as if he never existed.

Rose's features came together in a peculiar way, just like her grandfather's, severe and at odds with each other, her expression seemingly harsh and judgmental, when that wasn't her disposition at all. She was small, very small, like a tiny female version of Grampa Cow Tom. But whenever her mother called her Scrawny Chicken, her grandmother was quick to call her Little Warrior right after. She would grow prettier in time. That's what Gramma Amy said, and her grandmother knew many things others didn't.

"Just wait. I will have a husband and he'll be so strong he'll live almost forever. And it'll be me who saves the family from the curse. We'll have boys and girls both, not just girls. My ranch will be twice as big as Grampa Cow Tom's. And then you'll come live with us, Twin, but Ma'am can only visit."

The blue light around the gravesite grew deeper, darker. It was always like that with Twin, taking the pain into himself, and leaving her with new resolve.

"I have to go. Gramma Amy counts on me to find her herbs."

The grave clean, she left Twin behind and entered into the woods softly, paying close attention to sight and sound. It was easy to go unseen in the pasture, to anticipate surprise, but the forest was a different story. She searched for a suitable tree.

She welcomed the prospect of the woods

under the dripping umbrella of trees. A slippery elm was easy to find, and she selected one quickly, pulling her knife and stripping two long pieces of bark, checking the color of the inner layer to make sure it was cool gray, not red, perfect for boiling down to make a poultice. Satisfied, she tucked the strips in the basket and began her search for the more elusive yellow flowers of life everlasting.

Aunt Maggie's baby cried and coughed the night, and Gramma Amy used the last of her stash of the healing herb, and now the baby suffered spiking fever. In this search too, Rose was fortunate. Not far from the clearing where she picked with Gramma Amy last season, she found the same patch, and stepped carefully, searching the base of trees until she found the tiny yellow flower of the life everlasting plant. Despite the cold, there were fresh buds of new growth, and she added several shoots to her basket, careful not to damage the root in its removal or disturb the others in the ground. Her grandmother would be pleased.

What Rose knew of the outside world beyond the ranch she mostly learned from Grampa Cow Tom. Her grandfather was a man who knew the world, and carried the marks of his journey with him, using his two-fingered hand as deftly as anyone with the full complement of five fingers, as unmindful of that as of his ear nub, which Gramma Amy stroked for luck. He protected them and the land, whether from Confederates or predator or pest, and every time she looked at the jagged scar down his cheek, delivered by a Confederate Indian's knife, she felt safer. Most other men were gone, her uncles, the younger ranch hands, Chief Yargee, all run off to Kansas or serving in the Union's First Indian Home Guard army.

Last night after supper, her grandfather spoke to the children, an infrequent treat, all gathered round him at his feet as he recited the story of How Rabbit Fooled Wolf. First in the ancestral language, Mvskoke, and then in English. In Rose's opinion, the English version didn't sound as powerful. She liked the guttural sound of Mvskoke better, deep in the throat where language belonged, but Gramma Amy said English speaking brought great benefit to the entire family, and insisted all the children learn that language as well, even though Gramma Amy herself seldom spoke anything but Mvskoke or Hitchiti. Everyone had their place, that's what Gramma Amy said, both wolf and rabbit. If a character was open for the picking, Rose would choose rabbit. Clever, sly, fun loving. But that wasn't her lot. Hers was to be a mother of sons, and her sons could be rabbit, outsmarting and outlasting all the obstacles of the world.

Rose carefully packed the herbs in the basket, laid a large leaf of maidenhair spleenwort on top, and made her way out of the woods back to pastureland. The fields were miles of tall hay. Once again, she ran, but stopped, thinking better of her lack of caution so far from the ranch, setting off toward home at a walk. About halfway, she saw a flash of color in the field. There was a large patch of sage, stiff and prickly, but in the center, close to the ground and almost hidden, was a bed of wildflowers, spindly branches intertwined with its sage host. One double-lobed flower bloomed, a bold blue that made Rose's heart race, a blue to rival the most perfect sky of an Indian Territory summer day.

She'd seen this flower before, when out harvesting with Gramma Amy. Blue mouse ears. She picked her way through the sage, brushing aside the thorny growth to get to the supple branch holding the blue flower aloft. She knew she was foolish, but couldn't resist. The flower would neither serve useful purpose for her grandmother's herbal table nor at the serving table, but Rose loved the color and shape best of all the plants growing wild along the plains. She held the flower for a long time, admiring, savoring the bright blue, imagining herself surrounded by an entire field of beauty such as this.

She was still caught in reverie when she heard the hoofbeats of ponies. The grass was waist high, and she dropped to her knees, folding herself as small as she could, hoping she was hidden. They passed close enough for her to register a swish of the faded gray wool pants leg of a Confederate uniform as they rode beyond her toward the woods.

She didn't dare lift her head. The horses stopped a ways from her, and she heard cooldown snorts as they began to graze.

"We wait," a male voice said in Mvskoke, and dismounted. Rose heard him slide to the ground and walk in the opposite direction, followed by another man, who grunted his acknowledgment.

Two ponies, two men. The men spoke fast Mvskoke to each other, punctuated and hard. Not old but young men by register and tone. She couldn't catch all their words, but they bantered back and forth while she

294

crouched, frozen, and she wondered who or what they waited for and how long before they moved on. Whether safer for her to stay or try to make her way back home.

"Before the sun sets, the black man's ranch and cattle are ours."

"We wait for Little Eagle. Then wash our hands in Union blood."

Rose hesitated, unsure, her heart a hammer. She began to inch along on her hands and knees, picking her way free of the sage, careful to make no sound. She was patient, as her grandfather taught her, moving along at an irregular pace, neither too fast to attract attention nor too slow to get back to the ranch, keeping clutch to her basket of herbs. Just two weeks ago, the sandy-haired lieutenant in charge of Fort Gibson cautioned her grandfather to leave the ranch, and not for the first time. The Confederates had become more brazen, not less, since losing the Battle of Honey Springs. Maybe her grandfather was wrong. Maybe they should have abandoned the ranch two years back when Uncle Harry pleaded with Grampa Cow Tom to make a run for Kansas, a free state, alongside him and his family.

She remembered her uncle's words exactly, angry and despairing at the same time, flung at her grandfather as they stood toe to toe in this very pasture.

"Don't be a fool. You're grown too large in your own mind. The war will find you in the end. And you with nothing but women and girls and old men here."

Rose continued her winding path through the tall grass, listening for pursuit, but after the first cautious scans, the men's voices receded. The sounds that remained were familiar and everyday, of birds flying overhead, of animals in the pasture, of a coyote in the distance. She dared stand, still covered by the height of the hay-like grass, and peered out. No men in her sight.

Her basket lay at her feet. Her grandmother wouldn't have sent her from the ranch house unless she truly needed those herbs, so she scooped up the basket and broke into an all-out run, keeping to the tallest grass. She passed the corral and the bunkhouse and cut across the far north pasture, where she found her grandfather down in the clearing, his back against the thin base of a bois d'arc whose broad canopy overhung the banks of the Canadian River. Not far, five rawboned spotted cows grazed on the short grass near the lip of the clearing.

"Grampa," she cried, hardly able to push

the words out, so relieved she was to find him.

She fought back her tears. Her grandfather looked up in alarm, his face more lined than she remembered. He *was* old. Over fifty. Too old to join the Union army, but he would know what to do about the Confederate Indians. Everyone said they looked alike, grandfather and granddaughter. Full mouth slightly crooked under a broad nose; ears overlarge, though her grandfather had only a close-to-the-scalp stub on one side while she enjoyed both her flaps; brown eyes small and buried deep; wild, coarse hair framing a heart-shaped face. Like his, her skin was startlingly dark, but not for her the smooth, taut ebony her baby sister possessed. Her complexion was mottled, a random mix of coffees and chars and nut browns.

"The Confederates are yonder," she said, before he could speak. Her breath came hard, but she forced her story. "Just over by the south pasture. They're coming for us. I heard them."

Cow Tom's dark face, naturally unyielding and severe, hardly changed expression, but his eyes grew harder, and his cheek scar seemed to come alive. "How many? How long?"

297

"Two men, I think. But expecting more. They said they'd wash in Union blood."

Cow Tom didn't lose a moment. "Tell Amy to clear everybody out. Wait for us in the north hay field by the gristmill. We make for Fort Gibson."

Rose knew of Fort Gibson, the nearest supply town, thirty miles away. She'd never traveled that far, but her grandfather often talked about the fort. Because the Old Chief refused to learn English, Cow Tom regularly went there as Chief Yargee's translator. On horseback, the trip took a full day or even two. Were they supposed to walk?

Rose stood for an instant, waiting for more instruction, but her grandfather had already turned from her, headed for the bunkhouse.

"Git!" he ordered over his shoulder.

CHAPTER 30

Rose burst into the smoky kitchen, the basket still clutched to her chest. She would remember that moment of calm for the rest of her days, more clearly than hiding in the tall grass, or the men's voices, or her grandfather's command — Gramma Amy's ladle arrested in midair over the stew pot, Ma'am setting wood plates on the long, communal pine table for supper, Granny Sarah's white fluff of hair as she slept, chin to chest, in a chair by the fire, Aunt Maggie breast-feeding the smallest of the household's babies in one corner, her younger sister, Elizabeth, playing quietly with a corncob doll wrapped in strips of leather in the opposite corner, Cousin Emmaline and Cousin Lulu ferrying warm bread to the table. All eyes riveted to Rose. The comforting odor of stew meat bubbling in the pot over the fire consumed the kitchen and reminded her how hungry she was.

"Grampa says run," she said, her breath coming hard.

She repeated her story of the men in the woods, fast as she could.

Amy sprang to action first, organizing their escape, the long ladle clattering against the side of the pot where she dropped it, snapping her orders.

"Gather the children."

There was no debate. Each woman in the kitchen stopped midtask and demanded their children to their sides. Those old enough to understand moved quickly and waited obediently by their mothers' skirts. Rose smelled fear in the room, but there was something else she couldn't quite grasp that hung heavy in the cold air. Ferocity.

Ma'am grabbed a blanket and began to wrap as many kitchen utensils inside as she could.

Everything and everyone seemed suddenly in motion. "Only what you can carry at a run," Amy cautioned, and Ma'am abandoned all but the blanket. Rose thought to bring her bow and arrows, crafted by Grampa Cow Tom specially for her size and strength from bois d'arc branches, but they were awkward to carry, and she wasn't yet a good enough shot. She abandoned the idea. She had her knife.

Gramma Amy disappeared to the back of the house to snatch up herb pouches and her mortar and pestle, and dropped these in Rose's basket. "To keep the baby quiet," she said, and handed Rose a small cooking skillet as she scanned the room. "Elizabeth, go with Rose."

Elizabeth watched as if apart from the rising panic in the house, scooting back farther into the corner, clutching the corncob doll to her tiny chest.

Amy's quick hands continued to wrap dried jerky in oilskin.

"Come to me, Elizabeth," Rose said in Mvskoke, but the girl didn't move, poking out her lip and shaking her head.

Her mother and aunt gathered the other children, quickly bundling them against the cold, snatching up a stray moccasin. Her aunt deftly strapped the baby in a cradleboard, mounting it to her back. Cousin Emmaline and Cousin Lulu waited wide-eyed and silent by her side.

"You want to come with me, don't you?" Rose asked Elizabeth. She kept her voice steady. "You want to come with me and share my blanket?"

"I want to carry the basket," Elizabeth said, in a pout.

The medicinal herbs were too valuable to

entrust. "I'd rather carry this skillet," Rose said.

As expected, her sister shifted focus.

"I want to carry the skillet," Elizabeth said.

"All right." Rose said. "Put dolly in the skillet and come."

Rose held her sister by one hand and coaxed her out the back door, afraid to hear hoofbeats. She gave a last look as Gramma Amy dumped the contents of the cooking pot onto the fireplace ashes, leaving nothing for the Confederates when they came. Rose led Elizabeth through the tall grass toward the ranch's gristmill, aware of every sound, ready to drop and hide if the men came upon them. She took a chance and stopped, crouching to eye level with her little sister.

"Elizabeth. This is important. If I say run, you run and hide. If I say quiet, not one word or sound, no matter what. Like when we play hide-and-seek. Promise."

"Do the bad men want to hurt us?"

Rose decided not to lie. "Yes," she said. "So promise."

Elizabeth considered this. "I promise, Rose," she said.

They half walked and half ran the rest of the way, and arrived at the gathering spot where most women and children on the ranch waited. Rose tried to get Elizabeth to stand by Ma'am, but Elizabeth wouldn't let go of Rose's hand, her tiny fingers squeezing Rose's until her palm ached. Rose needed her hand free to get at her bark-stripping knife, but one look at Elizabeth convinced her to let her sister hang on. It was the same expression on everybody's face. Uncertainty. Fear. Panic. No one spoke. They waited a few minutes, not sure what came next, and Ma'am did a count. Eight.

"Gramma and Granny are missing," Ma'am whispered, and as if by force of thought, Amy materialized from the tall grass, leading Granny Sarah. She clutched a long, curve-bladed skinning knife in her right hand, and parted the grass with the other. A length of braided hemp secured the food-stuffed bundle wrapped in deer hide from the kitchen on her back. Gramma Amy smelled of the stew Rose watched her dump into the flames, and her apron was singed at its lower edge.

"I'd a mind to set the whole place afire," Gramma Amy said. "Leave them ash. But they'd come looking for us that much sooner."

Her grandmother surveyed the group, making her own count. "Cow Tom?" she whispered to Ma'am.

303

Ma'am shook her head.

They all looked to Gramma Amy for a decision.

"We wait," she whispered. "If they don't come soon, we head north like Lieutenant Phillips said."

Almost none of their neighbors remained on the tribe's land around them. Two weeks ago, several of the last Upper Creek holdouts passed by the ranch, accompanied by Lieutenant Phillips on horseback, a green-eyed white leader in the Union army. Rose had served the lieutenant before at her grandfather's table, but this time, there were two other heavily armed soldiers, one Seminole and one black Seminole, also on horseback, escorts to Fort Gibson. The military men's jacket and pants were worn and filthy, several different shades of badly faded and mismatched blue. North, Rose had thought. Union.

There were forty displaced Indians in that group, old men, women, and children, their faces a stunned stare of defeat. Lieutenant Phillips urged her grandfather to join the caravan, but he refused. While the two men argued, Gramma Amy whispered to Rose to bring *puska* from the storehouse to distribute among the ragtag group. Rose shook clumps of the parched corn powder into outstretched baskets, but one small boy, the same age as Elizabeth, snatched a handful and sucked greedily as if he hadn't eaten in a long while.

Once Lieutenant Phillips determined Cow Tom wouldn't dissuade, he sliced the air with two fingers, signaling forward motion to his men, and they spurred their horses and caravan away. The wagons creaked and rolled, come to life again as the mass of refugees plodded forward to the north in a slow march.

Lieutenant Phillips yelled, "Keep up with the Union soldiers," to the last stragglers in the line, and just as Rose formed the thought that probably none in the caravan could understand what the white man said, the black soldier repeated the warning in Mvskoke.

Later that night, Rose overheard Gramma Amy try to persuade Grampa Cow Tom to abandon the ranch.

"We are no more hid," Gramma Amy said. "We need to leave this place."

"Had we left for Kansas with Chief Yargee last spring, might be us massacred by Lower Creeks, not only one of Yargee's wives."

Rose had wondered which one of the five wives was killed. Hopefully not Milly, the youngest of three sisters married to the

305

chief, who had always shown kindness. Her uncle Harry made it through to Kansas with his family two years ago, and sent back word conditions were harsh at the army fort there, especially for black Indians.

Grampa Cow Tom refused to leave, and Gramma Amy backed down.

"Twin," Rose cried, the thought fresh and sharp as they waited in the tall grass. How could she have forgotten him? "I have to tell Twin."

"Hush now. You stay with us," said Gramma Amy.

"I can't leave him," Rose said. He'd be furious with her. Angry and hurt, no matter the reason.

"They won't bother with the grave," said Gramma Amy. "Twin'll be fine."

Gramma Amy didn't understand anything. Of course Twin would be fine. Rose was the one who wouldn't be fine without him.

Her grandmother turned her attention elsewhere, plotting an escape route, assessing their supplies, checking the health of the babies. Gramma Amy could master anything on ranch grounds, but her grandfather was more familiar with woods and trails, and knew how to speak to military men with their strange talk and stranger manners.

Gramma Amy motioned for Rose to bring the basket. She removed a green sprig and chewed until just soft, spitting out the juice and dividing the pulpy remains into pieces. "Rub this on the baby's gums and let her suck to keep her quiet," she instructed Rose. "Everybody else get ready to move."

Not too far away, the grass moved. Gramma Amy held up her hand for silence, turning her good ear first one way and then another to identify direction. After a moment of stillness, there came the sound of low-toned moaning.

Cooah, coo, coo.

Knife blade in front and ready to strike, Amy replicated the mourning dove's call.

Cooah.

The echoing response came closer. Rose set down the basket with her grandmother's medicines and put one finger to her lips to caution Elizabeth to stillness. The girl's almond eyes were wet with fear, but she didn't move or make a sound. Rose drew out her knife and tightened her grip around the handle.

The tall prairie grass parted, and Grampa Cow Tom stepped through the wild, damp pastureland, followed by the old cowpuncher who lived in the bunkhouse.

Rose bowed her head in thanks. Her

grandfather carried his hunting rifle and a powder flask at his hip, and the cowpuncher waved a small pistol. They came on foot, which meant they'd had to leave the horses behind. Even if larger numbers made the group easier to track, more people were better.

Her grandfather took everything in at a glance, the drawn knives, the hasty supplies, the tall grass that would keep them hidden but not cover the direction of their escape once someone caught their trail.

"Hurry," he said.

CHAPTER 31

They headed north, toward Fort Gibson, falling into routine for the first few hours. Grampa Cow Tom kept to the front, determining the path, always in the tall prairie grass, never on the trail in the open, and Gramma Amy guarded the rear, making sure no one fell behind. As the sun moved lower in the sky, they walked at her grandfather's pace. He never once slackened, refusing to be slowed by the fading stamina of the children or even Granny Sarah. One or another adult picked up a child if the little one couldn't continue. No one talked. Aunt Maggie put her infant daughter to breast, and the rest passed *puska* and gourds of water down the line, but still they moved forward.

There were twelve of them, men, women, children, babies, ranch hand, and Rose lost any sense of where they might be. The world had become dim gray sky above and mile after mile of spongy mud below. Wet grass slapped against her face and chilled air forced its way inside the woven blanket around her shoulders, and her ears filled with the steady footbeats of the others. Every step took them farther away from Twin.

At one point, they were forced to a narrow single file, and Elizabeth finally dropped Rose's hand. From then, Rose kept Elizabeth directly in front of her, or carried her, Elizabeth's arms in a sprawl around her torso. Rose was a good walker, but she was tired, and hungry, and feared they would never stop, but she trudged on, as did everyone else.

Just before nightfall, when the light was weak but they could still see, Grampa Cow Tom led them out of the pastureland and down an embankment to a stream. The water slipped over the rocks near the shore, frigid-looking and frothy.

"We cross here so they can't follow in the night."

The stream was at least as wide as two full lengths of the corral back on their ranch. There was no telling how deep. Rose could swim, if need be, but what about the baby? What about their supplies? What about Granny Sarah and Elizabeth?

Her grandfather handed his rifle to her grandmother and splashed into the water first, testing the bottom, and walked until the water reached his waist. He was less than halfway across. He inched his way carefully, his body disappearing a bit at a time until, midway, he was almost completely submerged, the water up to his neck. Still he pushed on, and with the next few tentative steps, he began to reappear. First his shoulders, then his chest, then his waist, and finally, he was whole again on the other side of the stream. The light was close to fading completely.

"Maggie, Malinda, Amy," he called on the other side. "Supplies first. Keep the guns and blankets dry."

He plunged back into the water toward the larger group on the opposite shore, taking up a waiting station at the deepest part of the stream. Five waded in and staggered positions, holding guns and food and blankets over their heads, handing them daisy chain as they went back for more. Once there was a pile of reasonably dry items on the other side of the stream, they ferried the children across, one by one, and floated the cradleboard with the baby to safety, passing from hand to hand.

"I don't want to," whispered Elizabeth to

Rose as they waited their turn, and Rose stayed with her as Cousin Emmaline and Cousin Lulu, her precious beaded doll clutched tight in one hand, forded the stream. Each time Rose thought Elizabeth ready, the girl panicked, and she let someone else take their place until they were the last two on the shore.

The night was almost fully upon them, the gloom settling in among the shadows. Rose thought of the Confederates in the woods. With darkness, they'd make their attack on the ranch house, and when they found it empty, they might well come after them. There was no going back.

"You've been brave," Rose said. "Pretend we're warriors."

Elizabeth remained unconvinced. "Where we going, Rose?" she asked.

Rose looked at her sister. Her small face was caked with grime, her hair tangled, wild, and filthy. Rose assumed she looked the same.

"Fort Gibson so the Confederates can't get us. They have soldiers there."

"I want to go home."

Rose shut her eyes tight, fighting the panic. She wasn't so much afraid of the water as of crossing a divide where Twin couldn't follow. They had always communed in the graveyard, and only there, but she tried summoning him wordlessly now. She needed him by her side. One minute passed, and then two, but he didn't come. She couldn't feel him at all.

"We can't go home," she whispered to Elizabeth. "It isn't safe at the ranch anymore."

"I want to go home now."

"We can't," Rose repeated. They could see the others on the other side, wet and cold, wrapping blankets around themselves.

In the weak light, Grampa Cow Tom signaled the two girls to the edge of the stream.

Elizabeth looked as if she would cry. "I dropped Dolly."

The corncob figure was no longer in her sister's limp hand, and as drained as Rose was, the sight of her sister threatened to undo her. "Elizabeth, you have to be a big girl now. Just a little longer. We cross the stream and when we get to Fort Gibson I'll make you a new Dolly. And we'll go back home once Union soldiers beat the Confederates."

Rose knew better, but promised anyway. She'd seen the look of finality settled into Gramma Amy's features when she joined them by the gristmill. There was no home to go back to.

Elizabeth didn't answer, but the willfulness abandoned her sister's face.

"You first, and I'll be right behind," said Rose. "Go to Grampa."

Elizabeth took a few tentative steps, shrinking back as soon as her foot touched the cold water, but Grampa Cow Tom grabbed her by the waist and pulled her toward him and swung her over his head. To her credit, Elizabeth didn't cry out as she passed hand to hand, and once Rose saw her sister transported safe and mostly dry to the other bank, she rushed straight into the stream herself, wading out as far as she dared. She'd seen her grandfather's tremble as he'd lifted Elizabeth. Even in the poor light, she'd seen the bluish tint to his skin and the rigidity of the muscles at his jaw, the involuntary chattering of his teeth and the beginnings of glazed eyes. He'd been in the cold water too long.

The iciness of the water penetrated Rose's moccasins and her bare thighs under her trousers, and then the shock of cold threatened to numb her brain as well as her limbs, but she was determined not to make her grandfather fetch her. He moved slowly toward her, and she began to paddle like a dog, furiously, keeping her head above the water. Her grandfather grabbed her arms to pull her toward the center of the stream, and she tried to help by kicking harder. She was last to cross over, and her grandfather didn't hand her to the next, but stayed beside her all the way to the other side. By the time she came out of the water, Ma'am had a blanket waiting for her.

Gramma Amy unwrapped the blanket from around her shoulders and bundled Grampa Cow Tom in it, wiping him dry. She ran her finger round the ridge of his nubbed ear, and he tilted toward her, laying his head on her breast for a moment before straightening again. Rose's blanket was damp, but warmed her nonetheless, and for a few moments, she was lost, unable to move or think, her nonresponsive body attempting to adjust to the freezing night air.

"Elizabeth?" Rose finally managed.

Gramma Amy brought her sister to her, eyes dull, her manner listless. Rose roused herself, and opened her blanket, bringing the girl closer, wrapping them back up together, folding her limbs around her sister.

"I'm hungry, Rose," said Elizabeth. "And cold."

"Me too," said Rose. "Lean into me."

Elizabeth collapsed into Rose, and fell immediately into sleep. By the light of the quarter moon, Rose took in the wet, be-draggled group around her. The adults had already begun to shake off the effects of the icy water, reconstituting themselves slowly into a group away from the children and whispering among themselves. For Rose's part, she wanted nothing more than to sit around a blazing fire, to have a proper meal and not take another step in any direction. She wanted to sleep, like Elizabeth, whose warm breath and clammy skin both comforted and alarmed her. Near the elm tree, Gramma Amy began to distribute shares of *puska,* enough to cut the pangs of hunger but not enough to satisfy. Rose shook Elizabeth awake and forced the girl to eat. Elizabeth chewed listlessly, as if from habit rather than hunger. She tucked herself into Rose and fell asleep again.

"We walk the stream tonight," Grampa Cow Tom announced.

Rose understood at once. The Confederates were on horseback, and if they followed them to this side of the river tomorrow, their tracks would be too easy to follow. But how could this group continue on throughout the night without sleep, in the dark, wet and cold?

Gramma Amy moved first. She picked through the supplies, assessing as best she could in the dim moonlight what was salvageable and what wasn't, and when she finished, she strapped her own pouch on her back before redistributing the supplies to carry among the tired refugees. Rose woke Elizabeth again. The girl looked at Rose, her eyes flat, but she stood when Rose stood, and accepted the blanket around her tiny shoulders when Rose enfolded her in it. She tried to grip the assigned skillet she'd carried so far already, but the pan fell from her cold hands and dropped to the ground, and Elizabeth stared at her feet, confused. Rose picked the skillet up and added it to her own items.

"Hold to me," she said to Elizabeth, and her sister grabbed onto the damp deerskin of Rose's tunic. When the group, with Grampa Cow Tom in the lead, started north, Rose kept up as best she could, and Elizabeth followed behind her, hand on tunic, even when they moved into the water near the shore in single file, their feet so cold they could barely feel them. They didn't walk fast, sometimes sloshing through the stream shin high, sometimes leaping from the exposed tops of rocks partially submerged in the water, but they walked steadily in the near dark, hour after hour, until her grandfather was satisfied they had put enough distance between themselves and the Confederates at the ranch. They filled their gourds with water and left the bank of the stream, and the road became darker than ever, without the water's surface to serve as reflector for the disappearing sliver of moon.

Rose was barely conscious of walking anymore. She followed single-mindedly, without expectation or thought. The air was too cold for her damp tunic to dry, and the stiff material clung to her with a sickening clamminess that made the piercing chill worse. She abandoned carrying Elizabeth, now in Ma'am's arms. Rose's feet were so tender each step pained and her limbs felt like dead weights. But still she trudged on.

At last a thin band of pink appeared along the horizon, so gradual Rose didn't identify dawn at first, but suddenly she was aware of more than the dark, hypnotic movement of shapes directly ahead, aware that she used her eyes to see as much as her muscles to move and her heart to pump. She forced herself to look forward and backward, craning her neck, luxuriating in the alien movement. The group was spread out in a ragged line, and she was almost at the tail end, the old cowpuncher up near the front, Gramma Amy, Ma'am, Elizabeth, and Granny Sarah just steps behind. She didn't see Grampa Cow Tom anywhere. Her knees buckled, and she stumbled, falling face forward into the prairie grass. Gramma Amy was by her side in moments, turning her over onto her back, whistling low for the line to stop.

"Can you get up?" Her Gramma Amy's voice.

Rose made her legs work, and stood, ashamed she had fallen.

At that moment, Cow Tom came from the east, his rifle slung over one shoulder, his bowlegged walk recognizable even through his new limp. Gramma Amy left her to meet him.

"They can't keep going," Amy said to him. She didn't pull him aside, or whisper, but merely claimed the fact.

Aunt Maggie sat cross-legged on the muddy ground hugging her baby to her chest. Cousin Emmaline's and Cousin Lulu's eyes were glazed. Many of the women had taken their moccasins off and were tending to their feet, wrapping and rewrapping strips of cloth striped with red.

"I found us a hiding place," said Cow Tom. "Not far. We rest until nightfall."

CHAPTER 32

They packed up supplies and followed once more into the face of the awakening dawn, limping, wincing with blister pain, shaking from the cold or fever. Those more able helped those less, and all moved forward. Cow Tom led them out of the tall prairie grass into a forested area, where tightly spaced oak trees formed a natural camp, dark and damp.

The group didn't so much settle in their campsite as collapse where they stood. The small warmth from the rising sun didn't reach under the trees, but lighting a fire was too risky. They worked out a watch schedule, and Ma'am and Aunt Maggie produced *puska* and dried deer strips. The meat helped push away the knifelike gnawing at Rose's belly. Gramma Amy pulled out her mortar and pestle and mixed up a medicinal concoction, her movements slow.

Rose's eyes were so heavy and her body

ached so deeply, she sat on the cold ground and stared at nothing. She wanted Twin, and recited his name over and over in her mind, but he didn't come. Elizabeth laid her head in Rose's lap and dozed, her stiff hair icy to the touch. Rose covered her sister's ears with the edge of the blanket. The next thing Rose knew, Gramma Amy was forcing her awake to drink down a potion, and she struggled to swallow the bitter-tasting brew before falling back into dreamless sleep. She missed all the morning and some of the afternoon. Elizabeth shook her awake, eyes bright with panic. Rose did her best to keep Elizabeth calm, tearing off a piece of deer strip she'd saved and giving it to her sister. Elizabeth devoured all of it.

They lay in their blankets together.

"Are they going to catch us?" Elizabeth asked again, as she had last night before they crossed the stream. Rose watched the chilled puff her words left in the air.

"No. Everything's better at Fort Gibson. We'll light a big fire and roast a whole pig."

Rose promised Elizabeth any number of impossible things. When she ran out of words, she sang softly to Elizabeth, snatches of lullabies and ceremonial chants, stroking Elizabeth's back, and Elizabeth fell off to sleep again, wheezing slightly. Rose dozed too.

Her grandfather finally returned, and led them out of the copse through close vegetation in the woods until they came to a narrow trail. Tonight, there was no stream to cross, but the moon sliver barely lit their way, and they were careful of every step, staying close to one another so as not to wander off alone into the dark. Once again, they walked all night, the pace not as punishing as the night before. They walked into the dawn, and waited in the dangerous sunlight hours. Amy caught a prairie rabbit, but everyone else stayed huddled close. Her grandfather came back to them in the full light of day, with as pleased a look as he ever displayed.

"Found it," he said.

He led them up a craggy hill and cleared away shrubs from the face of the ridge. On the other side was a cave, the fissure-crack so narrow each had to stoop as they entered single file. But despite the small crevice, the inside opened into a broader expanse, enough for all of them, though a tight fit. They pulled the shrub behind them to disguise the entrance, and posted a sentry. Here, they lit a small fire and cooked the rabbit, and the women produced a thin stew.

Gramma Amy treated the sick and the weary, which was just about everyone, and individuals tended themselves as well, rewrapping their feet, airing their clothes, smearing fat on their faces to stop the cold's penetration. Two had fevers, but other than tender and blistered feet, there were no more serious ailments among them. They listened to the wind howl and periodic bouts of rain, but with hot food in her stomach and the reminder of a fire's warmth, Rose began to believe they really would make it to Fort Gibson.

They rested in the cave for a full day and night, and until the next evening. When Cow Tom led them back into the prairie, their pace quickened. Tired though they were, they trudged through the mud without complaint. There was enough distance between themselves and the ranch to feel they were no longer in danger from the Confederates back there, but they worried about other roving bands.

By the fourth night's walking, Aunt Maggie's milk dried up, and the baby, who had remained so quiet, refused comforting. Elizabeth went from limp to hobble and had to be carried. Granny Sarah only walked at a turtle's pace. They tried night hunting, with poor results. Despite foraging nuts and berries along the way, their food store was low, and they cut back to half rations.

But the night finally came to an end. Rose spotted the thread of light announcing the sun's rise. The day was warmer than in all the time they'd been walking, almost like spring after a long, hard winter. They waited in the tall grass for her grandfather's return and pronouncement of the day's hiding place. When Elizabeth pulled at Rose's tunic, demanding attention, Rose had to stop herself from slapping her. She wanted a moment to herself, just a moment to relish the daylight and the prospect of sleep and quiet. She closed her eyes to better feel the warming sun on her face, and for an instant, she thought Twin had come, but the feeling slid away.

When Grampa Cow Tom returned, they followed him to a flat patch of land sheltered by trees, not far from a stream. He was more talkative than he had been for days. He had seen small groups of Indians of different tribes moving north toward Fort Gibson, some in wagons, some on horseback, but most walking, as they were. He had even seen two Union soldiers on their horses in the distance, scouring the landscape, protecting the territory from Confederates. He announced that after a rest, they would walk in the daylight, and arrive at Fort Gibson before nightfall.

Her grandmother came round, checking everyone. She got to them last, and Elizabeth was already asleep. Her grandmother brushed back some of the sleeping girl's hair with her hand, feeling for temperature. Permanent wrinkles grooved Gramma Amy's forehead and around her eyes, baked in by years of sun and wind and hard work. Gramma Amy lay herself down on the ground beside the girl, closed her eyes, and slept.

Now that they were close, Rose wondered what the fort might be like. She imagined an enormous structure with thick log walls, filled with soldiers and guns and horses, and vast storerooms of food of all kinds, dried meat, cornmeal, preserves like they stored in their own pantry at the ranch. She could almost feel the heat from a tall community fire, spitting sparks, and pictured herself with the other women in a circle, preparing warm meals with the fresh game and the fresh fish the men would catch. She would welcome seeing other Upper Creeks, listening to their stories of where they came from, what they left behind. She would welcome falling asleep at night instead of walking, without dreams of Confederates finding her crouched behind a bush and dragging her out by the ankle to her death. Maybe Twin would come to her once they settled.

They set out north one last time. Gramma Amy hummed as she walked, so Rose did too. Midmorning, they came upon a small group surrounding an overloaded wagon stuck on the open trail. A healthy, full-sized stallion trailed his reins as he grazed, and two women rolled out a new wheel. One of the men fixing the wagon was black, about her grandfather's age, but the rest looked to be full-blood Cherokee.

Her grandfather and the ranch hand rushed to lend a hand. Although close to the fort, they weren't yet within its protection. There were four children, including a pointy-nosed, dark-haired Indian boy a little older than Rose, and a girl about Elizabeth's age. They couldn't have been on the trail very long. Not only was their horse fresh, they all looked well fed. Once the new wheel was in place and they were ready to move on, their main man offered Grampa Cow Tom a wagon space, and he chose Granny Sarah to ride. The two parties took to the trail again together.

They fell into a rhythm walking in the daylight, and Rose gravitated to the middle of the pack, the road wide enough and the sky light enough they no longer had to follow single file. She listened to the worried squeak of the wagon wheels in front, and took solace from the men with guns behind. The Cherokee boy also walked in the middle, and they trudged along almost side by side without words. After an hour or so, the boy pulled out a piece of dried meat from his pocket and began to tear off chunks with his side teeth, chewing as he walked. Rose hadn't eaten since last night, and she couldn't help but stare at the deer meat. She tried to quell the desire by sipping a little water to trick her stomach. That only made things worse.

The boy held out his half-eaten strip to Rose, and said something to her. Grampa Cow Tom had taught her a few words of Tsalagi, but those weren't the words the boy used, and she didn't understand.

Rose was uncertain whether he offered the rest of the piece or one bite, but she took the chance to look at him squarely for the first time. He was full-blood. His long, dark hair was pulled back away from his face and stuck under his cap, his leathery skin a rich, coppery color and free of facial hair, his eyes a warm brown, set deep. His face was the opposite of her own, sharp nose, high cheekbones, thin lips, a profile so graceful it was almost feminine, and she suddenly worried about how she appeared to him.

She bit off a chunk and worked it in her mouth, savoring the tangy juice. She tried to hand the rest back to him.

"Chibona," he said, pointing to himself, watching her.

"Rose," she replied.

He pointed to her and then to the strip of meat, and back to her again.

Rose nodded and accepted the remainder of the chew. She knew she should save it for Elizabeth, but she wanted nothing more at this moment than to possess something the Indian boy had touched. And she was hungry. She bit off another piece, smaller this time, and stuffed the rest into her pocket.

He pointed to her once again and asked a question, but she couldn't catch the meaning of his words and shook her head.

This time, Chibona pointed to the black man who had fixed the wagon wheel, walking ahead of them, and then back at Rose.

"Gvhnige?" he asked.

Rose suddenly understood what he asked and bristled. "Yargee is our chief, but we're free," she said in Mvskoke. "Not slave. Creek and free."

Chibona studied her, uncomprehending.

"The Confederates came to take our ranch. I warned everyone just in time." Rose couldn't stop herself from talking, even though she knew he couldn't understand Mvskoke. "We've been walking five days."

They trudged along in silence for a time, but Rose ached to hear his voice again. She couldn't bear that he'd lost interest.

"My Grampa Cow Tom goes to Fort Gibson all the time. He interprets for our chief. I can speak English too."

"English," Chibona repeated. He shook his head and fell into an easy stride, and she kept up, but didn't initiate any more talk. When one of the older men called for him to help with the horses, he made his way toward the front of the group, leaving her behind.

For the first time since they started walking days ago, Rose shut out some of the ache of leaving the ranch and Twin, and the terrors of the trek. She caught a glimpse of the back of Chibona's head and, comforted by the gestures of a stranger, dropped back to walk alongside Elizabeth.

CHAPTER 33

The blended party journeyed on, rounding a bend on the trail, and in the distance, on a hill, a sprawling stone structure came into view, with wide porches running its length on both levels. They'd made it to the fort.

"Look, Elizabeth," Rose said. "One day, I'll have porches like that."

The fort didn't look at all like what she'd created in her mind, and as they came closer, word passed down the line that the building on the hill was a barracks for the soldiers, and not the main army post after all.

A bit farther, the fort itself rose up out of the flatlands. Rose had never seen so much stone. The walls were thick, and scores of soldiers carried rifles. But more jarring than the soldiers, which Rose expected and welcomed, were the Indians scattered everywhere, outside the walls of the fort as well as inside, sitting, standing, lying down, out in the open. Makeshift tents of blankets and pelts dotted every square inch of the terrain, intermingled with scrawny cattle, a few horses, chickens, and wagons of every sort crammed with personal and household items.

There were more displaced people at Fort Gibson than she could possibly count, many more than there were soldiers. Mostly Cherokee, judging from hair and beadwork and feathers, but also Upper Creek, Choctaw, and Seminole as well, as far as the eye reached. Since younger men were off fighting in the army, a majority of those surrounding the fort were women and children, or old men like her grandfather. Sprinkled in were family clusters with skin as dark as hers, but there was no way for Rose to know whether they were slave or free. Almost all seemed in the same condition of wretchedness — malnourished, shivering against the cold, ragged, weak, sick.

Grampa Cow Tom led the way through the motley sea of people, and pressed forward toward the front gate. Several bodies lay splayed on the ground in unnatural positions, not moving. Rose wasn't sure if they were dead or sick or asleep. There was something in the faces of the Indians who inhabited Fort Gibson as they stared back at the new arrivals, something Rose couldn't quite articulate, but instinctively grasped, at least in part. Fatigue. Despair. Resignation. But most of all, hunger. Clearly, most of the people here were starving. They shivered in the cold, damp mud and huddled together in family units, lethargic. For so many people in one place, there was remarkably little activity, as if everyone waited on something.

An army soldier on horseback yelled in English for a cleared lane to enter the fort. Few understood his words, but his intent was obvious, and people parted to open a path.

"Food," someone called out from the crowd in Mvskoke, and others picked up the refrain, in Mvskoke and Hitchiti, in Tsalagi, in other Choctaw and Cherokee dialects, hands reaching toward the man on the horse. The soldier spurred his huge mount forward. Rose understood only some of the petitions, but not all, the languages crowding one another.

"Nothing to hunt."

"Please. Medicine."

"Dead. My two children gone."

The soldier didn't respond, not to any, and kept his eyes purposefully forward and focused on the gate. Rose recognized him.

The man on the horse was Lieutenant Phillips, the white man who sometimes visited their ranch to talk to Grampa Cow Tom.

The black man riding with the Cherokee family called out to Lieutenant Phillips in English, and the lieutenant leaned down to hear him over the noise of the crowd. There was extended conversation back and forth, the black man acting as interpreter, and at the end, the military man agreed to something. The Cherokees they'd traveled with for the last few hours lifted Granny Sarah from the wagon, disentangled themselves from the crowd, and prepared to follow Phillips through the gate. Chibona caught Rose's eye for an instant but looked quickly away.

Before Phillips could disappear through the gate, her grandfather grabbed the bit of the lieutenant's horse. At first, Phillips seemed ready to lash him with the rein, but pulled back in recognition.

"Cow Tom. You made it to the fort," he said. "Bad situation all around."

Her grandfather switched to English. "Confederates came for us."

"Not many Indians left out there, Cherokee or Creek. Confederates are burning or destroying what they can. Most everyone not fighting in the army is in the fort now."

Cow Tom gestured toward the Indians surrounding them. "These people look starved," he said.

"Not enough food to go round," Phillips said. "Supply wagons don't always get through."

An old woman, full-blood Creek, hair done up in a traditional topknot, reached out to Grampa Cow Tom, pulling at his leather cloak with her thin, fragile fingers.

"You speak the white man's tongue," she said in Mvskoke. "Tell him how we die without food and warm clothes. They don't feed us and we can't go out to hunt without being killed by Confederate Indian. They don't give Creeks our rations."

A slave in Creek dress came at her grand-father from the other side. "Soldiers come, say get to the fort after the Battle of Honey Springs, but we belong to Indians don't got nothing now. And no way to raise food or make cloth."

A bone-thin woman, filthy, in a ragged scrap of dress, elbowed Rose as she pushed to the front. Rose fell to the ground, but no one noticed, and she scrambled to pick herself up. She grabbed at Granny Sarah's hand to try to shield her. A swarm of bodies and voices crowded in as attention chan-

334

neled to her grandfather, and the assumption he was linked somehow to the army man on the horse. Most had lost someone to smallpox or dysentery or stomach disorders, to pneumonia or other disease. Everyone had some story of uproot, of neglect, of starvation, but even her grandfather struggled to understand so many different languages and dialects.

"We can't tell what they say, but there's damned little we can do anyways," Lieutenant Phillips shouted to her grandfather, and he gave his horse a little kick, moving him through the crowd. He turned back. "Come tomorrow. Translator skills might prove useful," he said.

The lieutenant disappeared through the gates, the Cherokee family behind him, and the rest of the crowd fell back. The thin woman who knocked Rose down rushed forward and began to pick through the fresh horse droppings for bits of undigested corn. Another woman followed her lead, and they fought over the spoils.

All Rose wanted was to get warm and to sleep. She pulled Elizabeth under her blanket to share body heat. Grampa Cow Tom circulated among those outside the gates of the fort he could readily identify as Creek, whether black, mixed-blood, or full-blood, gathering complaints to present to the military about the cold, insufficient food, disease, and lack of supplies.

It was Gramma Amy who began the search for a place for the night. Rose's family never walked through the gates into the bowels of Fort Gibson. Her grandmother found a spot on a grass-trodden knoll outside the walls of the fort and formed a ring around what few supplies they had left. The grass was damp and the wind blew, but they lit a fire and ate the last of the cold tack and jerky. There wasn't enough to offer their neighbors, and Rose couldn't ignore the greedy eyes of want trained on all of them as they chewed. So tired she could barely think, she wrapped Elizabeth beside her, covered them with her blanket, and laid her head down.

Already, Rose didn't like their new home.

Chapter 34

Rose worried over granny Sarah. The trek to Fort Gibson drained them all, body and spirit, and the wretchedness of their situation weighed heavy all around, almost as searing as the persistent rank smell of open sewage and filth, the unpredictability of on-again off-again food rations, and the sickness girdling them no matter which way they turned. Hacking coughs pierced the darkness of the night, and a piteous chorus of moans came from several directions at once within the mass of humanity outside the gates of Fort Gibson. Someone died every day, a stiff body found in the morning after a long, chilly night, first loudly mourned and then stripped of their blanket to pass to the living. Deadly fever struck whole families, gone one after the other, dependent on strangers for the burying.

If only. If only Grampa Cow Tom could stop and talk to her, just the two of them, the steady drone of his voice in story a magic shield against the crush of the days and nights away from the only home she'd ever known. But he was always too busy, with strangers, with family, always in a group, always in demand. Not even a full moon had passed, and now Granny Sarah, weary, had lost the will to go on.

Rose stepped in to minister to her great-grandmother the best she could when Gramma Amy had others to attend, but Granny Sarah refused the little food or water they scrounged, and spent most of her time sleeping. Granny Sarah had been ancient as long as Rose could remember, but now she no longer made an attempt to rise each day, lying abed like so many others in the packed camp, her new routine one of sloth and resignation on the cold, damp ground. She perked up only slightly when Grampa Cow Tom came to sit by her side, for him and no one else, and slumped back into her own world when he absented himself to do his linguister work among the émigrés or camp officials. The weaker her great-grandmother became, the more Rose stayed close, struggling against her own loneliness in this world without Twin.

"I'm here, Granny Sarah," Rose announced one early afternoon, a week after they first came to Fort Gibson.

Her great-grandmother motioned to be pulled upright, her desiccated weight light and unresisting even for a twelve-year-old girl as small as Rose. The day was mild, and a bit of the sun's rays fell on Granny Sarah's face, and she luxuriated in it, as if it was a gentle, stroking hand at her cheek. She was in a talkative mood, and put her clawlike hand around Rose's.

"You got his face," Granny Sarah said. "I pray you got his grit."

"Yessum." What else could she say?

Granny Sarah seemed to lose her concentration, but then squeezed Rose's hand again.

"I was Bella before I was Sarah," she said.

Although Granny Sarah's eyes were age-clouded, there was a brightness behind, ravenous, fixing on Rose as if her great-granddaughter were the only person on earth, despite the filth and misery and anonymous thousands surrounding them. Granny Sarah pursed her dry lips and squinted hard, in search of what, Rose didn't know, and Rose lifted the gourd for her great-grandmother to drink, afraid to break Granny Sarah's mood. The moment offered the possibility of some glimpse of the past, something Rose longed for and seldom received. Once in a while her grandfather parceled out dribs and drabs of the exploits of his youth, the same few tales over and over, but he was miserly in the telling, and Ma'am never opened any parts of her life to inspection.

Rose knew so little about this frail woman whose wrinkled skin clung to her bony frame like an ill-fitted suit. "Who was Bella?"

A fine sheen of sweat covered Granny Sarah's face. She seemed at the edge of answering, but then released her grip on Rose.

"Wasn't my fault," she said.

"What?" Rose prodded. She wiped the moisture from her grandmother's forehead with her sleeve. "What wasn't your fault?"

"I see you with your sister, watching over her. You got it in you to do better than me, but hang tight to your children, hear? No matter what, keep them close. Don't let them go."

"Who was Bella?" Rose almost whispered, so soft, at first she wasn't sure her great-grandmother heard.

Granny Sarah released her grip and wiped at her eyes. They were dry.

"Don't even have any tears left," she finally said. "No use rooting in the past.

What's done is done and gone." She closed her eyes and quieted.

Rose fought the wash of disappointment, and prepared to help Granny Sarah lie back down, when her great-grandmother's eyes fluttered open again.

"I was Bella once, but Sarah's better."

"Please." Rose held her great-grandmother's hand. There was a secret here, she was sure of it, some meaning that might help her endure this terrible time at Fort Gibson if she could just keep her talking. Everyone in the family, so stingy with their stories. "What was Bella like?"

"Never you mind. Leave it be. Some things aren't for sharing," Granny Sarah said. "My story belongs to me." Granny Sarah made a great effort to focus, and tightened her grip on Rose's arm again. "Children matter. That's all what matters. You'll see when you have yours."

The moment was lost, and Rose didn't push further.

"Ma'am thinks I'm too plain to get a husband," she said instead. Amid the misery of Fort Gibson, she imagined herself and Granny Sarah alone and free to say anything.

Granny Sarah laughed, a short, dry sound that took much of her energy. "No need putting plain in your mind. You are Cow Tom's granddaughter. That's enough. You'll make it enough, and find a way, once decided what you want."

Granny Sarah lay back of her own accord, spent, her brittle bones a-creak. She closed her eyes and settled into a pattern of labored breathing. Rose pulled her blanket up to cover herself. As afternoon stretched toward evening, and Granny Sarah's breathing grew more ragged, Rose reflected on what her great-grandmother's words might mean, and what she most hoped for. Home. Husband. Family. Children. Enough, without constant want. Safety. She would sacrifice almost the world entire to have these things.

Shortly before dusk, Granny Sarah gasped, a sharp breath different from the others, and then gasped again. Rose thought to run to find her grandfather, but wouldn't leave Granny Sarah alone. Only one final rush of air in, and the old woman stopped breathing, mouth agape. Rose sat still, unsure what to do, and finally, with a trembling hand, pulled Granny Sarah's eyelids closed, as she'd seen Gramma Amy do once before with a neighbor's child, and worked at her great-grandmother's face to close her mouth until the lips touched. She straightened her on the blanket, and crossed her hands, one over the other, at her waist, until she looked more peaceful.

Only then did Rose run to get Aunt Maggie, who took charge as Rose drifted to the background and watched.

Not long after, Gramma Amy and Grampa Cow Tom returned from the day's scavenging, together. The rest of the family were all gathered around the body by then, and Grampa Cow Tom elbowed his way through the human circle, the dawning reality of Granny Sarah's passing clear by the wildness in his eyes. As he rushed forward to her body, his knees crumpled under him, and he sat limp alongside her where he'd fallen, just staring at her face, now stilled. Rose tried to describe Granny Sarah's final hours to him, but he wasn't listening. He never looked at Rose, even as she talked, his gaze only on Granny Sarah, and Gramma Amy wrapped her arms around Rose's shoulders and pulled her off to the side, putting distance between them. The rest of the family moved back too, Grampa Cow Tom's grief outsizing them all.

Her grandfather stayed next to Granny Sarah's body, refusing to move. Her grandmother brought him a blanket and cloaked him in it for warmth, but he didn't acknowledge his wife either. More than anything,

Rose wanted to comfort him, but didn't know how. If Gramma Amy wasn't able, what chance did she have?

And then she saw the rush of tears down his dark cheeks. He made no attempt to hide or wipe them away. His shoulders heaved, and he held his head in his hands, giving the gulping sobs full rein. Rose had never seen her grandfather cry before, but he wept with abandon, as if he'd never stop. Rose didn't think such a thing possible, Grampa Cow Tom in tears, and it terrified her, more than Granny Sarah's death. Her grandfather was always composed, always in charge. Finally, they left him there alone with the body and retreated to their bed-rolls.

"He needs come to his own peace," Gramma Amy told them.

Throughout the long night, Rose heard her grandfather speak in tongues she couldn't understand, sometimes shouting in anger, sometimes whispering in tones that sounded like begging.

He was still by Granny Sarah's side in the morning when Rose woke, but now he was quiet, more in control of himself, more the grandfather she knew. She brought him *puska* and fresh water, and offered the meal to him.

He accepted in silence, forcing down their precious ration without comment or connection.

CHAPTER 35

"We bury her proper," Grampa Cow Tom announced, his voice loud and thick.

He'd been gone three days, disappeared in the direction of the fort while Gramma Amy prepared the body, and finally returned. Rose smelled the stink of spirits on him, triggering vague memories of her father. She'd seen many men drink before, and women too, especially since coming to Fort Gibson, sometimes so deep in their cups that they stumbled as they walked, or soiled themselves and didn't care. Grampa Cow Tom wasn't to that stage, but she had never seen him drink at all.

He pulled a small pistol from under his coat, and waved it in the air.

An alarm ran through Rose at the sight of the pistol. She knew what came next, but not like this, not without ceremony. This wasn't right at all.

Gramma Amy rushed to Grampa Cow

Tom's side, easing the gun from his grip as she helped him sit on the ground. He handed the pistol to her without protest. His head rolled forward toward his chest as if too heavy to hold up.

"Proper," Gramma Amy promised him. "I'll hold to the gun till it's time."

"I have to give it back," he said. "And four bullets." He fished these out of his jacket and gave her those as well.

Amy pocketed the bullets and pistol, and spread her arms wide, circling one hand over her head, as if swinging an imaginary lasso, encompassing their encampment.

"Protect us," Amy said, her voice firm. "Keep us in the circle of family."

She gathered a handful of loose dirt and threw bits over her left shoulder, weaving around each family member in a snakelike dance as she softly chanted a wordless tune. Rose gave herself over to her grandmother's incantations, and followed along behind her, looping as she looped, shuffling as she shuffled. By the time Gramma Amy gave up her chanting, Grampa Cow Tom was already snoring where he lay on the ground, and Rose had worked up a fierce sweat. Rose covered her grandfather with a blanket.

That evening, before dark fell, they put Granny Sarah in the ground. Grampa Cow

Tom, more himself after his sleep, dug the hole himself, and after she was safely buried, and the dirt covered the body, he fired the pistol four times. First to the north, then west, then south, and finally east.

Granny Sarah was on her way home.

The next day, with her family still listless in the aftermath of Granny Sarah's service, Rose snuck away to find Chibona. She wasn't sure how to go about the task, but hungered for reconnection with the Cherokee boy. If only she could forge a bond outside the family. A friend of her own, now she had lost Twin. It needn't matter that they didn't speak the same language, only that he might be kind to her. That he let her talk to him.

There were thousands of Indians here, countless tribes represented, but Rose knew Chibona's family was allowed inside the fort's gates, and would be among the Cherokees there. That was at least a place to start. She slogged through the endless sea of communities of misery outside the gates, refusing to allow the suffering she witnessed to slow her resolve. She hadn't ventured very far on her own since coming to Fort Gibson, except under the protection of her grandfather or to fetch water, and she was

surprised to see so many pockets of play —
a small rectangular mudded field of children
younger than her getting up a game of stickball with dead branches and a lopsided ball
of moss, girls her age braiding one another's
hair, mothers tickling their lean babies until
they squirmed and twisted their faces into
smiles. Life went on.

Though soldiers in faded blue milled
about shouldering rifles, Rose slipped
through without incident. She'd been inside,
with Grampa Cow Tom, but it was different
on her own, as if the ominous weight of the
place was leavened by the scope of her small
task instead of the burden of the large duties her grandfather undertook.

Rose knew Chibona wouldn't be inside
the fort's buildings, reserved for military
and officials, and instead walked the muddy,
close-packed trails where so many Cherokee
families set up haphazard housing. She
looked for over an hour, peering over strung
blankets acting as walls, and small tepees in
zigzag formation, and crude huts to keep
off rain. Just like outside the gate, Cherokees
mostly sat idle, passing time. Her mood
flagged.

She heard yelling behind the company
commander's office, shouts of cheer and not
distress, and, drawn to the sound, anything

that might boost her frame of mind, walked until she saw a game of stickball, with dozens of young men running the small, cleared area. The only difference between the game outside the gate and this one inside was that here they had a real deerskin ball. They had jury-rigged a goal, and ran up and down the short field in teams, chests bare, feathers flying. Rose couldn't tell who was on which team, but the sheer purposefulness and the athleticism displayed were a joy to watch. As if they were young and carefree and not a part of the horror of Fort Gibson.

Rose almost forgot her mission, engrossed. And then she saw him. Chibona, one of the players on the makeshift field. He moved with the intensity of a warrior, whooping as he blocked a shot, emitting an intimidating screech as he stole the lopsided ball from another player and sped away toward the center goal.

She'd found him.

She waited for his time at the game to be finished. There were so many young Cherokee boys waiting on their turn to play, and they rotated in and out in shifts. Chibona came off the field with several others, bathed in sweat, his arm around the shoulders of another boy his age. There were several of them, laughing and joking, and Rose was in high spirits at her boldness, an act as bold as her grandfather might do, that she'd risked seeking him out, so happy for the opportunity to share in something lighthearted. She put herself in Chibona's path.

"Chibona," she said, and smiled her prettiest smile.

It took a moment for Chibona to place her. Rose read the confusion on his face, and saw it give way to uncertainty.

"Chibona," one of his friends mimicked, and the others took up the refrain, each interpretation more high-pitched and girlish than the last. The boy who'd come off the field with Chibona said some words Rose couldn't understand in Tsalagi, and made a gesture toward her face and then her body and laughed. Rose looked to Chibona for rescue.

Chibona hesitated, but then he laughed too, his words to his friends coming fast and matching their tone. Laughing.

At first, Rose was pinned to where she stood, frozen, until she had the presence of mind to run, their laughter at her back, calling out words she was thankful she couldn't understand. She ducked behind one of the buildings and pressed herself into the shadows, afraid to cross paths with any of them again. She wasn't sure what just happened, whether they laughed because she was a girl, or because she was Creek, or because she was dark, or because she was homely.

She stayed crouched there for some time, until she admitted to herself she needed to find her way home in the daylight, before darkness fell. Rose gathered herself and darted through the inner-fort trails, head down, retracing her steps until she came to the front gate. And there, waiting, was Chibona. He was alone now, none of his friends in sight, staring at her.

"Rose," he said. He shook his head and mumbled more cryptic words. He looked regretful, but what was that to her? He had laughed, when all she wanted was a friend. "Rose," he repeated.

Rose wouldn't look at him. She focused instead on a jagged rock by the gate's post, just the size to fit her hand. She could almost feel the spread of her fingers curl around the uneven edges of the rock, the heft as she lifted the stone over her head, and the driving force as she brought it down on Chibona's fine head, again and again until the blood ran. The light was overbright, a blinding blue. The air was overhot.

"Do it," Twin shouted. "Do it now. Now."

Twin's voice reverberated in her head, seemed to travel straight down her spine and back up again, shaking loose every other thought. She didn't move, not one inch in any direction, holding herself back. She tried to drown out Twin's voice, tried not to give way to the swelling rage, but the pounding at her ears kept directing her toward the promised justice that bloodied rock could bring. She took a step forward, toward Chibona, toward the rock, toward retribution, and Twin's voice grew louder still, excited.

But another voice competed, quieter, measured. A calm whisper instead of a roar, and suddenly, concentrating on that small spot of quiet, Rose's mind cleared enough to ask herself a question. What would Grampa Cow Tom do? The pierce of Twin's voice still rang in her head, but fell out of tempo with the wild beating of her heart. The blue surrounding her dimmed a shade.

Rose forced her gaze away from the jagged rock, pressed her hands into fists and kept them tight and in control by her sides, and ran as fast as she could through the fort's gate, never stopping once until she got home.

■ ■ ■ ■

Twin was back.

All the times she called on him since leaving the ranch, and he didn't come, and now he came and went of his own accord every day. Always pushing her to do terrible things. Hang around by the distribution center in the fort with the other ragtag children and steal part of another family's food ration. Hold Elizabeth's nose and mouth shut as she slept, until her sister woke up gasping for air. Throw her cousin Lulu's beloved bead doll, the only thing she had left from the ranch, in the sewer pit and watch it sink into the muck. Disappear from the encampment for hours without explanation to anyone. But mostly, Twin pushed her to go back into the fort and seek revenge on Chibona. Twin was obsessed with Chibona, and his remedies all involved blood. Slice off a finger. Bash in his head. Break his leg in two places so he couldn't play stickball. Twin came up with a new punishment every day, an evil spirit on her shoulder, whispering and yelling and demanding. Rose stopped sleeping more than a few hours at a stretch.

Rose stayed away from inside the fort,

even when her grandfather asked her to come along with him, as he often did now Granny Sarah was dead. She was afraid of what Twin might make her do. But after she dislocated Cousin Emmaline's shoulder in a fight over a handful of *puska,* Rose began to shut Twin out, one bad deed at a time, hollowing herself out, refusing him. When she felt him beside her, she ignored him, and attached herself to tasks from Ma'am or Gramma Amy or Grampa Cow Tom or Aunt Maggie, the more mindless, the better. She kept on guard with Elizabeth and the cousins, Lulu and Emmaline, and at that first seductive twitch to dole out harm, went off by herself. She gave up all thought of Chibona as a friend. She gave up thoughts of any friend. The remedy was simple. She'd give it all up. She'd starve Twin of her need until he went away once more, for good, and she would never call on him again. He was dangerous.

Rose hated Fort Gibson. She didn't want to know anyone else's story, full of hardship and suffering. She didn't know how her grandfather did it, listening to one bad-luck tale after the next. She didn't want to meet anyone new, or remember anyone's name she didn't have to. What was the point? They might be dead tomorrow, gone forever. She went about her tasks, but walled herself in, obedient. Something shut down inside her, and she felt it as a dimming flame. She wondered if that flame could ever burn bright again, especially without Twin as its spark.

CHAPTER 36

During the month of July, rains of extraordinary severity rolled through Fort Gibson, unattended by lightning or thunder. A scorching sun followed each fall of rain, and disease spread quickly in the Negro section outside the garrison. Many months had passed since Granny Sarah died, and despite the lingering sadness, at least her great-grandmother's passing felt to Rose more like a natural transition after a long life lived, not this foul thing that swept the camp without mercy, carrying the young and strong off after a day or two of suffering. They'd had a proper funeral for Granny Sarah, and observed the Creek power of fours — four days before being put to ground, four gunshots — but that was all before the cholera epidemic. The burials now were so frequent everyone in the settlement lived almost atop shallow graves hastily dug, not even three feet from the soil's surface, subject to uncovering by the next bad rain.

Twin was gone again, it felt this time forever. His voice grew weaker and weaker in her ear until one day she realized he wasn't there at all, prodding her toward this or that. Rose had so little investment in her surroundings, maybe Twin simply lost interest. Some part of Rose missed him, and she sometimes nursed her emptiness around the loss, but mostly she feared his return, and the havoc he could bring. Cousin Emmaline had forgiven her, and she put her misguided episode with the Cherokee boy behind her, a naive and desperate confrontation she regretted. She dug in with her own family.

Since the cholera, Gramma Amy kept Rose busy cleaning. Her grandmother was consumed with hauling out waste and garbage. The water in their kettle was always at a boil, to wash blankets and rags and tunics in shifts because there were no extras. The family lived in a hut now, in a settlement of almost all women and children about a quarter of a mile from the garrison, scant shelter against the elements but at least out of direct rain and sun and wind. Eleven of them made the area allotted to them work, grandparents, aunt, mother, sister, and cousins in a space not quite ten feet by twelve feet.

The ground itself was at a premium, along with food and medicine, and Gramma Amy made everyone clean the mudded hut continually. They all had diarrhea, a complaint so common as to be assumed, and Gramma Amy ordered them to do their personal business as far from the tight row of huts as possible, which often wasn't achievable, and bury the remains. Her herbs had run low, or out completely, but still she circulated among both Creeks and Negroes to minister where she could. Grampa Cow Tom spent most daylight within the walls of the fort, and fortunately, by day's end, sometimes came back with extra food or supplies or a mustard poultice or, occasionally, some Squibb's mixture for the diarrhea.

Rose obeyed whatever her mother or grandmother asked of her. Gramma Amy had a raft of instructions she expected everyone to follow. No fruit, sparing with water unless boiled for tea, no direct sun, avoid night air, avoid fatigue. And yet, all around them in nearby huts and beyond, new cases of cholera struck every day.

One evening, as the family gathered inside the hut and silently ate their dinner of green corn and cucumbers, Aunt Maggie was seized with a fit of cramping. Rose's grandfather hadn't yet returned from the fort. Aunt Maggie knocked over a stump of candle as she rushed from where she sat, her arms wild in clearing a path. Before she could make it outside, she vomited repeatedly and helplessly in the corner. Gramma Amy was on her daughter immediately, feeling for the cold of her arms and legs. Even Rose could see her aunt's eyes sunk into her face, deep and dark in the eyeholes, the leaden hue of her skin. Both cousins, Lulu and Emmaline, rushed headlong toward their mother, but Gramma Amy firmly pulled them away from Aunt Maggie, sending the children to the opposite side of the room, as if a few feet could protect any of them.

"Rose, be quick. Set stones to boil," Gramma Amy commanded.

Both cousins began bawling, lips trembling, hands intertwined, Lulu's fear feeding into Emmaline's and back again, but they did as they'd been told and kept their distance from their mother even as the horror filled them. Every member of the household had seen this disease, and knew its course.

The water in the black kettle outside was still warm, and Rose found several rocks and dropped them into the pot. She gathered what twigs she could find and built up the fire underneath. When the stones were hot enough, she fished them out with a branch and lugged them back into the hut wrapped in a blanket. Still, she'd burned her hands, but that was of no consequence now.

Back in the hut, Gramma Amy had Aunt Maggie on her back, and had already swathed her in a mustard poultice. She took the hot stones in the blanket and placed them on Maggie's abdomen. The room was small, and fear crowded it even more. Rose watched, helpless, and when Grampa Cow Tom came home at last, Gramma Amy was quick to block his way.

"Get them all out of here. Find someplace else to stay."

His face crumpled at the sight of Maggie, and he comprehended the scene in a glance. He moved to pack up some belongings for the move.

"Nothing from here leaves the hut," said Gramma Amy. "Nothing."

"What about you?" Grampa Cow Tom asked.

"I look after Maggie, and come if I can."

Gramma Amy's expression was stern. She cautioned him against coming any closer, but her eyes were liquid, as were Grampa

Cow Tom's. They held each other in a gaze for a second, no more, but even through her dread, Rose felt the tight bond of their connection, just the two of them, as though holding each other close.

"Get them to burn it all down," Gramma Amy said. "The officials. Make them listen. It must all burn."

Grim-faced, Grampa Cow Tom nodded.

Rose looked to Ma'am for comfort, but her mother's face was blank, barely registering. Grampa Cow Tom gathered all those remaining to him as if they were tiny children too young to fend for themselves, including Ma'am, and steered them out of the dim hut.

They went on foot into the hot, stuffy night without the few possessions they'd managed to accumulate since coming to Fort Gibson, twisting and turning among alleyways and passages between dwellings and huts until they were so far away that Rose couldn't recognize where they were. Grampa Cow Tom stopped in front of a crooked little logged house, but with a real door. He rapped, and whispered to the woman who answered, using his insistent negotiator voice, until finally she nodded in agreement.

"Only two," she said, and turned her back,

disappearing inside, but she left the door open.

Grampa Cow Tom squatted in front of Rose, eye level, and even in the moonlight, she saw herself reflected in him, that they were both terrified, but each knew to don the mask of courage in defense of those not strong enough.

"Take care of your sister, I'll take care of your mama. These are freedmen from the Canadian, and they owe me this favor. I'll come back for you tomorrow."

"Yes," said Rose, afraid that if she said more, she would break down and beg her grandfather to take her with him, wherever he went. She didn't want to be with strangers. She wanted Gramma Amy's warm arms around her, and for Aunt Maggie to get better, and to have enough to eat, and she wanted their ranch back. She wanted Ma'am to come out of herself, even if that meant a scolding. But what she didn't want to do was disappoint her grandfather.

Rose took Elizabeth by the hand and entered the small hut, without looking back. There were three inside, the woman and two children she held close to her on the other side of the room, a boy and girl, about the same age as Cousin Emmaline and Cousin Lulu. The woman kept her distance, and pointed to the far corner of the room. She offered neither blanket nor food. Rose settled her sister and herself on the floor in the corner and shut her eyes to gather strength.

Rose woke in the morning, unsure of where she was, Elizabeth snuggled up against her, still asleep. The previous night came crowding back, and she bolted upright. A dark woman sat in the opposite corner across the small room, watching her. In the light, Rose saw the woman was Ma'am's age, small and wiry, with a rag tied around her head and a long dress, stained and dirty, but of sturdy cotton. Her children were still asleep on either side.

"He said he's coming back to fetch you this morning first thing," the woman said. Her eyes never left Rose. "This is first thing now."

Rose shook Elizabeth awake. Her sister started to fuss, but sensed tension and sat up quietly, rubbing her eyes.

Rose was hungry, but somehow this didn't seem the right time to broach that subject.

"We can wait outside, missus."

The woman nodded.

She pulled Elizabeth by the hand and led her outside, and they heard a latch catch behind them. Dawn was barely broke, but the air already gusted hot, as if on fire. Rose settled them a few feet away from the hut, squatting in the dirt. Elizabeth didn't complain, and followed Rose's lead. They daren't go back to their own hut, not after Gramma Amy warned them away. If Grampa said he would come for them, Rose knew he would.

Rose and Elizabeth waited for hours until Grampa Cow Tom finally came down the path for them, daylight fully arrived. Rose thought he might be angry at the freed-woman for turning them out, but he seemed too preoccupied. She helped Elizabeth to her feet.

"How's Aunt Maggie?" Rose asked.

Her grandfather didn't answer. "We're going to a new place," he said.

Elizabeth started to cry.

"Is she dead?" Rose asked.

His face looked like he might lose control again, as he'd done after Granny Sarah died. When he spoke, his voice was flat. "The children took sick in the night too."

"Where's Gramma Amy?" Rose felt herself at the edge of something terrible, as if she was a river rising over the banks and yet the rains continued to pelt down. She was afraid she would call Twin. She was afraid she would call Twin and he wouldn't come. She was afraid Twin would come unbidden and make things even worse.

"All sick are back in our hut, and Amy won't leave, but I found a new place on a hill for us, away from the hut city. A tent. Your mother is there now, making things ready."

They followed him blindly, Rose and Elizabeth, trudging up the hill, putting more distance between their old home and the new, without knowing who might still be alive to inhabit the tent on the hill.

By the time Rose saw Gramma Amy again, Aunt Maggie was dead. Both Cousin Lulu and Cousin Emmaline were dead. Gone. Disappeared from this earth.

Several days later, before nightfall, just outside their new tepee on the hill, Rose stood between Grampa Cow Tom and Gramma Amy, and stared at the exodus on foot of all the people leaving the filth of the hut city. Her former neighbors.

At the end of the week, dry-eyed, she watched the settlement she'd called home for the last year and a half go up in flames, at the order of the commanding officer of the post.

CHAPTER 37

When Grampa Cow Tom squatted on the mudded ground outside the lieutenant adjunct's office, Rose did too.

"Take Rose on your rounds," Gramma Amy had pleaded with him several months back, after the firing of the hut city, when Rose could barely find the wherewithal to stand or sit or wake, every movement a chore, every thought leading back to death and hopelessness. "She rallies for you."

And so her grandfather often brought her with him when he did his work inside the fort, and those became her best days in this godforsaken place. At first she hardly cared, but now she hungered after these shared days, away from first the tent on the hill, and then their new location near Grand River. Rose considered herself lucky to shadow her grandfather, to be with him, to watch what he did, to pick up some of his language skills and the way he was with people, black, white, and Indian. She could be quiet, as if she wasn't there at all, and listen, and experimented with reading the expressions of people around her to report back to her grandfather later. Often it seemed waiting was her grandfather's main task. Waiting and bargaining for supplies. Pleading and delivering bad news.

Rose considered herself a different person from the raw girl she was before Fort Gibson, worse for wear like her tattered tunic, but tougher, more independent, smarter, and she saw a marked change in her grandfather too. He was outspoken to the military men, less patient, insistent that full-blood Creeks, mixed-blood Creeks, and Negroes all get their due at the fort. And he made great effort to spend time with her, though mostly in silence.

The adjunct finally emerged, in rapid conversation with another military man. Her grandfather scrambled to his feet, but the white man waved him away before he said a word.

"Too busy," he said. "Supplies coming in."

Her grandfather trailed the military men, and Rose trailed her grandfather, and from the parapet of the hilled fort, they all watched a caravan arrive below in the valley, a slow and seemingly endless string of clattering wooden wagons and squeaking carts.

Some refugees rode, but most walked, poor souls trudging silently alongside the rattle of vehicles, ankle deep in mud, or forced behind weary supply mules staggering under their load of corn or flour, with a few raw-ribbed horses sprinkled into the procession, almost as stumble-footed as their two-legged companions.

Her grandfather squinted. He told Rose his eyesight was worse since coming to Fort Gibson, and sometimes he saw the world as if through a halo. Rose was thirteen, which meant he was fifty-four.

"Is that Harry?" he asked Rose. She'd not heard so much excitement in his voice since coming to Fort Gibson.

Even at range, Rose recognized her uncle Harry, midpoint in the long queue on his cinnamon mare, with a small Negro girl no more than three or four years of age in front on his saddle. Harry Island was more family friend than blood relative, and she hadn't seen him for several years, but Harry and her grandfather were closer than brothers. In spite of Uncle Harry living in Kansas and Grampa Cow Tom in Indian Territory, they'd kept their connection through messages sent between forts.

"Yes," she cried. "That's Uncle Harry all right."

"They're come home from Kansas," he said.

The escorts were haggard Union military men, many of them African Indians of various stripe pressed to service, and some coarse-haired buffalo soldiers responsible for escorting civilians. Grampa Cow Tom made it his business to know most military men assigned escort detail, in order to understand what supplies came into the fort, and what went out. He used them to gather news from Fort Scott; he used them to pass messages to hold his connection with Harry Island, so they might strategize across the distance how to help keep Negroes alive, whether domiciled at Fort Scott in Kansas or Fort Gibson in Indian Territory.

Harry Island halted while the caravan proceeded at its snail's pace, and an old woman in a dark head rag claimed the girl, a small child in cloth so worn to shreds, Rose couldn't tell whether the garment was of a piece or the wrapping of random rags. The way the girl lifted her arms to the waiting woman put Rose in mind of Cousin Lulu, and Rose couldn't catch her breath. A rush of dread threatened to overtake her.

She closed her eyes tight, and forced out all thought of her dead cousin, imagining instead the contours of her grandfather's wide face, his calm, until the darkness passed and she regained control of herself.

Uncle Harry handed the girl over, and the waiting woman led her off and out of sight toward Grand River, where Rose lived now. Her fourth Fort Gibson home, after the open hillside, after the burned-out hut city, after the tent city.

The escorts neither dissuaded the stragglers nor urged them forward, content to let them orchestrate their own future from here on out. Close to done with this bit of their transport work, they proceeded to the fort on their horses, theirs in better shape than the civilian nags, but still so bony, ribs often visible beneath blanket and saddle. Uncle Harry went at a trot, lighter for the loss of the girl. Between valley and fort, first one group and then another peeled from the caravan, stopping well short of the fort's gate to search for a resting place in the landscape already crowded with dirty, lousy, half-starved squatters. New arrivals must surely wonder if there were more steady rations of food or clothing or safety at this latest place than the camps in Kansas.

Her grandfather broke for the courtyard

and Rose kept close. The scene was chaos, aswarm with military, livestock from the brigade train, sutlers, teamsters, commissary authorities, Indian agents, curious idlers, new refugees, and savvy squatters hoping to pilfer dropped foodstuffs in the midst of such confusion. Her grandfather fought their way through to a position close to the front gate. Some of the arriving party had already passed through, swallowed up into the buildings.

They didn't see Harry Island anywhere.

"Where'd he go?" Rose asked.

"He'll turn up soon enough," her grandfather answered, but his voice betrayed him. He was antsy too.

"Should we make petition rounds?"

"They'll all be busy logging in supplies and the refugee transfer. We wait."

Rose couldn't let go the thought that Uncle Harry was somewhere close. "Maybe Uncle Harry went to find us in Grand River."

"Then we see him tonight. We've no reason to go back with nothing fresh to report or distribute." Her grandfather found a small space where he could sit, his back against the building. "We sit tight. I'll welcome new arrivals to Grand River later."

But Rose couldn't be still. She ran to the

storeroom and back. No Uncle Harry. She ran to the sutler shop and back. No Uncle Harry. In the crowded fort near the stables, Chibona idled in a group of young Cherokee men. This wasn't the first time, running into him inside the gates. He glanced her way, and she looked through him, her shoulders back and her head held high. He could do her no more harm. She no longer pined for his friendship, nor feared him or his friends, nor sought revenge, nor felt the need for Twin to protect her. Yes, she was a different girl, hard enough to face the likes of Chibona without blinking. Rose had family, and that's what mattered, the dead spot in her heart sealed over and unavailable to anyone else.

Rose slowed and walked, knowing she was watched, lest Chibona think she ran from him again or thought of him at all. And there he was, finally, Harry Island across the crowded courtyard, riding his broke-down cinnamon mare, the selfsame horse he'd ridden off to Kansas, the poor animal now decrepit.

Harry hollered his old familiar whoop, and waved his hat in the air.

"Brother Cow Tom," Harry yelled, without regard for stares, though with the din at the fort, he was scarcely heard.

Her grandfather was up and on his feet, leaving Rose to scramble behind him.

Harry had shed all traces of fat, as had they all, his cheekbones sharp in his sunken face, two of his upper teeth missing. He was so dark as to look truly African, small of stature but handsome of face, with eyes like a lizard, heavy lidded and appraising.

He dismounted. No jumping off his horse in a showy flourish like the Harry of old, but a careful dismount, joints a-creak, and a clear favoring of one leg over the other. They hadn't seen him in more than three years, not since Harry followed Old Gouge Opothleyahola to Kansas and Cow Tom stayed in Indian Territory.

"Brother Harry," Cow Tom said. "Does my heart good." He grabbed Harry's hand in a firm shake.

Harry, unsatisfied with the greeting, caught her grandfather up in a bear's hug and danced him around the compound. Rose giggled at the folderol.

"Who's this?" Harry asked. Harry Island spoke with an inconsequential lisp, not enough for him to be considered damaged, but enough to make him overcareful in his speaking, intent on making himself clear. "Too grown to be my little Rose."

Rose turned shy. "Yes, Uncle Harry.

That's me. Rose."

Harry reached out and turned her face one way and then the other. "Blamed if it isn't you after all."

For the first time in a long while, standing within the warmth of these two men, Rose thought it possible that things might turn to the better.

CHAPTER 38

"I made you for an earlier convoy," Grampa Cow Tom said to Harry Island.

Uncle Harry became serious, his attention turned from Rose toward her grandfather. "They kept me at Fort Scott as go-between till the ragged end. They're cleaning the camps of Indians in Kansas," he said. "Seems we wore out our welcome. This is about the last of us, returned to mother country."

Uncle Harry looked around the fort and beyond to the valley, taking in the running sewage, the tight press of thousands of bodies for miles in each direction, the rank smell of foul air and unwashed humanity. "Still better than Fort Scott," he pronounced.

"You think it a contest?" asked Grampa Cow Tom, his temper at instant boil. "Suffering is suffering. No need to assign grade."

Uncle Harry stopped short at this last. He

turned his head, and his voice when it came was muffled. "None do well, but some do better," he said.

Her grandfather shook off his upset and clapped Uncle Harry on the back. "You'll see soon enough what work needs done here." He fell silent, giving Harry Island space to right himself. "Where's Chief Sands? I thought he required you by his side. Specially surrounded by the white man's English."

"Took fever the last days on the trail, the hindmost playing out now. I've left him to his bed, and resume duty at the morning. Tonight, I'm free to catch up, see what you call home."

"You're a welcome guest," said Grampa Cow Tom. "But home it is not."

"You and yours?"

"We lost Sarah last year. Pneumonia. And my daughter Maggie and two of her children to cholera six months ago," said Cow Tom.

"Sorry," said Harry. He shrugged. "Dinah's gone. Dysentery. It was quick."

Rose had never met Uncle Harry's wife, but heard of her through her grandfather. Uncle Harry clearly didn't want to dwell on his wife's passing, which suited Rose fine. Death was hard enough to live beyond without having to talk of it. The two men let the silence build, as tribute.

"We brought supplies," Uncle Harry finally said. "I thought it plenty, but they can't last long. We were five thousand in Kansas. Looks three times that here."

"Problems getting through?"

"A scrape with Confederates near Honey Springs, and a charge by a cattle gang, but the military boys fought them both back."

"The First Indian spends more time herding cattle to feed military and refugees than they soldier," Cow Tom said.

"It's the cattle gangs the bigger threat than Sesech, like small armies," said Harry. "Once past Kansas, rustlers came at us hard. Musta been insulted we brought back cattle they already stole once from us in Indian Territory and sold to beef contractors in Kansas."

Her grandfather's anger flared again. "Nobody beats us as stockmen. That's why there's so many African Creeks in the First Indian. But still our cattle disappear into Kansas while we starve here."

Harry Island played the good friend, letting him rant. He ran his hands over his horse, still sweaty from the ride. "Rose, wouldn't you think a man fresh off the trail would be offered something to eat?"

"Where's my head?" Her grandfather

beckoned to Harry. "Let's walk. I'll come back to the fort later. Amy'll coax something from the pot. Might be nothing more than roots and water, but what we have is yours."

"I can lead your horse, Uncle Harry," offered Rose.

"His name's Bucky."

Uncle Harry handed her the reins and they both followed along beside Cow Tom. They were barely free of the gate when a ragged full-blood Creek woman with a pocked face approached, dressed in a faded flour sack. She waited for them to notice her, and they broke off their talk.

"Micco Cow Tom," she said. "Thanks be to Amy. My baby got through the night."

"That's fine, Jane," her grandfather said.

The woman proceeded on her way, into the fort.

"Micco?" Uncle Harry asked. "They think you chief here? Don't that beat all."

It was as if Uncle Harry complimented Rose herself, the gift he gave her of seeing through new eyes the high regard her grandfather and grandmother garnered.

Her grandfather ignored him, and they continued walking the twisted trails toward Grand River.

"How's rations work at Gibson?" Uncle Harry asked.

"If wagons get through, might be corn, flour, sometimes cattle to slaughter or dried beef and bacon, canned goods, coffee, calico, candles, shoes, but first mouths fed are officer, then other military, random white, Cherokee, mayhaps Creek, last comes any other tribe and Negro. When I first come, wasn't Creeks nor Negroes considered to any rations at all, and no protest listened to, though it doesn't take words to reveal starvation."

"And now?"

"Now when supplies come, leastways I get somebody to break off a piece. They know I won't leave them be about the Negroes. I haven't forgotten our pledge."

Rose wanted to ask what the pledge was, but it wasn't her place to speak up in the men's conversation.

"We're still bad off," her grandfather went on, "but get our little bit. The others, they got their representers in the squabble over rations. Cherokee agents are strongest since Gibson lies in their territory, and Creeks specially forgot, with most chiefs Confederate or in Kansas, but Negroes worst. I watched how other agents done it, and made the same case for Creek. And Negro. In English."

The smell of smoke hung heavy. They

passed campsite after squeezed campsite, successive precincts of idled folks. The cadence of different dialects and languages confused Rose, but her grandfather quickly readjusted his ear and answered back in kind. The more fortunate defined space with a weave of blanket or stretch of cowhide, dung fires burning, open space a premium. There was little occupation or industry, no hunting in the played-out vicinity, no material to card or spin, or equipment on which to do it, and only meager foodstuffs to prepare.

A Creek woman, her naked child on her lap, sat on a sloped patch of ground and called a greeting, holding up her palm to acknowledge their passing. It wasn't long out of snow season, and the child had no protection, but he'd held to life thus far, and stood more chance of hanging on until spring if he had a scrap of blanket. Her grandfather promised nothing, indicated nothing, answering back with his raised palm to the woman, but Rose had seen this before, and knew he made a mental note of her location, should he prove successful freeing a blanket from the new shipment.

They walked, the vast grounds around the fort a reflection of territories before the war. Cherokees here, Upper Creeks there, Arapaho over there. They crossed one invisible border after another in quick succession — Cherokee, Chippewa, Creek, mostly women and children, since all healthy military-age men were forced to enlist and had disappeared into the war long ago. Her grandfather spoke to legions of people as they passed their camps. To those whose language or dialect he hadn't mastered, he gestured.

"How many languages you speak now, brother?" Uncle Harry asked.

"Did you go soft in Kansas?" asked Grampa Cow Tom. "Cherokee rules at Fort Gibson among Indian, so it was learn Tsalagi or not understand the dealings of the back room. I muddle Chippewa and Osage to get by, but they aren't players here. In the rations war, English trumps all else in shaking free provisions, from general to supply clerk."

"I see why they didn't pull you into the military," said Uncle Harry. "You made your place."

At last they came to a view of the Grand River, squatters inhabiting every space from wood to riverbank. Everywhere they turned was another dirt-crusted body in ragged garb, another pair of heavy-lidded eyes. Rose slowed her pace, falling behind the two men who provoked such interest as they walked, the better to study the faces of those they passed.

From one campsite to the next, people greeted her grandfather, some to complain, some to chat, some in mere acknowledgment.

"Micco."

"Micco Cow Tom."

"Micco," Harry repeated. "Chief. Chief of the wretched."

"Sometimes, when leadership is not given, it must be taken," said her grandfather.

Uncle Harry nodded. "It's a fact," he agreed.

"They have no one else to represent them. I only plead what is due my people, African or Creek, the way the Cherokee chiefs do, the way the Indian agents do. You fought for Negro and Creek in Kansas at Fort Scott, only you had a Creek chief by your side already in the title. There was no voice but mine here." Her grandfather stopped. "We're almost there. Amy will be glad to see you. Run ahead and give the alert, Rose."

Rose didn't want to leave them. Their men's talk made her feel better than she had in a long time. But she did as told, pulling the horse behind her, and her family greeted Uncle Harry, and welcomed him into their camp. Uncle Harry reacquainted with Gramma Amy, and Ma'am fussed over him for a meager supper of dandelion soup and meal bread.

"I'll find a way to free added rations," Uncle Harry assured Gramma Amy.

After supper, Rose took charge of Bucky once more and followed the two men toward the river, where Uncle Harry staked out a sleeping spot.

"You've grown ever more useful, Rose," Uncle Harry said, taking the reins from her and tying a length of rope from the horse's muzzle. He wrapped the other end around his wrist. "They try to take the horse, they come through me." He laid his horse blanket on the cold ground and pulled his jacket tighter.

"I'm come to be official interpreter for the U.S. Army here," Uncle Harry announced to her grandfather. "Chief Sands decrees." Even in the darkness, Rose could see the tightness in her uncle's face, as if he was unsure how her grandfather would take this news. "You willing to share the load?"

Grampa Cow Tom laughed, loud and long. The very sound was strange. Rose couldn't remember the last time her grandfather laughed.

"You think this work a gift, to be hoarded?" he said.

Uncle Harry laughed too. "I've missed you, old friend."

CHAPTER 39

As squalid as Fort Gibson was, despite the unthinkable memories of death and deprivation of the last couple of years, Rose walked through fire and came out the other side a warrior. She missed her Granny Sarah and Aunt Maggie and the cousins, but refused to dwell on them or the sadness pulling her down. Maybe this was the weight Granny Sarah felt when asked about her past, the impossibility of revisiting what could neither be borne nor amended and therefore couldn't be shared. Rose locked the bad memories away and put other thoughts in their stead.

At Fort Gibson, by the end, she walked chin high around the fort, inside and outside the gates, acknowledged as the African Creek chief's granddaughter, the one he so often brought with him as he went about his duties. She couldn't witness the Micco ceremony when Chief Sands, the big chief over the Creek tribe, officially bestowed the title her grandfather had already claimed. No women were allowed, but Grampa Cow Tom's added prestige and respect from that day was like healing water, running downhill to cleanse her as well. And her uncle Harry was the official translator for all the Creeks. Rose was somebody by connection.

And then, not long after her grandfather was named a Creek chief, the war was officially over. They were declared on the winning side and told to strike off into the wilderness to make a new home for themselves. If this was winning, Rose couldn't imagine how it felt to lose.

The family endured a painful separation from Harry Island, who decided to head toward Grand Fork. Cow Tom led them all south, deeper into Creek territory, with a few iron pots, some hides, an ax, a shovel, the ragged clothes on their backs, and a thin stack of headright money issued by the government to get them started. What they carried in greatest supply was hunger — an unquenchable hunger for food, hunger for peace, hunger for someplace where the family could settle and rebuild their lives. Both Gramma Amy and Ma'am were clever with roots and herbs, and the farther they traveled away from Fort Gibson, the more they were able to forage from the forest and even hunt game. They headed toward the last place they'd called home.

But the closer they came to their old ranch along the Canadian River, the more a dull pain burrowed deep in Rose's chest. None of them could know what they'd find at their old homestead, but all Rose could think of was Twin, whether he was still there, and what he might do.

They approached the familiar land from the north side, where the gristmill used to be, and Rose was pulled to the past, when the family gathered so long ago, just before their flight to Fort Gibson, waiting in the tall grass for Grampa Cow Tom. She expected a surge of longing for the place she'd been born to, where she'd grown up, but none came. She bit at the inside of her cheek as the group walked along the Canadian, passing her grandfather's favorite thinking spot. The bois d'arc tree still reached in a delicate arch over the river, and she remembered the exact curve of the river where crappies used to run in abundance, though the stream looked narrower than she remembered. There was a small Indian boy there now, Creek, his pole in the water. When the boy saw them, he ran in the direction of the ranch house.

By the time they reached their old house, the group mood was sour. The log cabin itself was half a house, most parts burned completely or at least charred, left to seasons of neglect, as well as wind, snow, and rain. A majority of the stones of the central chimney still held, but the roof was caved or gone completely. An outdoor cooking fire blazed, with a large black kettle suspended on a tripod of branches. By the looks of the people about and the newness of some sections of the house, several families, all women and children of assorted age, had claimed this land, and begun the work of restoration, splitting trunks of pine for logs, hauling large branches, replacing missing stones with substitutes dragged from the river. The area around the house was free of weeds, and the dirt was swept. A small patch of corn was already put to ground.

The new occupants gathered as one in front of the ruined ranch house, the small boy to one side. There were eighteen.

"We can't house any more here," one of the women said. She was taller than the rest, and burly, like a man. She had a rifle by her side, though she made no show of using it. But still.

Grampa Cow Tom stepped forward. "We lived here. Before the war."

"The land was abandoned. We took it up."

"This was our home."

"Everyone was somewhere before. And starts again now," she said. "We start here."

Rose thought of all of her secret hiding places and the familiar pastures. She imagined them now, either overgrown or in the hands of others.

Her grandfather must have made the same calculation.

"If you were men, I'd challenge," he said.

She nodded, unfazed. "And we plan to have the place ready for our men when they return."

"There are those who'll come looking for us, now war is done. Tell them Chief Cow Tom is downriver. Still along the Canadian."

Just that quickly, her grandfather had bargained away their old ranch. Rose was relieved. This place wasn't what she remembered, no longer what she wanted, somehow spoiled.

"We don't have much, but you're welcome to share from the pot before striking off," the woman said.

It was odd, being hosted by these people who took their land, but Rose was grateful for the thin soup, hot and flavored with the flesh of some small animal.

"We have business in the graveyard near

the woods," said Grampa Cow Tom after the food was through, "and then we go." The woman agreed.

Rose ran ahead to the old family graveyard, and found the entire patch choked with thistle. Weeds and vines tangled in the dirt close to ground. The dull pain in her chest deepened as she cleared them away. Her hands stung with the plant's needles, but beneath, Rose found the three smooth river stones on Twin's grave, unmolested.

She waited, stretched tight, afraid of the coming bright blue light that was Twin, and the finality of his presence washing over her, taking charge of her. She heard the rest of her family coming up behind her, and still she waited. There was nothing. Twin wasn't here in this place.

Ma'am fell upon the grave, as if the thistle was nothing.

"I can't leave him again," she said. "I won't."

Gramma Amy went to her daughter, lifting her up from the ground to standing, but it was Grampa Cow Tom who spoke with authority, the voice that couldn't be challenged.

"This place holds nothing for us anymore. We can't stay. But wherever we go, we make a new family plot, and honor all those

391

who've passed over beyond our reach. We won't forget them. Twin. Granny Sarah. Maggie. Emmaline. Lulu." He lifted one of the smooth stones, leaving two in their place. "We carry this stone with us for Twin's new grave."

Rose kept close watch on her breath. If this didn't rouse Twin, the taking of his headstone, nothing ever could. Nothing.

Ma'am grew docile, and the family set out again following the Canadian downstream. After the first confusing wave of disappointment and loss, Rose wasn't as sorry as she thought she'd be. Every travel day they put between themselves and the fort, and away from their old home, the better she felt.

They traveled south following the river until Grampa Cow Tom raised his hand and called for them to stop. There was nothing but prairie grass and dirt and rock and shrub and close-grown trees in a nearby forest, uncultivated, and a narrow creek with slow-running water dotted with cane plants. Her grandfather gathered a handful of red dirt, lifted it to his nose to smell, and tasted a bit, letting the mass play on his tongue.

He planted his feet with purpose and gathered them all round in a circle.

"This is home," he said.

He pointed out where the house would

be, and a barn, and a corral, and where the family plot would dwell. They placed Twin's stone there first thing, before any of the real work began.

All of them, regardless of age or condition, spent hard months breaking ground and claiming the new patch of land, again along the Canadian River, but much farther downstream, south of Muskogee.

CHAPTER 40

Rose woke.

Gramma Amy's gait was heavy on the packed-dirt floor of the temporary tepee at their new homesite along the Canadian River as she shuffled outside into the approaching dawn. Despite the closeness of their bodies, squeezed together like carelessly thrown pick-up sticks atop the hard ground on pallet hides, head to toe or side to foot or knee to back, they were fortunate for shelter at all, the land so stripped and scarred from the war that both timber and cowhide were hard to come by. So her Grampa Cow Tom often said and so Rose believed, having survived the horror of Fort Gibson.

Rose knew it was time to stir, but lay nevertheless, eyes closed. Snores, labored breath, and peculiar coughs punctuated the quiet of the early morning. There were eight of them in all in the tepee when Grampa

Cow Tom was there, and Rose could identify the owner of each sound. Most of the smaller children stayed in the other tepee with her mother and aunts and uncles. Older, fourteen now, Rose slept in her grandparents' tepee, along with four other siblings, including her younger sister Elizabeth.

She heard a thud as Gramma Amy dropped a load of wood collected from the nearby forest, and she imagined the creak of Gramma Amy's knees beneath her aproned trousers as she coaxed the morning's flame. She listened for her grandmother's stoking of the cooking fire and the responding snap and sputter in the fire pit, blazing of its own accord, and finally the spank of palms as Amy patted the doughy mixture for Indian bread between the flat of her hands.

Dawn was barely upon them, a gentle stirring of all creatures on the land they'd come to settle, and yet Rose resisted leaving her sleeping cocoon, though summer's tail neared, and even early sun made everything too hot by half. She wasn't lazy exactly, but in need of prolonging the heady significance of this day. She corrected herself. Actually, yesterday. August 5, 1865. Yesterday was the official day to remember, but yesterday had been too full of rumor and uncertainty as to the truth of the news, and today was the first opportunity to bask in the wonder. So many changes in the last few years, one on the heel of the next.

Rose heard Grampa Cow Tom roll over on the buffalo hide he'd been presented when named chief, the most cherished possession in the household, and then her grandfather cleared his throat, long and hacking and harsh, a sound she well knew could signal postsleep but maybe only prewake. She waited for him to declare himself further, but he showed no indication to rise. There was a beat of energy flowing throughout their small compound, from grandparents to parents to children, and she decided the time had long passed to embrace her duties. She elbowed Elizabeth awake.

"Come on, sleepy."

Elizabeth tried to turn over and go back to sleep, but Rose wouldn't allow it.

"It's a big day. We'll have fun," she promised.

Rose guided her reluctant sister outside, wiping the sleep from her own eyes as they slipped into the open air. Their mother was there already, scraping corn kernels from a stack of cobs for a fresh batch of *sofki*.

"Long past time," Ma'am said to Rose. "Lazy isn't likely to ever get you married."

"Leave the girl be," said Gramma Amy. "We were all up past late."

Her mother motioned toward the corn, jaw hard, and Rose took up the knife in her stead.

Ma'am brushed back the tangles of Elizabeth's dark hair with one hand. "Come," she said. "Let's get some milk from the cow and fight that rooster for some eggs."

Gramma Amy was about her tasks, rock-pounding corn kernels, adding the maize to the pot, stirring the thick stew. But this particular morning, Rose had no patience for silence. The day was too important, and her mother wasn't here to tell her to hush, to be seen and not heard.

"When's Grampa Cow Tom getting up?" Rose asked.

"The man deserves his rest," said Gramma Amy. "Let him sleep. No one's to pester him today. No one. Hear?"

Rose nodded, disappointed. She wished her grandfather awake and in a mood to tell this new story. He was so often absent, for hours or days or even months at a time, constantly swallowed up with elders in business dealings and important strategy meetings. He had been gone this last time for three days, and first word delivered to them about the victory yesterday hadn't come directly from her grandfather, but from a freedman farmer neighbor who made his home on the patch of land next to theirs. Cow Tom hadn't returned to the compound until the middle of the night, and the sea of bodies in the tepee shifted and rearranged to accommodate him.

"Is it true?" Rose asked. She pushed a stack of spent corncobs into the dirt to save for the shoat and began husking a new pile. Nothing went to waste.

"Appears so," Gramma Amy answered. "Soon as you're done with those ears, bring out a jar of cha-cha from the smokehouse."

"Cha-cha cabbage? For breakfast?" Today truly was special.

"The least we can do on Emancipation Day. Appreciate the import, girl."

Last night, her grandfather stumbled into the tepee and without bothering to shed tunic or trousers, found his sleeping spot. He whispered to Gramma Amy, but anyone awake could hear. "They voted us in. Today, forevermore, is Emancipation Day." His voice was heavy with fatigue, but there was conquest in the delivery.

Though Rose waited for more, she heard only a growing chorus of snores. Often,

Grampa Cow Tom sat all day with other men, sometimes red, sometimes black, sometimes white, straight-backed and solemn, talking, smoking, arguing, and once he sat with Rose and tried to explain to her what the men talked about. All those meetings of his, his dreams of living as black and Creek, both at once in equal measure, all those words finally bore fruit.

"Emancipation Day," Rose repeated.

"Creek Council finally voted us African Creeks full citizens. Colored or red, born slave or free, now we're members of the tribe."

"All Creeks?"

Gramma Amy shook her head. "Not the ones went Confederate. Only Loyal Creeks. Now they're to treat us Indian as anybody else."

Gramma Amy picked up a discarded ear of corn on the ground for inspecting. Too late, Rose saw the short row of yellow kernels still clinging to the cob. She braced for her grandmother's rebuke, whether slap or tongue lash.

"Pay attention, girl. Don't matter whether you black or Creek, no hog gonna eat better than family." Amy took her knife and scraped the stubborn kernels onto her pile and tossed the cob to the ground. She went back to task with her pounding, humming low.

Yes, this was destined to be a good day, full of celebration and forgiveness both.

CHAPTER 41

Midday, and still her grandfather slept the sleep of the dead. Rose made excuses to pass the tepee, on her way to the newly built smokehouse put up at the beginning of summer, on her way back from picking blackberries beyond the pasture, off to the Canadian to fetch water, but each trip, all she heard from the tepee were snores. She daren't disturb her grandfather, or her next brush with Gramma Amy wouldn't go so well as this morning's.

As she wove a basket alongside Elizabeth, a lone man on foot entered their compound from the north side. Only one person on earth had such a strut, and if she'd been a slip of a child, and not so close to a grown woman, she would have given in to impulse to run to him full tilt.

The appearance of Harry Island always broke up routine, and everyone young and old competed for his attention. He enjoyed his popularity too, always playing to the crowd, whether audience of one or dozens. He had gained weight since she last saw him at Fort Gibson, a more healthy fullness to his bronze cheeks, his long wooly hair pulled back and almost tamed by a leather cowhide strip knotted at the base of his neck, his moccasins more new than old. She supposed they must all look better than they did in those dark days. Sometimes she thought overmuch, she decided, and ran to intercept him before all the others realized he was here, Elizabeth fast on her heel.

"Uncle Harry," Rose said. She turned shy, close enough to catch the stink of the road on him.

"What now? Who is this lady in front of me? Do madam have more children at home, or just this one?"

"It's me, Rose," she protested. "And this is Elizabeth. She's not my child, she's my sister . . ." Rose let her voice trail off as she realized he had funned her.

"Rose? You sure? Because the only Rose I know would surely offer a poor, tired man who walked all the way from Grand Fork some water and a bit of biscuit."

"Yes," said Rose. She was reluctant to leave his side. Harry Island popped up no matter where they lived, and was looser with his storytelling than Grampa Cow Tom, at the ready to share their adventures as young men.

She walked with him farther into the compound, and Elizabeth slipped her hand into Uncle Harry's.

"Leave him be," Rose warned her sister. "Men don't like being bothered."

Uncle Harry stopped to appraise the child. "This one is beauty in the making," he said.

Rose fought not to read anything into a comparison. Her younger sister *was* stunning, and fawned over for her ebony hair, her lively eyes, her smooth, dark skin.

By the time they reached Gramma Amy at the fire pit, they'd attracted followers, but Elizabeth had no intention of giving up her place beside Uncle Harry, playing with the soft of his whiskers, a-pout when he talked to anyone else. Gramma Amy dished their visitor up a big bowl of *sofki* and cha-cha, and he lit into the still-warm stew as if it were a feast.

"Go rouse your grandfather," Gramma Amy said to Rose, as beguiled as everyone else with Uncle Harry. "Time to see in the day."

Rose sped to the tepee and pushed at her grandfather's shoulder, quickly standing back. Sometimes Grampa Cow Tom woke hard, and woe to the innocent standing in the way when he came to himself from a dream.

"Yes?" he mumbled, without opening his eyes. His tone was neither friendly nor harsh, reserving the right to go either way.

"Harry Island's come."

Cow Tom opened his eyes then, looked her through. "Here?"

"At the pit, eating."

Her grandfather was up, not bothering to brush the twigs from his hair or tongue the night fuzz from his teeth.

"Why didn't you say so, girl?" But his tone this time was full of tease. "We got celebrating to do," he said, and she followed behind, running to keep up.

Harry Island whooped when he saw her grandfather come across the clearing. "We done it!" he proclaimed, and Grampa Cow Tom's grin in response was as wide as Rose had ever seen.

"We Creeks, proper," he said.

She thought the two men ready to hug, to lock arms in satisfaction to commemorate the moment, but they held back from that public display.

"We can't drink, and we can't fiddle. How we gonna mark the largeness of the occasion?" asked Uncle Harry.

"Remember Florida? That military parade?" Grampa Cow Tom said, pulled into the excitement. "We could rig one up our own self, with marching. Decorate the mule. All the little ones taking a part. Mr. Lincoln freeing the slaves, winning the war, the Creek Council meeting, and us, brought in as members of the tribe. Mix in some Creek stomp-dancing. How about that? And food. Whatever we have."

Rose held her breath, waiting to see if this met with Harry Island's approval. Even Gramma Amy, whose job it was to make the food last, parceling out stingy portions today in anticipation of tomorrow's want, paused motionless.

"Perfect," Uncle Harry said. "Long as the part I play is head of the Creek Council."

"Then let's get to work," her grandfather said. He gave Rose a playful pinch on her cheek. "What say we choose Rose here to carry the flag? We make our own traditions."

Rose could barely recall such pride and happiness.

Chapter 42

Rose found a clean break in the fence line and doubled back on her pony to discover one of the laying hens gone. She checked the inside of the henhouse, the condition of the setting straw, mostly undisturbed, and noted the faint trace of footprints in the mudded grounds outside.

"Doesn't look like coyote," she reported back to Grampa Cow Tom. "More likely wild Indian, hungry and on the prowl."

"Not sure what annoys me more, repairing this fence or the prospect of a meatless supper down the road."

"But chicken tonight, still? For the white men?"

Her grandfather grunted. "Agriculture agents. From the United States government."

"Agriculture?"

"Farming. Crops. They say they want to see how different tribes use the land."

"They'll try to make us change our ways?" asked Rose.

"That's my Rose. Always suspicious." Grampa Cow Tom removed the broken fence post, putting the plank off to the side. "The agents don't present threat or gain for us at this moment, but we'll show off a little anyway what we've managed in the three years since war's end. You have to learn how to talk to white people, Rose. Don't give them too much power, but don't cause them such unease they feel the need to respond in kind. Remember, keep to your own, but curry favor when and where you can. You never know when a friend comes in handy, and with the government, you can never be sure what they might be up to. So, hen lost or no, tonight we offer chicken to our guests."

"I best be getting back to the house to help," said Rose. "Ma'am's on the third day of a fresh batch of *sofki* and everyone's cleaning the ranch house top to bottom." Rose ran her fingers through her pony's mane. Her grandfather had returned not long ago from a month at Fort Smith in Arkansas, representing the Creek Freedmen. He'd been in a good mood since. "Or I could stay and help you mend the fence."

Her grandfather hesitated. "A few minutes

more out here won't hurt," he said.

"Ma'am won't like it though."

"You're with me."

Rose set straightaway to the shed, took up the stump ax, and split four lengths of wood for fence rails. She brought them back to where her grandfather waited.

"I won't always be here, Rose."

She froze. "Where you going now?"

"My time on this earth runs down. Don't fret. Not now, but someday."

Rose struggled to find words, but none came. She couldn't imagine a world without her grandfather in it. She thought of the night at Fort Gibson when Grampa Cow Tom came back to their camp and found Granny Sarah still and dead, and the bottomless well of his grief. She thought of the brightness Grampa Cow Tom brought to her days, no matter where they lived, how good or how bad the condition. She was sixteen, and sometimes she felt as if her grandfather was the only man who knew her. Who truly loved her. Who would ever love her.

"You understand the land, Rose. The sacrifices we have to make for the land. Land, family, friends, tribe. That's all we have. That's all we need."

"Are you sick, Grampa?"

"Not sick. Just getting you ready." He positioned the split rail in the fence, notching the wood in the groove at the post. "Go on. I'll finish up here. Help your mama now."

All the way to the ranch house, Rose thought about the last three years, how hard they'd all worked to build up this ranch. For the first time in years, there were younger men with them to help — some straggled back from the war with a limp or a distractedness or a new worldliness to their face, but useful.

Even so, her grandfather continued to include her in his everyday doings whenever he was home, whether tending cows or ginning grain or riding the fence line. Occasionally, he even let her sit off to the side when he met with other men, talking of the future of Canadian Colored Town. Her grandfather was an important man here, which made Rose feel important too. And time spent with Grampa Cow Tom meant less time under the disapproving eye of Ma'am.

Small puffs of dirt exploded in the air each time Gramma Amy whacked one of the rugs and quilts hung over a taut clothesline behind the ranch house. Rose waved to her grandmother as she passed. One of her aunts scraped at dirt caked on the outside of the real glass windows and, pail in hand, soaped them down after with a coarse scrap of rag. The moment Rose entered through the back door of the ranch house, her eyes teared and she smelled a sharp burn. Her sister Elizabeth sat by the fireplace, where the big, black pot hung above the flames, humming, playing by herself, some private game with beanbags.

Rose rushed to take up the long spoon and tried to stir the bubbling mixture. Great chunks of charred corn began to surface, and the burned smell overwhelmed. "Elizabeth, haven't you been tending at all?"

Elizabeth looked up, guilty. "Ma'am's going to be mad," she said.

"Didn't Ma'am tell you to stir?"

Elizabeth's eyes grew narrow and her chin quivered.

"I'm sorry, Rose."

Both Gramma Amy and Ma'am came at a run into the room at the same time, sniffing at the air. Gramma Amy carried in the quilts she'd cleaned and Ma'am's arms were full of firewood.

"Smells like the whole house is going up in flames," Ma'am said, as her grandmother threw open the doors to let the smoke out.

"*Sofki* looks to be ruined, Ma'am," Rose said.

Elizabeth started to cry in earnest, great gasping sobs, equal parts fear and performance. She positioned herself as far behind Rose as she could, trying to hide herself, grabbing hold of Rose's tunic and refusing to let go.

"It's my fault, Ma'am. I should have watched her," Rose said, diverting her mother's disapproval from Elizabeth.

"Three days wasted, and no time to start again," Ma'am said to Rose. "Short on looks and long on clumsy. No husband will want the likes of you."

"Malinda," Gramma Amy said sharply. "Enough. We've time to make corn stew instead."

"Always off doing man's work," Ma'am grumbled. "Putting on airs, trailing behind Papa Cow Tom. Well, there's corn in the crib for you to start over by yourself. Be done by supper."

"Yes, Ma'am."

"First take this mess and throw it to the hogs."

Elizabeth sniffled. "I want to help Rose."

"See what you've done to her?" said Ma'am, prying Elizabeth from behind Rose. "No need making the same mistake twice.

Elizabeth, you come with me, help me put fresh linen on the beds."

Ma'am led Elizabeth from the room, the girl piteous in the looks she threw Rose over her shoulder.

Rose wrapped her hands in dishrags and wrestled the hot, heavy pot off the fireplace latch. She heard the sizzle as the pot brushed her arm, and the jolting sting threw her off-kilter. She managed to right the pot before she spilled too much of the spoiled *sofki* on the kitchen floor, but an angry pucker marked the burn spot on her skin. She scanned frantically to make sure her mother hadn't seen. But it was only Gramma Amy in the room.

Her grandmother took a look at her arm. "Not too bad," she said. "We'll cool it down with cold water from the stream and put honey on it."

"What'd I do?" Rose asked. "What'd I ever do to her?"

"Your mama's wrong. Isn't true, the things she says. Those are her private devils talking. Started long ago. You just weren't what she dreamed up, is all."

Gramma Amy let her hand linger on Rose's arm. Her touch was firm and warm.

"You go on fix yourself up and get the corn started. I'll clean up here, take the rest to the hogs, and we'll get another pot going in no time. Go on, now. The white men be here soon enough."

CHAPTER 43

"Looking forward to supper," said one of the white men. He was taller than the other by almost a full head length.

From the first, the talky agent, heavily whiskered and a bit overbearing, took the lead between the two overnight guests, and tried to awe all of the family with his position as an agricultural agent. He addressed her grandfather as if they were longtime acquaintances, confidants in a conspiracy.

"Look here. How'd you come by so much tamed land so quick after the loss and want of war? Cows, corn, cotton, chickens. We seen many a citizen, Creek freedman or full-blood, trying to scratch a second-rate living from the soil, one step from starvation."

Rose watched her grandfather puff up, gravitating to the sound of admiration, welcoming a chance to impress.

"First time I come to Indian Territory was over thirty years ago, in a scouting party from Alabama. I know this territory, where's the good land and the bad, and so long as Creek law allows me all the land I put under fence and cultivation, I will run my cattle and plant my crops to the better of any man."

The agents exchanged a look, trying to figure him out. Rose enjoyed their puzzlement. Sometimes she couldn't figure him out either, so how could they? Absently, she touched the raw, red, tender spot of the fresh burn on her arm, now sticky with honey administered by her grandmother. The wound was minor. Her grandfather came to the kitchen shortly after their guests arrived and plucked her from her tasks, telling Ma'am he needed Rose as well as the younger men as he escorted their guests the width and breadth of the ranch.

"We put improvements back to the land, and the land before our comfort," her grandfather went on. "Took our headright money from Fort Gibson and saw it to good use. This ranch ate up $150 in cash and trade, building that herd, improving the dwellings, managing the fences."

They did work hard. But Rose also knew luck was on their side in the favorable weather of the last two planting seasons and a chance encounter with an old cattle trader her grandfather dealt with before the flight to Fort Gibson. The trader staked them a good deal on two steers and a dairy cow in exchange for almost every cent of their early monthly allocations distributed through the Creek government. If these agents had seen them then, ragged and gone hungry to feed the livestock and buy seed in hopes of a future, they'd sing a different tune.

The agents nodded their approval. "What kind of tools you using?"

Rose tagged along as Grampa Cow Tom toured them around the vast storage shed near the cotton field, more spacious than the farmhouse, eager to show his cache of seeds and assortment of farm tools.

The agents walked the shed, remarking on the crops, the carding machine, Gramma Amy's spinning wheel, fingering the tools and the spent corn around the mortar and wooden pestle. Far from the nearest mill, they pounded their own corn, ginned the cotton with their fingers, and carded by hand before Rose and the other women spun.

"You work at a disadvantage," the tall agent finally said. "In our travels, we see farmers nearer the States use more modern tools. Cherokees and Quapaws especially."

The other agent nodded in agreement.

Rose began to wonder if the short man had a tongue to speak at all.

"Can you deny results?" asked her grandfather, defensive. "Does modern beget taller corn or better payout of cotton? What fool bellyaches about old tools that yet yield bumper crops when the newfangled is not on hand or comes only with unneeded cost?"

The agent gestured toward the old plow in the corner of the storage shed to make his argument. The wrought-iron plow point, from constant filing, was worn all the way to the moldboard. "This puts more work on both steer and man," he said. "Might break the soil, but difficult to cut the furrow deep enough for seed without another go-round. There's easier ways now, a Wood Patent plow, iron, with parts that interchange."

Her grandfather seldom flared for strangers, but his offense took root.

"Easier isn't always possible," he said. His voice rose. "Easier isn't always better. The prairie needs breaking up, and that old bull-plow does the breaking."

It seemed as though the tall agent intended to go one better, but then he changed his tone entirely. "You have single-handedly worked a miracle here," he said.

Her grandfather calmed himself in the

417

ensuing silence. But Rose knew Grampa Cow Tom as they did not, and where they saw a tetchy family patriarch, she saw the idea of a plow that could till a furrow without a broke back at the end of the day fix in his mind.

"Time to move along to supper," her grandfather said. "My wife awaits us."

They adjourned to the ranch house, the agents now full of flattery and small talk. Rose shifted easily into her role of preparing food and serving, doing her best to avoid Ma'am's gaze and stay out of her reach, and shepherding Elizabeth around the kitchen, helping her with her tasks. Her sister was recovered, excited by the visitors, as if the burned *sofki* never happened.

The corn stew came out fine, thick and seasoned, with chunks of chicken, and Gramma Amy prepared cha-cha and Indian bread, followed by strong, black coffee.

"Quite a place you got here," said the quiet agent. "Good food, stable household." He paused. "I'm wondering about another helping of that stew."

Rose served him up another plate, and the agents continued their probing, including a few questions by the shorter man, who found his voice after all, perhaps loosened by his third helping. The agents complimented the household, the neatness of the handstitched quilts on every bed, the sturdiness of the tables and chairs, the cleanliness of the farmhouse, the harmony of several generations under a single roof. They were pleased to hear of the nearby schoolhouse, where her grandfather paid for the teacher's salary from his own pocket, and were impressed when Gramma Amy's potion calmed the quiet man's stomach upset, with no physician nearer than Fort Gibson, thirty-three miles distant. Her grandfather's earlier temper evaporated.

"This Wood Patent plow, you happen to come across any in these parts, used?" Grampa Cow Tom asked.

"There's a few around. North Fork. Muskogee. Don't know whether they're wanting to sell or not. Creek agency village be a good place to start."

"Might look into that," her grandfather said. "We're waiting on our share of Creek tribal money, supposed to pass on to us any day now."

When supper was over, the agents made faces at the baby until she smiled a gummy smile, enjoyed a smoke with Grampa Cow Tom and his son-in-law while Rose and the other women cleaned up, and retired to the storage shed, where they slept the night on hay, covered by hand-turned quilts.

The agents left the next morning, and Rose tackled her day with new resolve. After so many hardscrabble years, first in Fort Gibson and then starting anew, she imagined a breathing space. They were doing fine, and with the Creek payout soon to come, the family could put money away in reserve in case fortune turned her back on them with failed crops or animal disease or poor weather.

The only nagging botherment was recalling the white man's words, that her grandfather had worked a single-handed miracle. Without question, they could not have come so far without Grampa Cow Tom, but he was often absent at the ranch in his role as linguister, traveling for days and weeks and months at a time, particularly in that first year after Fort Gibson. It was the women who put so much sweat into the ranch, who kept everything going, whether household or crop or cow or trade, always in attendance. It was Gramma Amy, and Ma'am, and the aunts, and yes, Rose herself, her hands calloused, her skin burned and bruised from whatever needed doing.

Their ranch might be a miracle, but it was not single-handed.

Chapter 44

Rose examined the four-year-old cow, dewlap swollen just above her front legs, matching lumps the size of small grapefruits on both sides. Their cow didn't present sick, still eating and drinking.

Her grandfather waited alongside her in the corral, leaning against the split-rail fence. He'd barely paid attention all morning, every movement stiff and slow. After the agriculture agents left, he'd caught a lingering head cold and slept away most of four days. Today was his first day back to working the herd.

"Separate her out for a day or two and keep an eye on her?" Rose asked.

"That'll do, then."

Grampa Cow Tom didn't offer up anything more, no advice on how to dose the animal, or a guess how long before she could rejoin the herd.

"You feeling well?" Rose asked. She'd

heard Gramma Amy and Ma'am talking about her grandfather, how easily he tired now and how his legs pained him in his sleep. They worried he'd come to the point in life of feeling his years.

"As good as I got a right, I guess," he said.

"Still thinking on that plow?"

"My back is past working furrows, but it'd be great relief for the sons-in-law. No more filing down that metal point that can barely hold an edge, no more reforging the broken wedge, no more coaxing furrows from first-pass ground nicks. Yes. I surely would like to retire that old bull-plow."

"We have money enough?"

"Central Creek Council holds $200,000 from Washington for the tribe. Money should flow through the chiefs in the next day or so to all Loyal Creek citizens according to the Dunn roll. Then we have money enough."

Every member of her family was on the roll of Negro Creeks eligible for payments. She wanted to see her name for herself, Rose Cow Tom, officially printed, but her grandfather assured her he'd studied it with his own eyes.

A light rain fell, and the fields were mudded. She led the ailing cow toward the barn, and halted as a hacking cough seized her

422

grandfather. Two horses pulling a buckboard suddenly appeared and bore down on them at a gallop. The wagon, sturdy and late vintage, was most likely Ketch Barnett's, who favored the fancy in his women and his transport both. Uncle Harry yelled her grandfather's name the while.

"Cow Tom! Cow Tom!"

There were four in all, Harry Island, Ketch Barnett, Monday Durant, and her uncle John, all four a-scowl. Rose and her grandfather waited on them to cover the short distance.

"They stripped us from the roll," Uncle Harry said. He planted himself in front of her grandfather as if daring him to turn aside. "Gone, like smoke to the heavens. There's to be no money for freedmen."

"That can't be," said her grandfather. He wiped at his forehead with his kerchief. "I saw the list myself, last week. Almost two thousand African Creeks."

"And I saw the telegram last night," said Uncle Harry. "Sent by special messenger from Fort Smith, from Commissioner of Indian Affairs. Freed people excluded from payout."

"Agent Dunn himself prepared the roll. He's on our side," he said. "Two hundred thousand dollars to sell the western section of Creek lands to the United States, divvied up per head to all on the Dunn roll, full-blood, mixed-blood, or freedman, no distinction. Equal."

"Agent Dunn isn't here. The money's to be distributed tomorrow against treaty, while Agent Dunn is in Washington. Those buzzards expect us to lay down without complaint while they throw dirt over our face."

"We can appeal," said Grampa Cow Tom. Her grandfather dropped his kerchief in the mud, forgotten now, and Rose retrieved it. "Creek Council . . ."

"Council voted already, persuaded by the Confederate Creeks. Any excuse to keep us out of the tribe. And the superintendent went along too. Now there's two layers of white men saying no, one here in Indian Territory, and one at Fort Smith. Doesn't matter what's right."

Rose's mind raced to keep up. These were the most powerful men she knew, all part of Creek Council. Her grandfather was in the House of kings. Her uncle Harry in the House of Warriors. They represented all five of the Creek colored towns.

"We're outnumbered," Uncle Harry said. "And we been outplayed."

"The treaty —" began her grandfather.

"No need schooling me on the treaty," snapped Uncle Harry. "Wasn't I there? Weren't we all there?"

"I'm talking the Seminole treaty," said Grampa Cow Tom. "Almost same as the Creek treaty as to freedmen and our right to Washington money. Blazes, they used our wording. Same words, same superintendent, and their freedmen already got their payout for selling Seminole lands to the United States, no argument." Her grandfather threw up his hands in disgust. "How many times we need prove to be Creek citizen?"

"Many as it takes," said Uncle Harry. He spit in the mud. "Or should we lay down and die?"

Harry calmed himself and took hold of her grandfather's arm, gently, as if cradling a baby. "Washington is the only place to right this," he said. "We come to ask you to go there to protest. Your name still carries currency."

"An old man past his prime?" said her grandfather. Except for Uncle John, the men surrounding Rose were all old guard, entered the sixth decade of life. "If the distribution comes tomorrow, the hour is already too late."

"An old man?" Uncle Harry repeated, laying thick his mockery.

"Who else goes?" Grampa Cow Tom asked.

"Two is enough, so long as departure is swift," said Harry. "The rest stay behind, put up a fuss here, give time to pull Washington in."

Her grandfather said nothing.

"I'm going," Uncle Harry volunteered. "Old or no. Have you forgotten the pledge? One last time, brother."

Rose saw a flicker of a smile play at the corners of her grandfather's lips. He finally nodded.

"One last time," he agreed.

To Rose's ear, her grandfather didn't sound defeated at all.

What she heard was excitement.

CHAPTER 45

The train jerked and gave a mighty heave.
It had been a long trip north to the station
at Lawrence, Kansas, and Cow Tom relaxed
as best he could against the stiff back of the
wooden bench. Through grimed windows,
he watched the monotony of flat landscape
pass, slow at first, then with increased
speed, as they put more distance between
themselves and home. He still fumed, but
Harry, in the adjacent seat, had fallen asleep
almost immediately after they'd stowed their
bags and settled in the Negro car. Harry's
mouth was open, his breath a whistling
monotone, his neck at a precarious angle,
his head resting on his own shoulder, and
he showed no signs of waking anytime soon.

When Cow Tom tired of the sameness of
the outside view, he assessed the interior of
the stuffy train, the multiple cigar burns on
the wood, the squeaking of the wheels, the
acrid smell of smoke from the boilers that

drifted into the car from the rear door of the train. They'd been traveling for four days, by horse, and by wagon, but neither Cow Tom's mind nor body could rest. This was potentially the most important job he'd ever undertaken, bigger than chief of the Creek Freedmen, which was, after all, merely a title, and a title couldn't stave off a lifetime of work coming unraveled.

His back ached from sitting upright in the uncomfortable seats so long, his fingers swollen and tender, his knees cranky, whether from use or disuse he could no longer tell. He remembered his year of tracking and interpreting in the swamps of Florida as a young man, when he could fall asleep anywhere for minutes or hours and wake refreshed, when danger meant hostile attacks or disease or, if truly unlucky, scalping. Nowadays danger meant the potential for falling and the breaking of bones, the ever-present aches and pains of age, the tender stomach that craved the blandness of *sofki* rather than a full bowl of rich venison stew.

Still, there was excitement being on the move with Harry, pitting their collective will and wits one final time against the disloyal Creeks trying to cheat freedmen of their place in the tribe. If there was a last stand to make, he welcomed making it with Harry Island. They had both done better than most Creek or African Creek, he with his modest ranch and Harry as interpreter in a store in North Fork, and they were part of Creek Council. Now when they visited, talk turned more toward days of old and shared adventures than current affairs, something missing. It didn't seem possible the kick of the old days was gone forever.

The train lurched again and, amid screeching, came to a stop. Harry jerked awake, and narrowed his eyes in disapproval.

"This train stops more than it goes," he grumbled.

"Something on the tracks again, I expect," Cow Tom replied.

He heard his own gruffness, and was glad Harry didn't shut his eyes to go back to sleep. Harry was hatless, and although dark-ish strands streaked the hair pulled back tight and fastened with a leather cord at the back of his neck, for the most part his long, coarse hair was grayed. A cloudy halo rimmed the pupils of his eyes, and he squinted often, especially when in direct sun, but his mind was as sharp as the first time Cow Tom met him. Cow Tom compared the Harry before him now, shorter, fleshy, with sag to his jowls and slowness to his movements, with the young Harry of their youth, and conceded how both of them had changed. When did they become old men?

"No need going sour," Harry said. His friend always could read him well. "We'll get there the same time whether sitting here or up front."

"We've the right to sit where we want," said Cow Tom, "and I could sure use a cushion about now."

Odd, hotheaded Harry consoling him instead of the other way around. Time did, indeed, change many things. They hadn't objected when relegated to the last car on the train, the color of their skin trumping the cost of their train ticket, and they settled into the dirty carriage restricted to Negro, little more than a boxcar. No words were spoken on the platform as the tight-lipped station agent barred access to the forward cars, he and Harry in instant and silent agreement. They needed to arrive in Washington without incident, where the real work waited to be done. A few days of injustice and discomfort was the price.

"Why so tetchy?" asked Harry.

Cow Tom lived in reflections now. They thought him a man of influence, Amy and his children and grandchildren, his sons-in-law, the people of Canadian Colored Town, his colleagues at Council. The clock had wound down on what he could yet accomplish. What if he failed, and became pitiable in their eyes?

"Our task is big," said Cow Tom.

"I'm more worried about these wasted hours while the blamed train sits here on the tracks. We can't beat them if we don't get to Washington," said Harry.

As if Cow Tom needed reminding what was at stake. "Long as we get there before Council figures out we're gone," he said. "I hope Washington listens."

"We have to make them listen," said Harry.

They left the train and regrouped outside the station, figuring how best to find a place to stay and start their search for the senator. A neatly dressed colored man in a suit and small cravat approached them.

"You gentlemen need transportation?" he said. "A nickel gets you and your bags wherever you need to be."

"Congress. You know where that is?" asked Harry.

The man looked doubtful. He scanned Cow Tom and Harry, from their deerskin leggings to their turbans, forming some opinion Cow Tom feared wasn't favorable. "I can carry y'all to where Congress meets, but you might need more particulars. What's your business?"

"We're here to find Mr. Harlan. Mr. James Harlan. Senator James Harlan," said Cow Tom.

"I don't know any Mr. Harlan," the man said.

"He's high up," said Harry. "Works for the government."

"That describes a lot of men in this town," the man said. "I can carry you to the buildings where most politicians set up offices. They're close to the Senate chambers."

"Good enough," said Harry. "We have to start somewhere."

"That nickel is up front."

Cow Tom fished a shield nickel from his coin bag and paid the driver, which the man inspected and pocketed before throwing their small bags in the back of the carriage. The carriage parts were old, but clean and cared for, and once Cow Tom and Harry climbed in, the man clicked the pitiful city horse to a sluggish pace.

The streets of Washington were nothing like Cow Tom imagined. On wide man-made avenues they passed several multistory buildings rising unexpectedly out of the mud, tightly girded within elevated wooden-planked sidewalks for long stretches. They saw mostly white men, almost all hatted, in shirtsleeves and in suits, but there were also black men, and women too, dressed fine, purposeful, and as far as he could tell, treated as proper citizens. His hopes rose.

The young man called over his shoulder from the front seat as the horse kept a steady, clip-clop pace. "What's your business?" he asked.

"We're from out West, Indian Territory," said Cow Tom. He was anxious to make this man understand the urgency of their important mission. "Come to Washington to speak up for the freedmen in the Creek Nation."

"That explains the clothes."

They'd brought their best, but suddenly Cow Tom understood the roughness of their coats, the foreignness of moccasins and leggings and turbans common at home. These were city people, even the carriage driver, black like them, but different. He was refined. Cow Tom was a good judge of people. By bearing, by speech, by the way the young man looked him directly in the eye, he was free long before war's end, familiar with liberty, wearing it like armor. Both he and Harry projected the same, and he was pleased at the brotherhood.

"This isn't such a big town," the brown-skinned man said, "but I don't know of any Mr. Harlan."

Cow Tom didn't agree. Washington was big and crowded and chaotic, full of movement and activity, everyone with their place carved, whether teamsters loading and unloading wagons, jacketed men spitting tobacco juice in the dusty street, or women walking parasoled on the wooden sidewalk.

The carriage driver was chatty. "With the Reconstruction and all, for the first time, I been carrying colored over to the Congress now, as gentlemen, just like white. Didn't used to be that way. This James Harlan. He one of those?"

"No," said Cow Tom. "He's white. Used to be Senator, but no more. We worked with him years back. As translators. He used to approve treaties from the Washington side."

"Well, if you gentlemen plan to stay the night after finding Mr. Harlan, and have need of a place to stay, my sister rents out rooms in her house in the colored section of town. Meals included. Reasonable and clean."

The carriage driver dropped them off in front of a cluster of small buildings and helped them unload their bags, and agreed

434

to come back in a few hours to carry them to his sister's boardinghouse. The pace of the city unnerved Cow Tom, so many men coming in and out of each of the buildings with such purpose, as if they had no time to waste.

A white man carrying a small satchel had stopped and openly stared in amusement at Cow Tom and Harry as they sorted through their things and tried to figure out their next move. His checkered three-piece suit was a loose fit, a bit of a mismatch for his slender shoulders, as he was a small man, but he looked respectable in his pointed leather shoes, and seemed in no great hurry to be one place or the other. Cow Tom approached him.

"Good afternoon," Cow Tom said.

"Good afternoon," the man responded. He didn't seem to be unfriendly, only overly interested in the spectacle of their arrival in the capital city.

"My partner and I are looking for Senator Harlan. Would you know where he is?"

"What department?"

Cow Tom shook his head in confusion, trying to puzzle out what the man was asking.

The man talked louder and much slower. "Freedmen's Bureau?" the man guessed, drawing out every syllable. "That would be the War Department."

"No, no," said Cow Tom, "the Bureau of Indian Affairs. Department of Interior."

The man looked back and forth between Cow Tom and Harry without comment, not once but several times, as if repeatedly staring at their moccasins and turbans would suddenly reveal some inner truth to him.

"Indian Affairs, eh?" he finally said. "And I thought I'd seen everything."

"Do you know where the Department of the Interior is?" asked Cow Tom, as politely as he could manage. He wasn't sure why this stranger was willing to be so helpful, but they had little time to wonder.

"I do," the man said. "Can't say I know a Senator Harlan, but least I can get you to the right building. We can walk from here."

"Obliged," said Cow Tom.

"Follow me," the man said, as they hoisted their bags to carry. And then, "Wait'll I tell the missus about this."

They were glad for the man's assistance, who steered them to the right building, but not sorry to see him go on his way once they found themselves in a warren of offices claimed as the Department of the Interior. From there, Cow Tom and Harry were referred and directed and passed from hand to hand, until they convinced a man sitting behind a wooden desk stacked high with papers to let them in to see former treaty commissioner James Harlan himself. The assistant personally led them into a small and drafty office, one of many along a long hall.

"Senator Harlan," Cow Tom said in introduction. "Cow Tom and Harry Island. We worked on several treaties for the Creeks with you? Last time at Fort Smith in '66?"

"Yes, yes," Harlan said. "Ex-senator now. Ex-secretary of the interior too, for that matter. Come in." He eyed their baggage, their clothes, dusty from the long trip. "I remember you both."

He invited them to sit in the cramped office space. They exchanged a few pleasantries, and memories, until the senator pulled out his timepiece, flicking open the case to check the hour.

"So. What makes you seek me out now?" he asked.

Harry took the lead. "We thought to get to the current secretary of the interior, to right a grievous wrong."

"The secretary of the interior," repeated Harlan. He seemed cautious, a politician's nonstatement. "What is the wrong?"

Harry launched into the actions of the

renegade Creeks in violation of the treaty, and the omission of the freedmen from the payout, and Cow Tom added the name of the new commissioner in Indian country who looked the other way when freedmen were dropped from the rolls.

"I see," said Harlan. He leaned forward, fully engaged now, his timepiece forgotten. "Both the secretary and the commissioner are Andrew Johnson's appointees."

"Yes?" Cow Tom waited for him to explain.

"The president is no friend of the freedmen, and his appointments reflect his thinking. You'll make no headway with either the secretary or the commissioner. But you may have come at exactly the right time. This could prove useful for us."

"Us?"

"Radical Republicans. Reconstructionists. A year ago, there would have been nothing we could do, but now we have a majority in Congress. Two-thirds, enough to overturn Johnson's vetoes and pass civil rights legislation. The Senate came one vote shy of impeaching Johnson last week. Yes, exactly the right time, just what we need to throw fuel on the anti-Johnson fire."

The senator seemed almost giddy at the prospect, and Cow Tom felt their cause suddenly swept up into some larger fight he was only beginning to understand. But Cow Tom was a politician too, in the Creek government, and understood there could be several different paths to victory. What matter how or why it happened, if they could come away with reinstatement?

"There are men for you to meet," Harlan said. Once again he eyed the bags. "Are you staying in town? We'll need you to testify in front of the Senate's Committee on Indian Affairs. As soon as we can arrange it."

Cow Tom wasn't nervous, even when he was led into the cavernous room to testify, even when he saw the collection of white men, somber and forbidding in their dark suits at the front of the large space, and he and Harry were led to sit behind an opposing table, as if facing accusers. It all came down to this, and he was ready. He had been making himself ready for fifty-eight years. He'd practiced his arguments for several days, consumed by laying out an irrefutable case, but a sudden single image crowded out all else. His mother's port-stained face, and her insistence that he was special. This was his moment.

"We come to talk about Article Two of the 1866 treaty between the United States government and the Indian nations," he began.

One of the senators on the panel had a horn trumpet to his ear, and a colleague at his elbow repeated almost everything Cow Tom said, as soon as he said it. It reminded Tom of his linguister days, but here it was translation of English into louder English.

"Can't say I ever heard of an Indian of African descent," the senator with the ear trumpet interrupted in a booming voice. He was a very large man, wearing a light-colored suit, barely able to fit in a single seat.

"That's why we came to Washington, sir, so you can see with your own eyes," said Cow Tom. "We exist, there are many of us, we're citizens of the Creek Nation, and we're part of the treaty you already approved."

Cow Tom's boldness elicited a chuckle, even from the almost-deaf senator, once the remark was repeated to him.

In the more respectful silence that followed, Cow Tom made his case for treaty violation, point by point, and ended with the statement Senator Harlan insisted would surely get the Radical Republican majority on their side.

"We assert that presidential appointees

are helping the Confederate Creeks to deprive us of our promised funds," Cow Tom concluded.

He heard murmurs of outraged whispering as he returned to his seat. They were excused from the room, and Senator Harlan saw them out to the hall while the committee decided whether to take up their claim.

"You did well," he said. "Now we wait."

It was only then that Cow Tom's nerves started in, once his testifying was done and they sat on a bench in the drafty hall.

"Leastways this time you didn't have to give up a body part," Harry joked.

Two hours passed before word came out that there had been a unanimous vote.

"The senator from Kansas brought a resolution before the Senate," Senator Harlan told them, "that the secretary of the interior must inform the Senate, as soon as possible, why a large number of persons registered as Creek Indians by the Creek agent in the spring of 1867 were stricken from said rolls and payment of their per capita dividend refused." He clapped Cow Tom heartily on the back, and then Harry, his delight too big to hide. "Let President Johnson try to ignore that."

The pronouncement was only the beginning of a long process — Cow Tom knew that — but he and Harry had exposed the Confederate Creeks' trick to the light. They had done all they could here, and needed to get back home. They might be caught in the middle of a bigger battle being waged in Washington, but they'd fought for what was theirs.

Cow Tom only hoped it was enough.

Chapter 46

The morning passed slowly, full of the usual chores and necessaries on the ranch, but long before noon, someone set the triangle bell to ringing. It was too early for the midday meal, but whoever continued to work the triangle, long and insistent, intended everyone to come to the house. Rose was in the henhouse, her apron full of the day's collection of eggs, and she came running. Her grandfather was at the triangle, a smile so wide on his face she dialed back her alarm.

Her grandfather had been off to himself all morning, some mystery afoot. Yesterday, he'd disappeared to meet with the Indian agent, but when she tried to talk to him, he waved her off, in the highest of humor.

He stood tall by the long wooden table in the kitchen, Gramma Amy beside him, and beckoned them round. Rose emptied her apron of the eggs in the kitchen. There was a great drying of hands on smocks and questioning looks, and Uncle John picked at a clump of mud from the pasture stuck to his moccasin. Once family was accounted for, all seven of them residing under one roof, her grandfather held up his two-fingered hand, as if calling a meeting to order. His hair had gone completely gray now, yet he seemed an overeager young boy with a secret too big to keep to himself.

"Last year, Harry Island and I went to Washington, DC," he began.

All eyes were on him. Rose knew the look well. He waited in silence until satisfied everyone had shown proper respect, and finally pulled an envelope from the inside pocket of his old cotton work jacket.

"Seventeen dollars and fifty-seven cents," Grampa Cow Tom announced.

Seventeen, thought Rose. Her age, at least for six more days until her birthday. She thought for a moment he meant to recognize the coming of her eighteenth year, but this was something larger, more significant than that.

He placed a small stack of money on the wooden in front of him, smoothing each bill as he gave it its own space on the tabletop, placing coins beside the bills in an exaggerated flourish. The bills were still crisp and uncreased. He held up the top paper certificate.

"This one is worth ten dollars," her grandfather said. He was careful to handle the bill by one edge.

All of them crowded closer. Elizabeth reached out to touch the money, but one quick swat on the arm from Gramma Amy stopped her, and she drew back, pouting. Rose interlaced her fingers with her sister's, and Elizabeth settled down.

"Who is that man?" Rose asked, pointing to one of the bills. A stern-faced man dominated the left side of the note.

"Same question I asked the Indian agent." He held up the bill. "That one is Mr. Daniel Webster. He's dead."

"Who is Mr. Webster?" Gramma Amy asked.

"I don't know," her grandfather confessed. "But the white man thinks he's important." He held the bill for closer inspection, though no one was allowed to touch the tender except him. "And the woman here is an Indian princess, Pocahontas." Her grandfather pointed at what looked like an eagle beginning flight at the bottom. "This is a funny one. Turn it upside down and the eagle becomes a donkey. The Indian agent called it the jackass note."

He performed the trick a few times until everyone seemed satisfied they had seen an eagle turn into a floppy-eared donkey, and he moved on to the next piece of currency, a crisp five-dollar bill with a scowling white man in one corner and a pioneer family and hunting dog in the center.

"This is one of the white man's presidents," Grampa Cow Tom said, pointing to the small portrait of a caped man with a sour face and unruly mane of wild white hair. "Andrew Jackson. No friend to the Indian, that one. He's dead too. I asked for Abraham Lincoln instead, but the Indian agent said it didn't work like that."

Her grandfather laid out a two-dollar bill, of odd greenish-brown color, unnatural, different from the five-dollar note. It featured a sharp-nosed Thomas Jefferson in profile and powdered wig. He turned the bill over to the other side to show a white building on the reverse.

"This here is where Harry Island and I traveled," Grampa Cow Tom said, "where they make the white man's laws." His eyes grew wet. "Washington." Rose had never seen him so shaky, at least not since Fort Gibson. Her grandfather usually had control of himself, but he seemed suddenly overwhelmed. "We stood up, we argued our case. It took time, but at last, they honor the treaty between the white man's government and the Creek Nation. This is back pay for what we, as citizens of the Creek tribe, are owed. They couldn't strip us from the rolls forever."

Silence grew until Elizabeth began to fidget. "Can we see the donkey again?" she asked.

Rose pinched her arm. "Hush," she said.

Elizabeth glared at Rose and then her mother in appeal, but Ma'am gave her a warning look and Elizabeth pouted in silence.

Her grandfather continued on, producing a silvery round coin, a piece worth half of a dollar, depicting a seated woman in a flowing gown. Again, the family was allowed to look, but not touch.

But Grampa Cow Tom saved the best for last. He fanned the stack of pennies out, one at a time, until each lay flat and nested in its own copper puddle. He called everyone in the room forward by name and handed them one of the pennies, seven in all. Rose didn't know exactly what she was supposed to do with the coin. She studied the reddish-brown profile of a young woman in a headdress, a band of spiky feathers that looked almost but not quite like a proper war bonnet.

"Miss Milly?" Gramma Amy asked. She brought the coin near her face, inspecting the image more closely, and ran her finger along the small rise and fall of the coin, back and forth, as if expecting it to rub away. "A Creek chief's wife on the white man's money?"

Rose also caught the resemblance to Chief Yargee's youngest wife, at least what she looked like in profile when still very young.

"No, that's not Miss Milly. They call her Lady Liberty. Liberty, like freedom," Grampa Cow Tom said, voice aquiver. "Each keeps a coin of your own, so you remember who you are."

Rose had never touched money before, and gripped her coin in a tight fist. Gramma Amy dropped her penny into the pocket of her apron. Elizabeth flipped her penny in the air to try to catch before it hit the ground. She missed, and scrambled under the table to retrieve the spinning coin, and when she reemerged with a scuffed knee and endearing grin, she held the penny overhead in triumph.

"Your penny isn't for spending," her grandfather said to them all. "Your penny is for reminding. We are Negro, and we are Creek, not one or the other but both, and we share with the tribe. When the tribe gets, we get. It is our right. We payed our dues to the nation, suffering alongside in every Removal, every war, every betrayal."

Suddenly, her grandfather faded. He'd dealt in words all his life, spoken or unspoken, he'd formed and clarified meanings and agreements and understandings, but at this moment appeared incapable. His sudden silence drove home the import of his gift to Rose, in a way words could not, what it must mean for a man like him to give each member of his family the symbol of his life's work. She vowed to cherish her penny always, a piece of him, and keep it near.

Her grandmother pulled gently at Grampa Cow Tom's arm, sensing his changed mood. She urged him into a chair and he sat.

The room stayed silent. Not even Elizabeth made a sound.

"This is celebration," he finally said. "We're on the Creek rolls again, part of the tribe. We have received our due."

"Our due," Gramma Amy agreed.

"After taking out the pennies, that leaves us seventeen dollars and fifty cents from the back payment," he said. "We'll use this money to improve on our land."

Rose took Elizabeth's hand. Today's windfall proved what she'd always known. Her grandfather could conquer anything.

CHAPTER 47

Rose dreaded entering the tepee alone. Grampa Cow Tom demanded they construct a last way station for him distant from the main house once certain he was going to die. What was the use of all of Gramma Amy's herbs if she couldn't cure her own husband? What started with the fall off a horse riding to a Council meeting and a broken leg had become this, first the march of gangrene up the leg and now a grim procession in and out of the tepee as her grandfather said his last good-byes to every member of the family, each by each.

He'd saved her for last. Rose breathed deep until her heart's pounding slowed. She raised the flap and entered. The interior was dark, and smelled of salves and rotting flesh and something damp and musky she couldn't name. She adjusted her face into acceptance and drew closer. He looked smaller than normal on a pallet on the floor, no longer fierce, the curlicue scar on his cheek sunken in sagged flesh, his missing earflap hidden by the pillow at his head, the putrefying left leg wrapped in bandages to the thigh, his favorite buffalo pelt underneath his body.

He beckoned her forward with his two-fingered hand, and patted the cover thrown over him, expecting her to sit. She'd not thought of it before now, but he favored his bad hand, as if challenging that old injury to try to get the better of him. Gramma Amy nodded to her, as if giving a blessing, egging her forward. Her grandmother tended him in between visitors, refusing to leave his side. Grampa Cow Tom and Gramma Amy were models for Rose, their devotion to each other palpable whether together or apart.

"Amy, just leave me to talk with Rose alone, eh?" said Cow Tom.

Gramma Amy seemed surprised, but she excused herself and left, lowering the tepee flap behind her. Rose kept her arms to her sides, tight. She was alone with the man she admired most in this world, yet she was ashamed to admit, she would rather be anywhere but here.

Rose didn't want her grandfather to die. If she could give up her own life for his, she

would. He was fearless, important, respected. And what was she? Destined to be
a spinster, someone to whom things happened, not someone who claimed their own
path, like him.

"Grampa, I am so sorry," she began.

He waved off her words.

"I ever tell you how you come to your
name?"

It was as if something kneaded at her
heart like so much dough to shape. She
squeezed back tears.

"No, Grampa Cow Tom."

"Now there's so little time, I see what I
should have done." He kept her gaze in his.
"Rose."

Her name held promise when her grandfather said it.

"Was me named you Rose," he said. "A
rose of beauty."

She flinched at the pain of his words, the
cruel falsity, and the sting made her speech
harsh.

"Elizabeth has beauty. I am plain. A
scrawny chicken." Elizabeth was already
shapely, with her dimpled cheek, smooth
ebony skin, and flashing eyes.

A change came across her grandfather's
face, a sudden grimace that held for a brief
moment before disappearing. In the dim

light of the tepee, Rose couldn't tell whether he was in pain, or angry, or disappointed. But his voice, when he spoke, only sounded sad.

"From early, I had to aim higher than my name, an offhand thing tossed out to make it easier for somebody to call me. The name fit, far as it went, but I was more than a tender of cows. I was a tender of words, and of people, and master of myself. I built a path to freedom with my words. And now I see you ignoring the name I took such care to give to you. Listening to the wrong voices. Listen to me now so you can learn to listen to yourself." He struggled to pull himself more upright on the pallet, and Rose helped him settle in a new position.

"My Rose has plentiful beauty," he went on. "My Rose survived what so many others couldn't. My Rose is special, and brave enough to make her own way."

"I'm not brave," said Rose.

Grampa Cow Tom laughed. He bore the physical ravages of sickness, but his voice was light. This death business had released something in him, set him loose and free.

"Brave is only doing a thing needs doing, no matter how hard, no matter if you're not ready or you're afraid."

"I want to be brave," Rose admitted.

"My mama told me I'd be special from a small boy. It looked impossible then. But I chased after my mother's opinion my whole life long. That search served me well. She made me braver than I was."

"I'm not destined for any such thing," said Rose. Her grandfather talked of glory. She just wanted her world small. She wanted snug and safe.

"And yet you sit here and not Twin."

Grampa Cow Tom adjusted himself again on the pallet, pulling forward to sit upright, and his movement let loose a stink so sharp and unexpected from beneath the bandages that Rose's eyes watered. She coughed to cover her face, hoping he hadn't seen her wince.

"I tell you things I see, even if you do not. I won't be here to remind you later. 'Twas me, Rose. 'Twas me that carved the life I wanted, whittling at the thing till the shape came clear. Like you must do for your life now. Find your own way. Go out in the world to know what waits there, if only for one year," he said. "To Muskogee or Haskell or Okmulgee. Or beyond. Come back to this ranch after, if need be, or build another, and protect the land as best you can. Make a family of your own. Make sons. Give my Amy the great-grandsons she deserves and break the curse. You are braver than you know."

Rose could barely absorb his words. How could he know of her dream of sons? Already she played each statement back in her mind, as she knew she would for years to come, committing all of them to memory, testing each as she pondered whether she believed these things her grandfather told her about herself, if she could live away from the ranch, if she really could fashion a family of her own.

"I'm not you," Rose said, her voice small.

"Not much time remains," he said. "This body tires. But you will sit with me each day. You will listen until my voice gives out. My mother never gave me her stories, and now they are lost forevermore. I was an orphan. I blundered. I sometimes hid my fear inside like slow poison. I did things of such deep shame, I never told anyone, not even Amy. But I made my life. I chose family and tribe and fixed to that choice. I did my best to atone. And that needs to continue with you. You can make my shame right. Stand tall, Rose, and know you will be knocked down. When knocked down, there is only the matter of how to get up again. In these last days, I aim to give you the gift of my stories. All of them. Some you know. Some no one knows. Hold them. Keep them safe."

Grampa Cow Tom was her bedrock, the perfect man, above reproach, her moral compass. Rose couldn't imagine his wrong-doing, or what part she could play in righting some unshared shame. She'd sought his stories all her life, begged for them, but was uneasy at the thought of secrets big enough to change her opinion of him.

"Yes, Grampa."

"I'll tell you all, the good and the bad. Judge me, but you mustn't tell anyone else. I can't go with the shame weighing down my spirit. Promise me."

She didn't want that burden, whatever he wanted to tell her, not if it began like this. She'd rather he be what he'd always been for her. Strong. Brave. All-knowing. A hero.

"You're a great man, Grampa. Everybody knows that."

"Amy must never know. Ever. Promise."

She wasn't sure what exactly she promised. Hide his stories? All of them? Some? But still, she knew she'd do anything he asked.

"I promise."

He lay back on his buffalo hide, exhausted.

"We begin tonight. Come alone, after supper."

Rose prepared to leave him, his eyes already heavy, but he stopped her before she stood, his hand on her arm.

"One thing more. I choose you, Rose, to shoot the gun south for me," he said.

Rose couldn't believe her grandfather asked her to do this, with such honor involved. She was a twenty-two-year-old woman, not a man of the family, not an elder. And yet he invited her, as one of four he would so ask, to shoot the bullet at his funeral that would guide his way home. A lump in her throat threatened. Whoever could love her again like this once her grandfather was gone?

"A woman can't —" she began.

"We make our own tradition," Grampa Cow Tom interrupted. "Remember?"

"Ma'am won't —"

"Will you do it?"

She'd made too many promises already, promises she didn't quite understand, but keeping secrets was different from standing up to everyone and demanding to break with tradition, without him there to guide her. Rose couldn't make a false promise, not now, not to him, and yet she knew to claim this honor would require more courage than she possessed. The family would surely object, insulted she would put herself forward in such a way, at her grandfather's request or no.

She was wedged, somewhere between duty and personal failing and dread. Her grandfather had hold of her arm, waiting for her answer. She closed her eyes, tight. She couldn't speak.

Please. Please. I can't do this alone. Help me. Please.

For the first time in years, she called on Twin, as if he was no longer a place of peace in a single-stoned grave to sweep and pay tribute to, but of this world and not the next. Hers was a silent, desperate plea.

The tepee grew warmer, all things suspended. He came to her side with a swiftness that surprised her. She couldn't see Twin, of course not, she never had, but she opened her eyes and the contours of the tepee's dark interior seemed to fall away, as if she observed them from a great distance instead of close on. The kerosene lantern gave off inconsequential light, yet the blue brightness almost blinded. He was here, by her side, and Twin was fearless. Twin was wild. Twin was very, very angry. He frightened her, threatened to overwhelm her, but at least she was not alone.

"I will shoot the gun south, Grampa," she said. "I promise."

459

Chapter 48

Rose's gaze wandered upward toward the white dome atop Cane Creek Baptist Church in Canadian Colored Town, framed by the brilliant blue of the cloudless Oklahoma sky. Her grandfather built the church himself, with his own hands. She needed a moment of relief from the freshly crowded hole at her feet. Off to the right lay Twin's river stone. For years, she'd kept it free of invading weeds in summer and spent leaves in fall, but the stone without a body beneath became harder to honor. But after these last days listening to her grandfather's failing voice, raspy but steady, she had greater understanding.

Rose reclaimed herself and bowed her head, eyes closed, a proper mourner, but still she couldn't force herself to peer downward into the gaping hollow. They'd surrounded him in pine, in a six-by-four box of her uncle John's making, and now they all stood around the clotted earth, lost in their own memories. She'd tried without success yesterday to busy herself, with cooking and sewing and plucking chickens, closing her ears against the pounding of nails as they prepared his final resting place. The very thought of her grandfather enclosed and stationary in one place caused her physical pain, even though she knew the body that lay before them was only the shell of the man she'd known and depended on her entire life, nothing more now than a collection of soon-to-be-gone muscle and skin and hair ripe to slough.

"Gramma?" Rose questioned.

There was no answer. Rose felt her grandmother's heavy weight against her arm.

Rose held tight, providing a counterbalance for the gray-haired woman's stooped stance, helping her remain upright. She avoided the wide plains of her grandmother's face. She'd glanced once when first leaving the church and filing toward the cemetery, seeking out the familiarity of Gramma Amy's dark eyes, always so reassuring, so stoic, no matter the circumstance. But today, there was no trace of the daily comfort from her grandmother that Rose expected. Gramma Amy seemed lost and confused, as if unsure where she was or how she came to be standing at the lip of a yawning graveside hole with her husband shut away from her, separated after all these years by a handful of thin pine planks and the impossible gulf called death.

At Rose's elbow, Elizabeth cried softly, cloth in hand to blot at her eyes. Her little sister was still not fully grown, but even so, it was easy to decipher the telling promise of a woman's guile just below the surface, awaiting bloom. Rose resisted the urge to comfort Elizabeth, staking out these moments as her own communion with her grandfather. Let Ma'am see to Elizabeth this time.

When the moment came, she broke away from the other mourners and took her place before the open hole with the other three, all men, awaiting her turn. It had been almost easy, asserting her right to fire the gun. She'd envisioned herself as a bullet, encased in a hard shell, ready for discharge, unwavering, and calmly declared what she planned to do. And her family yielded to Grampa Cow Tom's last wish in the face of such resolve, even Ma'am, with little protest.

Her uncles shot first, and second, and then she gripped the pistol as firmly as she'd been taught and took aim toward the south. When she pulled back on the trigger, her shot rang true. After Uncle Harry fired the final bullet, she returned to her place beside her grandmother.

"Gramma Amy," she whispered again.

Her grandmother looked to her then, her face blank, no longer elder to ward, but with the fullness of giving way and letting go.

"Time for the farewell handshake."

Gramma Amy didn't budge.

"Time to throw the dirt," Rose urged, and led her to the foot of the grave. At the reminder, her grandmother shuffled forward a few steps, obedient to the sound of Rose's voice, and stooped to grab a handful of soil to throw into the open grave.

"He's gone," her grandmother said, to no one in particular.

"Yes, Gramma. Gone." She wasn't sure what else to say, what else could be said, and she helped Amy stand again as others filed past to throw their own fistfuls of dirt into the hole.

"It came too soon," Gramma Amy said.

True enough. But Rose believed her grandfather's soul already freed. He himself taught her that concept, the certainty in his voice reassuring to the girl she had been at twelve, in those terrible Fort Gibson days. Surrounded by sickness and starvation and suffering, he had described death not as a physical place but as transition, a natural next step that came for everyone.

"He's free now," Rose said, keeping judgment from her voice, but her grandmother didn't respond. *He's free because he handed his shame to me,* Rose thought, *loading me down with this burden.*

Elizabeth's turn, and Ma'am motioned her sister forward. Rose watched Elizabeth's delicate fingers release a scattering of dirt into the gaping hole, and with the effort, begin to sob, her slender shoulders shaking violently. Rose checked to be sure. Her sister's tears were genuine. Sometimes they weren't, and Elizabeth used them as a weapon, a bargaining chip that brought her more reward than punishment in getting her way, especially among men, young and old, family or stranger. Ma'am comforted Elizabeth, gathering her to her side until the short service finished and it was time to go back to the ranch house to immerse themselves in all the particulars and demands of everyday living awaiting them there.

But Elizabeth couldn't be consoled, not by Ma'am, not by Gramma Amy, not by Rose, and after each took their turn trying and failing, her mother finally put the girl to an early bed.

Rose was dead inside. She tended the big pots of bison stew and lima beans on the stove, already at simmer for the noonday meal, and prepared big bean dumplings. There would be drop-ins to the ranch all day, paying respects, and grief or no grief, everyone expected to eat. She challenged the ache of her heart by rolling out *sofki,* by hauling out a barrel of pickles from the basement, by using the clabbered milk yeast to prepare enough flatbread no matter how many visitors came. She walked into the field and harvested cucumbers, and peeled enough to start the next rendering of a twenty-gallon-barrel of cha-cha cabbage. Her hands were almost raw, and the heavier the load, the harsher the ingredient, the harder the pounding, the more she craved some task even more punishing.

She said nothing, working all day, nodding politely at those trying to engage her in conversation. But she drew no comfort. With the passing of Grampa Cow Tom came the passing of an era. For the first time since Fort Gibson, Rose thought seriously about what it might be like to live a life elsewhere, beyond the reach of this ranch house and outbuildings and barns she'd marveled at as they came up out of the ground from nothing, her grandfather's vision. She considered what daily life might be without the sounds and stink and dust of lowing cattle herds in the distance swelling in number each season before being driven eastward for sale. Whether a city might hold promise for her, even if it meant working for hire in someone else's kitchen. She gave herself the freedom to ponder what it might be to one day have something of her own, to make her own rules, instead of following someone else's plan.

In her mind, she tested the concept of distance, as Grampa Cow Tom suggested, of a journey far from the familiarity of the rutted paths of her youth, but it was too much to hold, and she had to leave it go. There was no room for grief and bravery both.

For the first time in her life, Rose harbored anger toward Grampa Cow Tom, his forcing her to question what kind of man he really was. Yet, she missed him as a fierce ache. She'd made it through the morning so far, through the preparations and the service and the condolences, unwilling to call on Twin again. He'd helped shore her up in Grampa Cow Tom's tepee, but she'd taken care not to summon him since, especially not during these last bittersweet days when her grandfather's hoarse voice spun stories of his life she'd never before heard, including the one that sent her reeling, tarnishing her image of the man she thought she knew. And she'd stood strong, and fired the gun despite Ma'am's disapproval, without Twin's aid.

But by early afternoon, her mood had fallen so low and the hurt was so crippling, Rose left the busyness of the ranch house and made the short trip back to the graveyard, to conjure Twin there. All family and visitors had left, once the hole was filled, and she was alone with the new, loose-dirt grave that was her grandfather and the false grave that was Twin. She dropped to her knees in front of Twin's smooth river stone, and closed her eyes.

"Twin, help me," she said. "Help me know how to keep on."

She waited for the signs, but there was only nothing.

"Stand with me, Twin," she implored.

She tried to make her mind clear, to give her brother room, waiting for so long she felt the shift in the air as the day advanced toward evening. Still Twin didn't come. What if Twin was escorting Grampa Cow Tom to wherever he needed to go? What if he sought revenge for shutting him out at Fort Gibson? What if she could only call him to her once, and no more? Had he abandoned her too, in this time of all times?

Emptiness threatened. She was alone.

"Damn you, Twin. I don't need you. I don't need anyone." Granny Sarah's words came back to her, and she forced them into the hostile air. "What's done is done and gone."

As if to refute her claim, images crowded in on her with the immediacy of warm flesh, spilling out faster than she could sort, a jumble of quick flashes in no particular order, one after the other. She had to open her eyes and hard-press her palms to the dirt to stop the dizzying array. A boy with a cow named Hadjo. A smashed fiddle. A bloody ear flap held aloft by a murderous Seminole. A young slave mother stolen on horseback. Creeks drowning by the hundreds. Black men signing Indian treaties. A dying black Seminole brave. A sweet courtship.

Twin might have abandoned her again, so soon after his return, she didn't know. But all she had left of Grampa Cow Tom were his stories and the promise she'd made him, and she resolved she would hold his revelations close, hoard them, lock them deep in her heart to keep what should be hidden safe. The stories were hers now, to keep her whole. Hers and no one else's. Her burden, but her refuge too. Some things weren't for sharing.

She didn't bother to brush the mud from her tunic after she found her feet, a little afraid to believe. She stood taller.

Not yet, she told herself.

She returned to the ranch house, and served the visitors and ranch hands until the last of them straggled back home or to the bunkhouse.

Not yet.

She scrubbed out all the pots and set them to dry before pulling out her evening sewing.

Only then did she give herself over to the sorting out of heroics and shame, to the slow healing, to the stories, as if Grampa Cow Tom himself was still talking to her in the tepee. She vowed to mend herself, alone, no matter how long that might take, through what he'd left behind for her.

His voice was strong.

CHAPTER 49

Time slipped past, some months at a crawl, but most vanishing in a blur, disappeared as fire smoke carried off by the wind. Looking backward, Rose characterized each year since her grandfather's passing. Year one, when rolling stabs of grief surprised and engulfed her whenever her mind fixed too long on Grampa Cow Tom's airy laugh in the death tepee or a stray recollection of the familiar hitch to his walk. Year two, and that moment of unspeakable panic when she couldn't remember whether it was her grandfather's right or left ear that bore only a stub. Year three, when she let her mind go blank, and ranch chores washed over her like one of the numbing potions in her grandmother's medicine bag. And year four, when her Gramma Amy shook her awake early, before the dawn's light.

"Let's go," Gramma Amy whispered. "Horse is already hitched."

Her grandmother bent over her, and Rose brought Gramma Amy's face into focus only inches from her own.

"Go where?" asked Rose. She rubbed at her eyes in confusion, not yet fully awake, her brain sluggish. On the other side of the bed, Elizabeth still slept soundly, her soft, whistling snore uninterrupted.

"Okmulgee," Gramma Amy whispered. "I got our breakfast in a basket."

Gramma Amy was gone as quickly as she came. Rose stumbled out of bed, threw on her day dress, laced her shoes in the darkened room, and grabbed a thick shawl. She trailed the light of Gramma Amy's lantern ahead of her toward the barn, almost slipping once in the darkness, sidestepping some small scurrying animal, probably a prairie dog. She could hardly see, but took in the crisp smells of morning, musty hay, steaming cow patties, dew. The chickens hadn't yet roused themselves, still quiet. In front of the barn, the buckboard was hitched to one of the ranch's horses, and her grandmother held the reins. Rose hurried, scrambling up the other side to sit next to her on the hard plank, gathering the folds of her dress around her.

Gramma Amy clicked them forward, and they rode for almost four hours in silence, well past first light, north along a main road. Gramma Amy finally stopped. Rose's stomach churned, both from hunger and from not knowing where they were going or why. She helped her grandmother down from the wagon. In the back was the breakfast basket and a large carpetbag satchel, fastened. Her grandmother came round to the wagon bed and reached for the basket.

"What's in the satchel?" asked Rose.

"Enough of your things to last a month," said Gramma Amy. "Should you need."

Rose's breath almost stopped in her chest. "Are you turning me out?"

"Never. You're always free to stay home or come home."

"Why won't you tell me what's in Okmulgee?" Rose couldn't keep the panic from her voice.

"You'll see soon enough."

Gramma Amy picked through the contents of the wicker basket, and pulled out a firm green apple. At Gramma Amy's demand, Rose had been baking for the past three days, and inside were four of her loaves wrapped in cloth — one each of shuck bread, sour bread, pumpkin bread, and fry bread. Rose started to unwrap the sour bread, her favorite, but Gramma Amy stopped her.

"That one's not for us," she said. "Only the fry bread."

Rose was an excellent cook, so good that Gramma Amy seldom bothered her in the kitchen anymore, having taught her all she could, but for the last few days she had fussed and hovered over Rose as Rose baked, ordering her to make batch after batch until the loaves came out perfectly.

Gramma Amy ate her apple quickly, core and all. Discomforted by the silence, Rose picked out an apple and bit into the tart fruit, and wiped away the juice that dribbled down her chin. The only thing she was sure of was that her grandmother would never do anything to hurt her. They finished off the fry bread and *puska* balls, and only then did Gramma Amy first belch and then clear her throat.

"He'd want more for you," Gramma Amy said. "From you."

"Who?" asked Rose, but she knew.

"Your grandpa set great store by you. He always bragged on the fire spirit in the girl who warned us to run to Fort Gibson."

"I'm doing my part on the ranch," said Rose, defensive. She could neither describe how much she missed Grampa Cow Tom, the heaviness of each day, nor reveal that Gramma Amy didn't know as much about her grandfather's past as she thought. She didn't want to talk of him.

Gramma Amy brushed her comment aside as if it had no import.

"Time to choose, girl. Try to be the Rose he thought you could be, or play out your days like you been doing."

"Why are we going to Okmulgee?" asked Rose.

"To get you a future," she said.

Okmulgee wasn't what Rose expected. The dirt streets were wide, and though the single-story houses were mostly built of wood and sturdy, they were haphazard, as if a random tornado deposited one here in the middle of a grassy field, and another over there by the creek. They stopped the horse at a small building with a hand-painted sign over the narrow door that said General Store. Three old Indian men slumped outside, idle in mismatched chairs, and Gramma Amy called out to them.

"Morning," she said. "You know where the Pennymans stay?"

"Just round the bend, third house down, double-log, two stone fireplaces. You can't miss it."

They had no trouble finding the house, bigger than the others they'd seen, and

Gramma Amy grabbed the basket and marched toward the front door. Midway, she called, "Rose," and Rose clambered down to follow.

An attractive, middle-aged Creek woman answered Gramma Amy's knock. She was both full-figured and stiff-backed, dressed in European clothes, a cotton blouse high around the neck and long dark skirt, and she didn't smile, her plump face betraying nothing of what she thought to find these two women on her front stoop. She waited, the door open halfway.

"Mrs. Pennyman?"

"Yes."

"I'm Amy. You been buying our beef and our preserves from Cane Creek for years. We're here to make good on our new arrangement."

The woman swung the door open wide, and moved to one side so they could pass. "Come in then. I been expecting you."

Mrs. Pennyman led them back into the kitchen. Rose caught glimpses of the house as they walked. The rooms were small but well kept and clean, and someone had bunched a bowl of fresh purple windflowers on a little wooden table in the front room.

"This her?" Mrs. Pennyman asked once they got to the kitchen.

"Yes," said Gramma Amy. She took three of the loaves of bread out and arranged them in a line on the table. "You'll want to try these. Just a sample of what she can do."

Mrs. Pennyman pinched off a small piece of the pumpkin loaf and tasted. She nodded once in satisfaction. She repeated with the shuck bread, and again, she seemed pleased. But when she tasted the sour bread, she made a noise deep in her throat, broke off a much larger piece, and closed her eyes as she chewed. They waited silent until she finished, and dabbed at her mouth with a napkin.

"She talk?" asked Mrs. Pennyman.

"Rose?" Gramma Amy urged.

"Yes, ma'am. I talk and I cook both." Rose tried to keep the challenge out of her voice. She still didn't understand. What exactly was the new arrangement, and how could her grandmother bargain without explanation?

"We have a small room in the back," said Mrs. Pennyman. "Your grandmother tells me you cook just about anything, and we can see if this works out for the next month or so before we all decide. It's me and my husband and two boys and a girl. We entertain a fair amount. Room and board included. Wages go direct to you. You ready to work?"

Rose looked to Gramma Amy in alarm, but her grandmother just returned her look with a level stare.

Suddenly, Rose wanted nothing more than to be back at the ranch, buried underneath an avalanche of chores she'd repeated thousands of times before, and would repeat thousands of times again, sleepwalking, invisible. Her safe haven.

But another voice rose in her head, and she thought of Grampa Cow Tom's words to her, that she should go away for a time, and figure how to carve out her own life, and make her own traditions. She thought about Gramma Amy, and how disappointed she would be if they took the buckboard ride back to the ranch together, and she left the Okmulgee position without trying. A month. Hard work was a given no matter where she lived, and she'd survived a war, burned-out homes, hunger, the death of people she loved. She'd always had her family around her, but a single month unmoored from constant reminders of the past held its own appeal. She'd managed to stand up for herself and shoot the gun south for her grandfather. She could do this.

Rose found Gramma Amy's gaze again

and held fast until the drumming of her heart quieted. She trusted she could go or stay, of her own choosing.

"Yes, ma'am, I'm ready," Rose said to Mrs. Pennyman. "My satchel is in the wagon."

Gramma Amy came to fetch her at the end of her thirty-day trial with the Pennymans, and they returned to the ranch together to collect the rest of her things. Unlike the trip from the ranch to the Pennymans, Rose talked almost without pause on the way back, eager to impress Gramma Amy with all of her newfound knowledge. She'd been surprised by the deep satisfaction that came with running her own kitchen. They'd agreed already that Rose would return to Okmulgee and the Pennymans in three days.

"I made us dog heads for our trip," Rose said. "Wait until you taste, corn and beans wrapped in husks, with butter. They're better when they're hot, but fine cold. It's Cherokee, not Creek, but I bet you like them. Mrs. Pennyman learned how to make them from her grandmother."

"I see," said Gramma Amy, and Rose thought she saw a small smile. "Always more to learn, eh?"

From the moment Rose recognized the

landmark cattle pen in the north field of their ranch, she realized she was viewing her home through different eyes, as if a mist had thinned. Only thirty days, and the ranch seemed somehow smaller, as if it had shrunk in her absence. She was both drawn to and repelled by the familiar. Her first thought was to go to Twin, to share her ponderings with him, but Gramma Amy headed straight for the main house.

They arrived back at the ranch house just before supper. Rose stepped into the kitchen, still flush from the long trip and trading recipes with Gramma Amy. Ma'am, caught up in the preparation of the meal, was the first to see her. Her mother was in charge, pointing and directing, but she stopped, wiping her hands on her apron, and stood straighter.

"Welcome back," Ma'am said to Rose. "You visiting or staying?"

"I'm come to get my things, then back to Okmulgee in a couple days."

"Too good for your own family, I guess," said Ma'am.

Rose felt the lightness of the last few hours leave her. "No, Ma'am. I have a job."

"Plenty to do around here."

Elizabeth came into the room just then, her arms full of firewood. "Rose," Elizabeth squealed, and threw the logs down near the fireplace. She propelled herself onto Rose, throwing her arms around her older sister.

"Enough," Ma'am said to Elizabeth. "Go look after the bread. See it doesn't burn."

"We're just all glad to have Rose home for a few days," said Gramma Amy. "Why don't you set the table, Rose? We'll visit over supper."

Rose grabbed an apron and made herself useful. The stew was soon ready, and dished up, and though it felt good to sit around the table with family, Rose was restless, as if unsure now where she fit.

Later that night, after the dishes were scrubbed and they'd sat with their needlework long enough to signal bedtime, she and Elizabeth were finally alone in their own room.

"Please don't leave me again, Rose," Elizabeth said. "Please. It's harder without you here."

Elizabeth began to cry, and Rose gathered her up and rested her little sister's head on her chest, as she hadn't done for years.

"Don't waste what time we have," said Rose, but the girl's tears began to loosen her resolve to go back to the Pennymans. Still, she kept firm. "I'll come visit, but tomorrow, you'll help me pack up. I've only a few days before I have to go back to Ok-mulgee."

"But you don't have to," Elizabeth insisted. "You can stay here, like always. Ma'am says you're just a cook for a family of rich Creeks. What do they have that we don't?"

Rose felt the years between them, a girl's perspective versus a young woman's. She wanted to try to make Elizabeth understand.

"It was impossible here after Grampa died. I was drowning. They're not my family, the Pennymans, but there's a place for me there. A simple place, without weight, without secrets, where I can breathe again."

Elizabeth narrowed her eyes. "What secrets?"

"Not secrets." Rose tried to laugh off her blunder. Her promise to Grampa Cow Tom needed to remain safe. "You know how tight-lipped Ma'am and the rest are with family stories. That's all. The point is I miss you terribly," she said. "I think about you all the time. Okmulgee seems far, but I won't be gone forever."

She almost said "I promise," but she held herself back. She wasn't at all sure what would happen in the city, a city without her family around her. Rose remembered all of the promises she'd made to Elizabeth when they were girls and fleeing in the night to Fort Gibson, how she'd said anything that came into her mind to keep Elizabeth moving. They weren't girls any longer, but despite the difference in age, they were connected. Elizabeth wasn't a shadow from beyond the grave, like Twin, but Rose's flesh-and-blood shadow in this life.

"We'll always be sisters," Rose said, "and I'll always be there for you. That I can promise."

PART III
ROSE

–1880–

CHAPTER 50

Rose only just secured the lid atop the simmering pot of beef stew on the stove when she heard the knock at the back door. Possibly a hungry ranch hand returning early for supper, or a stray cowpuncher begging scraps, or an itinerate salesman. Her employers had plenty, but they weren't particularly generous to those they didn't know. She'd been warned to provide something, as was the way, but not waste too much on the inevitable passerby arriving at the back door, tired from traveling the plain, eager for food, drink, and rest. But Mrs. Pennyman knew Rose as likely more begrudging with a handout than she was, and left food distribution to her cook's discretion. Rose took the time to set the cucumbers to soak for cabbage and dried her hands on her apron before answering the knock. Whoever, it most likely meant more work for her.

She found a gangling Indian man, young,

hat in hand. At least she thought him Indian. By feature, he might even have been white, but her guess was mixed. He carried himself with a confidence not matching his age. Not even out of his teen years, he stared openly at her before he spoke, a look bordering on familiarity, if not insolence. The startling color of his eyes reminded her of the spindly-vined wildflower that grew in the pasture through the summer and into the fall on her grandfather's ranch, with flamboyant blue flowers lasting only a day, petals shaped like mouse ears. His eyes held her fast, but Rose didn't look away. He intruded on her domain, on her kitchen. More precisely, the Pennyman kitchen, but by extension of responsibility, her own as well.

"Excuse me, ma'am," he said. "You must be Rose."

His grin was impish, as if he knew her, both puzzling and rankling.

"Yes."

She waited for him to state his business, impatient. He was a cocky one, blue eyes or no. She was probably ten years his senior, and while she didn't expect deference, she did expect something more than this attempt at casual chumminess. He bordered on disrespectful, and made her nervous, though in the last six years, after her grandfather passed, she'd fortified herself, refusing to let anyone, family or stranger, bully her. The young man was definitely a cowpuncher. He wore the telltale high-heeled boots that kept his feet from slipping through the stirrup on a saddle, and chaps to protect his trousers, and carried the bow of leg identifying so many of the cowpunchers she served meals to since a small girl on her grandfather's ranch or now, around the Pennyman table. He'd mixed personal touches in with the typical cowpuncher outfit — a small white feather tucked in the large brim of his high-crowned hat, a checkered, sweat-soaked handkerchief around his neck tied with a fancy double knot. He'd made an attempt to brush the trail dust off his long-sleeved shirt, heavy and bright red to shield against both sun and insects, and although Rose was sure she smelled the remains of lye soap, she also caught the deeply embedded scent of cattle dung and sweat that clung to his clothes and his dark hair.

"I heard you're the best cook in the territory and I'm come to meet you," he said. "My name is Jake Simmons."

"The Pennymans sent you round?"

"No, ma'am. You underestimate your

reputation. You fed a household of men from the Lazy U a couple weeks back, and when they visited my employer up in Haskell, that's all they talked about, that amazing supper the African woman cook served at the Pennymans'. I had to see for myself."

"This is a private home," said Rose, "not a boardinghouse."

Jake laughed. "Which is why I wrangled an invitation to supper here tonight through my boss," he said. "I thought I'd introduce myself to you first so you know who I am."

"And who are you?" asked Rose. She was confused by whatever game he played, and had too much work to do preparing the evening meal to waste time on a stranger. And yet, she found herself transfixed by those blue eyes, as if she couldn't turn away.

Jake stepped back and looked Rose over. He cocked his head, and again produced that maddening grin. "A man come courting," he said.

"Courting who?"

Jake went on as if she hadn't spoken. "I've been on my own since twelve, and look now for a wife. My father was a white man, Scottish, adopted Cherokee, and my mother Negro and Creek. I been interested in the cattle business since a little boy, and plan to study every part before I'm through. I don't have much interest in farming, and aim to get my own ranch soon as I can."

Rose was a practical woman, able to tally her plusses and minuses as well as her prospects with a clear eye. She knew some called her a childless old maid, twenty-eight, unappealingly tiny and trim while other women of the tribe were large and voluptuous, and a glance in the mirror confirmed her probable future. Rose had no illusions. And yet, over the years, she'd seen other tribe women who weren't beauties selected as wives, but those women were at ease with socializing, able to talk about small subjects, able to flatter and cajole. Not Rose, more traditionally Creek than American, like her grandfather. She'd carved a place for herself in the tribe's busy capital town of Okmulgee, having left the family ranch to forge her own way in the world, using her culinary skills in a wealthy Indian family's kitchen.

But neither was Rose so blinded by her shortcomings she couldn't appreciate those things in her favor. Everyone sang the praises of her cooking, she could weave and card and sew and stand in as midwife and herbalist. She could shoot a gun, had a head for fancy figuring, and could run a ranch given the chance. Her grandmother taught

Rose how to be independent even while under a man's protection, and how to stretch a dollar, and Ma'am taught her how to can and pickle and preserve. Gramma Amy insisted all her grandchildren get an education, and Rose, as oldest, had looked after her sister and taken her to the integrated school every day. And her ace in the hole was her grandfather. Grampa Cow Tom had given her his looks and his resourcefulness. And an inheritance. She was relatively wealthy, both in her future portion of land and the successful settlement of her grandfather's claim with the government. She was confident that fact alone had brought Jake Simmons to her.

Rose gestured for Jake to come into the kitchen and shut the door behind him.

"Who says I'm looking for a husband?"

"Are you married?"

"No."

"Then I'm not saying you're looking. All I'm asking is if you're open."

Rose paused to gather her wits, the pace of this conversation too fast for her. She wished she wasn't wearing her stained apron, and had on her Sunday dress. She even thought about removing the plain scarf covering her cornrows.

"I'm Creek," she volunteered. "And Cow

Tom was my grandfather. I assume you know that."

"I do," answered Jake, without pause. "His ranch was on Cane Creek, about a thousand cattle a year, branded with a half-moon and mule-shoe X."

"How do you plan on getting this ranch of your own?" Rose asked, as calmly as she could manage. She cared more than she wanted to admit that he quantify his expectations of her land and her finances with honesty, and not insult her by treating her like a young, impressionable girl ripe for the fleecing with a few flattering words and the promise of passion. Better to get things in the open quickly, before other distractions came into play. Already she'd begun to think about those blue eyes in a different way than she had when he first knocked on the kitchen door.

"I have a sponsor, my employer, willing to get me started," Jake said. He pulled out one of the kitchen chairs for her to sit, but she shook her head and remained standing, crossing her arms in front of her chest. Jake took her refusal in stride, twirling his hat in his hand. "When I was ten, I landed my first paying job on a ranch. Earned me six dollars. I worked hard, and learned, and got me ten dollars. And so on. Over the years, I got to know my cattle and became buyer. I've bought thousands of head of cattle for my boss, running them from Texas to Kansas, and now he depends on me. Next step is do the same for myself."

"And what is that to me?" Rose asked. "Surely you could court someone closer your age, Indian or black."

"When I marry, I'm going to marry me a black-skinned lady," Jake said. "I been knowing that always. The closer to African, the better. None of my children going to grow up with slave ways, thinking they're less than anyone else."

There was something about Jake that reminded her of her grandfather. Not looks, one dark as a crow's wing, the other pale as fresh-wove cotton, but in such easy acceptance of who she was, who she could be. Six years gone, and still she thought of her grandfather every day, the contradiction of him, the unfairness of handing her his shame alongside the bedrock of his righteousness. Most times she thought of Grampa Cow Tom as inspiration, replaying his stories in her mind, first as building blocks of grief's recovery, and then to propel her into the world. Other times she resented him, a tainted man she was forced to protect.

"Sounds like you have hereafter all figured," Rose said.

"Coming up, I moved from place to place, shuffled from one relative to the next when my mother couldn't manage, one tribe to another, near starving most of the time. Early on, I made my way, but I've no interest in scraping by. I'm going to build a big ranch, and run cattle, and keep my family in one place. A big family. My wife has to help with all that."

A family in one place, Rose thought, afraid to believe this stranger's goals could match so closely to her own impossible dreams. She slowed down her breathing, brought herself in line. She composed her face, as she had so often seen her grandfather do when he negotiated. But she couldn't believe her grandfather ever had to stare into eyes the color of wildflowers.

"What kind of help?"

"Whatever it takes," said Jake. "A sensible woman wanting the same things I want, not afraid of hard work."

"I don't tolerate lazy," Rose said.

"Me neither," replied Jake.

Rose tried to tamp down the hopefulness blooming in her chest, spreading as fast and dangerous as Russian thistle on the prairie. She saw potential in this young man — lik-

able, even charming, but rough and unso-
phisticated. Yes, he was young, but he came
to her, as no other man had. Jake Simmons
was intrigued enough on the basis of her
pedigree and stories he'd heard about the
unmarried black woman with money in Okmulgee to ride all the way into town to offer
himself up, and he hadn't scared off once
he saw her.

"Can you read?" she asked.

A defensive flicker crossed Jake's face. "I
never had a chance for school. I get by on
the trail. Not many cowpunchers read."

"Maybe not, but running a ranch is different. People cheat you in a minute unless
you let them know they can't," Rose said.
There was no point to coyness. Charm
wasn't what she possessed to win him over.
"I could teach you to read and write. It's
not hard. You probably know some basics
from branding letters on cattle."

Jake nodded. He stared again, his eyes on
her in a new way. A small smile lifted the
edges of his lips, and he looked even
younger than before. "So, should I come
back again to see you?" he asked.

Rose fought back a schoolgirl simper,
dazzled anew by the intensity behind his
eyes and the magnetism of his quick grin. A
heavy door to an undreamed future swung

wide to her, in the space of a single hour, miracle enough, but her heart's pounding had surprisingly little to do with ranchland and cattle. Jake himself triggered this deep and unexpected longing, the lean-bodied hunger of him, the rich man-smell of him standing close.

She couldn't gather herself to answer. After a life of guardedness, she was fallen, so fast, so hard, and dizzy with the possibility she could open her arms wide and reach for everything she wanted. How easy and wondrous it would be to slide and lose herself completely. Rose knew, with certainty absolute, that this was the beginning at last, the passageway to the life she'd waited so long to clarify. Jake.

Rose forced her thoughts to Grampa Cow Tom, and the command required for any successful negotiation, the need to hang on to oneself and mask inner thought in favor of outward deportment. She imagined herself surrounded by hostile Seminoles, facing a sure death, while Jake held her bloody ear aloft. Rose found her voice.

"If that's what you've a mind to do," she answered softly, with as much control as she could muster, "I'll be right here."

CHAPTER 51

Rose watched Jake trace his finger under each line as he read the newspaper by lantern light, a slow and laborious procedure. Sometimes, he moved his lips in determination as he sounded out a sentence until it fell into place. If they were alone, just he and Rose, he'd call out to ask her what a certain word meant, and Rose would drop whatever she was doing to answer. She considered these moments among her favorite times with her husband, but there were so many pieces of her life with him she cherished, she couldn't confine her joy to only one. Teaching him to read had taken years, not because he was slow, but because they had so little time left after the avalanche of building a life together. He'd been a good student once he settled into the process, putting in the effort no matter how tired he was, but in the years since they married, there were long stretches when reading had to take second place to all the other demands — scrimping, saving, buying land, erecting a house, building a herd, cattle drives, crops, mending fences. Not to mention the children, who came quickly, one after the next, two girls in as many years, more Rose's responsibility than Jake's, though they adored their father.

As Jake promised Rose at their first meeting, they started a small ranch of their own half a day's ride from Cane Creek, and managed in only a few years to grow and add improvements — house, barn, corral, fencing, garden. Cash money was always tight, but Jake often joked he could ride onto a stranger's ranch sometime in the late afternoon, stay overnight in an unwilling seller's barn or camped on the prairie, and by the next morning, have a handshake deal and cattle exchanged with all parties smiling.

Jake put aside the newspaper, closing his eyes and massaging the bridge of his nose. Reading by the flicker of the lantern light took its toll.

"Say, Rose," Jake said. "What say you and me go to the church supper Sunday?"

"That'd be all right," answered Rose.

"But I know something to make it better than all right. Hold on."

Rose put aside her needlework. Jake was up to something, and sure enough, he disappeared into the back room, and returned with a loaf-sized bundle wrapped up in old newsprint. He presented the parcel to her, watching the expression on her face.

Rose peeled back the edges of the wrapping. Inside was a pair of high-top black leather shoes, fancy. A curved row of covered buttons ran up the side, each in its own buttonhole, with a small sateen bow at each toe, and dainty little heels. The shoes were so beautiful, Rose was almost afraid to touch them. She set them down carefully.

"Jake! So many things we need. We don't have money for this kind of foolishness. What were you thinking? What if the crop doesn't come in?"

Jake pulled back. "I knew you'd fight me on this," he said. "But I was thinking it time my scrawny chicken shows the other ladies a thing or two."

In the beginning, years before, Rose had been sorry she'd told Jake about her mother's careless comments as she grew up. But somehow, Jake had turned the insult on its head, and when he called her scrawny chicken, she felt bigger and bolder. And safer. Rose was Jake's scrawny chicken, his anchor, and Jake was her freewheeling cow-boy.

"Surely you can take them back to the store and get our money?" asked Rose.

"I could," answered Jake. "But I won't." He was working himself into a state. "We been squeezing every penny till there's nothing left, but this once, you're going to show out. You can wear them to church, and whenever we visit Cane Creek. And you tell Ma'am *I* got them for you."

If the gift were any other extravagance, Rose would have been able to resist, easily, but shoes were her weakness. Jake knew as much.

Rose marrying Jake provided everyone an opportunity to be nicer to one another. Even Ma'am had come round, charmed by her daughter's new husband, and then by the grandchildren as they appeared. Rose was happiest when Jake was home, but he was often gone away, chasing their fortune, buying or selling or both, that was his part of the bargain. Hers was to make a home for him to come back to. Home meant everything to him. And to her. Who could have believed the two of them fit so hand in glove? That the dead spots in her heart could soften, and give rise to new bloom?

Rose picked up the shoes again, and ran

her finger across the smooth surface of one of the sateen bows. She sniffed the leather, a raw, heady smell that filled her with satisfaction, and placed the pair in her lap, picking up her needlework again.

It was impossible to imagine keeping such a firm hold on her book of dreams without Jake on every page.

CHAPTER 52

Rose missed Jake, gone away this time along the Old Texas Trail in search of ten steers to add to the herd before winter set. With Jake away over two weeks already, the almost-baby occupied her thoughts most days and nights. Jake wouldn't be much help with woman's business even if he was home, but at least she could talk to him in Mvskoke. The bluntness of the language suited the occasion, and Rose always thought in Mvskoke in the days before a birth. Sometimes she'd rather live in the calm of no talk than navigate the trickeries of words, but she spoke to the little ones in English nonetheless. She and Jake agreed Mvskoke acceptable only between the two of them, their secret language. The children would be brought up with the language of the wider American world.

She rubbed her belly, soothing, stroking, the far end protruded like one of the overripe watermelons in the north patch. The baby was active, and already dropped. This one didn't feel like the other two she'd carried, so she hoped for a boy, but the all-girl family curse had held true thus far. She wondered if she was destined to break the string and finally produce a son in this, the third generation, or if she tempted fate by asking for too much. Whatever, the child was due soon, very soon.

When the knock came on the front door, she had just put down the oldest for her afternoon nap and turned to putting a stew to boil for dinner for the ranch hands. She'd heard neither horse hoof nor wagon. The nearest neighbors, several miles downstream, seldom visited, and when they did, they knew to come to the back, where she would most likely be. Transients weren't frequent, but common enough, black, white, or Indian, asking for water or bread or a hayloft to sleep in, and Rose always complied, unless she sensed danger, in which case she shooed them off, her rifle never too far from reach.

"Can you spare water?" the stranger asked. "I've come far."

The woman at the front door was young, too young to be carrying such a bundle. She was taller than Rose, as were most women, full-bosomed, her straight, black hair in a long, single-plaited tail down to her waist, tall moccasins visible beneath her dusty, sweat-stained cotton dress, her fawn-colored skin blemished but aglow. Her clothes, speech, and carriage indicated a woman from an Indian family. Rose wasn't sure which tribe, maybe Cherokee, maybe Creek, neither well-to-do nor brothel, but something in the middle. Most probably a farm girl, but with some little education. Clearly she'd walked a distance, and she leaned on first one foot and then the other, finding relief in neither. As much as Rose would rather shut the door and go about her business, she invited the woman inside, helping her sit on the upholstered chair, Jake's chair, and rest. Rose brought her a bowl of *sofki* and water from the pump, and waited until she drank down the last of the cup to inquire the reason for her visit.

"I'm Angeli," the woman said. "From Cow Hollow."

Rose had never been there, but she knew of the town, as described by Jake, one of many small clusters of tiny, remote ranches and wide-open spaces where he bought up cheap cattle one or two at a time to increase their herd. Sometimes he struck up partnerships and ran the ranchers' cows along with their own to market, for fee of cash or cattle.

"I know of it," said Rose.

"I'm looking for Jake Simmons," the woman said. "Some directed me here."

Rose felt her baby kick, once, twice, a demanding claim. She held her side in counterweight to reassure it. "Jake's gone with the cattle drive," she said.

"Is he soon back?"

"No way to know," said Rose.

"You the wife?" Angeli asked.

"I am," said Rose.

Angeli looked around the front room for the first time. Both of Rose's daughters slept, the oldest, three, in a crib in the corner, the youngest, sixteen months, in a woven basket nearby. Rose didn't believe in the waste of fancy, but they'd built the ranch house large, to accommodate the life they intended, and she had decorated, albeit sparely, with needlepoint headrests on Jake's stuffed chair and braided rugs on the floor. She worked each day to keep grime and dust outside where it belonged, and not on her inside possessions.

"This baby is your husband's work," the young woman said.

Rose was caught with a polite smile frozen on her face. All turned muffled inside. She stood, not sure why or where she could go, and turned her back to the woman as she tried to find some thought to latch to. Other than that she was a fool. A fool. If the woman said something more, she didn't hear.

She searched for some anchor place in her mind, something to stop the shattering. She'd called on Twin years back as Grampa Cow Tom lay dying, but he'd never appeared to her again. Only that once had he come at her beckoning. He was gone, almost forgotten completely, pushed aside by the blue of Jake's eyes. She fixed on her children. On her home. But thinking thus only sent her further into her despair. What would happen to them now? Grampa Cow Tom had gone from Gramma Amy for days and months and years on end, but there were never any babies finding their way back to his ranch door.

For no reason, she thought of the cast-iron cook stove they'd just bought for sixteen dollars, she and Jake together, plotting like children until they had the money saved, how proud and happy they'd both been. There was no anchor there. She couldn't think on Jake. Not yet.

She thought of Grampa Cow Tom, spiriting his mother onto the ship bound for Indian Territory, under the nose of the slave catcher. How her grandfather had turned disaster into advantage, in defense of his family. She could learn from his boldness.

A familiar voice asserted, stronger than any other, stronger than her own.

Make your own family.

Grampa Cow Tom's words came to her, and she felt a slight loosening, a small clearing of mind. Her family was what mattered, the family in her power to make. She pulled herself back from the brink, composing her face as she did so. Composing her resolve. Never show your enemy your true face. Grampa Cow Tom taught her that.

She turned to Angeli. "Why should I believe you?" Rose asked.

"His name is Jake," Angeli said, as if revealing a winning poker hand.

"That proves nothing."

"Look at him then. Look close."

Rose accepted the baby, settling him into her arms, balancing him on the curve of her belly, and she pushed back at the flimsy blanket wrapped round his body, obscuring his face. He couldn't have been more than two weeks old, a weak, defenseless thing. He opened and shut his eyes, unfocused, but already they reflected back Jake's eyes, and the jut of the infant's jaw followed like a tracing the jut of Jake's jaw. A ruddy baby, more Creek than black, dark hair sleek and plentiful. A boy child, in a family that didn't produce sons.

"I can't keep him," the woman said. "They'll throw me out, and where would I go? You have plenty here."

Angeli cried at this last, making no attempt to hold back. This young woman had walked to the ranch with her birth wounds still fresh, and the math of the situation worked, coinciding with Jake's road-time schedule. He had, indeed, passed through Cow Hollow last fall. Who could deny Angeli's story?

Rose thought about Angeli's words. It was true. She did have plenty. She had food and shelter and late-life babies of her own and a growing ranch with a husband she was bound to in ways she never expected. But what did this young thing know of the devastation of their very first crop nearly destroyed by hailstorm and the bank's threat of default? Of Jake's early scramblings for cash the year after they married, cutting rails for twelve hours a day on remote ranches farther and farther away while Rose tended cotton, corn, and children alone? Angeli saw the house now, but not as when first constructed, a twelve-by-fourteen-foot log cabin built on a foundation of borrowed money. What could she know of the harshness of the early years, before they made their first purchase of forty head of cattle and two horse teams, and their first hires to help bring in fifty-five acres of corn and ten of cotton?

Yes. Now was plenty. And she intended to keep it all. Children, husband, ranch. Her domain. She intended to claw out a life side by side with Jake, a bold cowman with a man's strong nature, and he would come back to her, regardless of his doings on the road. Her heart might shred now, but she would keep it intact with the force of her mind.

"Leave the boy, then," said Rose. "Leave him and go on your way. I'll pack up food for your trip home."

Angeli seemed taken aback, as if she hadn't expected the exchange to go so quickly, so smoothly. "You'll raise Jake?"

"Rest for awhile to get your strength, and then be on your way," Rose repeated. "There'll be no coming back for the boy later. Never."

"No, ma'am."

Rose left Angeli in the front room for a last moment with the child while she made her preparations from the larder. But Angeli waited no longer than it took Rose to fashion a basket with big bean dumplings to take with her. The woman set out as abruptly as she appeared, a determined figure becoming smaller in the distance as Rose, from the front porch, watched her retreat down the path. Rose stood for a time, holding the baby, staring toward the copse of trees at the edge of the prairie, until she realized the front of her dress was wet, and her milk had come down.

"Kindred," Rose whispered to the newest addition to the household, stroking his tiny face with her finger. Was this the only way to break the curse of no boy in the family line? "Your name is Kindred."

He was fast asleep, peaceful, and Rose put him in the basket-bed she'd already fashioned for the new baby coming. Tomorrow, she'd construct another from the elm branches that grew behind the bunkhouse.

She rang the supper triangle, just one go-round. They'd know the time wrong for noonday dinner, and only one of the hands would come in from the pasture to see what she wanted. An old cowpunch came, and she sent him with a message for Gramma Amy's place on the Canadian River, one half day's trip going, and a half day back. Elizabeth would read the note to Gramma Amy.

She needed her sister. Elizabeth must come here to live, now, to help her. She wasn't worried about the delivery, but what came after. Four babies less than four years old. She had support from the sister of a ranch hand, a recent widow living on the property, but the woman had given notice of her intent to move to Okmulgee, where more people passed through, and she might have more chance to build a life than on a remote ranch in the middle of nowhere.

Rose moved through the rest of the day slowly, her chores mechanical, but as soon as darkness fell across the prairie, she lay down. She cried quietly in her room, out of sight, her heart an alien enemy that raced one minute and went numb the next. The wind kicked up, rattling the roof shingles, so strong she worried how many might blow off. She brought Kindred into the bedroom with her, and for the second time, opened her top to feed him.

He took to her quickly, as if he knew no other way.

CHAPTER 53

In the night, the pain bit into her, refusing to let go. Almost a relief, such physical pain that it sometimes drove out thoughts of Jake. Rose wrapped her hands around the bedpost and squeezed so tight her fingernails sank into her own flesh, carving deep half-moon craters of dark blood. She made herself calm, willing herself not to cry out. This delivery would be easier than the others, she decided. This baby wouldn't fight her. She had endured much worse with the other two, and determined to stay on her feet and deliver Creek-style, squatting, half standing, letting gravity draw the baby out.

Her first, Laura, was physically perfect in every way when she finally appeared, but the girl had taken sixteen hours to come out into the light of the world, as if Rose's womb was where she wanted to hide forever. Despite Rose's early skill as a midwife, and all the birthing she witnessed or aided, the force of those stabbing pains still surprised her when the assault came to her own womanly parts. Her second, Lady, another girl, came quicker, but she was working in the orchard and couldn't make it all the way back to the house. She delivered two miles from the ranch in a field of hay, using an upright pitchfork she anchored into the ground to steady herself as she squatted. But she knew her body now, she knew how and when to demand, and she knew what she was capable of. Everyone on the ranch accepted that she would shut herself in her room to deliver alone. Not once had she called for help and she wouldn't for this one either.

With calm, Rose reassured herself that her tools were ready. She'd held the pair of newly whetstone-sharpened scissors over the open flame and wiped them down with alcohol, and now they lay on the stand beside the bed on a pile of clean rags, in place and waiting. The widow would have to look after the babies, and cook for the hands, and bring Rose food and water if the birth dragged on too long. She considered letting the widow cut the cord when the time came, but in this one thing, Rose was selfish. She loved the cutting herself, that first separation of mother and child, and could boast, if she had been so inclined, at the perfection of the belly buttons of both her daughters. No ruptures, no protrusions. Kindred's had been a sloppy cut. She'd inspected him for defect, and all save that seemed satisfactory.

She passed the night in fits and starts of waiting, with the contractions continuing to promise, falsely, an imminent birth, and she watched through the little glass window in their bedroom as the sun began to rise in the sky. When tempted to dwell on Jake's betrayal, she shut those thoughts out as best she could, making plans for all that needed doing instead. She heard the familiar commotion of the ranch rumbling to life, the fires started, water pumped, the coffee set to boil, the grease spitting in the pan, the horses married to saddle, the ranch hands clanging dishes, doors banging. Finally, a moment of complete quiet passed, blessed quiet, but then Rose heard a baby's sudden squeal somewhere in the house, an outrage of hurt, and the swift movement of a comforting rescue as someone picked her up. The widow was on task.

As the sun climbed higher, she knew the ranch hands were outdoors doing the daytime chores, tending the animals, mending fences, harvesting crops. But the babies were left behind, and Rose was confident the widow wouldn't stray too far, hovering nearby the closed bedroom door, careful not to intrude, even as she prepared noon dinner for the hands and oversaw the girls. Only Kindred was allowed in the bedroom with her, and his mere presence comforted her, in ways she didn't quite understand.

She gasped at the next sharp contraction, her time near, her baby finally impatient. She suddenly remembered last night's windstorm. Someone needed to ride out to the east gate to check the fencing. She didn't want to risk her milk cow wandering off again beyond her protection. As soon as she finished here, she'd have the widow run the order to one of the ranch hands. She had to be on top of them every minute.

Rose bore down. She couldn't hurry the process, but she still had a ranch to run. Their ranch. Hers and Jake's. They built it, and they'd hold on despite drought or flood or rascals or soulless bankers or human weakness, their lives intertwined. She was still his scrawny chicken. He was still her cowboy. They would pass the ranch to their children and grandchildren, preserving and improving. Rose would make sure of that.

Once the pushing started, the baby came fast. He was a big boy, long, featured like her grandfather, like her, Africa-based, sturdy of body and broad of face. In this baby, she saw more of her than of Jake. His eyes were brown, his hair dark, thick, and frizzled, his skin the shade of caramelized sugar in the pan. Rose was exhausted, but she relished the first astonished cry, the chest-to-chest contact of skin on skin, the wiping of the body, the ceremony of cutting, the gentle wrapping of layered protection within the blanket she'd scrubbed clean in the washtub and dried in the sun, set aside for just this moment.

"Jacob. My Jacob," said Rose.

The curse was broken. And now there were two sons to protect.

Kindred woke in his basket, hungry, searching for her, and as if in response, Jacob began rooting too, so quickly after birth.

It took some getting used to, positioning first one and then the other across her body at the proper angle, intertwined, each at rest on the other and dependent on Rose to support the heaviness of their heads, but Rose gave the first breast to Jacob, waiting for him to latch. Once he did so, she offered the other to Kindred.

CHAPTER 54

Before leaving the ranch house to pick peaches in the east field for supper, Rose asked Elizabeth to make butter from the cream held back from the broker in Haskell. She put her oldest down for a nap in the front room, fed the two boys, and strapped the youngest girl to her back. She craved time, however brief, to be away from the close-in walls of the house. She could force her hands to busyness, dawn to dusk, but managing the perturbations of her mind was another matter entirely.

"Keep an eye out," Rose reminded Elizabeth. Her sister had been a blessing to Rose the last three months, with Jake away. "I'm back to feed them again by the time they wake."

Her sister returned a tolerant smile. "They're safe with me," she said.

Eager as she was to get gone, she lingered, watching Elizabeth lug a cream bucket from the larder, set up the wooden butter churn on the front porch, and pour the thick mass from one container to the other. Once done, her sister brought out Jacob and Kindred, placing their two baskets side by side on the stoop in easy view, and began to turn the crank until she got a rhythm going.

Rose checked one last time on both babies, fast asleep, the two sons Jake didn't yet know he had. Kindred was the bigger of the two, Jacob the most active. Not even three months old, and already Jacob gurgled and chuckled often, smiling when she came into his line of vision. Kindred, older than his brother by two weeks, was more cautious, studying all around him with a seriousness that reminded Rose of herself, although he carried not one drop of her blood in him. Kindred rationed his smiles, as if he wanted to figure everything out first before taking such a risk.

Rose set out at last across the meadow, more careful of step since twisting her ankle in a prairie-dog hole last month. She felt moodiness in the air, a beginning or an ending, she couldn't tell which, but the day was alive with possibility. They were going to do well, she and Jake. She'd decided. The last few months had been difficult, full of reminders that she would need to think in new ways, but she considered her lot. Since Kindred arrived, she'd endured occasional, unexplained spells sometimes lasting an hour or more, when she could barely catch her breath and was forced to sit motionless until her heart and lungs unseized.

But their blessings were so many. Their acreage prospered. The herd increased each year, land improvements were more extensive, cultivated fields more productive, the mortgage always paid on time out of cattle or milk sales. And now Elizabeth.

Elizabeth was heaven-sent, arrived on Rose's ranch just days after Jacob was born. Rose offered no explanation of Kindred, and her little sister didn't push her to admit the words of his origin aloud as Rose struggled to prepare herself for Jake's return. Elizabeth was lively company, and talked to people Rose didn't care to spend time on. With four babies, Rose couldn't imagine how she would have managed without her younger sister's help, especially once the widow moved to Okmulgee. Elizabeth surprised Rose with her willingness to be of service and her eagerness to make herself a part of their ranch. Although Elizabeth too was born to dust and cattle and prairie, she'd always been sheltered from the worst, either being so young, or so timid, or so spoiled. She'd come of age after the horrors of Fort Gibson, and after the hardest work and uncertainty of building Grampa Cow Tom's ranches were far behind. Rose steadied the papoose, gathered her collection baskets, and continued on until she reached the orchard of peach trees, just started to come into their color for the picking.

Rose wasn't sure what day Jake would return, but she sensed the time near. Today, this week, maybe next, surely sometime this month. When he did come back to the ranch from the cattle drive, Rose was determined he find everything better than when he left. The field harvested, fences in good repair, the livestock groomed, corn, peas, beets planted, watermelon rind and okra canned, a season's worth of wheat taken to the mill and ground for flour, the pig fat and ready for slaughter, tubs of excess milk sold to the buyer in Haskell, and the gold coins safely deposited in the cedar box below the floorboards. And upon Jake's return, he would find a new balance to the household. Not one but two sons. She'd had to think long about how to introduce him to both. She'd been practicing.

Rose picked as the sun rose higher in the sky, until her hands were so wet with peach juice that the baby too became tacky with the sweetness when she handled her. Rose filled as many baskets of the heavy fruit as she could carry. With the sun of such late-summer potency, she would be glad to find shade while she did the rest of her late-morning chores.

She started back at a languid pace, the girl baby awake but content at her back, and when she came within sight of the house, she made out Elizabeth's outline on the front stoop, still cranking, the steady rise and fall of her full bosom, her home-made cotton dress splayed out around her legs, the butter churn between her knees for leverage, her face flushed with the exertion of the almost-butter in late stage.

She was beautiful.

Elizabeth was young and vibrant, with smooth, clear skin the color of a beaver's winter pelt fresh from the stream, her hair pulled up in a frizzled topknot that some-how made her eyes seem even larger. The boys were at her feet, out of their baskets, Kindred lying on his back, clutching at his own hands, Jacob naked on his stomach, practicing his newfound art of raising his head and shoulders off the blanket, in response to the rhythm of the crank's monotonous melody.

Rose stood transfixed, struck with the image of her sister, fully grown. Only after a moment did she widen her scan and notice Jake, come from the other direction, alone, astride his tall black horse, sweaty and weighed down with dusty saddle, saddlebags, and rifle. Jake was motionless amid the scrub and brush of the prairie, staring toward the ranch house too, eyes affixed on Elizabeth, as though she were evening prayer.

Rose may have moved, she wasn't sure, or the baby may have made some sound, but suddenly Jake looked in her direction. He broke out into a grin, and spurred his tired horse hard, closing the distance between them in moments. He jumped off the horse and scooped Rose into the broad expanse of his arms, twirling her, papoose and all, laughing.

"Nothing beats home," he said, and skimmed her lips with his own.

At any other time, she would have waved off his foolishness, pleased by the words but refusing any public reply to his charm. That was the way between them. But today, she glanced toward the porch, at all the changes signified there, the babies, her life in potential upheaval. Elizabeth was straightening her skirts and running a hand over her hair, tucking loose strands in place. She had seen them too, Rose and Jake, and watched the reunion of husband and wife.

Rose kissed Jake back, in broad daylight, a light peck, nothing more, but something never before done. When he looked to her in surprise she felt foolish for the impulse, but over his shoulder, she glanced furtively in satisfaction toward the porch. Elizabeth had seen it.

Jake peeked into the papoose at Rose's back. "Lady's growed," he said. The girl clapped her hands, delighted, and Jake did a little jig in the dirt while she giggled at his antics. "Where's my littlest one? Boy or girl? I'm itching to see."

Rose motioned toward the porch.

"What's your sister doing here?" he asked.

Rose slipped into Mvskoke, the relief of the language reassuring to her tongue, restoring her power. "Elizabeth helps me with your two sons," she whispered.

She waited for this news to sink in.

"Two? You carried twins then?"

"They are brothers, but not twins," said Rose.

Jake paused, his body still. "Speak plain, woman." His tone sharp, she saw the tired-ness of the road in his eyes, the red rising at his cheeks and neck, the slight telltale hitch of his shoulders toward his ears when he became tense or impatient.

Rose refused to be rushed. "One came of me. His name is Jacob. One came to the front doorstep, delivered from Cow Hollow. His name is Kindred. Both yours. Now we have four children."

Rose watched the features of Jake's face change as he puzzled her message. The progression was swift, from confusion to comprehension to guilt to something she couldn't name. She'd had ample time to prepare herself. Jake had not. As she'd anticipated in her months playing variations to this scene, Jake now ran through his options and the consequences in his mind.

"What are you saying?" he asked.

"My words are clear. He will be raised on this ranch as one of us, older brother to Jacob, younger brother to Laura and Lady. Son to Jake and Rose. Let no one tell him different."

Jake stayed quiet for so long Rose almost spoke again. She'd watched her grandfather sit across from opponents at Fort Gibson and let his silences work for him. She intended the same.

"Rose, how do you know —" Jake finally began.

She cut him off. "Truth is plain to see,"

she said. "There is no question."

Jake took out his dusty handkerchief and wiped his flushed face. By the time the sweat dried, he'd regained his composure. "I'll not deny," he said. "But the trail has nothing to do with us. With this ranch."

"How can you think that?"

"There's no attachment, no promises," Jake said. "They know I come home to you. I will always come back here, to you. Always. We are man and wife."

They. He'd said this as reassurance, and his assumption delivered her an icy chill. She might have preferred the lie, or at least an admission that he considered his offense a weakness he would fight. But in the end, she held fast to the fact that he told her truth as he knew it, his truth, and she knew where she stood. She tried to convince herself she was safe on her own ranch, and the outside world didn't matter overmuch.

"There is no need to speak further about this," Rose said. There was a sanctity and joy to marriage, regardless of circumstance, though she knew now she'd chosen a flawed man. A man she loved still, regardless. "But on future trips, you'll not tarry overlong in Cow Hollow."

"No," said Jake. And then, "I must see them."

"We have other matters to attend before you meet your sons."

Rose saw the flash of anger, the discomfort, the moment's hesitation on Jake's part, but he let them pass and ceded to her.

"My sister. She's a godsend. But I'll send her back to Gramma Amy and manage alone if need be."

"No," he said. "I'm glad you have family here while I'm gone. Your sister can stay."

She nodded. "Start me off with a few cows of my own," Rose said. "A small herd, separate from the ranch's brand. You can run them with yours come sell time."

Jake frowned. His body went rigid, arms folded across his chest, his lips thinned and pressed tight. "What I have is yours," he said. "No call for separate."

"Couldn't hurt," said Rose, and then let the stillness build.

Her absolute dependence was no longer an option. What was hers was his by law, but not the opposite. She remained wordless behind a mask of reason and negotiation.

Finally, Jake broke. "I'll cut out a couple steer need special attention. See what you make of them."

"Ten," said Rose.

Jake looked toward the porch, the tableau

waiting there, as did Rose. The boys were awake. Jacob was noticeably darker in this light, even from a distance, and he clutched to a cob of corn Elizabeth had given him. Kindred pulled at his blanket. Elizabeth made great show of engaging the babies, of purposefully not staring at the pair of them standing out in the prairie, a couple bereft of joy after such long separation.

Jake said nothing, yea or nay, and neither did Rose. He stared at her, searching her face, as if he didn't know quite who she was. Suddenly, she was terrified she'd gone too far.

Chapter 55

Spoiled, Rose thought in the stillness, standing in the prairie facing her husband, with one child strapped to her back and three more waiting on the porch. The marriage. The family. The ranch. Jake brought this upon them. It was Jake, she reminded herself, not her. All the compromises she'd made in her mind over the last few months, all her generous forgivenesses she'd brought to bear for the sake of a shared life, and now Jake caught out but not contrite? In all her considerations, all her practicing for this moment, he'd always been more sorry.

What would she do if he wouldn't capitulate to the few things she asked? Was she ready to take the babies and Elizabeth and move back to Gramma Amy and Ma'am? Give up on her own family? Carve Jake out of their lives like so much bruised fruit as if he didn't mean even more to her than this land they sought to tame? Ma'am had softened toward Rose over the years, especially after she married Jake, but to go back under that roof a failure instead of running her own ranch? The thoughts gnawed, the panic rose, but she kept her tongue.

"Ten cows," Jake finally agreed.

She blocked the relief from finding expression on her face, giving her away. "And a padlock with a key," Rose said. Her grandfather always taught her to make the most of an advantage, however brief. Should the padlock come with two keys, she intended to hold them both.

"What for?" Even the tone of Jake's speech was distorted, his words pushed through gritted teeth.

"For valuables."

"What valuables?"

"We have gold coin and silver, and too many coming and going here when you're away. Just makes good sense to put things under lock and key. We work too hard for our things to go missing."

Again Jake nodded, tightly. "I'll bring a padlock back from Okmulgee next time I pass through."

Rose relaxed a little. She'd pushed as far as she dared. Further. Time to move forward, away from the quagmire of the past.

"The cattle sold?" she asked.

"Most," Jake said. Rose saw his shoulders inch downward, just a hair, both of them in need of safer territory, but she knew he was still trying to regain his footing. "We ran into trouble on the Texas Trail, some rustlers trying to get at the herd, but we drove them off and made it almost straight through to market. Price is up this year. There'll be profit."

"We can settle the books later after everyone turns in," Rose said.

"The girls?" Jake asked.

"Both strong. Both healthy. Laura got bad fever early summer, but I herbed her, and she came round after a week of worry. Both boys get normal colds and such, give it back and forth."

She pretended not to see him look at her, searching for any signs that might indicate that she hadn't put the quandary of Kindred behind them.

"The property?"

"Most hands are out now fixing fences in the east pasture. Big windstorm came through two nights ago. Can't say I took a liking to the new hand you brought on before you left. He used up a horse without watering him after, and was shoddy with the currycomb. I sent him packing."

"You might have waited," said Jake.

As good as Jake was with cattle and cowpunchers and buyers, he would give away the ranch to the first visitor with a sad story if Rose wasn't there to prevent it. She barely caught herself from saying as much to him, uncertain what other accusations might tumble from her lips should she take to that road.

"Better to nip a vexation at the onset and move on," said Rose instead.

"I guess what's done is done."

"You must be hungry," Rose said.

"I could eat."

"I'll come with you to put up the horse," Rose said. "Then to meet your sons. Re-acquaint with the girls and my sister."

She expected they would, at last, go to the ranch house together, his understanding and acceptance of where they stood clear.

"I'll see to the hands first," he said, "and be in directly."

Rose hadn't counted on this, his reluctance to face either son. He needed time alone, she could understand that, as she had needed days and weeks and then months to adjust after Kindred came to her. She considered telling Jake that her anger was as good as spent, manageable, and Kindred such a gift, and how much she'd missed him, how glad she was to have him back, but that felt like begging. After so many months without him, she wanted to walk to their ranch house together, her husband by her side, sweeping past Elizabeth on the front porch and reclaiming their sons, and into her kitchen to feed her husband, the area she felt safest.

She wavered, succumbing to a false vision of her as the one in the chair on the porch, not sticky from peach juice and dried breast milk and sweat and dirt and veiled ultimatums, but a cleaner, fresher version of domesticity, like her sister. Alongside Elizabeth, Rose suddenly felt old. Old and ugly.

But Jake remounted his horse and rode out in the direction of the east pasture, leaving her there, alone amid the buzzing insects and wild blooms of the prairie, one child strapped to her and three more waiting. He hadn't seen his sons up close yet, either one. Was he too angry? Or suddenly afraid to confront them? Humiliated? Unwilling? She thought she knew Jake so well, but what did she know, really? How well could anyone occupy someone else's mind? Rose was certain Jake appreciated her. Desired her as his wife. She kept a fine house, ran the ranch, kept the books, had proven fertile and a good mother. And now a forgiving wife. Jake's job was to engage with the world outside their ranch, and she would leave him to it, so long as he didn't bring that world home to her.

Rose hitched up the papoose and headed for the house without her husband. She barely paused at the front porch, ignoring Elizabeth's bewilderments so obvious on her face, and escaped to the kitchen and her stove. Rose could barely handle her own emotions, let alone her sister's, whether pity or protectiveness. Her hands shook as she undid the papoose and transferred the baby to a blanket on the kitchen floor. But her nerves were much settled by the time Jake came in later, so filthy from time on the road and making his rounds on the ranch that he generated clouds of dust whenever he moved. She served him a large portion of hot limas with pork and a generous wedge of *sofki*. They didn't talk.

Elizabeth joined them in the kitchen after getting both boys down to sleep and the oldest girl settled at play. Jake had already devoured one plateful of beans and was working on his second.

"Jake, you remember Elizabeth," Rose said. Something so simple, yet she stumbled over the words.

Jake barely looked up from his plate, but his tone was civil, if not warm. "I hear you're a great help to my Rose," he said.

"Your Rose has always been a great help to me," Elizabeth said. She gave a demur nod.

Jake pushed back from the table, giving her full measure. "Rose says you'll stay with us on the ranch, keep her company while I'm gone."

Elizabeth laughed softly. "Whatsoever I can do," she said. "Rose tended to me when I was young. Now's time to return the favor."

"Well then," said Jake. "Whatsoever I can do too."

"There is something," said Elizabeth.

"Yes?"

Rose couldn't imagine Elizabeth making demands so early, especially with such unease in the air. Her boldness was unthinkable.

"I wish you would bring more newspapers here," Elizabeth said. "I'm so keen for the advertisements."

Now it was Jake's turn to laugh, but he avoided Rose's eye as he did so, their business not resolved.

"Easy enough," he said.

Ten, Rose thought, watching this exchange, like one of the math problems from the Indian school after the war ended. Rose was ten years older than Jake, and Jake and Elizabeth were almost the same age. The image unsettled her, two people so young and beautiful both.

"Pleased to have you on our ranch," Jake said. He sounded sincere, and they chatted awhile, the talk small and without strain.

The kitchen had turned sanctuary, and Rose was thankful they got on so well so quickly, Jake and Elizabeth. But the babies stirred, Kindred and Jacob on the same schedule, and within minutes, filled the ranch house with full-on hunger cries. The mood reverted, tight and fragile.

"I want to see my sons," Jake said.

Rose pulled her apron over her head to get at her top, leaving the kitchen and unbuttoning as she went to them. She didn't wait for Jake, though she heard the scrape of dish on wood behind her as he pushed his plate away, and the tumble of a chair he didn't bother to right.

He followed close behind Rose, all the way to their bedroom at the rear of the house. She didn't try to discourage him. For months, she'd imagined the introduction of father and sons.

She finished undoing the top of her dress, letting it fall. She was expert in feeding both at once now. Each week, as the boys grew in shape and size, she figured new ways to accommodate them. She used a pillow of late as their weight increased, easier on her arms, and positioned the bawling babies, one at each breast. They held hands, the two boys, staring defiantly at Jake the entire while. Daring him. Daring him not to love both, as she did.

He sat in the stiff-backed chair in the bedroom watching until the babies filled and drowsed, and he watched as Rose rubbed their backs to relieve gas from their bellies, one after the other, and put them back into their baskets. Rose buttoned her dress.

"This one here is Jacob," Rose said. "Took me eight hours." She brought the basket and laid it by Jake's right foot. "And this one here is Kindred. Older by two weeks." She placed his basket at Jake's left foot. "Two sons."

Jake looked from one to the other, Jacob and Kindred, the wonder so plainly written in the sunburned etches of his face, she knew she'd done the right thing.

CHAPTER 56

Sunday, and Ma'am and Gramma Amy were coming for an overnight visit, leaving their own ranch to the hired hands until their Monday return. No matter this was Rose's farm, larger than her grandfather's, that she'd been married now seven years, that she and her husband ran over fifteen hundred head of cattle, that she was mother to five healthy children, girls and boys both. It was as if she had become again that young girl, the scrawny chicken too plain for any man to want.

This year, the third in a row, showed every sign of another prosperous one — a bumper crop of cotton and corn, another hand hired and added to the bunkhouse, both her herd and Jake's free of disease, market prices in Kansas anticipated to be high, the children well except for normal ailments. Even after taking out Creek Council's share, they were still well ahead and able to save a little.

They'd worked hard to get to this point on the ranch, and settled into a routine. Elizabeth brought them much-needed help, especially with Jake so often gone, but not so often he didn't plant a new child in Rose each year or two. Yes, Elizabeth had brought them both her hard work and good luck.

Jake and Elizabeth got on from the start, and there was lightness around the table after supper whenever he was home before leaving again on the road to Kansas or Texas or within Indian Territory. Elizabeth was chatty where Rose was not, and could coax a smile from Jake at will. He relaxed when she was around, and they even eased into the habit of inviting some of their closer-in neighbors to share supper with them on an occasional Sunday. The ranch still demanded, but there was a vitality to offset the constant choring, a cheerfulness somehow connected to Elizabeth. The children without exception adored her, Laura, Lady, Kindred, Jacob, and now Ned, all eager to gain her attention, eager to please her, and where Rose set the bar high in her expectations of her children, Elizabeth gave that journey a taste of fun. Of play.

Rose and Jake never dwelled on Kindred's addition to the household, as if talk could cause an unraveling neither was willing to test. For a while, in the beginning, they tiptoed round each other. For the most part, Rose's hurt burrowed deep and scabbed over, but when she couldn't shake off a mood, she'd spend long, solo hours canning or at the spinning wheel, relying on Elizabeth to serve as conduit between her and Jake, safe haven. And as months passed, and then years, they were all swept back into the necessary ebbs and flows of growing the ranch, and Rose let go some of her distrust of her husband, sometimes forgetting for days at a time to be uneasy of his weeks away on the trail and what he might be doing there. The winds that threatened to destroy them three years before with Angeli's visit had quieted, and what settled across her heart now was as close to peace as she was likely to ever get.

"Don't let the *sofki* burn," Rose said to Elizabeth, suddenly reminded of a time so very long ago when she took the blame for her little sister's carelessness when preparing *sofki* for the white agriculture agents on Grampa Cow Tom's ranch. Now the dark kitchen was her own, clean and orderly, though they'd been cooking for days in preparation. She stirred the big pot on the stove to test for the mixture's consistency, and tasted from the ladle. Perfect. As good as Ma'am's.

"I'm not a child," Elizabeth snapped. She wiped her hands on her apron and studied Rose. "Why so skittish? It's only Ma'am and Gramma Amy, and not like it's the first time."

"It comes so easy for you."

"What comes easy?" Elizabeth asked.

"Everything."

Elizabeth grimaced, but Rose pretended not to notice. She didn't have time or patience to backtrack and explain herself, even if she could, or to calm feathers. There was too much still to do before her mother arrived. She wasn't sure who softened over the years, her or Ma'am, but things were improved between them now. Somehow her life with Jake allowed each of them to change into more accepting people. Still, everything need be perfect today.

"Rose," Elizabeth said. Her voice was soft but firm. "The visit will go well."

Rose stopped where she stood and closed her eyes, tight. When she opened them again, the flutters had calmed.

"Of course it will," she said. She brushed a few stray bread crumbs from the table. "I don't know how I'd manage without you here."

"No need to find out anytime soon."

"Someday you'll marry and have your own place. Whatever will I do then?"

"Someday," Elizabeth said. "But not today. Everything I need is right here with you."

"I forgot the cha-cha!"

Rose called Laura away from her scrub brush on the wooden floors of the front room, and sent her for a big jar of cha-cha from the storehouse. Rose could count on her daughter to assist with the babies and the boys when they woke from naps. Jake was in the south meadow with the hands, branding season almost at the finish, but he had promised to be back well before supper.

They were almost ready.

Ma'am and Gramma Amy arrived in a cloud of dust. They rode in on the same split-oak wagon her grandmother drove when she left her grandfather's ranch to go to Okmulgee as a cook, twelve years ago, each dent and nick in the wood bringing its own memories. At least the wheels looked safe, and newly crafted.

Age brought Ma'am's looks closer to Gramma Amy's, a fuller face, a fuller figure, gray-white hair, though her mother still carried the sour expression Rose remembered from childhood, and Gramma Amy the same calm.

She helped each down from the wagon, and showed them round the place and the new purchases added since their last visit, careful not to brag on the hand water pump in the kitchen or the new spinning wheel in the barn. She left them to freshen up in the room in the house she'd cleared for them for the night, and rushed to finish the rest of her chores.

By the time they sat to supper, Rose worried less that something might go wrong. Everyone ate with a hearty appetite, and asked for more. She busied herself, back and forth from the kitchen, insisting on filling each plate herself, her nerves smoothing as the chatter around the table grew comfortable.

Jake was in his element, and entertained as if he were king and the women his subjects. She marveled again at how at ease Jake was with everyone, how he drew them in with the energy of his talk and his enthusiasm.

"Cow 'most took a plug out of my arm today," said Jake. "Almost didn't see that back leg coming at me until too late to get out the way."

"Sounds like Hadjo," Gramma Amy said.

Rose laughed, the image of her grandfather's cow coming to her. "The trickster."

"Who's Hadjo?" Elizabeth asked.

"I haven't set my mind on that old cow for a long time," said Gramma Amy. A dreamy, faraway look crept to her face, and made her look years younger. "Your Grampa sure was fond of that animal. Treated him more like pet than cow. He practiced his courting words on Hadjo before coming for me."

Abruptly, Rose's mood soured. Everyone smiling, laughing, only skimming off the good parts of her grandfather, while she was left isolated in her knowledge, shackled by the promises of silence she'd made to him as he lay dying. Not for the first time, she resented her grandfather, the unfair burden he'd piled on her. What he'd asked of her was too much, and wrong. She wanted her grandmother to stop talking about him.

"There's gooseberry cobbler," she said, standing. "Elizabeth, help me dish up."

"Wait," Elizabeth said. "I want to hear Gramma Amy."

"What kind of cow?" asked Jake. He leaned forward in his chair.

"Spotted, black and white, not scrub either, but bred right." Amy smiled at the memory. "Broad haunches, and ornery when she wanted to be. She had her moods, but with Cow Tom she was at her best. He kept her till she dropped of her own at pasture. Wasn't long after that Old Turtle passed over."

"Old Turtle?" Now Ma'am was interested. "Wasn't he blind, taught Papa how to bring a sickly cow back into health?"

"Elizabeth, dessert?" reminded Rose.

"Honestly, Rose," Elizabeth said. "You'd think these were your stories. They belong to all of us. Just because Grampa carted you along wherever he went doesn't mean you're the only one deserving to hear them. You wouldn't share then, you won't share now." She looked around the table. "Who wants to hear Gramma?"

Laura raised her hand, shyly, and Lady followed her big sister's lead. Kindred and Jacob waved their arms in the air. Baby Ned, in his basket in the corner, was still too small to understand.

There was a hard glint in her sister's gaze that Rose didn't like, an anger there that matched her own. She looked away.

"I been trying to pry stories about her grandfather out of Rose for years," said Jake, "but she clams up."

"Always been that way," said Ma'am.

Rose motioned Laura, and her daughter

reluctantly followed her into the kitchen to serve up the plates. Everything felt ruined. This was the ultimate betrayal, them ganging up on her. She could hear her grandmother's voice from the other room, reaching back through the years, remembering, telling, and each word was as if someone chipped away at the very bedrock on which she stood. She'd kept the stories locked down so long, she felt stripped bare.

Rose sent Laura with plates of cobbler, but stayed in the kitchen, washing, tidying, storing. She couldn't make herself go back to the others. Jake's voice drifted in to her, loud and in high spirits, weaving tales of his last cattle drive, and laughter followed. Still, she couldn't rejoin them.

Her grandmother came alone into the kitchen, but said nothing at first, looking around at the neatly stocked shelves, the scrubbed floor, the clean aprons hanging from hooks on the wall ready to use. She ran her hand over the top of the brand-new cookstove.

"You've come far," Gramma Amy said. "A solid home. Children. There's pride to that."

Rose remembered how broken her grandmother was at her grandfather's funeral fifteen years before, how in that moment she'd felt she was the parent and her grandmother the child. Over time, Gramma Amy found a way to recover herself, and Rose was secure in her grandmother as guide again. And yet, Rose couldn't find words.

A burst of laughter came from the other room, and then the children's giggles. Once more, Jake's voice, and Ma'am and Elizabeth egging him on.

"You draw your power from Cow Tom, like water from a well," Gramma Amy said quietly, "as do I. Our family needs that power too. Let it go. You won't break."

How much easier for Rose if she could talk to her grandmother, tell her about the torching of the Seminole villages. Her grandfather as murderer. If she could explain why she remained silent.

"But Grampa chose me," Rose said, her voice small. Grampa Cow Tom had gifted her his shame, the darkness in his soul forevermore twined in with his goodness, such that she didn't know how to sort them out for herself, let alone for anyone else. Could Gramma Amy love Grampa Cow Tom the same if she told? Rose hated this burden. What started as a promise to her grandfather was now a way of being she couldn't control.

"Let go the needs of a child," Gramma Amy said. "You are equal to anyone. But if you think you're not, you're not."

Gramma Amy didn't understand. Couldn't understand. This was nothing to do with worthiness, but Rose accepted her grandmother's words, burying ever deeper her grandfather's shame beneath her own.

CHAPTER 57

After a long night in the barn at the spinning wheel, Rose looked forward to a hot meal and a bit of shut-eye before tackling the day. Elizabeth would already be up and had surely taken charge of the early morning kitchen by now, and started breakfast for the ranch hands. She'd need help with the children, especially Kindred and Jacob, unmanageable four-year-olds who made mischief everywhere. How different to have such male energy in the house, after so many generations of girl babies. She was blessed.

This wasn't the first full night spent at the loom by lantern light, an activity that soothed her like no other, strangely peaceful despite the clack and bang of the shuttle wheel, with its added benefit of practicality, producing an end product of material she could use to sew clothes for the children or a new shirt for Jake or a dress for Elizabeth, or a piece to embroider for slip pillows. The last few months she'd had great trouble sleeping. No matter how early she turned in, or how tired she was, her hold on sleep broke after an hour or two abed, and she woke to vague, feverish memories of chased dreams gone uncaught.

She had made her own family, as her Grampa Cow Tom predicted; a successful husband, children, sturdy and strong, and her sister, radiant and plump, content with her new life with them. They'd made the ranch a going concern, with money padlocked and buried beneath the floorboards for when bad years came. Rose congratulated herself on fighting through that dark time with Jake.

Weary, Rose slipped into the house, picking at the stray wisps of fluff settled on her dress from the carded wool she'd spun. She heard them before she saw them, Jake and Elizabeth, and although they whispered in frantic, low tones to each other, the words traveled across the distance as if meant for her ears alone.

"With child."

There sometimes comes a moment of comprehension when everything clears at once, and although the reality was there waiting to be seen, the recognition remains murky, just below the surface. After, it seems impossible the truth had not revealed itself before. For Rose, one moment her sister was her greatest ally, and the next, her mortal enemy, with the utterance of those two damning words, and the immediate certainty that Jake was the father. She'd played the fool for the past two years, again, with her husband, with her children, with her life.

Rose came out of the shadow into the glow of the kitchen so they could see her. They stood close to one another, her sister and her husband, not touching, but with an intimacy that threatened to knock her to her knees.

"Whose baby?" she demanded. She needed to hear the words to force the reality.

Elizabeth looked to Jake, her fear so thick she reeked of it, and Rose needed no further confirmation. Alongside, Jake distanced himself slightly from Elizabeth, his eyes on Rose, a bear caught in a trap. Rose couldn't stand still. She turned to flee, where, she didn't know, but anywhere away from the sight of the two of them.

"Wait," Jake said.

"Wait?" Rose asked. "Haven't I waited too long?"

"I've only found out myself," he said.

Rose didn't dare look at Elizabeth, her rage too large to control. "My sister? You brought this to our ranch?"

"I'm sorry," said Jake.

"It just . . . happened," said Elizabeth. "A mistake. Please, Rose. I would never in my right mind hurt you. You're everything to me."

Rose bolted from the room, back to the barn. The tears came and she couldn't choke them back, and after a time she stopped trying, letting them stream until the front of her dress was damp and her throat grown raw from her moans.

She heard the creak of the heavy barn door, and knew it was Jake, come to her. She didn't interrupt the course of her mourning, crying out her agony until she was spent, and he waited, not far from where she had thrown herself on a bundle of hay. At one point he tried to come closer, but she stopped him with a look.

When at last she thought her voice steady enough, she turned her face to her husband.

"Choose," she said.

Midwifing came naturally to Rose, trained from the time she was a little girl by her Gramma Amy, but there was nothing natural about the prospect of delivering Elizabeth's child by Jake. Elizabeth waited in her bedroom alone, labor progressing, while Rose lingered on the other side of the door, steeling herself to go in. Rose knew her sister was terrified by the prospect of delivering her first baby, and equally terrified that her only source of comfort and help came in the form of a sister who had barely spoken to her or looked her in the eye since the day the nature of the relationship between Jake and Elizabeth came to light.

The tools of her trade were carefully laid out beside the bed, cleaned and checked just that morning when labor first started, but try as she might, Rose couldn't force herself to go in to Elizabeth. She knew her job, the job of every midwife. Not only assist in the delivery of a baby but gain the trust of the mother, assuring her that as midwife, she understood her craft and all would be well. But that seemed impossible in this circumstance.

The last few months had been hell on earth, watching Elizabeth bloom to readiness, the child taking on burgeoning shape under her tunic. Each day, Rose blocked her ears to Elizabeth's appeals, gaining strength from the righteousness of her own pain-filled silences until Elizabeth, beaten, retreated back into silences of her own. Jake's frequent absences made things easier. Still, Rose played over and over in her mind the image of the two of them together, unable to stop herself. But with Jake gone, Rose went about her daily tasks and focused all of her wordless anger in one direction. Elizabeth.

She pulled up the floorboard in her bedroom, hers and Jake's, wrenched out the heavy strongbox, and fit the key in the lock. Inside were items precious to her, documents, gold, silver, and in the corner, a cream-colored linen handkerchief twisted into a double knot, identical to one Elizabeth possessed. She wasn't sure where Elizabeth kept her totem, but of all the valuables that might go missing through flood or fire or theft, this was the only thing she could never replace. Rose unknotted the handkerchief and held the single penny her Grampa Cow Tom had given her in her palm. She held the coin so tightly and so long that her hand began to ache. Carefully, when she felt herself ready, she returned the penny to the handkerchief, drew the knot taut, and put the strongbox back in its hiding place.

She knew she must do what had to be done.

Rose entered the room set up for the

birthing and closed the door tight behind her.

CHAPTER 58

Rose circled the front room and peered out the window, waiting. Elizabeth still sat in a rocking chair on the front stoop of the ranch house, handkerchief in hand, sniffling. Every once in a while, she broke into great sobs, shoulders heaving, producing fresh tears from her red-rimmed eyes. Her belongings lay piled in various bags and pouches at her feet, and she wore her best dress, the stiff gingham with both hoop and bustle, as if a proper lady, not a twenty-five-year-old child of the prairie who at one time picked out undigested kernels of corn from horse droppings for nourishment in order to survive.

Jacob and Kindred played in the packed dirt of the front yard, each intent in their separate games. They often played in just this way, not exactly together, but so aware of the other that if one walked away, the other followed, not far behind.

"Auntie Lizbeth," Jacob called out, and

held up his hoop for her comment. When she didn't respond, Kindred padded over to where she sat and laid his head in her lap. She stroked his hair, absently, and sobbed afresh.

How often in the past had Rose softened to her younger sister's tears, until she came to recognize any wellspring of concern only served to engulf her by the end? She refused to be fooled this time. She returned to hands and knees, hard-scrubbing the planks of the front room floor, only leaving off once she heard the approach of the cart's wheels on the gravel path outside the ranch house door, the whinny of the fatigued horse, the harsh set of the hand brake as wood scraped wood. Still, she waited indoors.

"C'mon, dear," she heard Gramma Amy say to Elizabeth, her voice more kind than Rose thought Elizabeth had a right to expect. Certainly more kindness than Rose intended.

"I'm not leaving without my child," Elizabeth said. Her voice was surprisingly strong.

Rose gave her sister credit. Defiant to the end, even as she was thrown to the mercy of family who would still have her.

"That cannot be," said Gramma Amy. Rose heard a new weariness. Her grandmother had seen too much, lived through too much. "We talked of this already and agreed. You promised your mother. Six months to weaning."

"He's mine, not hers."

"She has a claim," said Gramma Amy. "As you know."

"I am the boy's mother. He came from my body. Help me, Gramma. Please. It wasn't only me to fault."

"And mistakes carry a price. Six months come and gone. Grab hold to your things and get to the wagon. We're going home."

"My home is with Eugene."

"Not here," said Gramma Amy. "Not anymore."

Heavy-booted footsteps and then a thudding on the flatbed. Her grandmother must have asked a ranch hand to help load the wagon. Rose refused to hide herself any longer, not on her own ranch, the ordeal almost to an end.

From today, they would all move forward again, without the constant pall of reminder. The awkward silences, the accusations, the sickening aftermath of betrayal, the pleas for forgiveness, all relegated now to a tapestry of the past. She gathered up the baby from the crib in the corner, still drowsy with sleep, and stepped out onto the stoop. The sun was bright, and although a harsh glare rendered her sister a squinted obscurity, she took great care to affect calm and stare in that direction, as if made of stone. In this last year, she had decided stone was the safest state of mind around Elizabeth.

"Gramma Amy," Rose said in greeting.

"Rose."

Her grandmother walked toward the stoop in a slow, halting gait. From uncovered head to moccasined foot, she looked brittle and ancient. Her hair was totally white, in thin, coarse plaits curled tightly at the back of her neck, and she'd lost weight. She limped as she moved, the lameness more pronounced than when Rose saw her last, two months prior when she traveled to her grandfather's ranch to bring her case before the family. Ma'am. Her grandmother. Gramma Amy's sunken cheeks highlighted her wrinkled, sun-baked skin. Instead of fishing and dozing in the sun, surrounded by children and grandchildren and great-grandchildren, now she started over with a wayward, man-stealing granddaughter.

"The child?" Gramma Amy asked, holding out her hands.

"Of course."

Rose transferred Eugene to her grandmother's arms. He was awake now, and before long would cry in hunger. They needed to make this brief. Rose might be stone, but had no interest in this kind of cruelty, in the spectacle of a baby crying for mother's milk as the mother was forced to keep her breast from him.

Gramma Amy fingered the features of Eugene's face. Already he showed promise of a pretty child with delicate features, the cocoa of his smooth skin a perfect blend of Jake's light and Elizabeth's dark, his hair a mass of ebony curls, a sunny disposition doubled-dipped from both. Six months ago, Rose played dutiful midwife to her sister, Elizabeth's young body needing minimal assistance, a fast birth. Eugene was a good baby, an easy baby, as if he'd decided early he didn't want to make undue trouble for anyone.

Eugene started to fuss, and Elizabeth bolted from the wagon.

"No," commanded Gramma Amy. Elizabeth stopped, the plea on her face plain. But she didn't come closer, tightly wrapped arms around her chest as if hugging herself. She stood, unsure.

Rose put herself in Elizabeth's place. If one of her children needed her, especially a helpless baby of six months, nothing and no one could stop her. Not man nor woman nor beast. Certainly not one single word spoken, no matter by whom. Elizabeth was weak.

Gramma Amy handed Eugene back to Rose. "We are family still. This wasn't easy to decide, what was best for the child. But Elizabeth can still see Eugene."

Rose nodded. "After another six months," she said. "As agreed."

"She is mother," Gramma Amy said. "And sister. Those can't be forgot."

"How could I forget?" Rose said bitterly.

Now her grandmother nodded silently. She limped toward Elizabeth, and led her to the wagon.

"I'll fight for him, Rose," said Elizabeth. "And I'll never give up. I wronged you, and I'm sorry, but you've turned hard and cold. Eugene deserves better."

Rose ignored her sister, as she had for the last few months, pretending she wasn't there at all. Silence was all she had to wield. She promised herself to never speak to Elizabeth again.

Elizabeth stared over her shoulder, not once taking her eyes from the bundle that was Eugene. Not when Amy flicked the rein for the horse, not as they disappeared from sight of the ranch.

The entire business hadn't taken but a

small part of the morning. There were animals to feed, meals to prepare, gardens to tend, children to mold, ranch hands to monitor. Jake was on a cattle drive, and the everyday doings of the ranch fell to her.

She fed Eugene first, in the same rocking chair Elizabeth vacated. He slapped his hands against the nippled bottle she fashioned, unhappy with the blend of cow's milk and honey of his new diet. He was fussy, expecting his mother's smell and his mother's milk, but not inconsolable. He finally sucked at the substitute in defeat and fell once again into a drowsed sleep, succumbing to her will.

Let the rest of the ranch wait, Rose thought. The regular chores went undone as she acclimated Eugene to his new life. To his new mother.

CHAPTER 59

A freakish afternoon sun beat down on the prairie as if in full of summer, though the season registered only late spring, the ranch's busy season for calves, colts, and fawns. The glare was intense and the air so still and hot that even the littlest ones, usually afflicted with too much energy, kept rooted, neither breaking rank to tug at Rose's skirt nor to bedevil one another. They sat cross-legged in the shade, their sweat-drenched backs against the wall of the barn, watching their older brothers and sisters.

The centennial would soon be upon them, one century playing out and replaced with another. Rose tried to tease out her future, and found she couldn't guess what 1900 would bring, whether it would be better or worse for her family. She told herself the transfer of century was nothing but a date, one day's slip to the next, but anyone could smell the change riding the wind sure as dust following stampede. If Jake weren't gone on a drive, he'd reassure her. She wished him home.

"I set up the cans, Mama Rose," Eugene said.

Eugene was tall for almost nine, but no matter his desperation to bridge the gap between himself and Jacob and Kindred, to his older brothers he was merely a child, relegated to picking up the tin cans they shot off the fence during Wednesday target practice, someone to shoo away if he tried to tag along after them for too long.

"All right," Rose said, "Jacob first."

Rose had yet to get used to the invasion of the last couple of years, so many unfamiliar faces, mostly scruffy white men come to Indian Territory to claim what they now called unassigned land, stopping briefly for a night in the barn or a bit of food or water before pushing on, strangers setting their sights too close to Indian land. These settlers had a look about them, determination edged with entitlement, forcing her to mindfulness of all she and Jake had, as well as what could be taken from them and given to others. The talk of power struggles within tribes, between tribes, and between tribal governments and Washington unsettled her.

But short of flood or tornado, regardless of a merciless sun in a cloudless Oklahoma sky or a parade of humanity traipsing across their land, Rose refused to cut short the regular Wednesday lesson behind the red barn. Her barn. Her ranch.

"Take your time," Rose said to Jacob. "Find the can in your sight and pull steady."

Jacob hitched up his trousers, squared off, took rapid aim between each shot, and hit only two cans. He shrugged and deposited the spent six-shooter into Rose's hands.

"You satisfied for Kindred besting you again?" she said.

Rose's trick of playing to the competition between the two brothers had become less effective of late. The boys were twelve, Jacob and Kindred, as close as twins in their early years, but that bond had begun to notice-ably fray.

"Who's good at the gun isn't necessarily good where it matters. Or mayhaps a *gen-u-ine* Indian's aim is better. Ma'am." Jacob ambled toward the shade, unapologetic.

Her son perched on the ragged edge of sass, but Rose held her tongue. It was just too hot. She shook her head at her too-charming, too-bright son, willing to work hard at things that interested him, but almost impossible to engage in what did not.

She signaled Eugene with a wave of her hand. The boy took off at a trot and scooped up the cans his older brother managed to hit, and placed them upright along the split-rail fence alongside Jacob's misses. Six cans, six tries for each child.

"Kindred."

Kindred, shirtless, wore a breechcloth, buckskin leggings attached to his hip belt, and moccasins. His hair usually fell straight downward in a braid almost to his waist, decorated with feathers, shells, and strings, the sides of his head shaved, but today, he donned his deerskin-strip turban. Rose noticed a new indigo owl tattoo on his forearm.

Rose handed Kindred the pistol without comment. She no longer tried to coax him in his dress, nor did she have instruction for him on Wednesday afternoons. He didn't need her advice to improve. And he didn't want it.

With detached calm, Kindred took careful but easy aim, and squeezed back on the trigger lock. One can after another flew off the fence, until there were six lying on the ground, a new rent in each.

Kindred checked to make sure Jacob acknowledged his feat, but Jacob stared purposefully elsewhere.

"O mvl kv, Ecke," Kindred said, handing Rose the pistol.

"English," Rose warned.

"Faultless, Mother."

There was something in his tone Rose didn't like. What was it in the air, for her sons to border on such disrespect? Her best milking cow, due any time, had been off feed for two days, and she couldn't shake her foreboding about the impending birth of the calf. And last week, the entire crop of cucumbers in her garden quit blooming, suddenly, the leaves turning an ugly yellow before shriveling and falling to the ground.

Eugene retrieved the cans. "I want a turn too," he complained.

Rose had been at the business of educating her children long enough, mindful of contrary natures as well as abilities, to understand that short-lived desire and long-term persistence were two entirely different things.

"This is no game," Rose answered, as much for the benefit of the younger children listening as for Eugene. "Everyone learns to shoot a gun to protect the ranch. Eugene is still too young, but his time comes next year. When he's ten."

Eugene poked out his lower lip. Rose winced at the stab of recognition of Elizabeth in his features. She'd grown up with that look, a sullen expression her sister assumed when she didn't get her way. Seeing that mirrored in Eugene reminded her of too many things best forgotten. Rose shot Eugene a mother look, and he quickly straightened up his face and ducked his head, not daring to lift his eyes to meet hers as he set the cans up again. He was still malleable, fearful of her disapproval. If only she could keep them all that way.

She called Laura next, also an excellent shot. Her eldest was as conversant with pistol and rifle as with a needle. Rose mechanically reloaded the pistol for her daughter, and watched Kindred and Jacob, standing side by side, not quite facing each other. If this had been just a year ago, they would be banded together, in unison against the world, whispering secrets or without words, communing in a code of their own making that didn't include anyone else. But today, they stood apart, almost as if strangers.

She allowed all the older children their turns, then released them to their farm duties, pulling Eugene to the side.

"Take the pony. You be back home before the thick of choring tomorrow morning. Hear? That means setting out from Gramma

Amy's ranch before dawn."

She couldn't bring herself to mention Elizabeth's name. She'd had to agree to Eugene's time with his other mother, but she didn't have to acknowledge her sister aloud.

"Yes, Mama Rose."

In spite of the heat, she finished up the afternoon lessons with the smaller ones, guiding them in spelling out their letters or reciting their sums. Rose checked the cow, already separate from the herd. She led her to the barn, slowly, before the animal could lie down in the field, and settled her in a stall. She expected the calf by morning, and set off to the kitchen to oversee her daughters in preparing supper.

CHAPTER 60

The household quieted, supper finished, the hands returned to the bunkhouse, dishes sudsed and towel-dried, the little ones already in bed, and the girls busy at their needlework. Jake was due home tomorrow. Rose missed him, his physical presence, his easy domination of the hands who preferred their orders coming from a man. Rose decided to make one last check on the cow before turning in.

"Kindred," she ordered, "come with me."

As hot as the day had been, once the sun disappeared, the air turned cool and a howling wind kicked in. Rose wrapped her shawl tight around her shoulders and handed Kindred the lamp to light their way to the barn.

As soon as she pushed open the wide barn door, she heard slow, heavy breathing. Kindred affixed the lantern to a hook on the stall's hardwood post while she determined what stage the labor took.

"Cow's still standing," she said to Kindred. "A while yet."

To be safe, Rose shoveled clear an area of manure and led the animal there. The cow looked at her, eyes glassy with dismissal. Most cow births required no human intervention, the mother taking the natural course, but Rose worried over this one, for good reason or no she wasn't yet sure. She settled herself on the milking stool in the corner. Kindred sat on a bale of hay, his legs crossed over each other. Just today, between shooting practice and supper, he'd found the time to add another crude indigo tattoo on his right leg, this one of a vine wrapping round his shin. She made a mental note to assign him more to do.

"Why you so set on dressing that way?" asked Rose.

"This is the way Creeks dress," said Kindred.

"Don't forget we're a little of this and a little of that," said Rose. "Even most of the full-bloods save the turban and the rest for ceremony. You and me, we think the old way, but you the only one who dresses to it."

His face betrayed nothing, and they lapsed into silence, save the loud rhythm of the cow's breathing. Despite the flickering gas lantern, only the fusty stink of manure and disturbing eddy of her mind kept Rose awake. Robbed of chores, and confined with a sullen son, she let her thoughts turn dark. She should have brought embroidery, something to occupy her hands. A crush of worry stole up. She had responsibility for ten children, with her childbearing years apparently not yet done. She and Jake had a fifteen-hundred-cattle ranch to manage, and crops to bring in, and smallpox to guard against, and brutal weather of one type or another always descending on them full force, never safe to predict.

She'd almost forgot Kindred was there, when he spoke.

"Why can't they leave us be?"

"Who?"

"White boomers."

The last century had brought blessings, overall, that was certainly true, but not without severe setbacks along the way as Jake took risks to expand the herd and make improvements to the ranch, spreading ever outward on tribal lands along the Canadian River. More cattle, more hands, more fencing, more mouths to feed. More. But now there were white boomers and others from outside the nation, pushing steadily into

Indian Territory, laying claim to land supposedly set aside for tribes. Land appetite by noncitizens was unquenchable. The governments, both United States and tribal, forced themselves more and more into their lives.

"We aim to keep living on this land," Rose said.

"They'll come after the freedmen first," said Kindred. "There's nothing you can do."

She studied her son in the lantern light, this pale man-child struggling. The boy needed grounding, something gone missing in him, always trying to out-Creek the full-bloods. Rose wrestled with the notion of sharing one of Cow Tom's good stories with Kindred, here in this barn, tonight. Stories she'd withheld for years. The tale of how her grandfather bought his freedom might spark Kindred's pride in their family. Or Grampa saving his mother from slavers. Or how he gave an untested girl the courage to shoot a gun at his funeral, and convinced her she could take on anything.

Kindred knew of his great-grandfather by name and reputation, of course, but possessed no sense of how Cow Tom gloried in all parts of himself, Creek and African. All black Creeks knew Cow Tom signed a treaty to protect the freedmen. That he was a chief. Should she describe more than the man of public legend? Break the promise? A story might help Kindred find his way.

"No," said Rose. "There's always something can be done. One man's determination can thread the needle for all that come after. Your great-grandfather was such a man."

Kindred pulled himself erect on the bale, spine straight. He barely breathed, his surly mood suddenly evaporated. He stared at her, waiting.

Rose couldn't decide how to begin, where to start. The image leaped to her mind of a black Seminole brave, dead in the Florida swamp, her grandfather's doing, and the silence grew long.

The cow suddenly gulped at the air, a startling sound, her sides caved, labor finally started.

"Run get a bucket with water from the pump and a bar of lye soap," Rose ordered.

An eerie quiet except for the cow's distress folded around them in the barn as they waited for the second stage of labor. Rose couldn't make herself speak, concentrating on the cow instead, and Kindred didn't push. Two hours passed, the cow contracting but showing no further progress.

Finally, Rose rolled up her sleeves, lathered her hands in the wash bucket, soaped her arms to the armpit, and slathered on petroleum jelly. She soaped the cow's hindquarters as well, speaking in a gentle voice. The cow delivered the water bag and began straining. She reached inside the cow with both hands, feeling her way until she found the calf in the birth canal, pinching lightly. Movement. The calf was alive. She felt a leg, and ran her finger down the bones. Only one joint between hock and hoof. A back leg, not front. She'd delivered posterior before, trained the first time by Grampa Cow Tom. The effort had been hard on all three, cow, calf, and Rose, and she'd lost two calves this way. She centered the calf in the birth canal, clasped her hands, and moved her arms in and out for several minutes to speed delivery.

Rose was drenched with sweat. She worked steadily the next half hour, pulling in steady motion whenever the cow pushed, advancing the calf down the canal. With the next contraction, both the calf's hind feet emerged. Rose continued to pull and guide, and on the next push, the calf's body came into view, and finally forelegs and nose. Rose picked through the gummy gore to pinch the calf's tongue. The tongue retracted, the calf fine. Rose stepped back into the shadows to let the cow finish her work on her own.

The cow found her feet again, afterbirth hanging, and began to lick her baby. Her calf shook its head, wet ears slapping, and kicked its feet, and the mother continued her raspy-tongued cleaning. The calf stood unsteadily, then fell, again and again until balancing upright, seeking first milk.

With calf sucking, and cow in satisfactory health, she and Kindred were free to return to the ranch house. But Kindred hesitated, scratching at his owl tattoo, stalling, looking to her.

Rose could not bring herself to open her mouth to speak. She despised herself this weakness, but the weight of the promise trumped the need reflected in her son's eyes.

She was so tired. She'd try again some other time. Maybe tomorrow.

The moment was past.

CHAPTER 61

While thunderstorms built to the east and the west, and the wildflowers in the meadow competed, coming into their own dazzling displays, Rose dozed in her rocking chair in the full of the day, protected by the shade on their wraparound porch, beans unsnapped in the big bowl at her feet. After her long night in the barn, up to her bloodied elbows in the cow's delivery, only raw will and stubbornness prevented her from locking herself in her bedroom, drawing the shades tight across the windows, climbing under the quilt, and giving in to sleep until she felt herself again. And she couldn't erase the image of that last yearning look on Kindred's face before they walked back to the house in silence.

The thump of horse hooves and squeal of wagon wheels signaled Jake's arrival from the dry-goods store in Haskell. Only one week gone this trip. She watched him roll barrels of salt and syrup off the wagon, and then shoulder two bags of sugar before one of the hands arrived to help. Together, the men unloaded the rest, toting all to the storehouse in several trips. The wagon emptied, Jake dug out a parcel wrapped in newspaper under the buckboard plank, tucked it under his arm, and joined Rose on the porch.

Jake smiled a knowing smile. "For those beauteous feet," he said.

He handed her the package, and she carefully unwrapped it, smoothing out the newspaper and folding the edges into a neat square for future use. Inside was a pair of women's black shoes, new, the style slightly different from her last. They were leather, high-topped, with four small buttons on each shoe and black corded laces. Rose was tempted to kick off her old shoes, run-over at the heels and scuffed, to try on the new, right there on the front porch, but decided to wait until she was behind locked doors, where she could enjoy them at her leisure. Jake watched her.

She nodded her acknowledgment and put the shoes aside, bringing the bowl of beans once again to her lap. She began to snap them into bits.

"The calf?" Jake asked.

"Calf and cow are fine," answered Rose. She thought again of the long stretches of anxious waiting amid the soak of blood and gore in the barn last night. The moment beforehand when she almost pulled down the walls of the safe house where she kept her memories of Grampa Cow Tom. "For a time, I thought I'd lose both."

He dragged a chair over close to hers and sat, taking off his leather hat and shaking off some of the dust, running his fingers through his hair. Rose noticed a strand of gray mixed in with the brown. Jake wasn't so young anymore, but still closer to young than to old, and he yet exuded a powerful attraction. Her husband was eager to talk.

"There's news," he said.

She waited for him to get to it. News meant interruption, interference, an unwelcome reaching from the outside world into what they'd built. Rose wasn't partial to most news.

"Everyone's in an uproar about the Dawes Roll in Haskell."

"What's that?" asked Rose.

"The government wants us to come in and register on the Dawes Roll. They're listing each person in the nation, every member recorded, child or chief. In town, some are for, some against."

"We're already on the list," said Rose. "Been listed since I was nothing but a girl."

"That's Canadian Colored Town payroll," Jake corrected. He shrugged. "This is different. Payroll is our fair share of tribe money from Washington. Tribal Council decides who's on that list. Full-bloods tried to outfox the government by refusing to turn over names. Foolish. Now Washington sidesteps the tribes to make their own list. Payroll is by Creek Nation government, the Dawes Roll is United States government. Showdown's coming."

"Can't we sign up on both?"

"Full-bloods claim the right to decide who's enrolled and who isn't. They say this is another step by white men in Washington to break down the Indian and take power away from the tribe."

"Break down the Indian?" asked Rose. Her mind was quick to see the trap in any plan. "Indian or members of the nation?"

"So far, members of the nation," said Jake. "But the Dawes Roll is to be all citizens of the nation too. Full-bloods, mixed-bloods, and freedmen, according to treaty. Even adopted citizens."

"Full-bloods would gladly shed us." She picked out a worm in the bowl of beans and threw the wriggler into the dirt. "More for them."

"But your grandfather's treaty holds so far," said Jake. "Full-bloods aren't the only ones against. Big cattlemen and land companies weigh against the Dawes Roll too, hiring marplots and boodlers and lawyers to slow the census down, to keep things as they are. But it isn't working. Agents from Washington swell the towns. Flyers everywhere you look setting dates for enrollment, and men out surveying, making maps of all the land. I tell you, Washington will carry the day this time round."

"Land maps?"

"That's what I been trying to tell you. The Dawes Roll comes first, then Washington uses their list to give out land to the people. An allotment. Land not to the tribe like always, but direct to each person, free and clear, belonging to us by name and no other."

"Free land? What do they need from us to give out free land?"

"Proof. Proof of citizenship in the nation. That's the only way to get the land. The allotment goes to citizens only. The call's out to members of all nations, but they start with Creeks first. Some full-bloods threaten harm to anyone accepting allotment."

"What do you think?" asked Rose.

"That the old ways are done," said Jake. "One by one Washington will break tribes down and take what we have away. We best make good while we can. First enrollment, then allotment. Government will give out bits of land and keep the rest, surround us with immigrant boomers, and then fold us into their country, force us to give up our territory. That's the talk, anyway." He paused. "We're Indian, and we're freedman, both. But no one, Creek or government, will look after us better than we look after ourselves."

Rose admired her husband this. He might not possess formal education, he might have a heart so soft he gave away too freely what was theirs, but his mind was keen and penetrating, and he understood large-scale motivation and trickery long before others did. Things even her suspicious mind didn't always grasp.

"So we'd do best under a United States list?"

"Maybe, maybe not. Whites always been treating us worse than Indians. Full-bloods are stalling. Not likely to do much good though. Not against Washington."

"What of allotment?" Rose asked. She tried to shake off a wave of pure panic.

"What about the ranch?"

"That's the root of the fever sweeping town," said Jake. "For each and every person in a family on the roll, babe or grayhead, the government promises one hundred sixty acres."

"One hundred sixty acres?" Rose asked. "But we number thirteen, with babies and Laura's man."

She sprang from her chair and into the house. Beans spilled from the bowl onto the porch, but she didn't care. When she returned, she wet the tip of the pencil she'd brought and made the calculation on the reverse side of an old store receipt.

"That's more than two thousand acres," Rose figured. "Added to what we already have." She was dizzy with the thought.

"No," said Jake. "Allotment starts with land where you already made improvements. They transfer those to your name, and for the rest, you choose plots not belonging to anyone else. No guarantee where additional plots are, but everybody gets their full allotment."

Rose's mind was already at work. The oldest boys, Jacob and Kindred and Eugene, would soon need plots of their own to work until the time came to go off to live with their wives' families. Maybe a distribution of land in the boys' own names could keep Jacob, a self-declared businessman with an aversion to the manual practicalities of ranching, closer to home, could bind Kindred to his freedman family instead of chasing after the ways of the full-bloods, and could vanquish some of Eugene's restlessness, a man-child caught between Rose as mother and her sister, Elizabeth, as birth mother. Eugene's increasingly frequent trips to see Elizabeth left him off balance and resentful. Rose worried about slipknots of connection loosening between brothers. Between each of them and the rest of the family. Between them and her.

"You sure? Each?"

"That's the talk."

"Under our name? Nobody can take it?"

"Not unless we sell."

"What of the tribe? We'd be members still or no?"

Wasn't Grampa Cow Tom's last official act to ensure inclusion of the freedmen? For decades, her family had been solid members of the tribe.

"Members still," said Jake.

"There's some hitch," Rose said. She couldn't yet conjure the trick, but whenever something was offered to the Indians by the United States government, something else was sure to be stripped away. "Is our ranch safe?" she asked again. "Can they turn us out?"

"The Washington man said we lose the ranch if we don't sign up on the Dawes. That once we enroll with them and get allotment, the land is ours," said Jake. "Unassigned land won't belong to the Creek Nation in community anymore. Or the Cherokee Nation. Or any of the tribes. That land falls back to Washington, to turn over to white boomers, or do with as they will."

"We can't lose the ranch," said Rose.

"We're in a trap," Jake said. "Washington wants more land, and they'll get it. The Indian is used to giving up land, and in the end, they'll do like always. My worry is how they treat freedmen. There's talk of registering by blood quantum. Once they separate us out, they could decide to treat us like State Negroes or too-lates, like we haven't lived here all our lives."

"We're already separated out by town," said Rose. "We manage."

"They left us be, and we always got our payroll share. But we need to sign the Dawes. No Dawes, no land. Simple as that."

In this, Rose trusted Jake's instinct.

"Times change too fast," said Rose. Immigrants, both black and white, threatened everything they'd worked to build. More people stopped by the ranch each year that passed, and Jake reported a crush in the cities at least ten times increased from just a few years before, people buying bags of salt or shovels or packets of seed. Visitors told stories of non-Indian settlers on civilized tribe lands, staking out land claims, as if entitled.

"And talk of turning us into a state grows louder," Jake said. "Mark my words, it's coming. At least this way we have something official. Something harder to take away."

There was no good to come from turning Indian Territory into a part of the United States, Rose thought. At least nothing good for freedmen. But land in their own name. She wished her Grampa Cow Tom could have seen the coming of such a day.

"How do we enroll?" she asked.

"No plan yet, but the agent in town said word will come. Next year. Or year after."

Rose nodded. "Whenever," she said. "We'll be ready."

CHAPTER 62

They cleared the full day, leaving shortly
after sunup, once the boys milked the cows
and the most pressing chores were done.
They clambered into the wagon, Rose and
Jake on the buckboard with Lady between,
Jake driving the horse team, the rest in the
dusty bed behind. Rose wore her best dress
and a beaded jacket for the big day, and
though her fancy shoes pinched her feet,
she would wear no other.

"Kindred?" Rose asked. Rose put her
hand on Jake's wrist before he put rein to
horse. "Where's Kindred?"

"He said he'd see us in Okmulgee," Jacob
answered from the back. "That he'll get
there on his own."

Rose last saw Kindred at supper the night
before. He'd mentioned nothing about
breaking away on his own. This trip was
planned for weeks. "Why isn't he going with
us?" she asked.

Jacob just shrugged. The time of brothers covering for one another was past. Her sixteen-year-old son kept his own council, but he didn't shut her out the way Kindred did of late. Possibly Jacob really didn't know why Kindred absented himself on this important day. There was nothing to gain by pressing. Rose let it go.

They left Laura behind, too fresh from childbirth to travel well, in care of the smallest ranch children. Jacob and Eugene and the others bounced about in the wagon bed until they came to smoother roads leading to Okmulgee. Rose held tight to a bundle of papers she'd kept safe beneath the floorboards in her bedroom hiding place, all the formal proof of citizenship she'd accumulated over the years. The family Bible with the listing of the birth of each of her children. Her marriage certificate to Jake. The receipt from the Canadian Colored Town payroll of 1895. She wished she had her listing on the Dunn Roll from 1869, but she knew she was registered and would testify to it. Jake insisted she didn't need all these things, that they both were well documented over the years and therefore the children were as well, but if land was to be had, Rose didn't want a technicality to deny their acceptance.

Rose didn't expect the enormity of the convergence on the tent village in Okmulgee, the Creek capital. It was years since she'd been back and the town had grown beyond her imagining. The bustle and commotion hurt her ears and her eyes. From atop a rolling hill, she saw a great canvassed expanse spread out over the southwest corner of Okmulgee like an armada of ships at sea. But even before they got close enough to see the first tent pole, they began to choke on the dust of all the other families pouring into town. Now there was land to be had, suddenly everybody claimed Indian citizenship, valid or wishful thinking, including State Negroes from the old South and boomers who lost out in the land rush. Swarms of people matched swarms of dust, the air thick as if cattle were on stampede, and no matter which way she looked, Indians were everywhere, coming from every direction, on the move or idling.

All were accounted for but Kindred in the wagon bed. Absent again. Defiant again. The town's congestion would make a rendezvous with him close to impossible. How could they ever meet in the chaos that was this registration, where families, according to rumor, spent half the day or more waiting to be seen? To be tallied. To be authorized as true.

The noise deafened. Families squatted in the dirt everywhere, biding their time. On the main entryway into the heart of the tent city, a white man with a wild, black beard and squashed-down hat pulled low on his head to keep off the sun sat in a chair in the middle of the dirt road. He was surrounded by baffled questioners, and pointed them in one direction or another. The bearded man appeared to be an official, and Jake joined his line to make sense of the process. When Jake's turn came, he asked questions, first in Mvskoke, which the man didn't understand, and finally English. With the English, the bearded man responded with some degree of good cheer, pointing to one of the tents not far from where they stood. But when Jake motioned to his family, and Rose and the children joined him, the bearded man took one look at the pack of them, at Rose most especially, and suddenly shook his head, almost angry.

"No, no," he said. "Freedmen to the freedman tent," he said. "Over there."

He pointed this time in the opposite direction, on the far side of the square, to a tent at the edge of the clearing.

"My mother was blood Indian," said Jake. "I thought registration followed the mother."

The man stared briefly at Jake, a moment's hesitation, and then pointedly at Rose and the children. He stroked his beard, using his body as if to block entrance to the pathway, and again he shook his head. "Freedman tent is yonder," he said, and turned his attentions to another questioner, a full-blood in traditional regalia, from feathered turban to moccasined feet.

Jake hitched up his pants, a gesture Rose knew all too well as precursor to either bully or charm, and Rose thought he meant to argue them into the other tent, but to her surprise, as if thinking better of the effort, or convinced of the futility, he backed down without confrontation.

"Let's go." He stormed off, leaving Rose to collect up everyone in their group and follow.

They made their way as a family to the tent where the bearded man pointed. The people waiting were clearly darker. Most were obviously freedmen by complexion or feature, but ranged wildly in color, some as fair as Jake, some as dark as she. At least, Rose thought, even if they were separated out, as Jake had feared they would be, at least this was one way to reconnect with Kindred in the massive crowd. She could only hope he showed up soon to the freedmen's tent.

They joined the others squatting in the dirt waiting their turn. There were many ahead of them, and for a time, Jake didn't speak, nursing a private hurt. He'd come around, Rose thought, he always did, and she busied herself distributing the water and foodstuffs she'd brought, seeing to her family as best she could. Rose kept constant lookout for Kindred, nervous after the first passed hour, and more upset as two and then three slipped by. Their turn would come sometime today, and what if her son still hadn't appeared?

To their right was a family of blacks waiting for interview, a middle-aged man, a rag-headed woman, and six children ranging in age from toddler to old enough to tend the rest. Rose overheard them talking, and from the accent, she knew they were State Negroes from the South, outsiders, new immigrants, not native blacks from Indian Territory. They were on the hunt for free land without the qualifications. She wondered if they would be found out, a day's waiting for no gain.

Each time someone exited the tent, a frisson of excitement infected the waiting crowd. One family closer to registration, and the opportunity to hear impressions of what happened inside the tent. Freedmen emerged to tell the same basic tale, and the rumors Jake brought home were confirmed. They could expect to find two white men, clerks dispatched from Washington, sitting behind a table, their job to examine whatever documentation the petitioner had and ask questions until satisfied of citizenship. If the official representatives of the United States government weren't convinced one way or the other, they kept the case open, calling witnesses to confirm a family's claims.

At one point, Rose got up to stretch her legs, and wandered a bit from the tent. By then, they had waited well over four hours, and she resigned herself to registering Kindred in absentia. She walked dust-clogged lanes between one area of the vast tent city to the next, careful to keep her orientation. When her head cleared enough, and her muscles loosened, Rose headed back again to the freedmen's tent. Her family still squatted in the dirt, toward the head of the line. Their turn was closer, but not close, so she set out again, in the opposite direction, toward the area where they first entered the tent city, near the crossroads guarded by the bearded man.

Within the mass of humanity milling around the tent city, it wasn't her son she first registered, but his beloved deerskin turban, strips patched and replaced over years of wear. The hat fought its way into her consciousness even before the sheen on the pale face beneath, or the intricate tattoos covering his arms and legs and trunk. He'd come in time after all.

An enormous wave of relief coursed through her, and she started to rush to Kindred, but then froze. He wasn't alone, but strolled with purpose next to an older woman. It was years, sixteen, since she last saw Angeli, and then for only less than one hour's time, and yet she recognized her immediately. Older of face and body, her dark hair severe and pulled tight away from her face in traditional Creek style, no longer the desperate young girl who walked for days to give away her baby but an assured and almost matronly woman.

The two of them walked side by side, Kindred and Angeli, and even through her confusion, Rose thought again to yell out to him, to let him know his family waited for him, and where they were. But she was suddenly struck with the image, now not as mother but through the eyes of a stranger, observing her son as others would see him.

Kindred stood straight and tall amid the throng, surrounded by both full-blood and mixed-blood Creek Indians. Now that he was no longer in the context of their ranch, and coupled with a mother who could truthfully testify she bore him, Rose saw clearly what others must see. He could be by-blood Indian if he chose and no one else denied. As could have Jake this morning. Kindred could declare himself one thing or the other, at his whim. He could deny the family that bore him, as well as the family that raised him, and in either case, pass over to a different life. Or he could say nothing, and let young whelps from Washington who decided their fates and recorded these claims make up their own mind. Rose had no idea what Kindred would do. She was gripped with a sudden foreboding.

The cry died in her throat, a tainted thing, and Rose fell helplessly mute. Just as she had watched the gatekeeper, the bearded white man, banish Jake to the freedmen's tent because of his family's coloring, she saw the same man admit her son to the other side of the tent city.

And she watched as Angeli led the way, taking the turn to the right, away from the rest of them, and Kindred followed behind her in the same direction.

CHAPTER 63

Rose didn't know how her son found Angeli, or how Kindred persuaded her to come with him today, but hows no longer mattered. Kindred had chosen, and he hadn't chosen his family. Hadn't chosen her. She hurried back to the waiting place around the freedmen's tent, threading through the families clustered there, and sought out Jake. He was closer to the opening of the tent, their turn coming soon.

"Kindred," she began, but she couldn't continue without squatting down and shutting her eyes for a moment. "Kindred's gone to the by-blood camp."

"So he showed up," Jake said. He didn't seem overly concerned. "They'll send him here soon enough."

"You don't understand," said Rose. She expected Jake to jump up and do something, to go retrieve their son and bring him back where he belonged. But Jake didn't move.

"That woman is with him."

She couldn't bear to call Angeli by name, but from the expression on Jake's face, his guilt was clear. He looked on the verge of retching, leaning his head close to the dirt for a few seconds until composing himself. Rose couldn't quite place his response. Guilt? Shame? Despair? Defiance?

"What do you know about this?" asked Rose. It was as if there was a catching sickness in the air that leaped from Jake to her. Suddenly she felt ill, her stomach tensed and in wait for some heavier punch.

"I didn't think it would do any harm," said Jake, quietly.

Even as the question formed on her lips, Rose knew the answer. "What have you done?"

"He'd been after me for so long. He's no fool. His looks. Anyone can see he could be full-blood by look. He demanded to know who gave him birth. A few months back, I told him about Angeli. I never thought he'd look for her. I never dreamed he'd find her." He looked at Rose directly. "I never went back," he swore. "I haven't seen her for years."

Rose couldn't travel all the dangerous paths this admission created, not now. That Jake told Kindred about his birth mother without letting her know. That Kindred needed the mother who discarded him more than he needed her. She couldn't afford to dwell on whether or not to believe Jake had kept to his pledge to cut off communication with Angeli, an old wound reopened to everyone's peril.

"Do we go after him?" she asked, her voice atremble. "Or let him be?"

"We haven't lost him, no matter how they mark him today. Freedman or by-blood, he's our son."

There was little time for debate. A tall white man in an odd hat and too-small jacket barely covering his bulging stomach emerged from the tent and waved for the next family. Their turn had finally come.

Two white men sat behind a rickety four-legged table in the tent, surrounded by heavily bound books and sheaves of paper, as well as an inkpot and feathered nib pen. There were only two other chairs, and so Jake and Rose sat, the children fanned out around them, some standing, some sitting cross-legged on the earthen floor.

They looked young and unseasoned to Rose, both white men, and yet they went about their tasks with a certain absolute, if bored, authority. One of them finally looked up from his papers to where the Simmons family gathered themselves.

"English?" he asked.

Jake spoke up. "Yes," he said.

The clerk seemed relieved. Rose wondered how many of the petitioners coming through only spoke an Indian dialect, and how they managed to make themselves understood by these men.

"We are from Washington, and ask questions to determine citizenship. Understand?"

"Yes, sir," Jake said again. Her husband had encased himself in his charm shell. The stakes were too high to show annoyance with the condescending tone.

"You swear that all answers are true from here on out?"

"Yes, sir."

"You are now sworn in. What is your name?"

"Jake Simmons."

"Are you a citizen of the Muskogee Nation?"

"Yes, sir."

"What town do you belong to?"

"Canadian Colored."

"How long have you lived in the Creek Nation?"

"All my life."

"What did your mother look like? Full colored woman?"

"Oh. My mother was three-quarter Indian."

"You are willing to make affidavit to that?"

"Yes, you couldn't hardly tell the difference between her and full-blood. She could not use the English language whatever, hardly."

Some of his testimony was new information to Rose. Jake never talked to her overmuch about his mother, except to complain she didn't have the means to care for him growing up, and they were often on the edge of starvation drifting from place to place. She deposited him with distant relatives or sympathetic strangers whenever she could, which never lasted long before wearing out their welcome. Rose assumed his nomadic early life was at the heart of both his need to travel and his need for the stability of their family-centered ranch life to come back to.

"Have you been outside the territory in the last four years?"

"Only to drive cattle. I have a ranch and am known in these parts and could bring witnesses."

"Are you married?"

"Yes, sir."

"Her name?"

"Rose Simmons."

"Is your wife a citizen of the Muskogee Nation?"

"Yes, sir."

"How long has she lived in the Creek Nation?"

"All her life."

"What town does she belong to?"

"Canadian Colored."

"Has she been outside of the territory in the last four years?"

"No, sir."

"Are yours and your wife's names on the Dunn Roll?"

"Yes, sir."

Rose elbowed him, reminding him of the documents she brought, heavy on her lap.

"We have the 1895 payroll record too," Jake offered.

The clerk made a dismissive gesture, waiting for the other clerk to find the entry in the thick clutch of papers he flipped through, running his finger down the page until he found what he was looking for. Finally, the other clerk nodded.

"Names of each child previously registered."

Jake listed all their children, one by one, but didn't call out Kindred's name. Rose thought to correct the omission, but realized Jake's logic. If Kindred Simmons showed twice, once on the freedman roll, and once on the by-blood roll, Rose wasn't sure what happened, whether that invalidated their claim. Worst case, once they talked to Kindred, he could come back tomorrow to register under the family.

"Any new children to register?"

Jake gave him two names, their youngest child and their newest granddaughter.

"Looks in order. No further witnesses or documents required. Wait over there for the citizenship certificate," the government man said. "Take the certificate and go pick your allotments in the tent with the red flag markings." He scribbled something on the paper in front of him. They didn't realize they'd been dismissed until he raised his head and shouted, "Next!"

Rose's heart struggled to reconcile the unbearable sadness of Kindred's defection, and the euphoria of permanent ownership of their ranch. They left the first tent about thirty minutes later, the precious certificate stamped, certified and recorded in Jake's hand. Once outside, Jake asked Rose to read the document aloud. Although he could stumble through the words himself, he preferred Rose's voice.

As a family, minus one, they made their way to the red tent, to register for their land.

Chapter 64

Rose toiled in the late-morning sun on the near side of the garden, hoeing the weeds around the string bean vines, puzzling over the question of Eugene. Her son sat at the common table to eat when everyone else ate, and was a trusted hand tending the herd. Of age, he went with Jake on spring drive, proving his worth there, but still, she was afraid they'd lost him. That she'd lost him. The wound was still fresh from Kindred four years before, her oldest son's defection from the family permanent and final. She couldn't bear another child leaving them.

Eugene performed his obligations, faithfully, but there was little joy in the ranch life for him, anyone could see that. Neither Jacob nor Eugene had an innate gift for ranching, like their father. Eugene was dutiful, and Jacob adventurous, but with Jacob, the unsuitability didn't carry resentment, or shame, or desperation. Jacob would forge his own way, whatever that might be, but he would be in the pocket of family whatever he made of himself, Rose was sure of it. Eugene, on the other hand, was only biding his time. For what, she wasn't sure.

Eugene.

Her son was drowning in his dissatisfaction, and no matter how she tried to gauge his state of mind and mend fences between them, something stood in the way. She'd concocted a reason for him to be close at hand today, at the house, and yet she was out here, and him inside. She'd wanted an excuse to talk to him, find some words to bind him to her, the way it used to be. But the gulf was too wide, the specter of Elizabeth between them.

She stabbed at the weeds with a fury, row after row, and when at last she paused to take stock of her handiwork, saw a man in the distance approaching their property on a slow-trotting horse. He wasn't yet at the clearing, and she threw down the hoe and hurried toward the house, entering from the screened back door, unhooking the loaded rifle from the wall as she passed through toward the porch. She heard a noise from the kitchen, and stopped to check it wasn't one of the smaller children. At the top of the stairs off the kitchen was Eugene, bringing up the hogshead of sugar as she'd requested, and she motioned him to come with her. He eyed the rifle, and didn't hesitate, following along quietly and capably at her back.

She shouldered the rifle, more for show than expectation of use, but she distrusted the white man from the moment she first saw him set foot on their land and come straight for the front door. He wasn't freedman, he wasn't Creek, he wasn't Indian at all, he was white, a portrait of respectability from the point of his boots to the wide brim of his grimed hat.

"Say your piece," said Rose, from the protection of the front porch. She lowered the rifle but kept it visible at her side, not obscured by the folds of her apron. Eugene stood to her right. Though still not come to his full growth, he was tall, measured, deliberate. Whatever held between them, she was glad for him at her side.

"Ma'am," the man said, with a small tip of his hat. "Would this be the man of the house?"

"What would your business be?" asked Rose.

Eugene bristled beside her, as if he'd been dismissed, but he didn't speak, cleaving to her side. She'd deal with his feelings some other time.

The man looked back and forth between them, assessing the situation. She could imagine his simplistic computation; old freedwoman with a gun, young Indian man living on the property, ranch hand or drifter.

"Well, I could talk to you, then," he said to Rose. "No need for the rifle. No need at all."

Something wasn't quite right. Did he know Jake was away? Why didn't he come closer to evening, when chores were done, the man of the ranch more likely to be at the house? She kept the rifle in place, neither inviting him in nor offering water or *sofki*.

"State your business, then," she said.

"My name is Hawkins," he said. "Wade Hawkins. Come to offer my services."

"What services?"

"I could be great help to you and yours," he said. "You're Rose Simmons?" He didn't wait for her to reply, and instead, turned to Eugene. "And which are you?"

"Eugene Simmons," he said. Rose darted a warning glance to Eugene and he pulled back half a step, quieted.

"You appear knowing who we are," Rose

said. "So what is your business, Mr. Hawkins?"

"To the point, then," Hawkins said. "You're on the rolls. You and your family. And a large family it is. By law, you need a guardian to help make sure your allotments come to good use."

"We do fine by ourself," Rose said.

"That might be, up to now. Let me further introduce myself. I have a spread, ten thousand acres, outside Muskogee. People know me there. I have acquaintance with people who make things happen. No muss, no fuss. A land transaction needn't be hard as the government makes out. I can get you a good price for the land you sit on here, and you'd end with hard cash in your pocket."

"We live here, Mr. Hawkins," said Rose. "For over twenty years. Eugene grew up on this ranch from infant, and now he's a man." Rose felt a charge between them, her and Eugene, and prayed that this acknowledgment of him as a man come unto his own, though only midway through his teen years, held the possibility of thaw. "We are not in the market to sell."

"And a fine ranch it looks to be, if I may say so." Hawkins looked out over the expanse, from east to west. "I see why you'd hold on to forty acres for your homestead."

"We run cattle, Mr. Hawkins. Forty acres wouldn't even be enough for my herd, let alone my husband's."

Hawkins looked thoughtful. "With allotments coming for twelve members of your family, surely you don't need all the land?"

"Citizens," Rose corrected. "Creek citizens working the land we're entitled to."

"But surely not all your family wants to hold on to stubborn land taking more than it gives when there's good money to be made. You don't speak for every one of them, eh?"

He looked pointedly at Eugene, and Eugene hung on his every word.

"Why are you here?" asked Rose. "Everybody knows the land can't be sold."

"Forty acres of the allotment can't be sold. That's the law. But with a guardian's help, you could lease out the rest. Leasing's not same as selling. Leasing the rights for what's under the ground or on top of the ground brings you cash money while you still run your cattle, helps you keep up with what you have to pay the bank or other debt. Makes you a profit."

"We still own the land, and work the land, but somebody pays us anyway?" Rose asked.

"Yes," Hawkins said. "A little tricky, but

you put your trust in me as guardian, and I draw up papers and pay in gold coin. Tomorrow. Today. I take the risk of finding an interested party."

"What sort of interested party? Oilman? Timber stripper? Both leave the land worth less than nothing for a cattle rancher."

"Those are two options, but there are others. Remember, there's great risk for the person doing the leasing, and in five years, whether their bet paid off or not, the land comes back to you."

None of this sounded right to Rose. Nothing was painless. She would be glad when Jake returned in a couple of weeks. He had a better sense of this than she did, although one thing was certain. Neither of them would give up one acre of their land without a fight.

"How much?" she asked.

"Beg pardon?"

"How much per acre?"

"If you got each of the twelve to sign, or had me appointed guardian for the minors with a guardianship waiver, I could pay $500. Cash money."

Rose almost laughed out loud. If she'd had doubts before, she was certain now. He was charlatan, or worse. The land was easily worth $10,000. She was surprised to hear her son speak up.

"How much for one allotment?" Eugene asked.

CHAPTER 65

Hawkins stroked the full length of his beard before answering. "One allotment is not as valuable as a block of land together, as you can imagine, but I'd say I could get you twenty-five dollars."

Rose willed Eugene to quiet with a flinty look.

"Our signatures carry more worth than your quote. Your offer is of no interest," said Rose. "To any of us."

"Well, if leasing's not to your liking, there's selling."

"We're freedmen. This land is restricted. An appointed guardian must know as much. The government won't allow us to sell."

"Not yet," he said. "But those are the old rules. That's why you need a guardian. Someone to keep up with what you can do and what you can't." He looked to be enjoying himself. "The government changes rules when it suits them. I wouldn't expect you

610

to be able to follow all the ins and outs. That's what I'm here to do for you."

"What new rules?" asked Rose.

"Full-bloods still have all the old restrictions, but neither mixed-bloods nor freedmen will be banned from selling. Once restrictions on surplus land expire next year, freedmen can get rich."

He painted a picture of the good life to be had with money from a sale. He talked as if Rose couldn't possibly understand the complicated matters he dealt with. Eugene stood straight and tall by her side, but had the stunned, pathetic stare of a prairie dog in the seconds before his demise, hypnotized by a snake suddenly appeared, transferring venom to its fangs.

"I'll get myself appointed guardian to help with your money matters." He said this last in a solicitous tone, as if the welfare of every member of the Simmons ranch was his overwhelming concern. "Especially for the underage children needing guidance."

Rose kept her grip steady on the rifle, even though this was a threat that couldn't be resolved with a firearm.

"We advise our own," she said.

She thought of her smaller children at the ranch, aged four to sixteen. The older were a different calculus, champing at the bit to make their own decisions, but with the exception of Eugene, they were all so indoctrinated into the concept of family she was certain she could contain them. Speak for them. She'd brought them up under her protection, all of them, under her roof, under her rules. What could this man do for them she could not?

"You do the best you can, I'm sure," Hawkins said. "But much good can come from us working together. I take care of you and your family, get the best deal, whatever you decide. Once restrictions come off for freedmen next year, we can buy and sell more freely, without interference from the government. There's money to be made." He hesitated, a pause for effect. "Maybe it would be better for me to talk to Jake Simmons. He might better understand the opportunities."

"My husband is back in a few weeks. I assure you, his answer is no different than mine," said Rose. "But of course, you are free to try. Good day."

Eugene and Hawkins exchanged a quick look, an acknowledgment that excluded Rose. She didn't want Eugene anywhere near the influence of this man.

She waited until Hawkins left, merely a spot on the horizon, before she set the rifle down. "He's not to be trusted," she said.

"The government sent him to help us," said Eugene.

"He came today to help himself. Help himself to our land. Don't be fooled."

"He's an important man. He owns ten thousand acres and lives in Muskogee."

"Never want what other people have. You never know how they got it," Rose said.

Eugene didn't back down, as if his silent witness to this morning's meeting drained him of his full capacity for obedience. "I don't belong here," he said.

Rose's heart skipped. What did he mean? On the ranch? On this porch? With her?

"Not everybody wants to farm or ranch for the rest of their life," he said. "That's not what I want."

"What do you want, Eugene?" Rose asked. "Do you even know? Do you have any idea?"

She fully expected him to withdraw into himself, as he usually did when confronted, but he took a deep breath, and looked her directly in the eye.

"I want to live away from cows and mud and dust and chickens. I want to ride a train headed west. Or east. I want to live in a city, and meet people not knowing who I am or where I'm from, whose first question isn't 'who are your people?' Who don't peg me Creek or Cherokee, Indian or freedman, cowpunch or ranch hand. I want to sleep long in the morning and stay up with the moon at night, without a thought of a cow needs milking or a crop needs picking or a herd needs running. I want to see something new that man made. More than drinking enough rotgut whiskey to face another day of hard winter, or hard summer, and not use up my praying for rain during drought or sun during flood or calm during tornado. I want out."

This last rendered Rose mute. This was the most she'd heard Eugene say at one time, and the first he'd said aloud how little he wanted the farm life she had to offer. She'd failed him. Suddenly she knew it true. She wondered if he had shared his discontent with Elizabeth. She stood quiet for a long time before she spoke.

"Land is who we are," Rose said to him. "Land is our protection, land is our family, land is our life, from the time of Cow Tom. You'll do what I say. No one sells."

Eugene picked up the rifle from where she'd leaned it on the porch rail. He sighted down the barrel in the direction of the bunkhouse, before laying the old gun back to rest. When he looked to Rose again, his face bore such sorrow she could barely puzzle out the man he'd become. In her mind, she still saw baby fat and first steps and a young boy trailing after his brothers.

"How'd we get this way?" he asked.

The question made no sense, but she knew at once what he meant. She understood, but resented the impertinence from one so young and untested. How does anyone come to be what they are? Of necessity. By example. Day by day.

She didn't answer.

For once, Eugene pressed. "What was he like? My great-grandfather? Cow Tom."

"He was a great man," she said.

"I know the things he did. But what was he like?"

Rose remembered the conversation with Kindred in the barn the night the breech calf was born, the same hunger behind the question. She couldn't answer Kindred then, and couldn't answer Eugene now. She'd kept the stories so close by now, at first because of the promise, but now something more, that she feared something fundamental within her would break apart if she gave in to this impulse to open the past. Grampa Cow Tom was hers.

"There's work to be done," said Rose. "I want you to ride the east fence line today."

Eugene refused the dismissal. "We each come by our allotment, our hundred and sixty acres, made out to us, separate," said Eugene. "Each should do what they want."

"No one sells," Rose repeated. She wanted to shake him, slap him, make him see what was important. She modulated her voice instead to try reason. "That's how we stay strong. Your father will tell you the same. But if sell you must, come to family first. Only sell to family."

Eugene didn't answer her, and the silence deepened between them. He stood rigid as he stared out at the vastness of the prairie in the direction where the guardian disappeared, and then with the slightest of shrugs, he left Rose alone on the porch.

CHAPTER 66

Rose stayed close to home, as she had for the last six months since the guardian's visit, tending the ranch and the children. But even in her seclusion, rumors insinuated themselves into their everyday lives as the date approached to lift freedmen restrictions, and the government allowed all citizens other than full-bloods to sell their land allotments. The distasteful memory of the unctuous little man hadn't completely faded, but with busy season upon them, and so much to do, Rose almost convinced herself they were safe.

She watched Eugene closely, careful to respect his disappearances to see Elizabeth a half day's ride away. He performed his obligations, a dutiful son, but she detected a new gleam of eye, a more engaged carriage, an unexplained hopefulness Rose hadn't seen before. He didn't open up to her as the day he told her of his aversion for the rancher's life, nor express his dissatisfaction again.

The eve of the deadline, Rose worked herself into such distress about Eugene she put aside her needle and thread and retired early, leaving the older girls unsupervised to clear supper dishes and close up the house for the night. She hadn't yet changed into nightclothes, and sat on her side of the mattress, fully dressed, as Jake shed down to his long underwear. He sagged onto the bed, tired from a full day branding calves, and pulled the quilt over himself. Still, she couldn't force herself to begin her evening routines.

"I worry over Eugene," she said.

Jake opened his eyes. "If the boy wants to go, he'll go," he said. "We done all we could. You coming to bed?"

"He might still think to catch the last train to Muskogee tomorrow," Rose said. "We can't let him do it."

"No son of mine would throw in his lot with the ignorant mixed-bloods and liquored-up freedmen the grafters rounded up in the last few days," said Jake. "We raised Eugene smarter. If he's daft enough to go that direction, he'll lose the land sooner or later anyway."

The set of Jake's jaw convinced her he'd

618

settled on his thinking. Jake wasn't a man to turn his back on family, but he didn't always intuit truth even when directly in front of his face. There was more denial in his words than either acceptance or resignation.

"You need to talk to him. Forbid him. He'll listen to you. What if he still goes to town? He could give away his birthright for chicken feed."

"He's grown, Rose. I was on my own at his age. On my own with no help from anybody, least of all family."

She'd lost one of her sons. She refused to lose another. "After what happened to Kindred . . ."

Jake stopped her.

"That one is gone, and this isn't the same. Eugene isn't the same. He's older, and smarter. A man has to make his own choices, and be willing to live by them. Have faith in him."

Jake turned over and soon fell quiet, through with talking. Rose decided to try again in the morning. She changed to her nightdress and lay under the covers, and spent a goodly part of the night listening to Jake's soft snores before finally easing to sleep.

When morning came, Jake was up and out

early, and not long after, Eugene came to Rose.

"I'm going to Muskogee today on the free train," Eugene told her.

"The sharpers will try to strip your allotment and throw you a pauper on the government for support."

"I mean to hear the offer," he said.

"Please. Stand fast. Give up the notion of selling."

"We can't keep going round," Eugene said. "I'm telling you as courtesy, and I'm gone."

He left her in the kitchen. She listened to his horse's hoofbeats fade, and for a while did nothing. Finally, she roused herself. She wouldn't stand by idle while her son made such a serious mistake. Rose wrapped a bit of *sofki* and hardtack in a kerchief, left the older girls in charge, grabbed her rifle, and rode off on her pony toward Jake in the south field.

She found her husband with a ranch hand not far from the corral, tending a crippled calf, and when he looked to her on her pony in the fading light, it was as if she saw him for the first time. His eyes were still an arresting blue, more watery now than when he first captivated her in the Okmulgee kitchen all those years ago, and the crow's-feet around his eyes were so deeply etched from the sun they seemed a birthmark. He looked puzzled, not understanding why she was there.

"He's gone for the train," was all she said by way of greeting, trying to speak in code, not wanting to air their family business in front of the hand, although Old Sam had been with them for over ten years and was most likely as aware of their secrets as everyone else on the ranch.

"Then I'll go get him," Jake replied. He gave a few quick instructions to Old Sam, and stood to get circulation back into his legs from squatting so long on the ground.

"I'm going too," said Rose, and Jake didn't object.

They didn't put the horses to full gallop, but rode at a brisk pace for almost an hour through sagebrush and tumbleweed on the main road. The closer they came to town, the more people they saw on the dusty path, whether by horse, by wagon, or by foot, traveling in the same direction. Rose assessed every familiar-looking shape and face, in case Eugene was one of these pilgrims, but she didn't see him. By the time they came within sight of the Okmulgee train station in the distance, the road was choked with travelers. Rose didn't know what to expect, not having been to town for several years, since registration for the Dawes Roll. Before they got close, the press of so many people overwhelmed her. Even Jake gave a low whistle at how many people waited for the special train bound north for Muskogee that grafters chartered.

The town was thronged with clusters of mixed-bloods and freedmen lounging everywhere, on the few benches sprinkled in the station, leaning against the embanked wall, lying in the dirt in the middle of the outlying street, sitting on the planked sidewalks. They were of all descriptions, young and old, agitated and sedentary, ragged and well dressed, but there was one common denominator among those who waited — whiskey. More jugs and bottles than Rose could count were passing from one citizen to another. Liquor sellers didn't bother to hide themselves, alcohol hawked by both white and Indian grafters providing an endless supply to their recruits and keeping it moving. Many of the men were clearly drunk, whether in quiet stupor or boisterous engagement, so intoxicated they appeared to not know where they were.

They found Eugene's horse tied to an outlying hitching post.

"We need to find him fast," Jake said to Rose.

He sounded angry as he tied his horse to the same post and waded into the sea of men, leaving Rose several steps behind.

CHAPTER 67

Rose followed the best she could in her husband's wake, putting on more of a brave face than she felt. She had been around all manner of ranch hands, rough-hewn and sometimes dangerous. She'd grown up in the midst of competing Indian tribesmen, fighting for the last kernel of corn. She'd served middle- and upper-class Indians, privy to the secret depravities of the well-off, but she wasn't prepared for this.

They navigated and pushed their way through the men on the platform, many of whom were stinking drunk, falling-down drunk, sleepy drunk, mean drunk. One grabbed at her skirt, and another made lewd, slurred remarks, but for the most part, they'd drunk themselves into relative docility. The grafters among them were easy to spot, usually less inebriated, but not always, jealously guarding their marks, like shepherd to sheep, trying to keep another grafter from poaching their claimed territory, men persuaded to join them on the train ride to sell off their land allotments.

Rose heard Eugene's voice before she saw him. He stood with a motley assortment of rough-looking Creeks on the far side of the station, swaying, slightly apart, but his voice was loud and argumentative. Rose had seen her son at the jug at the end of a long workday, sipping, the hard edges of his face softened to slackness, but she had never seen her son this stage of drunk. He looked as though he might soon come to blows with a scrappy freedman a full head shorter but menacing-looking nonetheless. The only other person Rose recognized was Hawkins, the self-appointed guardian who had come to the ranch last year, watching over his collection of recruits.

Rose pointed to Eugene, and Jake strode over with such authority Rose couldn't keep up.

"Eugene!" Jake called.

Even over the din of the mob scene, Eugene heard his father's voice, confusion clouding his face as he tried to sort through the familiarity of the sound.

By the time Jake reached him, Hawkins, alert to threat, stepped between father and son.

"Eugene!" Jake repeated, his voice a command. Hawkins put out his hand to stop Jake's advance.

"He's mine," said Hawkins. He let loose a stream of tobacco juice in the dirt at Jake's feet. "Go find your own."

Rose arrived out of breath, caught up to her husband at last, and stood beside Jake. She watched the momentary puzzlement on Hawkins's face as he recognized her and pieced together the connection between the three of them — Eugene, Rose, and Jake. Immediately, Hawkins smiled wide, a fawning gesture, and put his hand out in greeting.

"We haven't met, but your son agreed to come to Muskogee with me," he said to Jake.

"No he won't," said Jake. He didn't extend his hand, and Hawkins's smile faded, his arm dropping limply to his side. Jake turned instead to Eugene, who watched with a certain amount of uncomprehending dispassion. "Come on home now, Eugene," Jake said.

"He's committed," said Hawkins. "He's coming with me."

Jake ignored him. "Come now, Eugene," he said, and like an obedient child, Eugene slowly separated himself from the throng of men in his circle. The freedman he was arguing with was so little invested in their squabble that, glassy-eyed, he dropped to the dirt and watched too, as if relieved to be off his feet.

"He's staying," Hawkins said. "He'll be back after he signs, at midnight."

Rose, so intent on willing Eugene toward them, missed what happened next, but did see Hawkins lay his hand on Jake's shoulder, and saw Jake draw back his arm. The next thing she knew, Hawkins was on the ground, looking up at Jake with a lethal determination. There was no compromise in his face.

She saw a quick motion, and the glimmer of something shiny as Hawkins scrambled back to his feet, and she realized how outnumbered they were in this dangerous crowd. Jake always carried both knife and gun, but she had gotten him to come straight from the pasture, and wasn't sure how prepared he was if it came to a fight. Other grafters didn't rush to back Hawkins up yet, more worried about protecting their own groups of citizen recruits, but they might come to his defense if they thought their marks could be inspired to desert.

She felt the weight of the rifle at her side, and raised the weapon, training it on Hawkins. "He has a knife," she said to Jake.

"Everybody has a knife," Jake said calmly, pulling his Colt from his waistband, keeping one eye on Hawkins while assessing the mood of the crowd. "Let's go, Eugene. Walk to me."

Eugene came toward them as if pulled by a string, unsteady but obedient, aware enough to give Hawkins wide berth as he staggered just beyond his reach. As he came close, Rose grabbed Eugene's arm to lead him away from the station in the direction of their horses, balancing her rifle with one arm and pushing her son in front of her. She looked back to make sure they weren't pursued, and for one long moment locked eyes with Hawkins, who stared after them, unwilling to leave the others gathered to retrieve the one he now lost.

The train rumbled as it approached, and the focus of the crowd shifted. The locomotive came to a hissing stop, and the station transformed. Grafters gathered their wards, prodding, pushing, threatening, cajoling, and prepared them to board the Muskogee-bound train.

Rose relaxed, just a bit, hoping the danger passed.

"Pa . . ." Eugene began. His voice slurred and he struggled to find the rest of his words.

"We don't sell, we don't lease," Jake said. He pointed to his horse. "Get on."

It took several tries for them to maneuver Eugene onto the horse, and once he was mostly upright in the saddle, Jake swung up behind and held him steady so he wouldn't fall. The set to Jake's jaw made clear his determination, but Rose saw the worry in his eyes. Rose mounted her smaller pony, and pulled Eugene's horse by the rein. They rode out of town single file, toward the ranch, against the tide of those still pouring in toward the station for the next train. Rose followed southward in the wake of her men.

Eugene snored, his head resting heavy on his father's chest. Jake's back was rigid, but his arms encircled his son, tight.

CHAPTER 68

Usually, this was the time of day Rose liked best. The heavy choring done for the day, children asleep in their beds, she fitting scraps for a quilt or busy with her sewing needles, Jake with his pipe. As if everything sought its place, and at last relieved, released a long, satisfying breath. But not tonight.

Rose picked up her darning needle and a hank of yarn to patch a pair of Jake's socks worn almost clean through at the heel. She slipped her stitch twice, like a greenhorn new to the capability. She thought to go to the spinning wheel in the back room for a session, sure to calm, but the hour was late.

"Mama Rose."

Her son stood tall before her. He was still growing, in height as well as brawn. Firm and muscled from ranch chores and cattle drives, he was a good-looking young man at seventeen. Eugene hadn't given the family any more trouble since they rescued him at the train station, but Rose didn't welcome a repeat of the argument they'd been having since supper. Jake sat in his favorite chair, eyelids closed, filled pipe at his side. He opened his eyes now.

"No more of that foolishness, Eugene," Rose said. "The matter is settled."

"The children all want to go to the parade. I'll take them myself, see that no harm comes." Eugene pulled up a straight-backed chair and set it across from them, between Jake and Rose, and sat, eye level. "*I* want to go to Muskogee to the parade."

"No Simmons child gonna hoot and holler and dance and carry on like a good thing's coming because they got fireworks or some parade," Rose said. "That's not for us."

"It's the future," said Eugene. "And a bit of fun. What's wrong with a bit of fun?"

Rose put down her needle and snatched up the newspaper from the side table.

"Listen," she said to Eugene. She smoothed the pages of the *Muskogee Phoenix* and extended the fusty broadsheet farther from her face until the blurred print came into focus. " 'There is a new light in the East,' " she read. " 'The brightest day in all the history of the Red Man's land has dawned.' "

Her whole body shook as she slammed the newspaper back onto the table. "This just makes it easier for the white man to figure a way to crush us."

"There's no stopping them making us a state," Eugene said calmly. "Oklahoma. Indian Territory. What's the difference?"

"You don't understand the evils that follow white man's thinking," said Rose. "Statehood is bad for Indians. Even worse for us, now that white majority rules. Grampa Cow Tom would be sorry to see this day."

"But tomorrow is just a parade, and everybody's going," said Eugene. He looked to Jake. "Papa?"

"Your mama already spoke her mind," Jake said.

But Eugene wasn't giving up. "We could all go, and you could tell us what Grampa Cow Tom would find so wrong. There's more than one way to look at a thing," he said.

"Nobody goes," said Rose. "Not you, not the children, not the growns." She took up her needle again. "Long as you're under my roof, you do what I say. I'll hear no more about it."

Eugene leaned back in the chair, jaw clenched tight, as if physically struck. But when he stood, abruptly, his face was a tight mask. "I am a man," he said, the words quiet but distinct. "I won't ask again."

In three long strides he was across the room and out the front door without once looking back, and a deep silence descended. Rose couldn't say exactly what, but something between the two of them had shifted and hit a new place, like a key finding home in its lock. There was a disturbing finality to the exchange.

"Why does he have to challenge?" she asked Jake. "Like he can barely tolerate me."

"Just trying to find his place," said Jake. "But don't drive him off."

"Me? Drive him off? I'm doing all I can to make him stay, see his fit on the ranch."

"There it is. You can't make him stay. You can't force him to do anything. He's right. He's a grown man."

When did it happen, so much sourness? First the statehood business and now Eugene in open rebellion. She thought briefly of Kindred, but refused to bring the old hurts forward to mix with the new.

"We built something here, you and me. Four days into August. That's when we'll celebrate, like we used to. On Emancipation Day. Why'd we ever stop? It was good enough for Grampa Cow Tom, it's good enough for them. And no Simmons celebrates statehood or they answer to me."

She pushed aside her worry about Eugene for the moment. Oklahoma statehood was another changing of the rules in answer to their mastery of the old system. As hard as things had always been, there was an additional layer of protection, albeit thin, within Indian Territory, something that gave them room to maneuver, defined them as off-limits to the full-on force of chattel politics, shielding them just enough from the crippling dismissiveness of Negro in the southernmost states of the country of which they were now an official part.

Rose took up the newspaper again and shook it, as if to make the words spill off the page and reverse themselves. "They try to make it sound good, and fair, but Indian Territory is supposed to be for us. We are Creek citizens."

"You know my thoughts." Jake relit his pipe, ingesting the smoke slow and deep. His very calmness stoked an even broader sense of wrong and fury in Rose.

"No different than mine," she said.

"The deed is done, Rose."

Jake refused to emote tonight on cue around the very thing he'd been worrying over and railing about for the last several years. And yet she couldn't stop poking at the notion of how much they had to lose, how yet again they'd been caught up in the giant maw of history and put at risk, as if they could never reach a safe place no matter how fast they ran.

"Leastways they could have kept Indian Territory and Oklahoma Territory separate," Rose said. "Haven't we suffered enough? Haven't enough promises been broken? There's only folly in this for us."

"Rose." Jake didn't raise his voice, but the tone was of warning. "No need fixing on how things coulda been. Shoulda been. Eugene was right about that part. Oklahoma is a state now. That's fact."

"Statehood," Rose said in contempt.

This time Jake didn't respond. Instead, he tapped out his hot pipe bowl in the dish and leaned back, closing his eyes again for a minute before hoisting himself from the chair.

He'd taken only a couple of halting steps toward the bedroom, the remnants of a limp from the recklessness of breaking a new horse two weeks prior instead of letting one of the other hands do it, when Rose spoke again.

"What's it mean, Jake?" she asked. "What happens now?"

Her husband turned around then and paused, as if considering how to answer. They'd been together far too long to sugar-coat, not long enough to lie outright.

"What it always means," Jake told her. "We mind our business; we pay what taxes come to us and what bills we owe; we pray for good weather and crops and a healthy herd; we answer to whatever the United States government asks, no matter they think us simpletons and incapable and ripe for misuse; we answer to the Creek government, no matter they think us less than Indian; we stay away best we can from the old-style white hate sure to come unleashed in our direction each by each; we remind ourselves and everyone else that this is our land as long as we work it; we raise our children to expect more and fight if we're not able; and we put as much as we can away in case we have to start over."

He looked tired, the contours of his once-unlined face deep and sagging, his shoulders stooped, his hair uncombed, still carrying the sweat-line indent circling his head from his cowboy's hat, though the hat itself lay flat against the hook by the door until morning. And Rose felt, deep and final, each one of her ten additional years of tiredness above her husband's age. How many times could a body start afresh, or be threatened with the possibility of needing to do so?

"What of the ranch? Will they come for the ranch?"

"Someone's bound to try." Jake was matter-of-fact. "Grafter or boodler, government or settler; the only thing we don't know is when. But we fight for what matters. We change as time demands."

What had Grampa Cow Tom said in the death tepee? Carve the life you want. She'd fought for Jake, and she'd fought for the land, with success at both, but at such cost. So much else had slipped out of her reach in the process.

"Yes," said Rose. "We're warriors. And we fight for what we want."

CHAPTER 69

At daybreak, months after the sting of statehood passed, Rose pulled two baskets'
worth of ripe cucumbers from the garden,
packed her pistol, left Laura in charge of
the house for the day, hitched up her favorite
pony, and set out for the pasture. She
selected four cows from her own herd,
including a milk cow and calf, and began to
drive them north.

"Cows!" she called out to get them on
their way, and again, each time they threatened to stray from the course she'd set.

She'd used this pony to move her cows
before, from grazed area to fresh pasture,
but never as far a distance as she intended
this morning. She gathered the four grace-
less cows in a loose herd and kept them
moving, zigging and zagging on her pony to
keep them calm but in motion, their hooves
clopping on the dry ground.

For the second time this week, Rose followed parallel to the creek until she came to the homestead of a distant neighbor, a widow with two small boys. Seminole. The woman had lost her husband in a gun accident the year before, and was struggling to hold on to her land. The family came to Rose's attention through loose ranch-hand gossip, and for the fact that she had never thought to search out such a family before, she was ashamed. But at least she was here now.

The trip took two hours, and when she arrived, the widow was already in the field outside, hoe in hand, weeding squash. Her dark, long dress had seen better days, but she wore rows of bright beads around her neck, Seminole-style, as she had when Rose talked to her the week before. Her young boys, from the look of them ten and twelve years old, worked lines of cornstalks by the side of the small log cabin. The widow put down her hoe when she heard the clatter of hooves, and Rose stopped short of the house to let the cows graze.

"I've beans if you're hungry," the widow said.

"I've somewhere else to be," said Rose, "but once the cows are settled, some coffee will send me on my way." She offered one of the baskets of cucumbers. "For you and the boys."

The widow accepted. "Your hand came round earlier in the week and helped me patch the fencing for the cows," she said.

She was even younger than Rose initially thought. She'd guess twenty-eight, no more than thirty. She'd gathered up her abundant hair in a topknot, but her work in the garden had loosened several locks that hung straight and limp against her damp skin.

"I still don't understand why you do this for us," the widow said. "I can't pay."

"If neighbor helps neighbor," Rose said, "fortune balances out."

The widow seemed puzzled, but didn't press further, perhaps afraid Rose's generosity would be rescinded. Rose didn't, she couldn't, explain that she strived to fulfill a commitment long overdue. How many years ago she'd sat in Grampa Cow Tom's death tepee and made him promises, and then went about her life picking and choosing which to keep. Over thirty years. A lifetime ago. Her early disillusionment that her grandfather committed shameful acts in wartime had vanished alongside her young womanhood, but he'd asked her to help him atone and she'd done nothing. Rose owed him that and more. She'd made too many promises she hadn't kept.

"There's grazing land enough here for now, but we'll check back from time to time to see what else you need."

"We thank you and yours." The widow glanced over at her sons. "It's been struggle for us."

Once the cows were driven to their pasture, and she'd had her fill of the bitter brew of the widow's coffee, Rose mounted her pony and rode until she found a small clearing in the woods.

She dismounted, and tied the pony to a tree so he wouldn't bolt. The pistol weighed heavy in her hands, but she was steady. She shot four times. Once north, once west, once south, and once east.

"Rest in peace, Grampa," she said aloud. "We make our own traditions."

Rose remounted. The next leg of the trip was not likely to be so easy.

She began to worry about what she would say, how the encounter might play out, whether she would be able to face her little sister after all this time. Over the years, her initial fury toward Elizabeth had turned to something hard and cool, a stony bitterness, and then bloomed again into jealousy as they battled over Eugene's head and heart, two mothers where there should only be one.

Rose slowed the horse's trot as she came near the tall-grass plain leading to the homesite where she'd spent a goodly part of her early years before striking out on her own. Now this was Elizabeth's home. The closer Rose came, the more her memories flooded, good recollections and ill, from this place and before. She'd have to hold those memories close to get through today, dealing with the living. Her Gramma Amy, in her nineties, body and mind both failing but still hanging on. Ma'am, now faithful caretaker of Cow Tom's ranch. Elizabeth, spinster. She thought of the departed. Aunt Maggie and the cousins, Lulu and Emmaline. Granny Sarah, lost and then found. Twin, of the blue light, who protected her as a child until, as an adult, she left him behind. Her Grampa Cow Tom, gone, but ever with her, her bedrock.

Though still morning, the day had warmed, and she saw movement at the front of the ranch house, on the wrapped porch, a solitary figure. Elizabeth, in a rocking chair, embroidery in her hand. She had changed much, and yet in some ways had barely changed at all. Older, yes, her face and body filled out, her dark hair streaked with silvery wisps, more matronly, but with the same promised charm of a smile waiting at her lips. Rose remembered clearly that day so long ago when a much younger Elizabeth churned butter on her front porch, and her husband, Jake, coming home from months on the road, laid eyes on her at their ranch. She should have known then what would follow. She should have sent her packing then.

Rose closed her eyes to wipe away the stale image, to reset her mind to an attitude that would serve better for her purposes today. She had to force the past gone. For Eugene.

Some children needed more than others. Her girls would marry, early and well. She had raised them thus, and they took the lessons to heart. Her son Jacob was already making a name for himself as an oil broker, taking full advantage of the booming industry literally bubbling up from beneath their feet. Kindred was lost to them, there was no bringing him back from his choice of slipped-life as Indian, and though it cut her to the core, she knew his mind. He had closed himself to them. But Eugene was teetering at a crossroads, and Rose refused to let him fall.

Elizabeth looked up from her needlework,

and stared at Rose as she slowed the pony and approached. Rose saw her whenever visiting Gramma Amy and Ma'am, but hadn't really talked directly to Elizabeth since the day she banished her from her ranch. Elizabeth wasn't as easy to read as she'd been as a girl or a young woman, and Rose had fallen out of the practice of trying. There was a moment of confusion on Elizabeth's face, come and gone in a twinkling, before her features settled to blankness.

"Ma'am's out back with Gramma Amy," Elizabeth said coolly.

Rose fought against her mind's picture, honed and burnished from years of imaginings, of Elizabeth and Jake together. She replaced the image best she could by setting young Elizabeth side by side with the woman before her now.

"I'll see them later," Rose said. "I come for you."

Elizabeth threw down her embroidery. "Something's happened to Eugene?"

"No, nothing." Rose pushed herself forward, closer. "It's time to talk about him, is all."

Elizabeth regained her composure, taking her time, picking up her stitch before responding. "Was a time I'da welcomed a word from you. Any word. All I got was silence."

"Those days are past. You been good to Eugene. He never gave you up."

"No thanks to you. You tried to poison him against me, but you couldn't," Elizabeth accused. "He's my son. From my body."

"I was there," said Rose. "Remember? Midwife to my sister with my husband's child."

The heat filled her, coming back as if she were still in that birthing room, helping Elizabeth with the final push. Rose willed herself to balance.

"Easier to think all the blame mine, eh?" said Elizabeth.

They had already taken a wrong turn. Of the many lessons learned from Grampa Cow Tom, she'd only just come to appreciate this last one. After her grandfather killed the black Seminole, he willed himself to change, to shed his old skin in favor of new, and become a different kind of man. A man of peace, and sobriety, and dedication to others, the grandfather she'd loved without reservation. If he could transform, so could she.

"There's too much time passed to capture right and wrong now," Rose said. "You are my sister, that doesn't change. It is Eugene at risk now, our battle spilled over to him, and him squeezed between Mama Rose and Mama Elizabeth. He threatens to go away, and leave us both."

"Not everyone is made for Indian country, for this life," said Elizabeth. "Not everyone is Rose Simmons. Perfect."

"Perfect?"

"Perfect wife. Perfect mother. Perfect rancher." Elizabeth could barely take a breath.

Rose fastened on a memory of Elizabeth in the kitchen at her ranch long ago, before Ma'am came to visit. Eugene wasn't yet born, and Elizabeth cajoled Rose out of her anxious mood, as only she was able. She remembered the dinner, with children laughing in the background.

"My children obey me but never brighten when I'm around the way they did with you. One of my sons is already fled and soon maybe another. We have to battle every day to keep our ranch from being snatched from under us." Rose could have stopped herself, but didn't, pushing the words out she'd never said aloud. "My husband takes up with other women and I look the other way."

Elizabeth sat back in her rocker, studying her sister. "Yet you stay," she said softly.

"Jake holds the key to the life I was meant for." Rose struggled to catch up to her own thoughts. "I want that life. I want him."

"Why are you here, Rose?"

"I'm come to say you were right, Elizabeth. I grew hard and cold without you, and only now try to find my way back." Rose fumbled with her handkerchief. Her voice, when it came, was barely a whisper. "Did you love him? Did he love you? Is that why you never married?"

Elizabeth put her embroidery in her lap, and a long moment passed before she spoke. "I am sorry for the part I played. Everything suddenly went wrong, and couldn't be called back."

Rose expected tears, but there were none. The young Elizabeth would have shed tears. Instead Elizabeth squared her shoulders and looked into Rose's eyes as she talked, a gaze so deep Rose had to force herself not to look away.

"I was young. Jake and me, we were both so young. There was only the one time, and we both knew at once what a mistake we'd made, but that's of no consequence now. The years on your ranch were the happiest I'd ever been. I was a part of something growing and alive. I looked up to you. You were everything I wanted to be. It was wrong, but I craved a taste of everything you had. Husband, children, building a ranch, making a home. I wasn't in love with Jake. Nor him with me. I wasn't trying to take your place. I just wanted to be a part. And after, I only wanted peace, and found that here. After all these years, I still can't explain, though it cost me everything."

"I didn't think I would survive it," Rose said.

"Yet you found a way to live with Jake, but not me, though we were both at fault."

"I'd built a life with Jake, and learned to live with who he was. I couldn't keep you both in my head, and chose Jake. But I didn't grasp the import of losing you. Losing who I was with you."

"And now you do?" A hard edge crept into Elizabeth's tone.

"I'm not sure I can change for Eugene without you." Rose forced herself to keep talking. "His place is here, in Oklahoma. I don't want him leaving because we can't forgive one another. Because I can't forgive you." She swallowed, and said the words she'd come to say. "I forgive you, Elizabeth."

Her sister was close to fury now. "Oh, and now all is well? You forgive me?" She laughed again, a mean little snort. "The great Rose Simmons forgives me? Well, after almost twenty years, I suppose I should fall to my knees in joy at my good fortune."

"Please," said Rose. "Please. I'm begging. Whatever I have to do. For Eugene. And for me."

Elizabeth stopped short, and Rose watched her face relax a bit, watched as some of the tightness melted. Rose had never begged her sister for anything.

Elizabeth put her needlework off to one side. "It's not like I want him gone away either," she finally said. "But you left here for years to live in Okmulgee, and came back. Why can't you see him do the same?"

"Grampa Cow Tom asked me to go. On his deathbed. I promised him that. I promised too many things."

Elizabeth shook her head. "How does Eugene know that? How would any of us know? You don't let him see you. Eugene used to beg me for Grampa Cow Tom stories all the time, any scrap, any clue, but there's only so many I heard or remembered. Grampa Cow Tom gave his stories to you, entrusted them to you day after day in his death tepee, and still you hide them, as much as you hide yourself. Eugene wants to see you, so he asks after Grampa. But you never budge, never give an inch. Hold a bird too tight and you end up squeezing out the life."

"I just want what's best for Eugene," said Rose.

"If that's true, then let him go, and work toward what he might come back to."

The words burrowed into Rose's brain. Could it be true? Was she squeezing the life from her son? Rose hadn't spent much time on her grandfather's ranch in years, only short obligatory visits to Gramma Amy and Ma'am or transporting Eugene back and fro. She looked toward the creek, remembered sitting on the bank so long ago with her grandfather, how full she used to get on one of his adventure stories, the fact he shared that kind of time with her almost more important than the story itself.

Shed one skin. Take on another.

"Bring Ma'am and Gramma Amy," Rose pleaded. "Come stay at the ranch for a couple of days, no more tug-of-war, let Eugene see us side by side, a family. Maybe we can hold on to him. Together."

Elizabeth was no longer the little girl she could trick into carrying a skillet by telling her she wasn't grown enough for the task. Too many years had passed, and Rose felt her sister's careful judgment.

"I'll think on it," Elizabeth finally said. "That's all I promise.

CHAPTER 70

The ride to the train station in Muskogee was long and taxing, not because of the distance, which was indeed far, or the poorness of the dirt road itself, full of ruts and bumps, or the jarring of the wagon, but because of the letting go. Rose would have liked to hold the reins, to give her something to put her attention toward, but Eugene drove, and guided the horse north, his going-away satchel in the wagon bed in back. She thought her heart on the way to breaking, but she'd thought thus before, and yet here she still was.

She sat straighter, trying to compose herself, when what she wanted to do was plead one last time, to beg Eugene not to go. Elizabeth sat on the buckboard next to her, and she was sure her sister faced the same inner struggle. But no matter how far the two of them had traveled down the path of reconciliation the last few months, this moment was too strained to imagine any small talking now. And so they rode in silence.

They'd come early. The first train west wouldn't leave for three hours yet, and both Rose and Elizabeth contributed to a basket of big bean dumplings and Creek corn pudding and cha-cha, all Eugene's favorites, for a last meal together, the three of them, and for him to carry off the leftover with him when he boarded.

They found a shade tree outside the station, spread a blanket, and sat on the ground eating, forming their own small circle. Rose could barely taste the food, although she knew she ought to be hungry. She promised Elizabeth she wouldn't bully Eugene to stay, and though the pledge was hard to honor, she knew it to be the right thing.

"There is much to speak before you leave," Rose said to Eugene. "Even if you may not make sense of it full-on yet, you must listen hard just the same. And remember this day."

Eugene's expression was severe, his mouth tight, in both his determination to go and in guilt for not being able to stay. Rose knew him well enough to know he didn't want to hurt them, but he did have to leave them.

He had to leave them both.

"Promise me . . ." she started, but corrected herself. "No, no promises. Listen best you can, and then go on and live the life you're meant to."

"All right," Eugene said, carefully.

There was too much to pass on. Where to begin? In the end, the twig had forced the trunk to bend, and Rose would play out her part.

"First, Mama Elizabeth has something for you," Rose said.

Elizabeth rummaged in the pocket of her apron and pulled out a knotted lace handkerchief, yellowed with age. Her fingers trembled as she worked loose the knot. She took Eugene's hands in her own, his big, hers smaller, both of theirs rough and calloused, and she opened one of his palms faceup. Elizabeth placed the old penny in the center.

Rose remembered her grandfather's touch as he gave the payout penny, from his hand to hers so many years before. One for each child. They'd tussled over this, Rose and Elizabeth, briefly, whose family penny would pass to Eugene to send him on his way, and Rose conceded the rightness of her sister's claim. They each had something powerful to share with their son.

"Never forget family," said Elizabeth.

"You can't give me your —" Eugene started in protest.

"Yes. I can," said Elizabeth. "This is yours now, to remember by."

"I'll keep the penny safe till time for me to pass it on," he promised.

Eugene reknotted the coin in the handkerchief and stuffed it deep in the pocket of his overalls. There was a softness to his face, and Rose worried once more about releasing him to a new life away from the ranch and her protection.

"You're a man now, Eugene. But no matter where you go, how far you travel, we are your family," said Rose. "We're your true home, and you can always come back to us, anytime. No questions asked."

"I have to leave here," said Eugene.

"Hush," Rose said, harsher than she intended. She might never have another chance. "We know, but there's barely time enough. Just listen."

Elizabeth gave a nod of agreement, slight but clear. Rose curled her hand around Eugene's, where the penny had been. They had three hours yet. She drew a deep, slowing breath, and reached inside herself to release the prison of words for the long telling. This was her gift to her son. And to her sister.

And to herself. First to them, and then to the other children, and to their children forevermore. A simple act really, once the gate unlocked.

Eugene's hand was hot in hers.

"When Elizabeth and I were girls," Rose began, "we were chased from our ranch by Confederate Indians set on murdering us." She stole a sidelong glance at Elizabeth, who leaned forward to listen, her face as open and receptive as Eugene's. "Took us days of walking to get to Fort Gibson, mostly in the deepest hours of dark, wading together through icy streams to cover our smell, and hiding in caves or woods or prairie once light broke. Grampa Cow Tom led us."

The stories mattered, but only if shared. And Rose would choose what she told and what she withheld, without passing down unfair burdens to another generation. She wouldn't wait till she was on her deathbed, or pick who might be worthy. Since Gramma Amy still lived, Rose wouldn't reveal the darkest parts of her grandfather's past.

"That's the kind of man your great-grandfather Cow Tom was. A loyal, seven-fingered citizen of the Creek tribe. He only had a nub for a right ear, and a deep-pitted scar from a Confederate Indian's knife that curled down one cheek like a pig's tail. He told me most of his stories from his death-bed, and later, remembering those stories helped me do whatever needed. If he pros-pered against all odds, how could I not?

"He passed before my twenty-third birth-day, yet still I conjure him, bleak days or bright. It took some time for me to under-stand my place, but once comprehended, I held firm, yielding to no one, man or woman, black, Indian, or white. For better or worse, I know who I am and where I belong. Know who we are, Eugene, your family, and you'll come to know who you are.

"Your great-grandfather Cow Tom was the first African Creek Indian chief. His blood runs in you, so now I pass these stories for your safekeeping. Use them, as I did, to give you strength.

"I begin by saying to you what he said to me.

"You are braver than you know.

"You are special.

"You will make your way in this world."

AFTERWORD

The often unbelievable account of the first black Creek Indian chief and his descendants intrigued me from the first moment I accidently and serendipitously stumbled onto this amazing family. I was in between writing projects, captivated in general by the black towns of Oklahoma in the 1800s that sprang up after the Civil War, and waiting for inspiration for my next novel. Hearing about my Oklahoma interest, a friend of my husband's, Steve Hicks, gave me an old, battered book about his family who had deep roots in Oklahoma, written by a well-respected journalist. I remember carefully leafing through *Staking a Claim: Jake Simmons Jr. and the Making of an African-American Oil Dynasty,* by Jonathan Greenberg, trying desperately to keep the pages from falling out as I read. The book centered on Jake Simmons Jr., who had an astonishing career as an oil broker and politician in the mid-1900s. But what captivated me more was the handful of pages devoted to Jake's mother, Rose Simmons, and his great-grandfather Cow Tom.

Yes, this story is based on real people who lived in the 1800s and 1900s, their lives unfolding around cataclysmic and rapidly changing American events. Their futures were bound up in the shifting political landscapes of an explosively growing country, a country that made its peace with exploiting black labor through slavery and later sharecropping, and pitilessly pushed west with an unbounded appetite for land. Native Americans' very existence stood in the way of expansion, and gave rise to an uneasy and often ruthless relationship with the U.S. government. And yet this particular family, beginning as slaves of Indian masters, continued to overcome every obstacle that stood in the way of their success. They not only prevailed, but Rose and Jake's son Jake Simmons Jr. founded what became an oil dynasty in Oklahoma.

So many stories with black protagonists chronicle poor, defeated, powerless, dependent victims. But I found myself totally inspired by the spirit at the core of this family, a spirit preserved from generation to generation. While each of these characters carried their own flaws, as all humans do, they refused to be defeated. They were self-sufficient, strong, proud contributors to their family and to their community.

Within a week of being given that book, I knew I wanted to find out more about the unique position held by certain black men in nineteenth-century tribes as translators and intermediaries between the Five Civilized Tribes and the U.S. government. And I was equally interested in the women in their lives who made it possible for them to succeed — mothers, wives, daughters, and granddaughters. Seldom has a single family personified so many different aspects of this country's history at once — the conjunction of slavery, the push west, and Native Americans. And in the course of research, I discovered that Cow Tom's descendants are many.

Three years seems to be the magic number of how long it takes for me to write a historical novel, a very long and serious commitment involving years of research, finding a narrative arc, and telling a good story. The subject matter, the characters, and the setting have to be fascinating, complex, vibrant, and surprising to hold my interest for such a long period of time. The story of Cow Tom and his family did not disappoint.

ACKNOWLEDGMENTS

So many people to thank, so little time.

To my agents at Inkwell, Kim Witherspoon, who never gave up, and Allison Hunter, for the final sprint.

To my editor, Malaika Adero, and the rest of the gang at Atria and Simon & Schuster.

I owe a great debt to the village of readers of various iterations of the first fifteen drafts. Thanks to my writing group, the Finish Party, my mighty sisters of the word. Farai Chideya, Alyss Dixson, Jackie Luckett, ZZ Packer, Deborah Santana, Renee Swindle, and Nichelle Tramble, my first line of defense for multiple readings and unflagging enthusiasm.

And to my other writing group: Rosemary Graham, Nina Schyler, Elizabeth Stark, and Ellen Sussman. Also for the insights from Veronica Chambers, Caroline Leavitt, Vicky Mylniec, Meg Waite Clayton, Joan Lothery, and Barry Williams.

Thanks to Willard Johnson, professor of political science emeritus at MIT, whose deep knowledge of black Indians and Kansas/Oklahoma history proved invaluable. To John Oakley, whom I knew as a law professor and turned out to also be a maritime expert, historian, copy editor, and gun collector. To Damario Solomon, a descendant who pointed me toward Cow Tom's gravesite in Cane Creek, Oklahoma. And thanks to the Okies who ardently helped me navigate the state of Oklahoma — Hans Helmerich in Tulsa; Judge Robert Henry, president of Oklahoma City University; Phil Kistler; and Bill Welge, director of the Research Division of the Oklahoma Historical Society, who allowed me to hold (with white-gloved hands) the original 1866 treaty Cow Tom signed as Micco Cow Tom.

I'm grateful for the gift of time and space at Ragdale, Hedgebrook, and UCross residencies. And for Susan Orr and Hilary Valentine who provided additional inspiring writing venues.

To Steve Hicks, who gave me the book about his family that piqued my interest to start this long journey, *Staking a Claim: Jake Simmons Jr. and the Making of an African-American Oil Dynasty*, by Jonathan Greenberg.

And finally, to Barry Lawson Williams, my amazing husband, who single-handedly kept me from giving up and shelving this manuscript so many years in the making.

ABOUT THE AUTHOR

Lalita Tademy is the author of *Cane River*, a *New York Times* bestselling novel and the 2001 Oprah Book Club Summer Selection, and its critically acclaimed sequel *Red River*. She lives in Northern California.

The employees of Thorndike Press hope you have enjoyed this Large Print book. All our Thorndike, Wheeler, and Kennebec Large Print titles are designed for easy reading, and all our books are made to last. Other Thorndike Press Large Print books are available at your library, through selected bookstores, or directly from us.

For information about titles, please call:
    (800) 223-1244

or visit our Web site at:
    http://gale.cengage.com/thorndike

To share your comments, please write:
    Publisher
    Thorndike Press
    10 Water St., Suite 310
    Waterville, ME 04901